Dear Reader:

The Sherbrooke family saga continues with James and Jason Sherbrooke, identical male twins who look exactly like their beautiful Aunt Melissande, and not at all like their father, the earl, which riles him to no end.

James, twenty-eight minutes older than his brother, is the heir. He is solid, is James. He's a student of astronomy, rides like a centaur, and unlike his brother, Jason, enjoys learning the ropes of managing his father's estates. He no longer sows excessive wild oats, as his neighbor, Corrie Tybourne-Barrett, a brat he's known since she was three years old, looks forward to doing since she turned eighteen. When she nearly shoves him off a cliff, sneering all the while, James hauls off and spanks her.

A promising start. Then, unfortunately, the earl, Douglas Sherbrooke, is shot at. This leads to Georges Cadoudal, a Frenchman in the employ of the English War Ministry with whom Douglas had dealings some years before. But Cadoudal died in 1815, fifteen years earlier. Were there children who might want revenge against Douglas? But the question is why: Georges and Douglas parted friends—at least Douglas believed that they had.

Adventures compound; Corrie hurls herself into the thick of things. As for Jason, he swims like a fish, loves horses, wants to start a stud farm, still sows more oats than a man should be allowed, but finally meets a girl who stops him in his tracks. And then what happens?

You will have to read the book to find out. I hope you enjoy yourself. The characters are rich, colorful, and a hoot to boot. The mystery will confound you.

Do let me know what you think. Write me at P.O. Box 17, Mill Valley, CA, 94942 or e-mail me at readmoi@aol.com. Keep an eye on my website at www.CatherineCoulter.com.

Catherine Coulter

**Don't Miss Catherine Coulter's
Sherbrooke Series**

(in order)

THE SHERBROOKE BRIDE
THE HELLION BRIDE
THE HEIRESS BRIDE
MAD JACK
THE COURTSHIP
THE SCOTTISH BRIDE
PENDRAGON
THE SHERBROOKE TWINS

The critics praise the novels of
New York Times bestselling author
CATHERINE COULTER

The Penwyth Curse

"Coulter is at her best with this historical romance that tells
the stories of parallel loves . . . Wonderful."

—*The Best Reviews*

Pendragon

"Coulter is excellent at portraying the romantic tension
between her heroes and heroines."

—*Milwaukee Journal Sentinel*

The Courtship

"This is a sexy . . . Coulter Regency-era romance . . . For
readers who relish the subgenre."　　　—*Booklist*

Mad Jack

"Catherine Coulter delivers . . . straightforward, fast-paced
romance."　　　—*Minneapolis Star Tribune*

The Wild Baron

"Catherine Coulter has created some of the most memorable
characters in romance."　　　—*Atlanta Constitution*

Rosehaven

"A hot-blooded medieval romp."　　　—*People*

"Bawdy fare, Coulter-style . . . romance, humor, and spicy
sex talk."　　　—*Kirkus Reviews*

Titles by Catherine Coulter

The Bride Series
THE SHERBROOKE BRIDE
THE HELLION BRIDE
THE HEIRESS BRIDE
MAD JACK
THE COURTSHIP
THE SCOTTISH BRIDE
PENDRAGON
THE SHERBROOKE TWINS

The Legacy Trilogy
THE WYNDHAM LEGACY
THE NIGHTINGALE LEGACY
THE VALENTINE LEGACY

The Baron Novels
THE WILD BARON
THE OFFER
THE DECEPTION

The Viking Novels
LORD OF HAWKFELL ISLAND
LORD OF RAVEN'S PEAK
LORD OF FALCON RIDGE
SEASON OF THE SUN

The Song Novels
WARRIOR'S SONG
FIRE SONG
EARTH SONG
SECRET SONG
ROSEHAVEN
THE PENWYTH CURSE

The Magic Trilogy
MIDSUMMER MAGIC
CALYPSO MAGIC
MOONSPUN MAGIC

The Star Series
EVENING STAR
MIDNIGHT STAR
WILD STAR
JADE STAR

Other Regency Historical Romances
THE COUNTESS
THE REBEL BRIDE
THE HEIR
THE DUKE
LORD HARRY

Devil's Duology
DEVIL'S EMBRACE
DEVIL'S DAUGHTER

Contemporary Romantic Thrillers
FALSE PRETENSES
IMPULSE
BEYOND EDEN

FBI Suspense Thrillers
THE COVE
THE MAZE
THE TARGET
THE EDGE
RIPTIDE
HEMLOCK BAY
ELEVENTH HOUR
BLINDSIDE

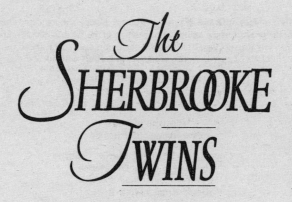

The SHERBROOKE TWINS

CATHERINE COULTER

JOVE BOOKS, NEW YORK

THE SHERBROOKE TWINS

A Jove Book / published by arrangement with the author

PRINTING HISTORY
Jove edition / March 2004

Copyright © 2004 by Catherine Coulter
Cover art by Gregg Gulbronson
Cover design by Brad Springer
Book design by Julie Rogers

For information, address: The Berkley Publishing Group, a division of Penguin Group (USA) Inc., 375 Hudson Street, New York, New York 10014.

ISBN: 0-515-13654-9

A JOVE BOOK®
Jove Books are published by The Berkley Publishing Group, a division of Penguin Group (USA) Inc., 375 Hudson Street, New York, New York 10014. JOVE and the "J" design are trademarks belonging to Penguin Group (USA) Inc.

PRINTED IN THE UNITED STATES OF AMERICA

10 9 8 7 6 5 4 3 2 1

To Judy Cochran Ward—

*You have a beautiful smile and
a beautiful heart to match.
I'm very grateful you're in my life.*

CC

CHAPTER ONE

⎈⎋⎈

Who can refute a sneer?

WILLIAM PALEY

NORTHCLIFFE HALL
AUGUST 1830

James Sherbrooke, Lord Hammersmith, twenty-eight minutes older than his brother, wondered if Jason was swimming in the North Sea off the coast of Stonehaven. His brother swam like a fish, no matter if the water froze his parts or cradled him in a warm bath. He'd say while he shook himself like their hound Tulip, "Now, James, that doesn't matter, does it? It's rather like making love. You can be on a grainy beach with cold waves nipping your toes, or wallowing in a feather tick—in the end the pleasure's the same."

James had never made love on a grainy beach, but he supposed his twin was right. Jason had a way of putting things that amused you even as you nodded in agreement. Jason had inherited this gift, if that's what it really was, from their mother, who'd once said as she'd looked lovingly at James, that she'd delivered one gift from God and now it was time to grit her teeth and deliver the other gift. This had gained her looks of sheer amazement from her sons, and, of course, nods, at which point, their father gave them both a look of acute dislike, snorted, and said, "Gifts from the Devil, more like."

"My precious boys," she'd say, "it's such a pity you're so beautiful, isn't it? It really annoys your father."

They'd stare at her, but again, they'd nod.

James sighed and stepped away from the cliff that overlooked the Poe Valley, a lovely stretch of undulating green, dotted with maple and lime trees and divided by ancient fences. The Poe Valley was protected on all sides by the low-lying Trelow hills; James always believed that some of those long, rounded hills were ancient barrows. He and Jason had built countless adventures about the possible inhabitants of those barrows—Jason had always liked to be the warrior who wore bearskins, painted his face blue, and ate raw meat. As for James, he was the shaman who flicked his fingers and made smoke spiral into the sky and rained flame down on the warriors.

James stepped back from the edge. He'd fallen off that cliff once because he and Jason had been fighting with swords, and Jason had flattened his sword button against James's gullet, and James had grabbed his neck and flailed about—all drama and no style, Jason told him later. He'd lost his footing and tumbled down the hill, his brother's yells blasting. "You stupid bloody bleater, don't you dare kill yourself! It was only a neck wound!"

He'd been laughing even as he'd landed. Hard. But thankfully he'd survived with just a mass of bruises on his face and ribs, which made his Aunt Melissande, who'd been visiting Northcliffe Hall, shriek as she'd run her hands over his face. "Oh my dear boy, you must take care of your exquisite and perfect face, and I should know since it's mine." And his father, the earl, had said to the heavens, "How could such a thing have happened?"

It was true. James and Jason were the image of their glorious Aunt Melissande, not a single red hair from their mother's head or a single dark eye from their father. All their features were from their Aunt Melissande, which made no sense to anyone. Except their size, thank God. They were both near the size of their father, and that pleased him inordinately. Their mother had actually said something to the effect that, "A boy should be almost as big as his father and almost as smart; it's what all fathers want. Possibly mothers too." And her boys had blinked at her and nodded.

James had heard a rumor many years before that his father had wanted to marry his Aunt Melissande, and would have, if it hadn't been for his Uncle Tony, who'd up and stolen her. James couldn't imagine such a thing. Not that his Uncle Tony had stolen her, but that his Aunt Melissande hadn't preferred his father. His mother had stepped into the breach, luckily for James and Jason, who, although they found their aunt very interesting, loved their mother to their toes. Fortunately, they had the Sherbrooke brains. Their father had told them many times, "Brains are more important than your damned beautiful faces. If either of you ever forget that, I'll pound you into the ground."

"Ah, but their beautiful faces are extraordinarily manly," their mother had hastened to add, and patted them both.

James was grinning at that memory when he heard a shout and turned to see Corrie Tybourne-Barrett, an annoyance who'd been in his life nearly as long as she'd been in hers, riding like a boy with more guts than brains up the

slope, bringing her mare Darlene to an abrupt stop not two
feet from the cliff edge and only one foot from him. To his
credit, James didn't even twitch. He looked up at her, so
angry he wanted to hurl her to the ground. But he managed
to say in a fairly calm voice, "That was stupid. It rained
yesterday and the ground isn't all that firm. You're not ten
years old anymore, Corrie. You must stop acting like a boy
with mud between his ears. Now back up Darlene, slow
and easy. If you're not worried about killing yourself, you
might want to think about your mare."

Corrie stared down at him and said, "I admire how you
can speak so calmly when smoke is coming out of your
ears. You don't fool me for one minute, James Sherbrooke." She sneered down at him, and click-clicked her
mare right into him, nearly knocking him over. He side-
stepped, patted Darlene's nose, and said, "You're right.
Smoke is coming out of my ears. Do you remember that
day you wanted to prove how skilled you were and rode
that half-wild stallion my father had just bought? That
damned horse nearly killed me when I was trying to save
you, which, fool that I was, I did."

"I didn't need you to save me, James. I was skilled, even
at twelve."

"I suppose you planned to have your legs wrapped
around that horse's neck, hanging on, screaming. Ah, that
was a measure of your skill, wasn't it? And don't forget the
time you told my father that I had seduced a Don's wife at
Oxford, knowing he'd be furious at me."

"That's not true, James. He wasn't furious, at least not
at first. He first wanted proof because he said he couldn't
imagine you being that stupid."

"I wasn't stupid, damn you. It took me a good two
months to convince Father that it was all your doing, and
you whimpered and whined that it was just a wee bit of a
little joke."

She smiled. "I even found out the name of one of the Dons' wives to make it more believable."

He shuddered, remembering clearly the look on his father's face. "You want to know something, Corrie? I think it's long past due that someone explained manners to you." Without warning, he grabbed her arm and pulled her down off Darlene's back and dragged her over to a rock. He sat down and pulled her between his legs. "This thrashing is long overdue." Before she could begin to imagine what he was going to do, James flipped her over on her belly across his legs and brought the flat of his hand down hard on her breeched bottom. She gasped and yowled and struggled, but he was strong, more than determined, and held her easily. "If you had on a riding skirt," smack, smack, smack, "this wouldn't hurt because you'd have a half dozen petticoats to pad you." Smack, smack, smack.

Corrie fought him, twisting, and yelling, "Stop this now, James! You can't do this, you idiot! I'm a girl, and I'm not even your bloody sister."

"Thank God for that. Do you remember the time you slipped that medicine in my tea and my bowels were water for a day and a half?"

"I didn't think it would last so long. Stop, James, this isn't proper!"

"Oh, now that's rich. It isn't proper, you say? I've been saddled with you all your blessed life. I remember seeing your skinny little backside when you were swimming in Trenton's pond. All the rest of you as well."

"I was eight years old!"

"You don't act much older now. This, Corrie, is long overdue discipline. Just consider me acting in your Uncle Simon's place."

James stopped. He just couldn't wallop her again, despite the overflowing memories of atrocious things she'd done to him over the years. He started to roll her off his lap, then saw the rocks on the ground. "Oh damnation, brat," he said, and lifted her off his legs to set her on her feet. She stood there, rubbing her bottom, staring at him. If looks could kill, he'd be dead at her feet. He rose and shook a finger at her, much in the same manner as a long-ago tutor, Mr. Boniface. "Don't be such a pitiful little sissy. Your bottom smarts a little, nothing more." He looked fixedly at his boots a moment, then said, "How old are you, Corrie? I forget."

She sniveled, wiped her hand across her running nose, stuck her chin up, and said, "I'm eighteen."

He whipped his head up, appalled. "No, no, that's impossible. Just look at you, a hairless young man who just happens to have a round butt beneath those ridiculous britches that no self-respecting young man would ever want. Well, I didn't mean to say it exactly like that."

"I am eighteen years old. Do you hear me, James Sherbrooke? What's so impossible about that? And do you know what else?"

He stared down at her, slowly shaking his head.

"I've had a round backside for at least three years now! And do you know what else?"

"How was I ever to notice, what with the breeches you wear, bagging off your bottom. What else?"

"This is important, James. I am having a sort of practice season this fall. Aunt Maybella says it's called the Little Season. And that means I'll wear fancy gowns and silk stockings with garters to hold them up, and shoes that will raise me off the ground a good two inches. It means I'm now a grown-up. I will put my hair up, smear cream all over me so I'll be soft, and show off my bosom."

"It will take buckets of cream."

"Just maybe. But I'll soften up sooner or later and then it will take less. So what?"

"Show off what bosom?"

To his absolute horror, James believed for one second

that she was going to rip her shirt open and show him her breasts, but thankfully reason prevailed and she said, eyes slits now, "I have a bosom, a very nice one that just happens to be hidden right now."

"Hidden where?" He looked around.

She actually flushed. James would have apologized if he hadn't known her all her life—seen her as a five-year-old with no front teeth trying to figure out how to bite into an apple, assured her she wasn't dying when she'd begun her woman's monthly flow at thirteen, and been the recipient of that sneer of hers too many times in recent years.

She poked her fingers against her chest. "They're all in here, smashed down. But when I unsmash them and frame them with satin and lace, a dozen gentlemen will very likely swoon."

He tried on one of her sneers and found that it fit him well enough. "Only in your twit's dreams will you be able to unsmash that much. Good Lord, I'm picturing a board with knots on it."

"A board with knots? That's very mean of you, James."

"Very well, you're right. I apologize. What I should have said was that the thought of your unsmashed chest boggles my mind."

"There's nothing but swamp water in your mind." She drew herself up, threw back her shoulders, stuck out her chest, and said, "My Aunt Maybella assured me this will happen."

Since James had known Maybella Ambrose, Lady Montague, practically since his birth, he didn't believe this for an instant. "What did she really say?"

"Very well, Aunt Maybella said something about when I was cleaned up properly I shouldn't disgrace them. As long as I wear blue, just like her."

"That sounds more like it."

"Don't you slap me in the face with your insults, James Sherbrooke. You know my aunt, she's a veritable mistress of understatement. What she really means is that I will knock them down in the street when I ride by in my very own curricle, holding, perhaps, a poodle on my lap."

"The only way you would knock down gentlemen is if you were driving."

It was a meaty insult. Shaking her fist in his face, she bellowed at him, "You listen to me, you codsbreath! I drive as well as you do, maybe better. I have heard it remarked many times—I have the better eye."

That was so patently absurd that James just rolled his own eyes. "All right, name one person who remarked that."

"Your father, for one."

"Impossible. My father taught me to drive. My eye is as good as his, probably better now since he's getting old."

She gave him a beatific smile. "Your father taught me to drive as well. And he's not old at all. What he is is very handsome and wicked—I heard Aunt Maybella saying that to her friend, Mrs. Hubbard."

That nearly made him puke. As for her driving, James remembered seeing the girl sitting proudly beside his father, hanging on his every word. He remembered feeling a stab of jealousy. It was mean-spirited, particularly since both Corrie's father and mother had been killed in a riot right after Napoleon's defeat at Waterloo. It was an unfortunate accident that happened during an official visit by Corrie's father, diplomatic envoy Benjamin Tybourne-Barrett, Viscount Plessante, to Paris to discuss the second restoration of the Bourbons with Talleyrand and Fouché.

Talleyrand had seen to it that Corrie, not yet three years old, was returned to England to her mother's sister in the company of her dead mother's heartbroken maid, and six French soldiers, who were not warmly treated.

When James finally brought his brain back, it was to hear her say, "And my uncle will have fits trying to decide which gentleman is good enough for me. I shall have my pick, you know, and that immensely lucky man will be strong and handsome and very rich, and nothing like you, James." Another sneer, this one very refined, meant to make him shake with rage. "Just look at your eyelashes, all thick and poking out a good inch, like a Spanish lady's fan. Even a little curl on the ends. Yes, you've got a girl's eyelashes."

He'd only been ten years old when his mother had come up with the right answer for him, and so he smiled now and said easily, "You're wrong about that. I've never met a girl who had eyelashes as long and as thick as mine."

She was silent, her mouth open. She couldn't think of a thing to say. He laughed. "Leave my face out of this, brat. It has nothing to do with your bosom. *Bosom,* for God's sake. Men don't say *bosom.*"

"What do men say?"

"Never you mind. You're too young. And you're a lady. Well, not really, but you should be since you're eighteen. No, I can't believe you're eighteen. That means nearly twenty, which would place you in the same decade as I am. It's just not possible."

"You bought me a birthday present just two weeks ago."

He gave her a perfectly blank look.

Corrie smacked her palm to her forehead. "Oh, I see now, your mother bought the present and put your name on it."

"Well, that's not really what happened, it's—"

"All right. Then what did you get me?"

"Well, you know, Corrie, it's been a long time."

"Two weeks, you bloody sod."

"Watch your mouth, my girl, or I'll smack you again. You talk like a damned boy. I should have gotten a riding crop for your birthday so I could use it on you when the need arose. Like right now."

He took a menacing step toward her, got hold of himself, and stopped. To his amazement, she walked right up to him, stood toe-to-toe, sneered up at him, and said in his face, "A riding crop? You just try it. I'll take it away from you, rip off your shirt, and whip you with it."

"Now that's a sight I'd like to see."

"Well, maybe I'd leave your shirt on you. After all, I'm a gently bred young lady and it wouldn't do for me to see a half-naked man."

He was laughing so hard he nearly fell backward off the damned cliff.

She wasn't done, humiliation ripe in her voice. "You used your hand when you whipped me—your naked hand. I'll wager I'm scarred for life, you bully."

He grinned down at her. "Your bottom still smarting a bit?"

To his amazement, she blushed.

"Is your face turning red as well?"

She opened her mouth, then tears welled up in her eyes, and she jerked away, climbed into Darlene's saddle, and straightened. She gave him a long, emotionless look, twitched Darlene's reins, making her rear on her hind legs, sending James stumbling back. He heard her shout, "I will ask my uncle what men call a *bosom*."

He devoutly hoped she wouldn't. He could picture her Uncle Simon's eyes rolling back as he keeled over in his chair, his glasses sliding off his face. Uncle Simon was at home with his collection of leaves. He had leaves, carefully dried and pressed, from every tree found in Britain, France, and even two from Greece, one of them from an ancient olive tree near the Oracle of Delphi. Leaves, but not females. Uncle Simon wasn't at home at all with females. James watched her ride away, not even looking at him to see if he'd survived her attack. Her long hair, tied up tight in a fat braid, slapped up and down on her back.

James dusted himself off, then shook his head. He'd grown up with the little twit. Since the day she arrived at

Twyley Grange, home of her mother's sister and husband, she'd followed him—not Jason, never Jason—only him, and how could a little girl possibly tell them apart? But she had. She'd even followed him once to the bushes when he went to relieve himself, an incident that had left him red-faced and sputtering with furious embarrassment when Corrie had said from off to his left side, "Goodness, you don't do that like I do. Would you just look at that thing you're holding! Why, I can't imagine how to do—"

He was only fifteen, humiliated, his breeches still un-buttoned, and he'd yelled down at the child who was all of eight years old, "You're nothing but a stupid worthless lit-tle girl!" and stomped off to his horse, and proceeded to nearly kill himself when a mail coach had come around a curve, spooking his horse, who threw him to the ground, senseless. His father had come to fetch him from the inn where he'd been taken. He'd held him close while the doc-tor had peered into his ears, for what purpose, his father told him later, he had no clue. James had settled against him and said in a slurred voice, "Papa, I relieved myself, but I used the wrong bush because Corrie was there and she watched me, and said things." His father, without hesi-tation, replied, "Little girls happen, James, and then they become big girls, and you forget about the wrong bush. Don't dwell on it." And so James hadn't. He let his father take care of him. He felt safe, his humiliation wafting out the open window.

 Life, James thought now, *was something that seemed to happen when you weren't paying enough attention.* It seemed to him that what you did right this minute became a memory all too quickly, just like Corrie turning eigh-teen—how had that happened? As he walked back to where he'd left his bay stallion, Bad Boy, he wondered if it was possible that one day he'd look at her and discover that she'd grown breasts. He laughed, looked up at the sky. It would be clear tonight, nearly a half-moon, a beautiful night to lie up here on his back and look at the stars.

As he rode back to Northcliffe Hall, James didn't hold out any hope that his mother had gotten Corrie a riding crop for her eighteenth birthday, from him.

CHAPTER TWO

⚜

*If there is anything disagreeable
going on, men are sure to get out of it.*

JANE AUSTEN

"YOU GAVE HER what? Mother, please tell me you
didn't sign my name to that."

"Now, James, Corrie has no notion of what is expected
of her when she goes up to London for the Little Season. I
thought a lovely book on proper deportment for a young
lady entering polite society was just the thing to get her
thinking in the right direction."

His mother already knew about Corrie's Little Season?
Where had he been? Why had no one told him? "A book on
deportment," he said blankly, and ate a slice of ham. He
thought of that sneer of hers and said, "Yes, I can see that
she would really need that."

"No, wait, James, the book was from Jason. I got Corrie a lovely illustrated book of Racine's plays from you."

"All she'll do is look at the pictures, Mama. Her French is execrable."

"So was mine, once upon a time. If Corrie sets her mind to it, she will become as remarkably fluent as I am."

The earl, who was watching with a half smile on his face from the other end of the table, nearly choked on his green beans. He arched a dark brow. "Once upon a time, Alexandra? And now you're fluent? Why, I—"

"You are interrupting a conversation, Douglas. You may continue eating. Now, James, about the plays. As I recall, the illustrations are in quite the classical style, and I think she will enjoy them, even if she can't make out all the ⌐rds."

James stared down at the chunk of potato speared on his fork.

His mother asked, "Why, James? Was there something else you wanted to get her?"

"A riding crop," James said under his breath, but not under enough. His father choked again, this time on a stewed carrot.

His mother said, "She is a young lady now, James, even though she still wears those lamentable trousers and that disreputable old hat. You can't treat her like your little brother any longer. Now, about this riding crop, why didn't you get it for her yourself? Oh, I remember now that Corrie said she'd never use a riding crop on her horse."

"I forgot her birthday," James said, and prayed his father wouldn't enlighten his mother.

"I know, James. As I recall, you weren't here to ask, so I had no choice but to supply your gift."

"Mama, couldn't you have gotten her some clothes— you know, perhaps a nice riding habit or a pair of riding boots and signed my name to it?"

"That, my dear, wouldn't be proper. Corrie is now a young lady and you are a young gentleman not related to her."

"Young gentlemen," said Douglas Sherbrooke, waving his fork at James from the head of the luncheon table, "only give clothes and riding boots to their mistresses. Surely you and I have already spoken of that, James."

Alexandra said, "Douglas, please, James is my lovely little boy. Surely it isn't the thing for you to speak of mistresses to him. Surely he needs years to ripen before he actually takes part in such, er, activities."

Both her husband and her son stared at her, then slowly, they both nodded. James said, "Er, yes, of course, Mama. Many years."

She said, "Douglas, I'm not a mistress and you've bought me clothes and riding boots."

"Well, naturally, someone has to dress you properly."

James said, "Just as someone needs to dress Corrie properly, sir. She's more boy than girl. If she does turn into a girl, she still has no notion of the way of things. She has no experience at all. She's never been to London. I don't think, Mama, that a book on deportment is going to be of much assistance if she doesn't know how to dress and rig herself out."

"Perhaps I can give her Aunt Maybella some suggestions," Alexandra said. "I've wondered many times why Maybella hasn't dressed Corrie properly. Both she and Simon have let her continue to roam around the countryside dressed like a boy."

"I've wondered that too," James said, and took a bite of his bread. "Maybe she doesn't like gowns. The good Lord knows she can be so stubborn, her uncle's probably given up and lets her rule."

"No," Douglas said. "That isn't it. There is no one more stubborn than Simon Ambrose in all of England. It's got to be something else."

"Would you like a peach fritter, dear?" Both dears looked at her. "Isn't that nice. I have your attention now, both of you. Would you two like to accompany me to Eastbourne this afternoon?"

Douglas, who'd wanted to go see a new hunter at Squire Beglie's, chewed more vigorously on his shrimp patty.

"Er, it's for your mother," Alexandra said.

"Excuse me, Mother, Father, I'm off."

"James is fast when he needs to be," Douglas said, following his son's speedy progress from the dining room. He sighed. "All right. What does my mother want?"

"She wants me to bring back at least six new patterns of wallpaper for her bedchamber."

"Six?"

"Well, you see, she doesn't trust my taste, so I'm really to bring as many as I can so that she can make her selection here."

"Let her go herself."

"Ah, and you would drive her?"

"What time do you wish to leave?"

Alexandra laughed, tossed down her napkin, and rose. "In an hour or so." She leaned over, palms on the snowy white tablecloth, and said down the expanse of table to her husband, "Douglas, there is something else—"

Before she could get out another word, her husband said, "By God, Alexandra, your gown is cut nearly to your knees. It's obviously a hussy's gown, what with your breasts nearly falling out of it. Wait—you're doing this on purpose, leaning over the table like that." He smacked his fist on the table, making his wineglass jump. "Why don't I ever learn? I've had decade upon decade to learn."

"Well, not all that many decades. And I really do appreciate your admiration of my finer points."

"You will not make me blush, madam. You are remarkably well put together—all right, I'm hooked good and proper, what is it you want from me?"

She gave him the sweetest smile. "I want to talk to you about the Virgin Bride. A serious talk, not one of your *you're an idiot to even mention that ridiculous ghost who doesn't exist.*"

"What did that bloody ghost do now?"

Alexandra straightened and looked through the tall windows toward the east lawn. "She said there would be trouble."

He held the sarcasm in check for the moment. "You're saying that our centuries-old resident virgin ghost, who's never appeared to any man in this house for the simple reason that our brains don't allow such nonsense, has come to you and told you there would be trouble?"

"That's about the size of it."

"I didn't think she spoke, just wafted about looking forlorn and transparent."

"And lovely. She is really quite incredible. Now, you know she doesn't really speak, she feels what she's thinking to you. She hasn't visited me in ages, not since Ryder got set upon by those three thugs that miserable clothing merchant hired."

"But Ryder managed to fell one of them with an excellent throw of a rock to the gut. He stuffed the other into a half-full herring barrel. I don't remember what he did to the third, probably because it wasn't amusing."

"But still, he was hurt in that fight and the Virgin Bride told me about it."

He paused. It was true that Alexandra had known about his brother's fight before he had, dammit. At least his sister, Sinjun, hadn't come tearing down from Scotland to see what had happened. She'd written a half dozen letters demanding all the facts. Ryder's wife, Sophie, hadn't written or sent a messenger, because she'd known that the Virgin

Bride would tell Alexandra and Sinjun. The Virgin Bride? No, he wasn't even going to consider it.

"Ryder wasn't badly hurt. It seems to me that your Virgin Bride suffers from female hysteria. You know, a fellow gets his fingernail broken, and she falls apart."

"Female hysteria? Broken fingernail? I'm serious about this. I'm worried. When she felt Ryder's situation to me, I actually saw the three men pounding on him."

He wanted to tell her to stop telling him tales that gave him gooseflesh, but he thought of her premeditated display of lovely cleavage, and because he wasn't stupid, he held his tongue. He would mock the wretched ghost only to himself. Her tactics should be encouraged. But this was difficult to bear. It seemed that since the unfortunate bride's demise sometime in the latter part of the sixteenth century—still a virgin when she drew her last breath—so the story went, that all the Sherbrooke women had believed in this wafting ghost oracle ever since.

Douglas swallowed the sarcasm that was still hovering just above his tongue, and said, "No mention of a specific sort of trouble?"

"No, and that makes me think that she doesn't know exactly what's coming, just that something is, and it's not good." She drew a deep breath. "I know that it has to do with you, Douglas. I simply understood that from what she felt to me."

"I see, but she sent you this vague understanding? No names? She's always known everything before."

"I think that's because it's already happened or is happening at that moment." Alexandra took a big breath. "Whatever she doesn't know, it's still enough to concern her, Douglas. Since it was about you, that's why she was warning me. She's worried about you, even though she didn't exactly come right out with it. It's you. There is not a single doubt in my mind."

"Nonsense," he said, "idiotic nonsense," then wished he

could bite his tongue. His wife withdrew. "All right, all right, talk to her again, see if she can give you some details. In the meantime, I'll have our horses saddled. My mother wants you to bring back six samples of wallpaper?"

"Yes, but I think we'd best have Dilfer follow with a small wagon since I know that if I only fetch six samples, she'll want more. I think we'll simply clean out the warehouse. Excuse me now, Douglas. I'm very sorry to have bothered you with my hysterical female nonsense."

Douglas threw his fork against the wall where it hit just below a portrait of Audley Sherbrooke, Baron Lindley. He cursed.

"My lord."

Douglas shut his mouth when Hollis, the Sherbrooke butler since Douglas's youth, appeared in the breakfast room doorway. "Yes, Hollis?"

"The dowager countess—your esteemed mother, my lord—wishes to see you."

"I have known all my life who she is. I had a feeling she'd want to see me. All right."

Hollis smiled and turned on his stately heel. Douglas looked after him, the tall, straight figure, the perfectly squared shoulders, still more white hair than Moses, but his step was slower, and perhaps one shoulder wasn't as high as the other? How old was Hollis now? He must be nearly as old as Audley Sherbrooke's portrait, at least seventy, maybe even older. That made Douglas blanch. Few men ever reached that age without shaking veined hands, a mouth empty of teeth, not a single hair left on the head, and perfectly hideous bent old bodies. Surely it was time for Hollis to retire, at least twenty years past his time to retire, perhaps to a lovely cottage by the sea, say in Brighton or Tunbridge Wells, and—and what? Sit and rock his old bones and look at the water? No, Douglas couldn't imagine Hollis, whom his boys firmly believed was God when they were younger, doing anything other than ruling Northcliffe

Hall, which he did with ruthless efficiency, splendid tact, and a benevolent, firm hand.

The fact was, though, that time was passing, no way to stop it. Hollis was beyond old now, and that meant he could die. Douglas shook his head. He didn't want to think about Hollis dying, he couldn't bear that. He called out, "Hollis!"

The stately old man slowly turned, a white brow arched at the strange tone in his lordship's voice. "My lord?"

"Er, how are you feeling?"

"I, my lord?"

"Unless you have a footman hiding behind you, then yes, you."

"I have nothing wrong that a lovely young wife won't cure, my lord."

Douglas stared at the small secret smile that showed a mouth loaded with teeth, and that was a good thing. Before Douglas could ask what the devil he meant by that, Hollis had removed himself from sight.

A lovely young wife?

To the best of Douglas's knowledge, Hollis had never looked at a woman with marital intent since the tragic death of his beloved young Miss Plimpton in the last century.

A lovely young wife?

CHAPTER THREE

❧❧

**KILDRUMMY CASTLE, SCOTTISH HOME
OF REVEREND TYSEN SHERBROOKE, BARON BARTHWICK**

The Honorable Jason Edward Charles Sherbrooke didn't
like this at all. He didn't want to accept it, but he didn't see
how he could ignore it.

It was a dream, nothing more than the result of losing
too many games of chess to his Aunt Mary Rose or too
much grouse hunting in the interminable rain with his Uncle Tysen and his cousin Rory. Or the natural consequence
of drinking too much brandy and having too much sex with
Elanora Dillingham in too short a time.

No, even those altogether splendid, excessively gratifying hours didn't explain it. It had been real. He'd finally
had his first visit from the Virgin Bride, a phantom his father laughed about, saying, "Yes, imagine this piece of
white nothing wafting around our house for three centuries. Only to the ladies, mind you, so you're safe."

Well, Jason was a man, and she'd visited him.

He remembered clearly that he'd awakened when Elanora had gotten up to use the chamber pot in the dressing room just before dawn. He'd lain there, half-asleep, and suddenly there was this very beautiful young lady with long loose hair, dressed in a long white gown, and she'd just stood there at the foot of the bed looking at him, and he heard her say as clearly as bells ringing, "There's trouble at home, Jason. Go home. Go home."

And he'd seen his father's face, clear as if he'd been standing right next to him.

Elanora had come back into the bedchamber, yawning, naked to her white feet, her beautiful black hair falling all over the place, and the young lady had simply vanished, not a sound, not even a ripple in the air. She was just gone.

Jason had lain there, dumbfounded, not wanting to believe it, but he'd been raised with tales of the Virgin Bride. Why had she come to him? Because there was trouble at home.

He whispered to the empty air where she'd stood, "I didn't have time to ask you whom I would marry."

Elanora was feeling amorous; Jason was a young man, but still, he gave her a perfunctory kiss and got himself out of bed. He'd met Elanora only a month before when his leg had cramped while he'd been swimming in the North Sea, and he'd managed to drag himself up onto her beach. She'd been standing there, twirling a parasol, a stiff breeze flattening her gown to her lovely legs when he'd emerged from the water stark naked. She'd looked her fill at what the sea had spit up for her, and was evidently pleased. She was a widow, the stepmother of three sons all older than Jason, who lavished gifts on their dear step-mama. Jason quite liked her, for she was clever, and even better, she loved horses, just as he did. He always left Elanora's house, a lovely Georgian set on the coast between Kildrummy Castle and Stonehaven, before dawn so he'd be back at Kildrummy Castle in time for breakfast with his Aunt Mary Rose and his Uncle Tysen. If either of them realized he wasn't sleeping in his own bed, they'd said nothing.

He'd heard his cousin Rory say several days before, "Jason must really like to hunt grouse. He not only hunts during the day with you, Papa, then he's out most nights as well, until nearly dawn." Thank the heavens that no one had asked him if this was indeed true.

This morning, over kippers and clooties, he told them he'd had a visit from the Virgin Bride. His reverend uncle didn't say anything, just chewed thoughtfully on a slice of toast. Aunt Mary Rose, her glorious red hair rioting around her head, frowned. "Tysen, do you think God knows the Virgin Bride?"

Her husband didn't laugh. He continued to look thoughtful. "I would never say this to Douglas or to Ryder, but I've sometimes thought there's a sort of window that isn't completely shut and sometimes spirits slip back into our world. Does God know her? Perhaps if she ever visits me, I'll ask her."

Mary Rose said, "I've never had a visit from her either, and that's not fair. You're not even a lady, Jason, yet she came to you. Did she say anything?"

Jason said, "She said there was trouble at home. Nothing else, just that, but the funny thing was that I saw my father's face clear as day. I must leave, of course."

Jason was on his way south by eight o'clock that morning, thankful that he'd managed to talk his aunt and uncle out of coming with him. He thought endlessly about what the trouble at home could be, and how his father was involved, and he thought about his uncle's words—a window not quite shut between our world and the next. It gave a man pause.

Life, he thought as he nudged Dodger's sleek sides with his boot heels, *could be going along nicely when suddenly the road closed, and you suddenly had to travel another di-*

rection. He wondered if the Virgin Bride had visited his mother. Very probably. Had she visited James? Well, he'd know soon enough.

He worried and rode and wished he could use the spirit window. It had to be faster.

On the sixth day, he rode a tired Dodger past the massive front steps of Northcliffe Hall toward the stables.

Lovejoy, a youth of sixteen summers, and Dodger's favorite stable lad, came running out, yelping, "My glorious big boy! Yer home, yer home, at last. Ah, would ye look at yer coat, all dirty and filled with stinging ickles."

Jason said, grinning down at Lovejoy, "Are you talking to me or my horse, Lovejoy?"

"Dodger's me boy, Master Jason. 'Tis yer mither who'll welcome ye awright 'n' proper."

Dodger, sixteen hands high, black as a moonless night except for the lightning streak of white down his nose, whinnied, and stuck his face in Lovejoy's shoulder and lipped his musty shirt.

When Jason walked into Northcliffe Hall, he stopped and looked around. No one seemed to be about. Where was Hollis? Hollis was always near the front door. Oh no, he was ill, or he'd died. No, Jason couldn't bear that. He knew Hollis was older than the oak tree he'd carved his initials on in the east lawn, but he belonged here, in Northcliffe Hall, alive and scolding and calming everyone.

"My sweet boy! You're home! Oh goodness, how dirty you are. I didn't expect you for another sennight. What's the matter?"

"Where's Hollis? Is he all right?"

His mother said, "Why yes, Jason. I believe he's in the village. Ah, I'm so glad you're home. Now, what's wrong?"

Hollis was alive and kicking, thank God. And Lovejoy was right. His mother had welcomed him all right and proper. Jason went forward to hug his laughing mother. He said against her ear, "The Virgin Bride told me to come home, said there's trouble. And I saw father's face, so he's got to be the one."

His mother stepped back and looked up at him. "Oh dear, it's lovely to have one's own visit confirmed, but still, this isn't good at all. Your father, you know how he scoffs." She tapped her fingertips to her chin. "Well, she came to you as well. We'll have to see what your father has to say now."

His father had hardly a thing to say, other than, "You ate turnips for dinner, didn't you, Jason?"

He assured his sire that he hadn't. He knew his father wanted to ask him if he'd been carousing, but he couldn't, not in front of his mother.

His father grunted, and waved him away. "Go take a bath. It will get rid of all your dirt and hopefully set your brain on the right track again."

As for James, he listened to what Jason said, then replied, "I don't understand this, I really don't. It makes my brain ache, Jase. She said there was trouble at home, nothing more, and then you saw Father? That's exactly what she felt to Mother too, but Mother didn't see Father's face, she said she just knew he was the one in danger. We shall have to be vigilant. Now, about this Elanora, did you buy her any clothes?"

"Clothes?" Jason's dark brow shot up. "Well, no, I don't believe I bought her anything at all."

"Hmm. I wonder what father would say about that," James said and walked away, whistling.

THERE WAS NO sign of trouble until two afternoons later.

Douglas Sherbrooke was breaking in his new gelding, Henry VIII, meaner than Douglas's mother when the mood struck. Henry was bucking, rearing on his hind legs, corkscrewing, and Douglas was having a fine time when suddenly there was a loud popping sound. Henry bucked wildly, and Douglas, distracted, was hurled out of the saddle onto his back into a mess of low-lying yews that broke his fall. He didn't move, just lay there, looking up into the blue summer sky, querying his parts. Someone had shot him in his upper arm. Just a graze, really. It was the fall that could have killed him. He admired yew bushes more than he ever had in the past.

He got to his feet, felt the sting in his arm, looked around for a sign of the man who'd fired the shot, then walked to where Henry was standing. The big horse was frightened and sweating. Douglas wrapped his handkerchief around his arm, hoping Henry wouldn't smell the blood.

Douglas spoke to him, soothed him as best he could, took off his riding jacket, and rubbed him down. He didn't know what his valet Peabody would have to say about that. "We're both all right now, Henry. Don't fret, boy, we pulled through this. I'm going to give you a nice bucket of oats when we get home. As for me, well I suppose I'll have to get that miserable Dr. Milton here, Alex will demand it. Then she'll hover over me, and she won't say it, but she'll give me that look that says very clearly, *'I told you she said there'd be trouble. I said it was you and I was right.'*

"Now, the question is, who shot me and why? Was it an accident? Some poacher whose finger slipped on the trigger? And if it was someone who for whatever reason hates my guts, then why did he fire only one shot? That seems ill thought-out, docsn't it, Henry, if he was after me? Well, let's see if he left something behind that could be useful."

As he rode back to Northcliffe Hall, his arm burning, he thought again of the Virgin Bride and her warning.

When he walked through the front door, it was to hear raised voices, several of them, all arguing. He was carrying his riding jacket since it was covered with Henry's sweat. He hoped no one would notice that he had a bloody handkerchief tied around his upper arm.

He saw Corrie Tybourne-Barrett standing in the middle of the vast central hall, looking as disreputable as a village boy in her ridiculous old breeches and boots, that old hat pulled down low on her forehead, her dusty braid hanging down her back. Shaking his fist at her was Mr. Josiah Marker, owner of a mill on the Alsop River.

"Ye went flying right into the mill, that horse o' yers spraying grain all over the place! Fer shame, missy! Fer shame!"

Corrie yelled back, waving her own fist in Mr. Marker's face, "Don't you dare say that Darlene sprayed your grain any place, she didn't! It was your son Willie, that good-for-nothing little blighter! I hit him when he tried to kiss me, and he's paying me back! Darlene wasn't near your mill!"

Douglas didn't raise his voice, he'd never had to. He simply said, "Quiet, everyone. That is quite enough."

He realized then that Corrie and Mr. Marker and four servants were standing in the great hall entrance. Where were his sons, his wife, for God's sake, even his damned mother? Where was Hollis, who could have dealt with this in a matter of three very calm seconds?

There was instant silence, but anger vibrated in the air. Douglas dismissed the servants and was just turning to Mr. Marker when James came through the front doors, windblown, lightly slapping his riding crop against his thigh. He stopped cold. "What is going on, Father? Corrie, what are you doing here?"

Mr. Marker started to open his mouth, but Douglas merely raised his hand. "No, no more. James, would you please deal with this? It's some sort of spurned suitor revenge, I gather."

"My boy would never seek revenge," said Mr. Marker furiously. "He's a sweet-tempered saint, my lord." Mr.

Marker added, his voice lower now because no one ever
yelled in the vicinity of the earl of Northcliffe, "He doesn't
even like girls, told me he didn't, so he would never try to
kiss Miss Corrie. And jest look at her, not even a girl, if ye
take me meaning. My Willie's niver done anything wrong
in his whole little life, bless him and bless his mother fer
birthing him."

James was staring at the handkerchief tied around his
father's arm, and the blood soaking it. The Virgin Bride
was right. What had happened? He watched his father walk
up the stairs, Mr. Marker's words flowing over him, but he
had no choice but to remain and deal with this idiocy. He
didn't like this one bit, but he had no choice. He turned and
smiled at Mr. Marker.

"I would like to hear what both of you have to say.
Would you please come into the estate room?"

CHAPTER FOUR

❧

What a woman wants is what you're out of.

O. HENRY

I T REQUIRED TEN minutes to pin down the basic facts. James finally said to Mr. Marker, "I regret to tell you, sir, that Willie, your sweet boy, has a very long road to travel if he is to attain sainthood in the next six lifetimes."

"Impossible, my lord. He tells me everything, Willie does, and he's a good boy, thoughtful and kind, even to this missy over here."

"You force me to be blunt, sir. Willie is known throughout the area as a young man who kisses any girl who isn't fast enough to get away from him. There is no doubt in my mind that Corrie smacked him, and that he wanted revenge. I suggest you make him work off what he has done. Now, good day to you, and I wish you luck with Willie."

"But, my sweet boy—"

"Good day, Mr. Marker. Corrie, you stay."

Hollis magically appeared in the doorway of the estate room. "Mr. Marker, it seems to me that you would like a nice glass of ale before you confront William. Isn't it always so that a man, regardless of his own high moral standing, must face bad behavior in his children? I do have some suggestions for how you might deal with him."

Mr. Marker folded his tent. He followed Hollis from the estate room, his old hat clutched in his fingers.

"Did Willie really try to kiss you?"

Corrie shuddered. "Yes, it was awful. I turned my head really fast and he kissed my ear. James, I had to do something—"

"Yes, I know. You clouted him."

"Right in the nose. Then I kicked him in the shin. You know these boots, the toes are really sharp."

"No wonder he wanted to get back at you. At least you didn't knee him in his—"

"What? You mean—" Her eyes fell, looking directly at his crotch. She frowned. "Why would I do that?"

"Never mind. Now, you look a fright. Go home and take a nice bath and get all the dust off your face and out of your hair. Why did you come here, Corrie?"

She fidgeted a moment, then whispered, "I came here to Northcliffe because I couldn't imagine what my aunt and uncle would have done faced with Mr. Marker. But I knew you would take care of things, or your father. Thank you, James."

Suddenly, the dowager countess of Northcliffe, a big woman with more than ample padding, who would outlive them all, appeared in the estate room door, pumped herself up, and bellowed, "James!"

"Yes, Grandmother?" *It needed but this,* he thought, dutifully turning to give his grandmother his full attention, hoping it would focus her eye and tongue on him. But of course it didn't. She was still tall and straight, her white hair thinning now, her blue eyes faded, but there was nothing at all wrong with the workings of her mouth, her brain, or her diction, unfortunately.

If a voice could be said to ring, hers did. "Coriander Tybourne-Bennett, your dead parents would be appalled! Look at you—you're a disgrace. You look like a ruffian. I must speak to your aunt and uncle, even though both of them are feckless creatures, but they must do something."

Corrie stuck her chin in the air. "They are."

"They are what, miss?"

"They are doing something. I'm going to London for the Little Season. They are not feckless."

The dowager's blue eyes glittered with anticipation. She saw fresh prey and wanted to dig in her claws and bring it down. She opened her mouth, but her grandson dared to insert himself.

"Grandmother, Corrie will be all ready to go to London. My mother will assist her aunt in seeing that she knows things and dresses appropriately."

The dowager turned on her grandson. "Your mother? That redheaded girl your father was forced to keep when that bad boy Tony Parrish stole your father's real bride, Melissande? No one can believe they are sisters. Why, all you have to do is look into the mirror to see the face of the glorious creature your father should have married. But no, he was tricked into remaining with your mother. May I ask, young man, just what your mother knows about anything at all? Why, it is your dear father who dresses her, who tells her how to behave, who scolds her, but not often enough, the good Lord knows, only he can't control her cutting her gowns down to her ankles. How many times have I told him—"

"Madam, that is quite enough!" James was so angry he was shaking with it. He'd never in his life interrupted his grandmother, but he couldn't stop himself. Corrie was forgotten as his brain sharpened itself up to go toe-to-toe with the old besom. "Madam, you are speaking about the countess of Northcliffe—my mother. She is the most beautiful lady I have ever met, she is loving and kind and makes my father very happy and—"

"Ha! Loving is right, or something far more lewd. Why, at her age, she still sneaks up on my dear Douglas and kisses his ear. It is disgraceful. Never would I have done that to your grandfather—"

"I am sure you would not, Grandmother. However, my mother and father, despite their advanced years, quite love each other. I do not wish for you to speak ill of her again."

"I like her too," Corrie said.

The dowager turned her cannon on Corrie. "You dare to interrupt me, missy? A grandson, the future earl, is one rudeness I must accept, but not you. Goodness, just look at you, a viscount's daughter and you're—" Words failed her, but only for a moment. "I don't believe for an instant that little Willie Marker kissed you. He's a sweet little boy. You probably tried to kiss him."

James said more calmly now, "He's sweet to you, madam, because he knows if he weren't, you'd have him boiled in oil. Fact is, he's a bully. He is the scourge of the neighborhood."

Corrie said, "And I would rather kiss a toad than Willie Marker."

"I don't believe that, James. He is a precious little fellow." She whirled on Corrie. "When he kissed you, you struck him? There, doesn't that show that you have no breeding, no sense of who or what you're supposed to be? You, supposedly a lady, struck him? That proves what I think—you are a pathetic ragamuffin."

With that parting shot, she flounced out of the estate room, her petticoats flapping.

Corrie whispered, "I'm not. I'm not pathetic or a ragamuffin."

James looked after his grandmother, shook his head. It was the very first time in his entire life he'd dished back some of her own sauce, and she appeared not to even have noticed. He felt like he'd failed. Upon brief reflection, James realized that if his grandmother were to apologize to anyone for her rudeness, such an extraordinary event would likely signal the end of the world. Still, to attack both his mother and Corrie like that. He said, "I'm sorry, Corrie, but if it makes you feel any better, she treats my mother worse."

"But I don't understand, James. Why would she be so nasty to your poor mother?" *Why hasn't the old bat croaked it?* That was what she really wanted to say.

"She's nasty to all her daughters-in-law," James said. "Her own daughter, my Aunt Sinjun, as well. She's nasty to any woman who walks into Northcliffe, except for my Aunt Melissande. If it was a matter of not wanting any competition why would she be kind to Aunt Melissande?"

"Maybe it's because you and Jason look exactly like her. That is so very strange, isn't it?"

James winced. "Yes. Now, is your name really Coriander?"

Corrie looked down at her scuffed and dirty boots. "So I've been told."

"That's unfortunate."

"Yes."

He sighed and lightly laid his hand on her arm. "You don't look like a ragamuffin." It was possible she looked worse, he thought, but she also looked flattened, and he'd known her forever, and oddly, he felt responsible for her. Why, he didn't know. Then he saw a little girl in his mind's eye, beaming up at him, wetter than the captured frog she held in her hand, a gift, from her to him.

Corrie blinked up at him even as she tugged on her old brown waistcoat, doubtless worn in a previous life by a stable lad. "What do I look like?"

James stalled. He wanted to go study all the farm accounts for the last decade, he wanted to calculate the price of oats and wheat for the next twenty quarters, he wanted to go count the sheep in the east pasture all by himself, anything but answer her.

She said slowly, "You don't know what to say, do you, James?"

"You look like you, dammit. You look like Corrie, not this wretched Coriander. Were your parents drinking too much brandy when they named you?"

"I'll ask my Aunt Maybella, although she and my mother evidently never got along very well. She's never called me anything but Corrie. Once when I was little, I'd been playing with my dog Benjie, both of us minding our own business all right, so Benjie had gotten just the littlest bit muddy, and so he did escape me and ran into my uncle's library. I'll even admit that he rolled around on top of my uncle's desk and tore up two leaves my uncle was pressing. Well, that was when Uncle Simon yelled out my full name for the first time." She paused a moment, looking out over the west gardens. "I didn't know who he was yelling at."

"Corrie, forget the nastiness. I will speak to my father; he's the only one who can do anything about my grandmother's meanness. I heard him tell my Uncle Ryder that my grandfather had doubtless hurled himself to the hereafter, just to escape her."

"It doesn't matter. I will simply avoid her in the future. I must be going. Good-bye, James." And she went out the estate room glass doors, out into the gardens. If she meandered far enough, then she'd run smack into the naked Greek statues, all of couples copulating in varied positions. He and Jason had spent many many hours staring at those statues, giggling and pointing when they were young, then looking at them through very different eyes when they'd gotten older. To the best of his knowledge, Corrie had never been in this part of the vast Northcliffe gardens. He yelled, "No, Corrie! Come back here. I want you to have some tea and cake with me."

She turned, frowned at him. Reluctantly, she came back into the estate room. "What kind of cake?"

"Lemon seed cake, I hope. It's my favorite."

She looked down at her boots, then up again, but not at his face, over his left shoulder. "Thank you, but I must go home. Good-bye, James." And she dashed out the doors. He watched her run into the gardens. There were paths leading out; surely she wouldn't explore; surely she wouldn't find the statues.

J AMES FOUND HIS father in his bedchamber, alone, bandaging his arm.

"What happened, Father?"

Douglas jerked around, then heaved a sigh of relief. "James. I thought it was your mother. It's nothing really, an idiot shot me in the arm, nothing more."

James's fear sliced right through to his belly. He swallowed, but the fear just kept bubbling up. "This isn't good," he said. "Papa, I really don't like this. Where's Peabody?"

James hadn't called him Papa for many years now. Douglas tied off the strip of linen that he'd ripped from his shirt, pulled it tight with his teeth, then turned and managed a smile. "I'm all right, James." Then because James looked afraid, Douglas walked to him, and pulled his precious boy against him. "I am just fine, it's just a bit of a sting, nothing to worry you or me or anyone, particularly your mother who will never find out about this."

James felt his father's strength and was comforted. He also realized that he was now as large as his father, this man he'd looked up to all his life, seen as a god, an omnipotent being, and now they were the same size? He said against his father's ear, "Did you see who it was?"

Douglas took James's arms in his hands and stepped back. "I was riding Henry out on the downs. There was a single shot and Henry knows an opportunity when he sees it, and, of course, he threw me. I'd swear that damned horse was laughing down at me lying there in the bushes where I landed, luckily. I looked afterward, but the fellow had left no signs. It could have easily been a poacher, James, an accident, pure and simple."

"No." He looked his father right in the eye. "The Virgin Bride was right. There is trouble here. Where's Peabody?"

"I got rid of him right away, sent him to Eastbourne to fetch some special pomade for me, I made up a name—Foley's Special Hair Restorer."

"But you have lots of hair."

"No matter. It'll drive Peabody quite frantic when he doesn't locate the pomade, something he deserves since he's always sticking his long nose in my business."

James drew a deep breath. "I want to look at your arm, Father. Jason is right as well—someone is after you. We have to do something. But first I want to see for myself that the wound isn't bad."

Douglas raised a dark brow at his son, saw the fear in James's eyes, and knew James had to see for himself that the wound was nothing.

"Very well," he said, and let James untie the linen he'd just wrapped around it.

James studied the angry red slash that had torn through his father's flesh. "It's nearly stopped bleeding. I want to wash it, then I want Hollis to see it. He will have some salve to put on it."

Of course Hollis had exactly the right nasty mixture. He also insisted, under James's watchful eye, on smearing it over the gash himself. "Hmmm," he said. "Hand me the clean bandage, Master James."

James handed him the clean linen. The old man's hands shook. From fear for his father? No, Hollis never was afraid of anything. "Hollis, how old are you?"

"Master James?"

"Er, if you don't mind my asking your age?"

"I am the very same age as your esteemed grandmother, my lord, well, perhaps she is a year older, but one hesitates to speak bluntly about such things, particularly when it involves a lady who is also one's mistress."

"That means," Douglas said, laughing, "that Hollis is older than those Greek statues in the west gardens."

"It does indeed," Hollis said. "There, my lord, you're tied up right and tight. Would you care for a tetch of laudanum?"

His arm throbbed, but who cared? He raised a haughty brow, looked disgusted, and said, "No I would not, Hollis. Are the two of you happy now?"

The door opened and Jason walked in, turned white, and blurted out, "I knew it. I just knew it was something bad."

James looked at the blood in the basin of water, swallowed, and told his brother what had happened.

"You know, sir," Jason said before the three of them went downstairs, "Mother will know there's something wrong when she sees the bandage on your arm."

"She won't see it."

"But you and Mother always sleep together," James said. "Surely she'll see it. I heard her say once that you never wore a nightshirt."

James said quickly, "She didn't know we were listening."

"Hmmm," Douglas said. "I'll think about that."

"We don't wear nightshirts either," Jason said, "once we heard that you didn't. What were we, James, about twelve?"

"Something like that," James said.

Douglas felt a lurch in his chest. He looked at his boys—*his boys*—and the throbbing in his arm became nothing at all.

Of course Alexandra found out quickly enough, not later than five o'clock that afternoon. Her maid, Phyllis, told her what the laundry girl—who'd washed a bloody linen strip—had told Mrs. Wilbur, the Sherbrooke housekeeper, who had rightfully passed it along to Hollis, who'd told her sharply to close her lips over her teeth, which, naturally, Mrs. Wilbur hadn't, and thus it had come to Phyllis's sharp ears over a cup of tea in Mrs. Wilbur's parlor.

"A bloody cloth?" Alexandra said, swiveling about on her dressing chair to stare up at Phyllis, who had mossy green eyes and a lovely thin nose that constantly dripped, necessitating a handkerchief in her right hand most of the time.

"Yes, my lady, a bloody cloth. From his lordship's bedchamber."

Alexandra raced out of the bedchamber and through the adjoining door to confront her husband, to run her hands all over his body, to even check the teeth in his mouth. Curse him—he wasn't there. And she knew when she confronted him, he would look down his elegant nose at her, call her a twit, and tell her it was all a tale invented by some silly girl in the laundry room.

Even though it was five o'clock in the afternoon, Alexandra hurried downstairs to the butler's pantry, a lovely airy room with black and white marble tiles on the floor. The only problem was, Hollis wasn't alone. Indeed, he was in the embrace of a woman. A woman she'd never seen before. Alexandra stared, then retreated, step by step, until she quietly closed the door.

Hollis hugging and kissing a strange woman? It seemed suddenly that everything was flying out of control. She forgot about nailing down proof so Douglas couldn't look down his nose at her, and burst into the estate room where her husband was in conversation with the twins. She looked at them all with new eyes. The twins were in on it, whatever it was. The three of them were in a *secret* conversation, she knew it, one that excluded her. She wanted to shoot all of them. Instead, she said, "Hollis is kissing a strange woman in the butler's pantry."

CHAPTER FIVE

❧

When you have no problems, you're dead.

ZELDA WERNER

DOUGLAS AND THE twins shut their mouths fast. Douglas said, "Er, Alex, my dear, did you say that Hollis was kissing a strange woman? In the butler's pantry?"

"Yes, Douglas, and she was much younger than Hollis, no more than sixty years old, I'd say."

"Hollis taking liberties with a younger woman," Jason said, threw his head back and laughed, then stopped. "My God, Father, what if she's an adventuress, after his money? I know he's well-heeled. He told me you'd been investing his money for him for years and he's nearly as rich as you are now."

"I will ensure that Hollis hasn't been snared by a rapacious grandmother," Douglas said.

James said, "You're sure they were actually kissing, Mother?"

"It was a rather passionate embrace, and yes, quite a bit of nuzzling and kissing," Alexandra said. "I'll tell you, it fairly made my eyes pop out of my head."

She took a step closer to her husband and whispered, "They both appeared to be enjoying themselves immensely."

Douglas said, "One hopes this is the young woman Hollis intends to marry."

His wife and his sons stared at him.

"You know about this, Douglas?"

"He spoke of marriage several days ago—something to the effect that a young wife would make him feel just fine."

"But—"

Douglas raised his hand to cut her off. "We'll see. After all, it really isn't any of our business."

James said, "It's Hollis, sir. He's been here longer than you have."

"Do not equate old with dead," Douglas said. "A man isn't dead in his parts until he's six feet under. Strive not to forget that."

Alexandra sighed. "All right, enough of this excitement. Now, Douglas, you will tell me what happened to you and you will tell me all of it. You will include all references to a bloody cloth found in the washbasin in your bedchamber, and you will not fob me off with a cut finger."

"I told you she'd find out, sir," Jason said.

"Mother even found out that I'd kissed Melissa Hamilton behind the stables when I was thirteen," James said. He gave his mother a brooding stare. "I've never figured out how you found out about that."

Alexandra looked at him. "I have spies who owe me their loyalty. It's best you never forget that. Just because you're men now doesn't mean that I've sent my spies into retirement."

"They certainly must be old enough," Jason said, and gave her a beautiful smile.

Alexandra said, trying not to melt under that smile, "Now, Douglas, speak and make it to the point."

"All right if you're going to make a big to-do about it."

Alexandra grinned at him. "I wonder, is that the Virgin Bride I hear applauding?"

**TWYLEY GRANGE,
HOME OF LORD AND LADY MONTAGUE
AND CORRIE TYBOURNE-BARRETT**

"My goodness, is it you, Douglas?" Simon Ambrose, Lord Montague, came quickly to his feet, blinked as he shoved his glasses up his nose, and nearly tripped over a journal that had fallen from the table at his side. He straightened himself and his vest.

"Yes, Simon, and I am here without invitation. I hope you will allow me to enter."

Simon Ambrose laughed. "As if you wouldn't be welcome to come into my bedchamber if you wished to leap through my window." Simon frowned. "Of course, you wouldn't be quite so welcome if you slipped into Maybella's bedchamber, but that is a possibility that isn't likely to occur, is it?"

"No more than you climbing in through Alexandra's bedchamber window, Simon."

"Now that is a thought that tickles my brain."

"Don't let it tickle too much."

Lord Montague laughed, waved Douglas to a seat. "It is very pleasant to see you. Maybella, here is Lord Northcliffe. Maybella? You are not here? How very odd that I don't see her, and I'd believed she was close by, maybe sewing in that chair over by the window." Simon sighed, then brightened. "Surely Corrie must be near. You know, she's quite able to entertain guests in her aunt's absence. Or maybe not." He threw back his head and yelled, "Buxted!"

"Yes, my lord," said Buxted, hovering at Lord Montague's elbow. Simon shot into the air, knocked his glasses off, and stumbled backward to hit against a small marquetry table. Buxted grabbed his arm and pulled him upright with such energy that Simon nearly went over on his nose. Once Simon was upright, Buxted handed him his glasses, and straightened the table. He then began brushing off his master, saying, "Ah, my lord, what an idiot I am, surprising you as I would a young lass who's hiked up her skirts to cross a stream."

Simon said, "Ah, yes, that is better, and quite enough. What happens when you surprise a young lady with her skirt up, Buxted?"

"It was a thought that shouldn't have traveled further than my fantasies, my lord. Wipe it from your mind, sir. Long white legs, that's all there can be at the end of that delightful thought."

Douglas remembered what Hollis had once said of Buxted, *"He is quite maladroit, my lord, altogether scattered in his brain, and quite an entertaining fellow. He and Lord Montague fit together excellently."*

Douglas smiled to see Buxted still brushing off Simon even as Simon was trying to push him away. "Buxted," Simon said, slapping at his hands, "I have need of Lady Maybella. If you cannot find her, then bring Corrie. Perhaps she is helping in the kitchen, the girl loves to bake berry tarts, at least she did when she was twelve. Douglas, do come in and sit down."

"I don't know who is where, my lord, no one tells me anything at all," Buxted said. "Ah, my lord Northcliffe, please do be seated. Let me move his lordship's precious journals from this lovely brocade winged chair. There, only three left, and that makes the chair look interesting, does it not?" Buxted hovered until Douglas sat himself on the three journals. Then he went flapping from the room, his bald head shiny with sweat.

Douglas smiled at his host. He quite liked Simon Ambrose. Simon was luckily rich enough so that he was known as eccentric, rather than batty. And he was as eccentric today as he'd been twenty years before, when, after his father had passed to the hereafter, Simon, now Viscount Montague, had taken himself to London, met and married Maybella Connaught, and brought her home to Twyley Grange, a neat Georgian house built upon the exact foundation of the granary attached to the long-defunct St. Lucien monastery.

Douglas knew that women vastly admired Simon until they came to know him well, and realized that his very handsome face and his sweet expression masked a mind that was usually elsewhere. But when, upon rare occasion, his mind did focus, Douglas knew he was very smart. Given Simon's mental inattention, he'd wondered upon occasion how the wedding night had gone, but surely something had transpired since Maybella had birthed three children, all, unfortunately, having died in infancy. Simon had a younger brother, Borty, who was as batty as he was, waiting in the wings. His brother was obsessively devoted to the collection of acorns, not leaves, like Simon.

Simon said, his glasses now firmly on his nose, "Truly, Douglas, I didn't forget you were coming, did I?"

"No, this is a surprise visit, Simon. I'm here because I fear my wife would come if I didn't."

"That's all right, isn't it? I quite like Alexandra. She could come into my bedchamber anytime she wished."

"Yes, she is likable, but you can forget her coming through your bedchamber window, Simon. The point is that my wife has no taste in clothes."

"I see. Goodness, I had no idea. I assure you, whenever

I see her, I am struck by how very round and white, er, well, it's best to stop right there, isn't it? She is very lovely, I will say, and wisely leave it at that."

"That is because I dress her," Douglas said.

"Now there is a thought that stirs the imagination."

"Don't let it stir too much, Simon."

"Yes, I can see that such an observation might quiver the embers of a man's passions. But she is really quite lovely—well, perhaps it is best that I put a period to that thought. Now, is there a problem with Maybella's clothes, Douglas? Or mine?"

Douglas sat forward, clasping his hands between his knees. "No problem at all. This is about Corrie. The thing is, Simon, Corrie is just like my wife in that she has no idea about clothes. When my wife told me she would speak with Maybella and advise Corrie, I knew that to avert complete disaster I had no choice but to come here myself and see to it. Now, if you will call in Corrie, I will tell her what it is she must wear. You know, the colors and styles of gowns and such. Of course, you want her to appear her best in London."

"Well naturally," Simon said, and blinked rapidly. "I've always thought Corrie dressed quite nicely, like her aunt, as a matter of fact, when she's not wearing her breeches. Isn't that odd that all her gowns are light blue, like Maybella's? And her boots—they are always highly polished, at least they were the last time I chanced to notice them. But, perhaps that was a long time ago. I don't often notice feet, you know."

"No, probably not. I agree with you. Her breeches, in particular, are doubtless of excellent style and cut. But the thing is, Simon, London is a vastly different place. Young ladies don't wear boots in London nor do they wear stylish breeches. You do remember?"

Simon sat back in his chair, closed his eyes, and sighed deeply. "Aye, Douglas, I remember all too well. It was only ten years ago that Maybella dragged me to London, to see a balloon ascension, she assured me. I was moved by her attempt to please me because I very much wanted to see the balloon ascension, Douglas, and it was indeed an incredible sight, but I fear I was taken in. It was six weeks before I could come home. There was only one other balloon ascension during that very long, tedious time. Do you mean that I must go there again?"

"Yes, you must. However, I fear that a balloon ascension isn't a certain thing. The weather in the fall is unpredictable, and as you know, balloons need to have clear weather and very little wind."

"Then why must I go to London if the weather is too uncertain for the balloons?"

"Because Corrie is eighteen, a young lady, and young ladies must be presented. They must attend balls and be seen and admired and taught to dance. James tells me that Corrie is going to come out in the Little Season, Simon, a sort of practice season, so she can learn how to go on. I fear, Simon, that you will have to go yet again to London next spring when Corrie is officially presented."

Simon moaned, then perked up. "Perhaps Corrie has no wish to go to London and be presented."

"She must be in the middle of things in order to find a husband, Simon. Young gentlemen are thick on the ground in London during the Season. Only then are there enough of them about to give a girl a decent selection. Alexandra and I will be in London this fall. We can assist you. Now, if you would call Corrie, I can begin advising her on her apparel. Also, James has offered to teach her to waltz."

Buxted cleared his throat from the doorway. "Ah, please regard me, my lords. I managed to snag some lovely cinnamon bread from the kitchen from under Cook's nose. It is Lady Maybella's favorite. When I found out she didn't consume all of it at the breakfast table, I moved quickly. Just look—there are six nice fat slices left. There were seven, but I must confess that I nipped one slice, to ensure its freshness, you know."

"Excellent, Buxted," Simon said, and pushed a quantity of scientific journals off the table at his elbow. "You didn't eat more than one, did you, Buxted?"

"Just one, my lord."

Simon never looked away from that plate Buxted was holding as he said, "Did you find Corrie?"

"Yes, my lord. In the middle of the upstairs corridor. She was tugging on her breeches that have become too short in the past months." Buxted fidgeted, looked over his master's left shoulder, then drew himself up. "I warned her we had a very august personage visiting. I even managed in a very roundabout manner to let her know that she might also want to change her stockings. She squeaked and ran to her bedchamber. I daresay the result of my words might be a pale blue gown, just like her ladyship's."

"Well done, Buxted," Douglas said.

Buxted drew himself up and gave the earl a blinding smile. "As to that, one would never wish to repel an earl, my lord."

"Naturally not," Douglas said. "I shall tell Hollis of your wily brain, Buxted."

"Will you, my lord? Will you indeed? Oh, to have Hollis know that I perhaps managed to bring something worthwhile to fruition. Perhaps you'd best not, my lord. One must wait and see."

"The cinnamon bread, Buxted. Now."

Buxted reverently laid the plate on the table beside Simon, gave one last wistful look at the artfully arranged slices, sighed, blotted the sweat on his bald head with a handkerchief, and walked out the door.

The instant Buxted was gone, Simon grabbed up a slice of cinnamon bread. "I thought he would never leave, Douglas. We must hurry and eat the cinnamon bread before Maybella comes down. Don't talk, Douglas, just eat, or else Maybella may appear and she will snag the other slices. She has a powerful sense of smell, does Maybella."

Douglas smiled, took a slice, bit into it. He realized this wasn't just any sort of cinnamon bread, this was cinnamon bread straight from the celestial realm. He was reaching for a second slice when his hand hit Simon's.

"There's a problem about this, Douglas," Simon said, and gently eased out the slice from beneath Douglas's hand.

Douglas snagged the next slice, managed to polish it off before he raised an eyebrow in question.

Simon sighed so deeply he nearly choked. "The money."

"Money? Isn't Corrie well-dowered?"

Simon looked on the point of bursting into tears. *Oh God*, Douglas thought, *what was wrong? No dowry? No, surely that couldn't be true*.

"That would be bad enough. No, Douglas, it is far worse than that. She's an *heiress*."

Douglas nearly laughed aloud. "Surely that isn't all that bad."

"You know what will happen when it's discovered she has bucketfuls of groats, Douglas. She will be hunted down like a rat."

"I wouldn't put it precisely like that, Simon, but I do understand that she will be the focus of any fortune-hungry young gentleman in London."

"If the young gentlemen don't have the wit to do it, then their parents will plot and scheme to get her to the altar. Not to mention all the old gentlemen who would want to get their hands on her money. You know the sort—womanizers, lechers, gamblers who will forbid her breeches and keep her breeding until she's thirty and likely dead of it. I don't want that to happen, Douglas."

"Is she really an heiress or does she have, say, in the vicinity of five thousand pounds?"

"She could drop five thousand pounds in a ditch and not even blink, Douglas."

"I see. I will think about this. Perhaps we can keep it quiet."

"Ha! When money is involved it won't remain a secret for long."

Douglas frowned. "Well, it has until now, but you're right, Simon. Once she gets to London and it's known she's looking for a husband, even burying her money in the kitchen garden won't help." Douglas sighed and tapped his fingertips together.

A lovely low musical voice came from the doorway. "Good morning, my lord. So you are our august personage?"

CHAPTER SIX

❧❦❧

There is no such thing as too much couth.

S. J. PERELMAN

DOUGLAS QUICKLY ROSE. "Maybella. You are looking fine this morning."

She looked as she always looked, wearing one of her many pale blue gowns that covered her from throat to toe. She nodded and headed straight to the cinnamon bread. The plate was empty.

Maybella merely held out her hand. With obvious reluctance, perhaps even a small whimper, Simon stuck out his hand. On his palm lay two slices.

She took both slices without a word, sat herself down on the small sofa facing Douglas, and smiled placidly at him.

"Corrie will be down presently," she said, and proceeded to eat, both men watching her avidly. "I believe she was searching for a stocking."

"As I was telling Simon, Maybella, you are going to have to take Corrie to London this fall."

She said matter-of-factly, "I hadn't informed him of it yet, Douglas, because he would figure a way to get out of it."

Simon said, "The weather is uncertain in the fall, Maybella. Perhaps Corrie can be presented when the weather is finer, in the summer, perhaps, two or three summers after this one."

Douglas said, "I have just recalled that the second week of October is always pleasant, Simon, and we will see every balloon ascension during that week. Perhaps several will be held. Trust me."

Buxted's throat cleared once again in the doorway. "Miss Corrie is here, my lord, and she is not wearing her breeches. I did not inquire about her stockings as such a query could be taken amiss."

Since Maybella's mouth was full, she only nodded. Corrie came into the drawing room dressed in a very old muslin gown the same pale blue as her aunt's. It needed more petticoats and fewer flounces and perhaps an inch of her neck showing. At least she was straight and tall, her waist small enough to please even Douglas's mother. On the other hand, probably not.

"Good morning, my lord," Corrie said and gave Douglas a fine curtsy.

"I taught her to curtsy," Maybella said, beaming at Corrie as she chewed on the cinnamon bread. "Isn't that shade of blue particularly fetching on her?"

"It always is on you, my love," Simon said, eyeing that final slice of cinnamon bread lovingly held in Maybella's right hand.

Douglas said, "Good morning to you, Corrie. That was a lovely curtsy. You're tall and that's excellent. No, straighten your shoulders. That's right. Never stoop. Small, mincing girls aren't to any gentleman's taste, unless he is very short himself. You do not wish to attract a short man, he will make you bow your shoulders. Hmmm, yes, your shoulders are nice." Douglas rose and made a circuit around her. Her hair was in a single fat braid down her back. "I think with your height you will enhance any gown Madame Jourdan can make for you."

"I don't understand why you are examining me, my lord."

Simon said, "Douglas is going to advise you on clothes, Corrie, for London. He is evidently superior to his wife in this. He is evidently renowned at it. We will listen to him."

"Pale blue is such a lovely color, don't you think, Douglas? What a girl needs is blue, a lovely pale blue, I've always said."

"She will have one pale blue gown, Maybella, no more. Your coloring is very different from Corrie's. Now, you must trust me on this."

Maybella bit into a slice of cinnamon bread, then said, "Perhaps you are right. Corrie has never had my radiance."

"Indeed," said her husband, and pushed his glasses back up.

Maybella, having finished the second slice of cinnamon bread, cleared her throat. "I say, Douglas, why is Jason skulking out there leaning against one of the lime trees on the drive? Or is it dear James? One can never tell since they are like two heads on the same Greek coin."

Corrie immediately whipped around and skipped to the windows. "It is James, Aunt Maybella. He isn't doing anything at all."

"Why is he outside, Douglas?"

Douglas gave Simon a harassed look and said, "Some idiot shot me in the arm yesterday and my sons must need keep me under close watch every waking hour."

"Such good boys." Maybella said. "I daresay Corrie would do the same for her Uncle Simon if some idiot shot at him. Do invite him in, Douglas. There isn't any more cinnamon bread. However, Cook hides food in the expectation that we will have an earthquake or a flood, so Buxted will find something else for James."

Corrie said, "I have noticed that young men are usually happy to eat anything one throws at them." She walked to the windows and tapped on the glass. When James looked at her, she waved him in.

He raised a perfect dark eyebrow, and nodded. A moment later, he was making his bows to Lord and Lady Montague.

"So you are protecting your father," Maybella said, smiling and nodding at the young Adonis who stood before her, all windblown, white-toothed, his lawn shirt open at his throat. "How very lovely. Your father is looking particularly fine this morning, James, don't you think?"

James, who had known Lord and Lady Montague nearly all his life, nodded and smiled. The overly admiring gleam in Lady Montague's eyes wiped the smile off James's face in a hurry. He supposed his father looked fine, but the fact was, his father looked like his father—an aristocrat, tall and lean, silver threaded through his black hair.

"Throw him some food, Buxted," Corrie said. James turned, eyed her up and down, and said, "Where is Corrie? I would swear I heard her voice, but all I see is a chit with a gown on that's too short and too tight and comes almost to her chin. Also the color makes her look sallow."

"I was looking at my eyelashes this morning, James, and they're quite long. Mayhap even longer than yours."

Douglas cleared his throat. "Be seated, James. I was about to tell Corrie that you were going to teach her to waltz."

Lord Montague gave his full attention to his niece and said in an austere voice, "You know, James, Lord Hammersmith, is a young man of excellent parts, Corrie. He was quite the scholar at Oxford, fast becoming an expert on celestial bodies and their movements. In particular he knows all three of Kepler's laws, the third one, simply stated, is—well I forget—but the fact is that Galileo observed that the moon is not a smooth, polished surface as Aristotle had claimed."

"He must have had very sharp eyes," Lady Maybella said.

"No, my dear," Simon said. "Galileo was using the telescope, just invented by Dutch lens grinders. What was the year, my boy?"

James started to say he didn't know when he happened to glance at Corrie and saw the sneer on her face.

"It was in the early seventeenth century," he said.

"A nice guess," Corrie said. "I don't believe that you have any comprehension at all about Dutch lens grinders, James. I think you made it up to make yourself look intelligent."

Maybella said, "James doesn't need to know about stars and telescopes, Corrie. All he has to do is stand rather still and let everyone look at him."

Corrie's sneer was near to overflowing. Truth be told, she knew well enough that James had looked into the heavens since he'd been a boy, studied and learned and built his own telescope, but any chance she could find to bait him wasn't to be ignored.

James was ready to run out the door, Douglas knew it, but there wasn't the chance because Simon said, "So you see, James is not too pretty, Corrie. No one can be too pretty who understands Kepler, even though I can't remember that third law. James has his father's jaw, which is the most stubborn jaw in all of England. And that little hole in his chin, that's his father's as well."

That was true, Douglas thought, pleased. *Not everything on his face belongs to Melissande.*

Simon bent then to pick up a journal off the pile on the

floor beside his chair, and paged to an article titled *The Workings of Black Air During an Eclipse*.

"Corrie," Douglas said, rising, knowing escape was imminent, "I know exactly the style and colors that will suit you. Mrs. Ann Plack's daughter, Miss Jane Plack, from Rye, is an excellent seamstress. She will make you several gowns. Then I will take you to Madame Jourdan once you're settled in London."

"Corrie's maid is a perfectly good seamstress, Douglas," Maybella said. "Why, she sewed this gown I'm wearing as well as the one Corrie is wearing. Surely she—"

Simon said, "My dear, you ate the last two slices of cinnamon bread. Now you wish to foist Corrie's maid onto good material. Corrie needs to be dressed appropriately. Wherever am I to get fabric, Douglas?"

"Don't worry, Simon. I will have Miss Plack deliver both the materials and various patterns, and herself, and I will make the appropriate selections. Are you in agreement, Corrie?"

She desperately wanted to ask him what men said instead of *bosom*. "I thank you, my lord."

"Good," Douglas said. "I knew you weren't a blockhead."

"Ignorant as a post," James said, "but not a blockhead."

Corrie opened her mouth to blast him, but Douglas was faster. "Now, James, are you ready to take your leave?"

"I will fetch our horses, sir."

After James bid his host and hostess good-bye and gave Corrie the tolerant look he bestowed on his grandmother's pug, he was outside, circling trees, looking behind bushes, and even peering down into a rain barrel.

"He worries," Douglas said. He walked to Corrie, cupped her chin in his palm, and studied her face a moment. He slowly nodded. "You'll do," he said, and then he smiled down at her.

CHAPTER SEVEN

*'Tis safest in matrimony
to begin with a little aversion.*

RICHARD BRINSLEY SHERIDAN

THE DOWAGER COUNTESS of Northcliffe said, "Corrie is a misfit, a ragamuffin, a disgrace to her parentage. Hollis, where is my dish of prunes?"

Hollis said, "I have frequently noted, my lady, that even the Norman church bells that chime so beautifully in New Romney need a bit of polish on the outside."

"Corrie Tybourne-Barrett isn't an old bell, Hollis, she is a new bell with excessive rust. Not acceptable. I would have nothing rusted in my house. What is wrong with you, Hollis? You are paying no attention to what is important, like my dish of prunes."

Hollis merely smiled and made his way to the sideboard

to fetch the prunes. He was humming under his breath when he poured Douglas some tea.

"At least you will be dressing her, Douglas, and that must certainly help."

"It will," Douglas said. "Who knows what we'll find beneath those absurd costumes she wears."

The dowager said, waving a slice of toast, "I have often wondered at Maybella and Simon. Why would they let the girl run around like a tart in breeches?"

Douglas realized he now knew the answer to that question, but he merely shook his head and smiled. Their strategy had worked—no budding fortune hunter would ever look in her direction—but at what cost to a young lady who'd never been a girl?

Douglas waited until his mother was concentrating her full attention on her prunes, then said quietly, "Hollis, when will we meet this paragon Alexandra saw you kissing in the butler's pantry?"

"Ah, I thought I saw a shadow of movement, sniffed the lightest of perfumes."

"Yes, it was her ladyship on a mission to discover what had happened to me. You routed her."

"I will introduce you to Annabelle very soon now, my lord."

"Annabelle?"

Hollis nodded and moved a small jug of milk closer to his lordship's elbow. "Annabelle Trelawny, my lord. A very fine young lady, one of immense good will and fine taste."

"Why don't you bring her by this afternoon? I believe my mother will be off to visit some of her cronies."

"That would be premature, my lord. Annabelle hasn't yet agreed to be my wife. Can you imagine? Indeed, I fear that I may have to resort to seduction to bring her to the mark."

There was a tic in Douglas's left cheek. "Seduction, Hollis?"

"Yes, my lord. I realize it is indeed a grave step to consider, but I believe it to be one I may have to undertake."

"I wish you luck."

"Thank you, my lord."

"You have never before been married, Hollis. My father said once that you'd been the victim of a tragic love affair. Was he correct, or didn't you appreciate the fairer sex until now?"

Hollis saw that the dowager countess was still concentrating on her prunes, but still he moved a bit closer to Douglas. "I was a victim of a love, my lord, and a sad time it was. Her name was Miss Drucilla Plimpton, and I worshiped the very air she breathed. It is an amazing stroke of circumstance—Annabelle actually knew my own dear Miss Plimpton. Ah, so many years ago it was.

"Ah, my lord, I have always appreciated the fairer sex. But after I lost my precious Miss Plimpton, I came to view wedlock as not enough wed and perhaps too much lock."

"No wonder. You lived here."

"There is that, my lord. However, I believe being locked up by Annabelle might be vastly amusing. So many stories Annabelle remembers about Miss Plimpton, even though she was younger than Drucilla. Drucilla, I believe, was very kind to her, teaching her stitching, correcting her manners. Of course, Annabelle also remembers me clearly as well, particularly my very fine head of hair."

"It has remained very fine. Are you certain that my mother hasn't kept you away from matrimony, Hollis?"

"Not at all, my lord." Hollis took another quick look at the dowager, leaned closer, and added, "Although the notion about too much lock—well, never you mind. Robbie has informed me that Master Jason is waiting for you at the stables."

"All right, curse him. At least James is in the estate room with Danvers."

"Poor young man. Danvers will work Master James until his head is an empty gourd, an exceptional empty gourd I might add."

Douglas sipped his tea. If Hollis only knew. James was not only enamored with celestial bodies and Kepler's laws, he was also fascinated in every facet of the estate's workings, had been from his earliest years, even before he'd fully grasped that Northcliffe would someday be his responsibility. No, it was James who would work Danvers to near exhaustion, not the other way around.

When Douglas rose, tossed his napkin on his plate, and strode from the room, his mother's voice hit him squarely in the back. "I need more wallpaper samples, Douglas. Alexandra is incapable of making selections pleasing to anyone blessed with extraordinary taste, such as I."

"I'll see to it, Mother," Douglas said, and wondered if there were any samples left in the warehouses in Eastbourne. Well, he supposed there could be samples found in New Romney, though he doubted it.

He met Jason in the paddock where Henry VIII was having a fine time trying to kill Bad Boy, James's horse. Lovejoy was trying his best to save his favorite of the two, but Henry wasn't having it. Douglas walked to the fence and whistled. Henry eyed Bad Boy for another moment, then wheeled about and came trotting over to his master, head high, tail swishing. Douglas patted his shiny black neck while he butted his head against Douglas's shoulder.

Douglas held out his hand. Weir, the head stable lad, slapped two carrots sharply onto his palm, and stepped back because he wasn't stupid. "All right, my big brute," Douglas said, and watched with a smile as Henry ate the carrots.

"I'll saddle him up, Weir," he said. Two minutes later, he and Jason were riding toward Branderleigh Farm to look at the new hunters that had just arrived from Spain. Douglas was very aware that Jason was trying to look in all directions at once for a villain bent on murder.

Jason said, riding close to his father, giving him as much protection as he could, "Mother told me that the Virgin Bride had visited you, Father, when Mother had been kidnapped by that fanatic Royalist, Georges Cadoudal. She said you hated it, but if you were pushed, you would admit it because you don't lie, at least not usually, at least not to her, usually."

Douglas rolled his eyes.

Jason sighed. "Did you really see her, Father? What did she say?"

Douglas turned in his saddle to look at his boy—tall, straight, an excellent rider, a big man now, not a boy. At least the twins' respective characters didn't appear to be ruined by their incredible good looks, and surely that was a victory over nature. Where had the years gone? "Forget that ridiculous phantom, Jason. Whatever happened in the distant past will remain there. It is forgotten. Do you understand me?"

Jason said, "No, sir, I can't forget, but I do recognize a granite wall when I see it. I believe I will go swimming later."

"You'll freeze your parts off."

Jason grinned like a bandit. "That, sir, is an image that truly appalls."

"It should. Forget that damned ghost."

"Yes, sir." But of course Douglas knew he wouldn't.

He couldn't for the life of him decide if the first shot had been intentional or not. Just because that damned phantom had predicted it—well, that made him want to dismiss it without another thought. However, he wasn't stupid, curse it.

LATE IN THE afternoon, three days later, a messenger arrived at Northcliffe Hall with a message for Douglas from Lord Avery at the War Ministry.

The earl left for London the following morning, alone, his wife refusing to speak to him, and his two sons, whom he suspected would follow him, staring after him.

MICHAELMAS WAS THREE weeks away, Douglas thought, as he rode Garth into the stable entrance off Putnam Square, and he would be a year older, and wasn't that the strangest thing. George IV had died in June, bringing his brother, the duke of Clarence, to the throne as William IV. William was good-natured, but, truth be told, he wasn't smart enough to give wise counsel or recognize it when it smacked him in the nose. He had more enthusiasm than sense, was indiscreet to the point of lunacy, causing one wag to say, *"It is a good sovereign, but it is a little cracked."* It remained to be seen what would happen, particularly since the duke of Wellington was at the helm and had offended Tories and Whigs alike. It was an extraordinary year, Douglas thought, as he walked into the Sherbrooke townhouse. Revolution everywhere—in France, Poland, Belgium, Germany, Italy, but thankfully not here at home, even though there were hardships, no denying that, grave hardships. After the duke had achieved Catholic Emancipation, he'd turned against all reform. His inconsistencies boggled Douglas's mind, but since he owed Wellington his allegiance, he would support him in the House of Lords, although he hated politics, would swear until he was out of breath that the vast majority of the Tories and the Whigs alike were power-mongering, flatulent liars. He recalled that his father had felt the same way. Douglas smiled at that. He would have to ask James and Jason their opinions.

He went to his club that evening, chatted with old friends, realized that there was more divisiveness in the government than he'd thought, won a hundred pounds at whist, and fell asleep with a warm belly, the result of a snifter of French brandy that, he would swear, had tasted much better when it had been illegal and smuggled into England in the dead of night.

He was surprised when he entered Lord Avery's large ornate office at the War Ministry the following morning to see Arthur Wellesley, the duke of Wellington, standing by one of the long windows, staring at Westminster in the distance, now visible because the morning fog had lifted. He looked weary to his bones, but when he saw Douglas, his eyes lit up and he smiled.

"Northcliffe," he said, turning. He strode forward to shake Douglas's hand. "You are looking fit."

"As are you. It is a pleasure to see you, your grace. I will not speak of either Tories or Whigs for fear there may be one hidden in the closet, ready to jump out and clout the both of us. I congratulate you on achieving Catholic Emancipation. You can count on me in the House of Lords, though to be honest about it, to listen to those weasels whine about any- and everything makes my belly cramp."

The duke smiled. "I have many times thought the same thing. I am a soldier, Northcliffe, and now I am called upon to perform a vastly different job. It is a pity I cannot have the opposition whipped with a cat o' nine tails."

Douglas laughed.

"But you know, I have decided that what will happen, will happen," he said, his voice more bitter than angry. "It is one of those newfangled trains that is now in motion. There is no stopping it. Further, I am no longer in control of it." When Douglas would have questioned him, he waved his hand and said, "Enough of that. I wish to speak to you because Lord Avery has discussed with me a threat to your life that comes from a trustworthy source. You have served your country well, Northcliffe. I wished to tell you that and to inform you of the nature of this threat."

Well, blessed hell. That damned phantom was right.

The bullet that hit his arm wasn't from a poacher's gun. He and the duke spent the next hour together.

When Douglas arrived back at the Sherbrooke town house some two hours later, it was to see his wife and two sons standing in the entrance hall, their luggage piled around them, surely denoting a protracted stay. All three of them stared him down, daring him to say a word.

CHAPTER EIGHT

The English never smash in a face.
They merely refrain from asking it to dinner.

MARGARET HALSEY

DOUGLAS DIDN'T SAY a single word. He just sighed and said, "Wellington met me at the ministry. There is indeed a threat, dammit."

Alexandra was in his arms in a moment. "I knew it, I just knew it," she whispered against his neck. "What sort of threat? Who is behind this?"

Douglas kissed the tip of her nose, hugging her tightly. The twins were practically *en pointe*, and that made him smile.

James said, "I don't understand, sir, you haven't been involved in any missions for a very long time."

Douglas nodded. "It is, I believe, a matter of revenge,

and the exacting of revenge is something that one can savor for years before acting. Enough now. Alexandra, call Willicombe and get us something to eat and drink. Come along, and I will tell you all about it. Oh, there you are, Willicombe. Please see to the valises and—"

"Aye, my lord, all is done. If you would repair to the drawing room, everything will be as you wish in but a matter of moments."

Willicombe, at fifty, quite young enough to be Hollis's son, wanted more than anything in his life to be just likc Hollis. He wanted to talk like him, he wanted to fetch up the perfect word at exactly the right time, he wanted to inspire the household staff to regard him as God. He wanted all of this, but he wanted to do all of it better and faster than Hollis. Perhaps Willicombe would be faster since Hollis was beginning to creak. Douglas wondered what Willicombe would do were he to tell him that Hollis was in love, mayhap even set upon seduction, just to see the look on his face. Would he then try to seduce one of the maids? Or perhaps Mrs. Bootie, the housekeeper, who had more hair on her upper lip than Douglas did before he shaved in the morning?

No one settled into comfortable chairs, no one relaxed. Tension flowed throughout the large room. Douglas looked around at his family and said, "Lord Avery received a letter from an informant in Paris that I was to finally get my just desserts. The informant believes it has something to do with Georges Cadoudal."

Alexandra was shaking her head. "No, that couldn't be possible, could it? You parted friends with Georges. Goodness, Douglas, it was years and years ago, before the twins were even born."

"Yes, I know."

"Who is this Cadoudal, Father?"

Douglas looked at James, who was standing, shoulders against the mantelpiece, arms crossed over his chest, exactly in the same way that Douglas stood, and said, "Georges Cadoudal was a madman and a genius. Our government paid him vast amounts of money to kill Napoleon. He killed a lot of Frenchmen, but not the emperor. I heard he'd died some time ago."

Willicombe entered, carrying a beautiful Georgian tea tray on his arm. Douglas remained silent until finally, seeing that Willicombe could think of nothing that would allow him to remain and eavesdrop, and thus know more than Hollis knew about this situation, whatever it was, raised an eyebrow.

But Willicombe didn't move, couldn't move. Something bad had happened, that was all he knew. The family was in trouble. He was needed. It was time to prove his worth. He tried manfully to dredge up a wise word. He cleared his throat.

"Yes, Willicombe?" Alexandra asked.

He could tell she was so upset she was white as the lovely lace at the neck of her gown. He drew himself up to his full five foot, six inches and squared his shoulders. "I am your man, my lord. I am resourceful. I learn quickly what is what. I could pick out an enemy from fifty feet. I am a man of action when the need but offers itself. I am the soul of discretion. Pull out my fingernails and nothing will pass my lips but an occasional scream."

James looked at Willicombe with great respect. After all, when James was born, Willicombe was a footman who'd occasionally played with him in the back gardens, tossing him a red ball, James remembered. "Nothing but a scream, Willicombe?"

"That's correct, my lord. I can be trusted to go to the grave carrying any secrets you would wish to confide in me."

Douglas said, "I thank you, Willicombe. Fact is, it appears that someone with revenge on his mind is out to cut my days short, something I really don't want."

Willicombe stood *en pointe*.

"I will assign the footmen to guard duty, my lord. I, myself, will take the first watch, eight o'clock until midnight, each and every night until the enemy is dispatched. No one will come into this house, this I swear."

"How many footmen are there, Willicombe?" James asked.

"There are three now, Master James. I will myself tell them what is what. You don't have to worry, my lord."

"Thank you, Willicombe," Douglas said. "I am certain that Hollis would be very impressed with your resourcefulness."

"Robert, the second footman, my lord, comes from a noxious area near the docks. He still knows some of the miscreants there. I will have him sniff around to see what he can learn."

"That is an excellent idea, Willicombe," Alexandra said and gave him a big smile.

They watched Willicombe stride from the room, taller, straighter, a man on a mission.

Jason stood. "Did Georges Cadoudal have family? Children?"

"I believe he married a woman whose name was Janine. I don't know about children."

Jason said, "We must find out. Now, I'm off to visit my club. I want to know if anyone has heard anything." He rose, straightened his waistcoat.

James said, "Father, we both have friends who will want to help. I don't think we should keep this a secret. I think we should announce to the world that someone—some *Frenchman*—is trying to kill you. Everyone will rally. Everyone will keep his eyes open. Jason and I will divide up the clubs between us. We will find this person, Father, and we will destroy him."

Douglas and Alexandra watched their sons walk from

the drawing room. She said quietly even as she burrowed against her husband's shoulder, "They are not boys any longer, Douglas."

"Yes, you're right about that. Where have the years gone, Alex?"

"I don't know, I just want them to continue going into the distant future. Our sons want to protect you now as you always wanted to protect them."

"I still want to protect them." He held her a moment, saying against her hair, "I fear they are too brave."

Alexandra raised her head, and Douglas saw that she was smiling. "I too have many friends. Ladies, you know, hear many things. We must find out about children Georges could have left when he died."

"Alex, you will not involve yourself in this!"

"Do not be a blockhead, my lord. I am your wife and thus I am more involved than anyone, with the possible exception of your stubborn self. Yes, I shall begin with Lady Avery. I wonder if her spouse ever tells her anything."

Douglas's face was red. "Alex, I forbid—"

She gave him a lovely smile and said, "Would you like a cup of tea, my lord?"

He growled and took his tea. "You will take no risks, madam, do you understand me?"

"Oh yes, Douglas. I understand you perfectly."

Sometime later, Douglas said to his wife as they walked up the central staircase, "Well, damnation. I forgot all about Corrie."

"It's all right, Douglas. I didn't. I selected several lovely patterns for her and some very nice white muslin and pale blue satin."

Douglas knew it wasn't going to be good. He cleared his throat. "Did Miss Plack sew up the gowns?"

"No, there wasn't time, but Maybella assured me that all would be well. She said that Corrie's maid could sew in a closed carriage. Indeed, I am expecting them to arrive in

London today—even though Simon was complaining that he had contracted the plague—and Corrie will be wearing one of her new gowns."

It was difficult, but Douglas did manage not to put his head in his hands. "Simon's town house is on Great Little Street, is that right?"

Alexandra nodded. She was thinking hard, not about Corrie but about Georges Cadoudal. She said, "It's been so long since Georges kidnapped me and took me to France. It was a matter of revenge then, Douglas, against you. But it isn't the same now. This is someone hiding, lurking in the shadows, trying to kill you without you seeing his face."

Douglas grunted.

"I wonder if Georges did marry Janine, that wretched hussy who betrayed you."

"We'll find out."

"Could he have spoken with such hatred of you that any children he might have had are now out to avenge him? It makes no sense for the simple reason that there wasn't any hatred. You and Georges parted amicably, like you told the boys, and I should know. I was there. I wonder, do you think perhaps that Georges is still alive?"

"I'll make certain, one way or the other. I agree with you. Given what happened then, Georges's involvement doesn't make any sense to me either."

She stopped in her tracks, halfway down the vast corridor, and grabbed his arm. "You were on a mission in France before Waterloo. I remember that since you tried to keep it from me."

"It was not a particularly dangerous mission, just the extraction of one of our highly placed spies."

"You told me that much, but nothing more. Now, was Georges involved in that?"

"I never saw him. Perhaps he was close by." He didn't say another word. He wasn't about to tell her the rest of it for the simple reason that it had nothing to do with this.

"Spill it now, Douglas, or I will do something you won't like."

He hesitated, and she said, "I even learned to speak French to help protect you. Not that it did me much good."

"The informant said something about revenge against me would be lovely."

Alexandra shuddered. "I knew it. It is what I expected."

He'd managed to sidetrack her, but not for long. She would remember that he hadn't told her about that mission to France before Waterloo, and what had happened. Well, it didn't matter. He'd survived.

J AMES WALKED TO Great Little Street, at the request of his father, to see exactly how bad Corrie looked in her maid-sewn gowns whose fabric and pattern his mother had, unfortunately, selected.

He arrived at Number 27 Great Little Street and rapped the bronze lion's-head knocker.

A red-faced butler took one look at him and quickly stepped back. "Please hurry, my lord, before it is too late! I don't know what to do."

James ran past the butler's flapping hand up the stairs and through the wide double doors into the Ambrose drawing room. He came to a halt in the doorway, scared to his toes, to find Corrie standing in the middle of the room, garbed in the most hideous gown he'd ever seen. It was pale blue, lace sewn nearly to her ears, row upon row of flounces sewn on the bottom portion, and sleeves the size of cannons. The only thing that looked good was her nearly invisible waist—she had to be wearing an iron corset beneath that belt because she looked ready to faint. She was crying.

James shut the door in the butler's face. He was at her

side in a moment, grabbing up her hand that fell out of that huge sleeve. "Corrie, what the devil is the matter?"

She swiped the back of her right hand over her eyes and gave him the most pathetic look he'd ever seen from her. Another tear trickled over her cheek to drip off her chin.

"Corrie, for God's sake, what's happened?"

She drew a deep breath, focused on his face, and sneered. "Why nothing, you fool."

He shook her. "What is wrong, damn you? The butler was really scared."

"All right, all right, stop shaking me. If you would know the truth, I'm practicing."

He dropped his hands. "Practicing what?"

"You'll just keep digging and prodding, won't you? Very well. Aunt Maybella said I must know how to turn down the scores of young gentlemen who will be proposing to me right and left. She said to think of something sad and it would make me cry. She said that gentlemen are most profoundly affected by a lady's tears. They would believe that I am desolate to refuse to marry them. There, are you satisfied?"

He was staring down at her, dumbfounded. The tears had certainly worked on him, and the butler. He said, "You will not gain a single proposal wearing a gown like that."

Her tears dried up in a flash. Her mouth seamed shut. "Aunt Maybella said it is very fine. Your mother selected the pattern and the fabric and my maid sewed it."

"In that case, you have to know that it is very bad indeed."

She stood there, trying to close the huge mouths of the sleeves, but they'd been stiffened and didn't move.

James wanted to laugh, but he wasn't a total clod. "Listen, Corrie, my father is going to take you tomorrow to Madame Jourdan. She will fix you up."

"Do I really look that bad?"

Sometimes the truth was good. On the other hand, sometimes the truth needlessly devastated. "No. But listen to me. London is a vastly different place. Look at me. I'm not wearing breeches, a shirt open at my throat. Not here."

"I like you better in breeches and an open shirt."

"Well, that's not going to happen here in London. Now, my mother wants you to come back with me for a visit. Er, do you perhaps have something else you can wear?"

CHAPTER NINE

❧

Men and women,
women and men. It will never work.

I AM THE *jewel of Arabie . . . I am the jewel of Ara-*
bie. . . . It was her litany, spoken over and over from the
moment she stepped in the carriage with Aunt Maybella to
come to the Ranleagh ball just two streets away on Putnam
Square, although she wasn't entirely certain what the jewel
of Arabie actually was. She'd thought it ridiculous to take a
carriage until she'd tottered down the front stairs in a pair
of lovely high-heeled white satin slippers.

She might indeed look fine, but the fact was that if
Willie Marker tried to kiss her again, she wouldn't be able
to run after him and smack him in the head. No, she'd ei-

ther stumble over her feet or collapse in a dead faint because she couldn't breathe.

On the other hand, she could kick him with a deadly heel.

On the second other hand, Willie Marker was an idiot she didn't have to worry about here in London.

No, her only worry here was to snag a husband, and if that meant looking fine through exquisite torture, her aunt was fully prepared to bring out an iron maiden. Maybella, looking very pleased, had patted her hand and told her a lady's lot wasn't an easy one. And what was one to say to that?

Who wanted a husband anyway? She'd rather have a white poodle on her lap when she drove herself down Bond Street smiling graciously at all the gentlemen swooning at the sight of her.

She saw a lady throw her head back and laugh at something a gentleman said. What could a man possibly say to make a woman laugh with such gusto?

Corrie had been looking around the Ranleagh ballroom, near to bursting with scores of laughing, beautiful people who had to be roasting it was so warm this evening, but it didn't seem to phase any of them. They waltzed and laughed and flirted and drank champagne while she stood, nailed to the spot, so frightened she knew she was going to erupt in hives.

She was wedged between James's mother and her Aunt Maybella, and weren't they having just the finest time, speaking to other ladies who floated by on lovely heeled slippers, some of which were more than two inches off the ground. And all the gentlemen, crooning over Lady Alexandra's lovely hand, whispering wicked things not an inch from her lovely ear. She heard her Aunt Maybella titter.

Both her aunt and Lady Alexandra appeared to take it all in stride, indeed, blossoming, as if this was the way things were done, and evidently they were.

If she were wise, she would watch and listen and imitate.

She was convinced she'd been introduced to every lady who wasn't on the dance floor, and said her practiced niceties to such a polished degree that she heard one lady say under her breath to James's mother that she was a prettily behaved girl. As opposed to what? She'd practiced in front of a mirror until she was fluent in politeness. She smiled and nodded and recited, trying to sound spontaneous, difficult after you'd said the same things twelve times.

By the time she'd danced with six young gentlemen in forty-five minutes, she couldn't believe she'd been such a twit to be scared. There was only one Willie Marker in the lot, but at least he was nicely dressed and his hands weren't dirty. All her aunt could talk about was finding her a right and proper husband, not one that was after *things* other than a wife, and thus because you never knew what lurked beneath a nice set of shoulders, Corrie was to be *very vigilant*. Since Corrie had no idea what those other things could possibly be, she was suspicious of every gentleman who asked her to dance until she reached the fourth, Jonathan Vallante, whose eyes bugged out just a bit, and made her laugh. Looking out over the ballroom, she realized this was like one of the big country fairs, except there were no pickpockets lurking and none of these people had to count their money. She saw a man with two gold front teeth. There was another lady with three chins and a lovely diamond necklace that looked in danger of choking her. Corrie realized that if you stripped off all the jewels, loosened all the stays, these beautiful people were much like the ones at home.

She hadn't danced in seven minutes, and she wanted to dance again, she loved to dance, she'd discovered, and so where were all these young gentlemen? She tapped the heel of one slipper. She was restless. She'd only attracted six of them. Surely there were more than a measly half dozen. She wanted a long line of gentlemen, queuing right in front of her, peering around each other to get a better view of her.

Then her ears perked up.

The duchess of Brabante was saying to James's mama, "There are the twins, just coming into the ballroom. Ah, what exquisite and delightful boys, Alexandra. You've done so very well. What a thrill it must be for you now that they are all so splendidly grown up, watching all the young ladies and their mamas dogging them, hanging on to their every word. Why, I saw one young lady swoon at James's feet. I was hoping he'd let her fall, but no, James is a gentleman, and before her elbow hit the floor, he caught her. He gave her a scare though, and I thought that was smart of him.

"I have the same problem, naturally, with my dear Devlin, such an exemplary young man. Being the heir to a duke—not just an earl—naturally all the very best families are after him for their daughters. And how is your dear sister, Melissande? Everyone finds it so terribly interesting that the twins are in her image. Tell me, what does Lord Northcliffe think?"

Alexandra simply smiled and cocked her head to one side. "Why, I believe he thinks of me most of all, then the boys, perhaps then the estates."

The duchess blew out an annoyed breath, but to persist would have made her look a fool.

That was well done, Corrie thought. Had this odd woman reached the end of her very singular monologue?

No, she had not. The duchess said, "However do you tell them apart? I swear they are like two stitches on a pillowcase."

"Trust me, Lorelei, if one births twins, one can easily tell them apart."

"Oh look, three girls are already twittering around them. Oh goodness, I do believe that girl is trying to pass

Jason a note. Poor boys! Look there—I see a convoy of white gowns steering toward them."

Where were they? Corrie craned her neck, but even in her two-inch heels, she couldn't see them, and she was tall. Were they already dancing? Was James already dancing?

The duchess cleared her throat. "My son would be delighted to dance with Maybella's lovely little niece. Since Maybella is gossiping with Sir Arthur, Alexandra, I will inquire of you since you appear to be a friend of the family."

"Oh? Where is Devlin?" Alexandra asked.

"There, by that huge pot of flowers that is making everyone sneeze. I do wonder why Clorinda needs to pollinate her ballroom."

Devlin? A duke's son? What would a duke's son want with her? She was practically a nobody from Twyley Grange.

The duchess gave an imperious nod toward a young man who smiled and nodded, and began a leisurely stroll toward them, pausing to chat with everyone in his path. *It will take him an hour to get here,* Corrie thought. How much could a man really want to dance with a lady if he didn't have a little snap in his step?

His name was Devlin Archibald Monroe, earl of Convers, heir to the duke of Brabante, and Corrie thought he was very nice-looking indeed. He wasn't much older than James, tall, black-eyed, and his face was as pale as the portrait of a vampire Corrie had seen in a forbidden book a century old, hidden at the back of her uncle's bookshelf. He had a dark voice that sent lovely shivers up her back.

He smiled and showed no fangs, and that was a relief. She said her rehearsed speech, he looked amused, and when he asked her to waltz, she lightly placed her hand on his offered forearm and headed to the dance floor.

Not many minutes later, Alexandra heard a beloved voice and turned, a smile on her face. "Mother, you look altogether lovely this evening. I see Father has deserted you."

"James, my dear. Your father escaped me after one dance to meet with some of his cronies in the library. It's past ten o'clock. You're here at last. Where have you and Jason been?"

James moved a bit closer since there were people nearby. "Jason and I wanted to meet with some men down at the docks. No, Mother, don't chew my ear, there was no particular danger. Besides, Jase and I are very careful now, so please don't worry or else I can't tell you what we're doing anymore."

That was a powerful argument, but it was difficult to keep her mother's worry and advice behind her teeth. She touched his cheek. "I won't carp at you. Did you learn anything?"

"Yes and no. One of the men had come from Paris. He'd heard that an English nobleman was going to get his just desserts, nothing more than that. Perhaps it was the same person who informed the War Ministry.

"I asked if he'd heard of any children, but he didn't know. He gave us another name, a captain on a fishing boat due up the Thames within the week. Will he know more? I don't know, but it's worth a try. Ah, where's Corrie?"

"She's dancing with Devlin Monroe, see over there, on the other side of the dance floor."

James shook his head. "No, I don't see her. I see Devlin, but not Corrie."

Alexandra said, "Ah, James, give your greetings to Lady Montague and Sir Arthur Cochrane."

James greeted Corrie's Aunt Maybella, who was wearing her usual pale blue. He greeted Sir Arthur Cochrane with the deference he automatically accorded an older gentleman who had claims on his father's friendship. Personally, he'd always believed that Sir Arthur needed to bathe more often and use less pomade on what was left of his hair.

He said to Maybella, "I've been trying to locate Corrie on the dance floor, ma'am."

"Perhaps you can spot Devlin. He's so very pale, you know, with those lovely dark eyelashes fanning over his cheeks. Ah, the dance is ending. Here they come."

"I see him, but I don't recognize—" James's jaw dropped.

CHAPTER TEN

❧

Love is a universal migraine.

ROBERT GRAVES

JAMES STARED, SHOOK his head, looked at every female near to that approaching female, who was laughing, nearly skipping, her step was so light, so filled with excitement.

No, that couldn't be Corrie Tybourne-Barrett. Not that creature with hair the color of rich autumn leaves, all piled up on top of her head with ringlets hanging in front of lovely little white ears that were pierced with small diamond studs. All right, maybe it was Corrie—but—his eyes were on her breasts, yes, there were breasts. How had she hidden this incredible creature so thoroughly? He pictured her breeches and old hat and shuddered. He looked at her breasts and shuddered again.

She was smiling at something Devlin said. She looked fresh and innocent, a babe ignorant of wickedness, and he knew he should warn her about Devlin.

"Hello, James."

"Hello, Corrie. Devlin, did you purchase Mountjoy's bay gelding?"

"Yes, I did, as a matter of fact."

"A bay gelding?" she asked. "A hunter?"

He nodded. "Yes, a fine addition to my stables. He likes to chase foxes at night, isn't that nice?"

"I suppose so," Corrie said. "My money's on the fox, though."

Devlin laughed.

James took a small step forward, crowding this interloper, his voice aggressive. "Perhaps Corrie told you that I've known her since she was three years old, Devlin. I suppose you could say that I know her better than I know the planets. And I know the planets very well indeed. Naturally I've always looked out for her."

"Ah, but perhaps she'd like to hunt sometime with me, you think?"

"No, she has night blindness," James said and narrowed his eyes on Devlin's pale, pale face. Then he smiled and offered his arm. "Would you care to dance, Corrie?"

Corrie ignored him, giving a blinding smile to Devlin Monroe. "Thank you, my lord, for the lovely dance." James watched Devlin's smile widen, and wanted to smash his fist into his pale pretty face.

"Perhaps another waltz later?" he said, half an eye on James.

"Oh yes," she said. "I should like that." When she turned back to James, he was still frowning as he watched Devlin disappear into the crowd.

"What was that all about, James? You were rude to Devlin. All he did was dance excellently with me, and amuse me." When he just kept looking ahead and said nothing, she was presented with a delightful opportunity: she was free to look at him. If she looked fine, then James looked beyond fine. Every feature blended with every other feature, as if by an artist's hand. His eyes looked pure violet this evening beneath the swarm of candles that shown down from scores of chandeliers.

"Your cravat is crooked," she said, placing her arm on his and walking to the dance floor, not looking at him, but at the gaggle of girls heading their way. Oh dear, would they walk over her and haul him away?

They stopped only when James had led her into the center of the dance floor. He said, "I would ask you to straighten it but I doubt that is a skill you possess."

She wanted to snarl at him, kiss him, maybe even hurl him to the floor and bite his ear, and so she twitched the cravat this way and that until it was as straight as it had been before she'd touched it.

All the while, he was looking down at her, a curious smile on his face. "Your gown is lovely. I assume my father selected the pattern and the fabric?"

"Oh yes," she said, her eyes still on the blasted cravat that wouldn't cooperate.

"I assume my father also thought that the gown is cut too low?"

"Well, he did gnash his teeth a bit, and he did point out that the gown was cut so low my knees were nearly on display. He started to hoist it up himself, like he does with your mother's gowns, but stopped fast when Madame Jourdan told him he wasn't my father, so his odd notions of bosom coverage weren't to the point."

An understatement. James could hear his father roaring.

She dropped her hands from his cravat, then lightly traced her fingertips over his shoulders and down his arms. "Lovely fabric, James. Nearly as lovely as mine."

"Oh no, surely not. Is my cravat perfect now?"

"Naturally."

"I also assume you learned how to waltz?"

"You certainly weren't around to instruct me, were you?"

"No. I had to come to London. There were things I had to do."

"Like what?"

"None of your business." He put his arm around her, actually touched her back, and she nearly fell off her slippers.

"Pay attention, Corrie." The music started and so did they.

"Ah, you have the steps down, that's good." And he whirled her about, making her nearly swallow her tongue with the excitement and pleasure of it.

"Oh, this is wonderful!" She was smiling and laughing, and he continued to dance her through every part of the dance floor, her wide skirt swishing around his legs, the lovely white of her attire like snow against the black of his trousers. She was panting for breath when he finally slowed. "James,"—pant, pant, pant—"if you are unable to do anything else of use in your life, know that you are excellent at waltzing."

He grinned into that shining face that had long since lost its rice powder. A face, he realized, he knew as well as his own. Those breasts, though, he didn't know them at all. One thick braid looked in danger of unwinding. He didn't think, just said, "Keep moving, slowly." And he reached up both hands and slipped the wooden pins skillfully back into the braid, anchoring it. Then he slid one of the half dozen white roses securely back in.

"There, that is just fine now."

She was looking at him oddly. "How do you know how to fix a lady's hair?"

"I'm not a clod," he said, nothing more.

"Well, I'm not a clod either, but I wouldn't know how to do it as well as you do."

"For God's sake, Corrie, I've had some practice."

"On whom? I've never asked you to braid my hair or anything like that."

James drew a deep breath. This was something he'd never encountered in his male adult life. Here was a girl he'd known forever, and yet she was now a young lady, and surely he should treat her differently. He said, "No, you've always stuffed your braid under your hat, or left it to flap against your back. What was there to do?"

"May I inquire upon whom you practiced?"

"Not that it's any of your business, but I've known quite a few females, and all of them have hair that occasionally needs fixing."

She was frowning up at him, still not understanding. He said, looking at her breasts, ready to swallow his tongue, "I see you unsmashed yourself."

She actually arched her back a little so that her breasts were pressed against his chest. "I told you I had a bosom."

"Well, yes, possibly. I suppose."

"What do you mean 'I suppose'? My bosom is quite nice, so Madame Jourdan said when your father took me to her shop."

Because he didn't know what to say to that, James picked up speed and danced her around the perimeter of the dance floor, laughing and panting at the same time, as other couples quickly danced out of their way.

Then the music ended.

He looked down at her and saw her smile turn into misery. She looked ready to burst into tears.

"Whatever is the matter?"

She gulped. "That was lovely. I should like to do it again. Now."

"All right," he said and thought that surely two dances wouldn't mean anything to anyone, for heaven's sake, since they were very nearly related. He saw four young ladies bearing down on them, and quickly took Corrie's arm and led her into the dozen or so couples still on the dance floor.

She said, "I swear that every gown in this incredible room is either white like mine, or rose, blue, or purple."

"Lilac, not purple. Lilac is much lighter."

"Ah, and what about violet?" Was that a hint of a sneer on her mouth?

"Why, I would say that violet is just about the most beautiful color on this earth."

Corrie swallowed, acknowledging the hit, and said, "Aunt Maybella's blue fits right in."

"Not exactly, but close enough." He eyed her, wanted to touch his fingertips to the tops of her breasts, looked at her white shoulders, and said, "Well, did it require bucketfuls?"

"What? Smeared on me. Well, yes, at least one and a half buckets of cream. Uncle Simon complained about it at first because he said I smelled like lavender compost, but Aunt Maybella said it was necessary or I just might never be able to crawl off the shelf and fall into a matrimony basket."

"As in no man wants a scaly wife?"

"I've been here now five days, James, and I tell you, I haven't met a single man I would want to have consider my scales."

He laughed. "How many have you met?"

"Well, I've danced with at least a half dozen this evening. Very well, counting Lord Devlin, it's now exactly seven. Of course now there's you to add to my list. Eight gentlemen. That's a rather nice large number, isn't it? You couldn't possibly consider me a failure, could you?"

"Er, were they all nice to you?"

"Oh yes. I practiced answers to every sort of question. You know, spontaneous answers. And you know what, James?"

"What?"

"They used nearly all of them." She frowned a moment. "I think the favorite question was about the weather."

"Well, that's normal, I suppose. It is nice and warm, worthy to comment upon."

She looked over his left shoulder.

"What's the matter? What did they do besides ask you your opinion on the weather?"

"Well, it wasn't all of them, but you see, ever since I've unsmashed my bosom and lowered my neckline—well, really, it was Madame Jourdan who wouldn't tolerate your father's criticism about my neckline—" she rose on her tiptoes and whispered near his ear, "they've been looking."

"This is something that surprises and astounds you? I'd like to know why any female on this earth could possibly be surprised at that."

"It surprised me at first, I'll admit it. Then I realized that I really liked them looking at me. I figure that if they're actually focused on my parts then it's obvious I don't look like such a country bumpkin. But you know, James, I never realized that males found that particular part of the female's anatomy so mesmerizing."

If you only knew, he thought. The music started up again and James said, "Are you ready to gallop?"

She laughed until her eyes were tearing.

Along the side of the dance floor, Thomas Crowley, the younger son of Sir Edmund Crowley, one of Wellington's cronies, said to Jason, "Who is that lovely girl James is dancing with?"

"You know," Jason said slowly, "I've been wondering that myself. Perhaps it's someone from his mysterious past."

"James doesn't have a mysterious past," said Tom. "Neither do we."

Jason poked him in the shoulder. "I've been thinking that it's time to start making one."

Since Jason had told him about the threat on his father's life, Tom said, "You're already on your way. Blessed Lord, who's that? Good God, what a beauty."

Jason turned to look where Tom was pointing. He smiled, that lazy confident smile that seemed to make ladies from the ages of ten to eighty perk right up whenever he came within fifty feet.

Jason said slowly, in that easy voice of his, "You know, Tom, maybe I don't need anymore mystery right now." Thomas saw Jason draw a bead on the dark-haired girl who was peeking at him over the top of her fan, and stride off in a very straight line toward her, paying no attention at all to the score of young ladies, and not-so-young ladies, who tried to put themselves in his path. He didn't mow any of them down, but it was close.

Tom shook his head and took himself off to where his mother was holding court. He tried to slink behind a palm tree when he realized she was in animated conversation with three dowagers with unmarried daughters.

"Tom! Do come here, my boy."

He'd been well and fairly caught. He drew a deep breath and went to his doom.

CHAPTER ELEVEN

❧

JASON SHERBROOKE GRINNED from ear to ear. His worry about his father shifted to the back of his brain. This female looked charming, and the good Lord knew he hadn't been this charmed by a female since he was fifteen years old and seduced by Bea O'Rourke, a clever young widow from St. Ives who'd been visiting New Romney and liked his smile and his lovely, very busy, hands, she'd told him while she nibbled on his ear.

This girl had dark, dark eyes, alight with intelligence and humor. Then she snapped her furled fan and those lovely eyes disappeared. He saw shiny black hair drawn back from a white forehead. He'd swear she could be Bea's daughter. But Bea didn't have any daughters, just two sons who were both in the king's navy, she told him when he'd last been with her in early August.

He looked about for her mother or her chaperone and found himself staring into the bony face of Lady Arbuckle, known for her lack of humor and her tedious piety. This charming young creature with the wicked eyes was a relative of Lady Arbuckle's? No, that couldn't be possible. But Lady Arbuckle did look like the dragon guarding the treasure.

"Lady Arbuckle," he said, turning on all the charm he'd learned from his Uncle Ryder over the years. *"Observe your uncle,"* his father had said to him and James. *"He can coax the wart off a lady's chin. If you find it inconvenient to use brute force, you might consider charm to gain what you want."*

"My goodness, is it you, James?"

"No, I'm Jason, ma'am."

"Ah, how terribly familiar each of you look when I see the other. How are your mother and father?"

"They are well, ma'am." Jason smiled toward the girl who was now gazing down at the toes of her very pale lilac slippers. "And Lord Arbuckle?"

The lady stiffened straight as a lamppost. "He goes as well as can be expected."

This made no sense to Jason, but he nodded politely before he said, "May I be presented to your charming companion, ma'am?"

Lady Arbuckle gave only an infinitesimal pause, but Jason saw it and wondered at it. Was she concerned that he wasn't exactly the sort of gentleman he should be?

"This is my niece, Judith McCrae, come with me to London to make her curtsy in polite society. Judith, this is Jason Sherbrooke, Lord Northcliffe's second son."

Jason was fully prepared to be disappointed when she opened her lovely mouth; he was prepared to see and hear silliness or simpering; he was prepared to wish himself a thousand miles away. But he wasn't prepared for the sock of lust that roared through him when she smiled up at him, the dimple on the left side of her mouth deepening.

"My father was Irish," she said, and let him take her

hand. Long, slender fingers, soft, so very soft was her flesh. He lightly kissed her wrist.

"My father is English," Jason said, and felt stupid. He'd never in his life felt stupid with a girl, but now he felt like he had nothing at all in his head but relentless waves of lust that were cooking his brain, and the good Lord knew there was nothing at all to lust but more lust. "My mother is also English."

"My mother was a Cornish girl from Penzance. She and Aunt Arbuckle were second cousins. She calls me her niece because she loved me from the moment I was born. She is my only living relative now. She is giving me a Season. Isn't that kind of her?"

Jason remembered now that Lord and Lady Arbuckle's country estate was near St. Ives on the northern coast of Cornwall. He said, "Oh yes, as kind as it is proper. You've lived in Cornwall?"

"Sometimes. My father was from Waterford. I grew up there." He loved the lilting voice, the soft vowels beneath the starchy English cadence. He'd never known English to sound so sweet.

"Would you care to dance with me, Miss McCrae?"

Judith looked toward Lady Arbuckle. The lady's lips were a disapproving tight seam. He wasn't a rake by any means—ah, he wasn't the first son, the heir. She probably wondered about his income. Why would she even think such a thing? It was just a damned dance he wanted, nothing more.

"I will bring her right back, ma'am. Or perhaps you would like to speak to my mother? To assure you that I am not rabid and have no overtly distressing habits?"

Lady Arbuckle seemed to study those arching palm trees for a good thirty seconds before she gave him a stingy nod. "Very well. You may dance with Judith. Once."

She was small, the top of her head barely reaching his

shoulder. "Do you look like your mother?" he asked as he slipped his arm around her and began to waltz.

"Ah, my coloring. Yes, I have her eyes and her hair, and I am short, like she was, but my freckles come from my dear father."

He didn't see any freckles, no wait, there was a thin line marching across the bridge of her nose. "Your mother was a beautiful woman."

"Yes, she was, but I am nothing compared to her, so my Aunt Arbuckle tells me. I don't remember my mama really, since she died when I was very young, you see."

Jason whirled her about, aware that she was a marvelous dancer, light on her feet, an armful that felt natural and— oh damn, the lust was poking and prodding at him, so he danced faster and faster. And very nearly slammed into his brother and his partner, who looked vaguely familiar.

Judith lost her balance when Jason suddenly jerked to the side, and so he simply lifted her off her feet. The thing was, once he had her against him, he didn't want to put her down. He wanted to press her against his belly through all those damned petticoats and imagine that she wasn't wearing any.

She gasped, even as she grabbed his arms to steady herself. "My goodness, that man looks just like you!"

"Ah, I believe it's my brother. James, Lord Hammersmith, this is Miss Judith McCrae from Cornwall and Ireland." Jason looked pointedly at the young lady who was breathing heavily next to James, her face shiny with perspiration, her mouth still smiling. She looked familiar, and those green eyes of hers, she—

"Jason, don't you recognize me? You lout, it's me, Corrie."

For the first time since Jason had seen Judith, he forgot his lust and stared at the girl who'd dogged his brother's heels from the age of three. "Corrie?"

She nodded, grinning at him. "I creamed myself down, unsmashed my bosom, and put my old hat on the shelf."

"Will you pound me if I tell you that you look quite acceptable as a young lady?"

"Oh no, I want you to admire me. I want every gentleman in this room to admire me, to metaphorically fall at my feet like dead dogs. James doesn't want to fall, much less be a dead dog, but I'm trying."

"Like she said, buckets of cream and unsmashing have much improved her," James said. "As for admiration, she laps it up." Because James had exquisite manners, he turned immediately to Judith. "Miss McCrae, you are new to London?"

Judith was looking back and forth between the brothers. "Even though Aunt Arbuckle mentioned that you were twins, I didn't realize that you were really such complete and utter twins," Judith said, "as in how nicely you're duplicated in each other."

"Actually," Jason said, "we're not at all alike. James here is a devotee of the planets and stars, while I am an earthbound creature."

Corrie said, "Jason swims like a fish and rides better than James, although James would never agree with that, and regularly beats James in footraces."

"I swim as well," Judith said. "In the Irish Sea in the deep of summer when you won't freeze your toes off."

Jason wanted to ask her what she wore when she swam. Surely a young lady couldn't swim naked, like he did.

Judith turned those dark eyes of hers on James. "Stars, my lord?"

Corrie said, "Oh yes, on fine nights, you can find him on this particular hilltop, lying on his back, looking up at the heavens."

Jason grinned. "He even knows all of Kepler's laws."

"Twins," Judith said, looking yet again from one to the

other. "How very convenient for you. Do you change places often?"

Jason said, "No, not since we were young." Actually not since James wanted to prove to him that Ann Redfern wanted him and not Jason, and so traded places and found himself in the barn with a naked girl, and Jason outside the stall door. However, to this day, neither of them really figured out who Ann preferred for the simple reason that she couldn't tell them apart.

"If I had an identical twin, I should practice until I could have fooled our mother."

Jason laughed. "Sorry, Miss McCrae, no matter how hard you tried, you would never fool our mother."

"Or our grandmother, who is so old that she shouldn't have such sharp eyes anymore, but she does."

Judith looked at them once again. "A challenge," she said. "I have always loved challenges. I believe I can see one in the making." Judith turned to Corrie. "Are you a twin as well?"

"Oh no," Corrie said, staring at the exquisite girl with her porcelain skin and those brilliant black eyes and wondered if she saw a bucket of cream she'd even know what to do with it. As for her bosom, she was well-endowed very likely without using stays to hoist her up. "I'm just me."

"Thank God," James said. "Two of you would drive me mad."

"James, I will see you at home," Jason said, smiled at Corrie as if she was still someone he couldn't quite place, and waltzed away.

James stood staring after him a moment before he turned, looking thoughtful, and said, "The waltz is ending. No, Corrie, not a third waltz. It wouldn't do your reputation any good."

"Whatever do you mean by that?"

"Didn't you read the deportment book my mother, er, Jason gave you for your birthday?"

"I enjoyed it as much as I enjoyed the Racine plays. You know, James, the birthday present you gave to me, with all the lovely pictures. You know, the pictures I could look at if my brain ached from all those big French words?"

"Naturally I remember. It was thoughtfully selected for you. Now listen to me, brat. You don't dance more than two dances with a gentleman or you're nearly as good as engaged."

"But it wasn't two dances, at least two full dances. Jason interrupted the last third. Can't we dance the first third of the next one?"

James shook his head.

"But why? How silly that sounds. You're a good dancer, the best of all my gentlemen tonight. You're perhaps even more accomplished than Devlin, maybe. I wouldn't mind dancing with you all evening."

"Thank you, but it isn't done even though I've known you forever, and you're very nearly my sister."

She felt the punch of those careless words and sighed. She touched her fingers to his cravat again, pushing it this way and that. "That's it then. Very well, if you're not available, then I'll dance with Devlin. I wonder where he is." She looked up at him. "Uncle Simon is really keen on me finding a husband now. The dear man really doesn't want to come back to London in the spring for another come-out. He says one month should be enough to do the trick."

"Look, Corrie, it's not really possible so don't think you're a failure if you're not standing in front of a vicar by the end of the month, this poor sod you've yet to meet shackled to your side. An offer now, I suppose that's possible. At least you're looking fine now, so there should be some unattached young gentleman ready to leap into your cage."

"That's an interesting image. James, what do you think of when you think about the jewel of Arabie?"

"The jewel of Arabie? What the devil is a jewel of Arabie?"

"I think it's a magnificent diamond that everyone coveted over the years."

"What does that have to do with you?"

"Well, perhaps nothing at all if you fail to see any obvious comparisons."

"Listen to me, Corrie. Don't dance with Devlin Monroe. I strongly advise you to avoid him."

"He looks like a vampire until he smiles, then he is quite nice-looking indeed."

"Vampire? Devlin? Oh, you mean his pallor." James looked thoughtful, rubbed his chin. "Yes, he's known for his pallor. A vampire? Come to think of it, perhaps, I haven't ever seen him during the day."

"Really? Oh goodness, James, mayhap—oh, you sod, you're teasing me."

"Of course I'm teasing you, Corrie. But Devlin—listen to me now—he's got a reputation for being involved in very different sorts of things—"

"What kind of different sorts of things?"

"You don't need to know that. Just obey me and you'll be all right."

"Obey you? *You?*" She threw back her head and laughed, just couldn't help it, and many female heads turned to see the source of that laughter—if they weren't looking already, their focus James, naturally.

"I nearly raised you. Yes, pay attention to me. I'm older, I've had more experience, and most important, I'm a man, and thus I know about other men and their base—well, never mind that. Just avoid Devlin Monroe."

"Base what? You mean wicked? You're saying that Devlin Monroe is wicked? Doesn't it take a man many years and a lot of concentration to attain true wickedness? Devlin is young. How can he possibly be wicked?"

James wanted to take that lovely white neck he'd never

seen before, he'd swear to that, between his hands and gently slide his fingers around that neck and squeeze.

"I didn't say he was wicked. He likes different sorts of things."

"Well, so do I. Is this what experience gains you, James? Wickedness?"

"No, don't be ridiculous. Forget Devlin. Now, I see Kellard Reems speaking to your Aunt Maybella. He is quite unexceptional. Dance with him. If he ogles your breas—your bosom—tell me and I'll kick his teeth down his throat."

She whispered, nearly choking, "Men say *breasts*?"

"Forget that."

But she wasn't about to forget it. Corrie was staring down at herself with new eyes. "It's, well, so very unambiguous, that word."

"Yes, that's true. Men tend to be unambiguous and straightforward, unlike ladies, who must sugarcoat everything with lace and frills and outlandish words, like bosom."

"Breasts," she repeated slowly, fully tasting that wicked word, and James grabbed her arms and gave her a shake, anything to wipe that thoughtful look off her face. "Listen to me, Corrie, you don't want to be saying that, particularly in front of a man. Do you understand me? A man might—very well, he will of a certainty get the wrong impression about your virtue and dwell upon activities you might share with him. It's *bosom,* Corrie. That's it. Do you promise?"

"Ah, there's Devlin the vampire. Look at that very nice smile of his. White teeth against that white face of his and those really dark eyes—just like Judith McCrae's eyes, don't you think?"

"No, I don't think."

"Yes, all dark and snapping and—I think I'll ask him what he's doing at midnight, and offer him my neck."

He remembered his hand pounding down on her bottom that day. That hand flexed, fingers tingled.

She left him, not even a nod of gratitude that he'd given her valuable advice. No, she'd walked off, fanning herself, because he'd danced her into the floor and she'd loved it. At least she hadn't given him one of her patented sneers that made him want to rub her face in the mud.

James stood there, frowning, until he felt some fingers on his sleeve and turned to see Miss Milner fluttering her eyelashes at him. He sighed, only a very brief sigh because he was a gentleman, turned, and dredged up a smile.

As for Jason, he danced Miss Judith McCrae toward the huge glass doors that gave onto the Ranleagh balcony and gardens below, and pictured her naked.

She was laughing up at him. What had he said that was amusing? He couldn't seem to remember. Yes, he pictured her laughing, and naked.

He slowed because the waltz was coming to an end. "Tell me how long you'll be in London."

"Aunt Arbuckle wants to return to Cornwall by Christmas."

"Do you have brothers? Sisters?"

She paused, then said finally with a smile, "Well, I have a cousin. He owns a stud farm called The Coombes near Waterford."

"Is this male cousin older than you, Miss McCrae?"

"Oh yes, he's much older."

The waltz ended. Jason smiled down at this beautiful young girl. He would like to take her for a nice meandering walk through the Ranleagh gardens, but it wasn't to be. He offered her his arm and escorted her back to her aunt. "My lady," he said, and gave her a slight bow. "I trust that Lord Arbuckle will feel better soon."

Lady Arbuckle said, "That is very kind of you, Mr. Sherbrooke," and Judith dropped her fan.

"Oh dear, I am so clumsy. No, no, Mr. Sherbrooke, I've got it," but of course, he swooped down on the fan and handed it to her, smiling as he did so. "It isn't broken. A pleasure, Miss McCrae, Lady Arbuckle." He bowed again and took his leave. He spied Tom walking toward the doorway, looking neither to his right nor to his left. He looked like a hound who'd just scented a stag, nostrils flared. It was lobster patties. Tom could sniff out a lobster patty from a good thirty feet. Jason joined him, and after Tom downed a good half dozen and drank two glasses of the suicide champagne punch, they left the Ranleagh ball to go to White's, Jason managing to avoid the troop of young ladies and some not-so-young ladies forging his way. He caught his brother's eye, and nodded.

That nod meant that they had more plans to make, but not right at this moment. James turned his attention back to the beautiful Miss Lorimer, probably the diamond of the Little Season, who waltzed very well indeed and hummed while she danced. James was charmed.

When James next chanced to look up, it was to see Corrie dancing with Devlin Monroe.

"Whatever is the matter, my lord?"

"What? Oh, nothing at all, Miss Lorimer, just looking out for my childhood friend who continues to disobey me."

"Hmmm," said Miss Lorimer. "It sounds more like you're her father, my lord."

"God forbid," James said as the waltz ended. He watched Corrie take Devlin's arm, and walk to the huge banquet table, right to the nearly empty bowl of champagne punch strong enough to wilt a girl's scruples after one glass. He cursed under his breath.

When he left Juliette Lorimer with her mama and a warm smile, Juliette said, "I think I will have him, Mama. Even if he were boring or dissolute—which he doesn't appear to be—one could still look at him, and that would bring enough pleasure, don't you think?"

Lady Lorimer looked at the magnificent creature to whom she'd given birth, and said in her matter-of-fact voice, "Given that you are the most beautiful girl in this ballroom, and James Sherbrooke the most beautiful man, I think such a marriage would produce children so beyond mortal people they would likely be shot so civilization could march onward."

Miss Lorimer gave a charming laugh. "There's only one of me, but Lord Hammersmith has a twin brother who is as beautiful as he is. I saw him dancing with a dark-haired girl who didn't look very interesting at all."

"I saw her as well. Very ordinary. But it doesn't matter. You must remember that his brother isn't the next earl of Northcliffe, now is he?"

Miss Lorimer gave another charming laugh and watched James make his way through the throng of guests, all, it seemed, wanting to speak to him, most of them of the fairer sex. It was a very good thing that she was the most beautiful girl in these as well as other parts. Otherwise she just might find herself feeling a bit concerned.

CHAPTER TWELVE

❧

The state of matrimony is a dangerous disease;
far better to take drink in my opinion.

MADAME DE SEVIGNE

ALEXANDRA SHERBROOKE SHOUTED at her
husband even as he eased himself through the front
door, "Sometimes I want to shoot you myself, Douglas!
Have you lost your wits? Look at you, walking down the
street, swinging your cane, yes, I saw you out the window,
even whistling, I'll wager, and not one single friend beside
you. I will shoot you myself!"

And she ran across the entrance hall and threw herself
into his arms, which opened just in time. He squeezed her,
kissed the top of her head, and said very quietly, "I suppose
it wasn't too wise of me, sweetheart, but I'm tired of shad-

ows and threats and worries that someone might jump out at me."

She looked up at him, holding him even more tightly. "You wanted the assassin to come and get you?"

"Yes, I guess that's about it." He reached into his pocket and pulled out a small silver derringer. "It fires two shots. My cane is also a sword. I was prepared, Alex." He hugged her again then set her away from him. He lightly stroked his fingertip over her eyebrows. She closed her eyes and moved closer. It was a habit of long standing. "Damnation, I want this over."

"I want your friends around you, do you hear me, Douglas?"

"What? All of us are nearly ready to dodder forward into old age and you still want them around me?"

"I don't care if they're drooling, their presence would protect you."

They walked into the library and Douglas quietly closed the door. "I fear that Willicombe will come running in at any minute, and I want some peace."

"He is taking your safety more seriously than you are, Douglas. Do you know that he asked me if he could hire his nephew, said he could pound in a nail with his bare fist. Of course I said yes. We now have another footman and guard. This Remie stands watch between midnight and three A.M., then Robert until six A.M."

Douglas fetched a bottle of brandy and poured each of them a glass. "I have thought and thought about this. I swear to you, Alex, I can think of no one who hates me enough to go to all this trouble—it's all so dramatic, this revenge scheme, if revenge is indeed what this is all about. Georges Cadoudal—I've certainly seen him several times over the years once we left him in Etaples in 1803. Since he couldn't seem to assassinate Napoleon, he set his sights on several of Napoleon's top generals and functionaries.

He killed at least six of them during the last years before Waterloo. But that was over fifteen years ago, Alex. Fifteen years. He died just after Waterloo, sometime in early 1816."

"When will we find out if he had children?"

"Soon, I hope."

"I've been thinking, Douglas. Remember that special mission you went on in early 1814? All you told me was that it wasn't dangerous, that you were bringing someone to the safety of England."

He suddenly looked much younger and very pleased with himself. "Yes, I did manage to keep that from you, didn't I?"

"Who was it, Douglas?"

"It was a gentleman who had enough money and offered enough information to the War Ministry to earn him safe haven in England. I swore never to divulge his name."

"So he would have no reason to hate you. You saved him."

"That's it."

"Did Georges have anything to do with this man you brought out from France?"

"My lord, Remie is now on duty."

Douglas nearly dropped his brandy. He whirled around, his hand already in the pocket of his jacket ready to pull out the derringer, only to see Willicombe standing at sharp attention inside the door.

"How the devil did you get in here without our hearing you, Willicombe? Good God, man, I could have shot you."

"You would have to hear me first, my lord, and that, I daresay, is well nigh impossible because I am almost a shadow, exactly in the manner as Hollis. I daresay as well that if you had felt my presence, you would have been flooded with warmth and well-being. Never would you have shot me, my lord."

Alexandra smiled. "You're right, Willicombe. Hollis

couldn't have moved more quietly than you. Where is Remie stationed for the night?"

"He roams, my lady, roams from the attic to the basement and out to the stable. He lurks in the shadows along the walkways and even slips into the park. He sees all, hears all. He is worth every groat you pay him, my lord."

"Well, that is reassuring. Go to bed, Willicombe."

"Yes, my lord. Have you found out any more information about the villain who seeks to shorten your life, my lord?"

"No, not yet. Go to bed, Willicombe."

When Willicombe walked on cat's feet out of the library, gently closing the doors behind him, Douglas turned to his wife. "Did I tell you that you looked quite fetching tonight, save that half of your breasts were on display to every lascivious debaucher in London?"

Alexandra looked at him beneath her lashes. "It is a remarkable thing to have a husband who still remarks with such earnest attention upon one's personal parts."

"It isn't funny, Alexandra. I was forced to take myself off to the card room, else I would have shot a good dozen of those lechers."

She smiled, hugged him, went up on her tiptoes, and said against his cheek, "Did you remark upon how very lovely Corrie looked this evening? The gown you selected for her was quite flattering."

"Isn't it amazing? I had believed her quite flat-chested. I fear though that there was too much of her showing as well." Douglas's lips thinned. "I told her and Madame Jourdan—you will stop laughing at me, Alex, or I will make you sorry."

"I had no idea she was so pretty, Douglas. Her smile makes you want to smile back at her."

"Yes, yes, who cares? Come along now. I'm an old man and it is after midnight. I have very few miracles left."

"Oh, yes, you do," his wife said as she walked up the stairs beside him.

*Very few men care to have the
obvious pointed out to them by a woman.*

MARGARET BAILLIE SAUNDERS

"You're being a moron, James Sherbrooke. Go away before I knock you in the head with that fireplace poker."

"No, I will not." He caught her arm before she could grab the poker. He even shook her. "You will answer me now and truthfully, madam. I want to know exactly what happened between you and Devlin Monroe last night."

She stepped toe-to-toe with him, tilted back her head, and said, a lovely sneer lacing her voice, "Nothing happened that I didn't want to happen."

"You drank too much of that champagne punch, didn't you? I knew after I tasted it that a score of girls would lose their virtue last night."

"Nonsense, James. Most girls have much harder heads than you give them credit for. Yes, I drank two glasses of that delightful brain-numbing punch, but Devlin was a perfect gentleman. Do you hear me? A *perfect* gentleman. Can a vampire be a gentleman? No matter. Now, I am going riding with him in the park this afternoon at exactly five o'clock, if it doesn't rain, which it looks like it might."

He took a step back, otherwise he might grab her and throw her over his legs and wallop her again, though he doubted she'd feel it. "How many petticoats are you wearing?"

"What?"

"How many petticoats do you have under that gown?"

A man's mind, she thought, *an astounding thing.* "Well now, let me see." She tapped her fingertips against her chin. "There are my drawers, then my chemise—you know, it's nearly down to my knees with really pretty lace around the neck, a soft, white muslin—what is this? Your eyes are crossing? You asked—"

"Tell me only about petticoats, not all the rest of it. For God's sake, Corrie, you don't talk about your drawers, much less about the soft white muslin chemise, particularly in front of a man."

"All right, I suppose I don't want to know about what you're wearing beneath your breeches either. Now, where was I? There's the flannel petticoat, just one, to keep me all toasty even when it's already hot. Then there are four cotton ones, and on the very top is this very pretty white lawn petticoat that, if my gown happens to flip up in the wind, will show even the most critical of ladies that I am well-dressed beneath my clothes. As for what the gentlemen would think, well, you will have to tell me the answer to that, won't you? There, are you happy now? Why the devil do you want to know about my petticoats?"

"I liked you better in breeches. I could see exactly what was going on with you."

"Just what does that mean?"

"I could see your bottom. Well, not really; those damned breeches were so loose."

This was her aunt's drawing room. Uncle Simon was hunkered down in his study not more than twenty feet away. Her Aunt Maybella, goodness, she could be right outside the door, listening.

"You are not to speak of my bottom, James. Surely that isn't the thing."

"It's not. I apologize."

"Well, forget my breeches too. You always made fun of them in any case. Don't you like my gown? Your father selected it. It's very white, all virginal, don't you think?"

"You hang around Devlin Monroe much longer and you won't have a virginal thought in your head. Not to mention the rest of you."

"Now you're accusing me of taking off my clothes with a man I scarcely know? Stripping off all those wretched petticoats?"

"I saw you drinking that champagne punch last night. It was dangerous stuff, not at all proper for young ladies. You waltzed with him twice, Corrie. That wasn't proper of your aunt to allow it."

"She was flirting with Sir Arthur. I saw you having a wonderful time with that Miss Lorimer, who, my aunt tells me, is considered the very best catch in London at the moment, and isn't it a pity that she had to show up when I arrived? Did you enjoy yourself with her, James? Did you?"

"Juliette—"

"Her name is Juliette? As in Romeo's doomed schoolroom girl? That makes me want to—" *Don't spit, not in your aunt's drawing room.* His eyes were gleaming. She didn't know if they were violet or the shade of blue that made her innards ache, but she saw them gleaming. She tacked right into the wind. "Ah, she's surely lovely, isn't she? But you know, James, I've heard that she prefers different sorts of things, just like Devlin Monroe, and I don't think it wise of you to spend too much time with her. You might find yourself without your breeches and wouldn't that be shocking?"

James could only stare at her, his mouth hanging open, his brain soggy in his head. "What different sorts of things? Are you calling Miss Lorimer loose?"

"You mean do I think she is wicked? Like Devlin Monroe?"

"I never said he was wicked, dammit."

"Well, I'm really not saying that Miss Lorimer is wicked either, James. I said she prefers different sorts of things and—"

"What sorts of things?" Those ridiculous words danced out of his mouth before he could tell himself that she was stringing him like a sea bass on a fishing line, slowly reeling him in, and he, fool that he was, was leaping toward her hand. He was an idiot. *Grab the reins, grab the reins.* "No, forget that, be quiet."

"But you're interested, aren't you, James? You want to know what young ladies who are leaning toward debauchery like to do. Admit it."

He was an idiot, an idiot she was reeling in without a single snag in her line. "All right, tell me."

She came up close, dangerous since he was perfectly ready to wring her neck, and whispered, "I heard it said that Juliette likes to perform lascivious parts in plays. Like Aristophanes's *Lysistrada*, you know, that Greek play where the women tell the men that they won't—"

He stared down at that face he knew so well he could close his eyes and set his fingertips roving over it and know exactly what he was seeing. The part of him that was still the sea bass being reeled in, said, "How do you know about this?"

She leaned even closer, not touching him. "I overheard some girls talking about it in the ladies' withdrawing room last night. And since I am interested in Devlin Monroe and the different sorts of things he prefers, I spoke to Miss Lorimer and told her I could perform too, particularly characters of great moral flexibility. She said that was her favorite sort of character as well. She told me that good people were boring, that stepping off the road just a bit was exhilarating. What would happen when she stepped off that road?" Corrie stepped closer. He could feel her breath on his cheek. "I thought about soiling the hem of my gown, and after that first big step, why then, mayhap losing the pins in my hair. What do you think, James?"

The fishing line snapped. James grabbed her shoulders and shook her. He wanted to beat her, but that wouldn't happen, at least not here in her uncle's drawing room. Mayhap the next time they were both home, he could take her back to that rock, then he might jerk those breeches of hers down her hips and—"Listen to me, Corrie. I've really had enough of this. You might consider forgetting Aristophanes and what those women in his play did, which of course you can't begin to understand, despite all your talk about moral flexibility. You might consider also forgetting Juliette Lorimer and her plays. You wouldn't want to perform in a play like that. You wouldn't want to step off the road and soil the hem of your gown."

"Why not?"

"You will not, and that's the end to the matter. Now, I absolutely insist that you forget Devlin Monroe. You will write him a note explaining that you won't be seeing him again. Do you understand me?"

"You're shouting, James. I like Devlin; he's the heir to a dukedom. Goodness, he's already an earl."

"Enough!"

"You're only the heir to an earldom." She leaned close again. "Is it possible that Juliette wants your money?"

It was too much. He finally pulled free of the fishing line. He roared, "If I see you with Devlin Monroe, I will beat you!"

She sneered, a full-bodied, insolent, utterly gratifying sneer. To further enrage him, she crossed her arms over her chest and began to whistle.

He got hold of himself. He said not another word. He turned on his heel and almost ran down Aunt Maybella on his way out of the drawing room.

"James? Jason?"

"I am Jason, ma'am, and forgive me, but I must go."

"Well, I—good-bye, dear boy."

Aunt Maybella walked into the drawing room, saw her niece standing by the front windows, her forehead against the glass. "Whatever was Jason doing here?"

CHAPTER THIRTEEN

❧

One should forgive one's enemies,
but not before they are hanged.

HEINRICH HEINE

IT WAS EARLY, barely seven o'clock in the morning.
Douglas and James were riding toward Hyde Park, comfortable silence between them, each buried in his own thoughts.

It was a cloudy morning, the early fog yet to burn off.

They turned onto Rotten Row and immediately set Bad Boy and Garth into a gallop. Wind whipped against their faces, making their eyes tear.

"Henry VIII would like this," Douglas shouted.

"Aye, he'd like it until he saw someone riding toward him, then he'd attack."

When at last Douglas reined in Garth, he was laughing,

exhilarated, ready to consign all the worry about assassins to Hades.

James pulled in beside him, patting Bad Boy's neck, telling him what a great, fast fellow he was. Bad Boy butted his head against Garth's. Garth tried to bite Bad Boy's neck. Both father and son were busy for several minutes separating them.

James was laughing when he turned to his father. Suddenly the laugh died in his throat. He saw a flash of silver glinting off a spear of early morning sun that had broken through the clouds.

He threw himself at his father, hurtling both of them to the ground as a shot rang out, obscenely loud in the quiet morning air.

James flattened himself over his father even as he tried to pull his gun from his jacket pocket. Another shot—a clod of earth flew up, not six inches from Douglas's head.

"Dammit, James, get off me!" Douglas managed to twist and wrap his arms around his son's waist. He literally lifted him off and rolled him onto his back, flattening himself on top of him.

Another shot, then another, and Douglas wrapped his arms around his son's head to protect him. But these shots weren't close, probably because Bad Boy and Garth were rearing and whinnying, breaking the assassin's line of sight. "Father, please, let me up."

Douglas grunted and rolled over onto his back, then came up to his feet and offered James a hand. They fanned the area with their guns, but saw no one. Suddenly, Garth, maddened, started to run. Douglas calmly whistled, bringing him back, Bad Boy was long gone. He stopped close, head down, blowing hard, lipping at Douglas's hand.

"James, it's all right now."

James slowly turned to face his father. "You must teach me how to call Bad Boy."

Douglas had tried to teach James to whistle for his horse, but James simply never got the hang of a nice ear-splitting whistle, which is what was needed to get any horse's attention. "I'll teach you," he said.

"Father, they were after you, not me. You tried to protect me."

"Of course I'd protect you," Douglas said simply. "You're my son."

"And you're my father, dammit." He fiddled with his gun a moment. "I think I'll go check those bushes where I saw that glint of silver."

"The damned fellow's long gone," Douglas said as he brushed himself off. His shoulder hurt where James had landed on him. He held his derringer loosely in his hand and walked with his son, who was also carrying a gun, this one big and ugly, a dueling pistol out of Douglas's library, over to the thick bushes beside the riding trail.

"Nothing," James said, and cursed. Douglas smiled. "Damnation, the bastard is gone. You can see where he was waiting—the smashed bushes. This isn't what—"

Douglas suddenly raised his derringer and fired. They heard a yell, then nothing. Douglas was off, James running after him. They came out of the narrow band of trees in time to see a man riding a horse out of the south gate of the park, blood streaming down his arm.

"Too bad," Douglas said. "I'd hoped to get him through the head."

"A small target," James said, so relieved, so surprised, that his heart was near to pounding out of his chest. His father was gently rubbing his thumb over the shiny silver derringer. "Actually, I'm surprised I even hit him. A bullet from six feet is a good range for this derringer and this was a good twenty feet."

"Oh, God, that was too close, far too close. Father, do you swear you're all right?"

"Oh yes," Douglas said absently, staring after the man who'd tried to kill him. He turned to his son, punched his arm. "Thank you for saving my life."

James swallowed, then swallowed again. His heart was finally slowing. Now the fear was seeping in, making his hands shake. So close, it had been so close. "If I hadn't seen that glitter of silver—" He swallowed again. "It was you who saved my life and—"

Douglas saw the fear in his son's eyes, and he wrapped his arms around him and held him. "We will get through this, James. You'll see."

James said, "I can't stand this, sir, I really can't."

"You're right. It grows tedious, James, I'll agree with you there. Perhaps it's time I did something about this myself. There's been no more word about Cadoudal's death or any children. I'm off to France in the morning."

"But that's where—"

"No, the enemy is here, James, not in France. I have friends there. It's time I met with them, tried to get the facts of this insane plot."

"I'll go with you."

"No, you and Jason are my eyes and ears here in England."

"Mother won't be pleased."

"I've a mind to take her with me," Douglas said. "It's sure to be safer in France. When I think of how she wanted to come riding with us this morning, it makes my innards cramp. We'll leave discreetly, before dawn tomorrow morning. I don't want our enemy to know that we're no longer here in England. Let the bugger continue to make his plans." He smiled as he stared toward the south gate. "The bastard will have to tend his arm. That will keep him away for several days, at least. Then he'll believe he scared me so badly I'm hiding in the house." Douglas walked to Garth, who was eating some grass beside the path, and said over his shoulder, "Come along, James. We have a lot to do."

Unfortunately it took them a good while to get home since Bad Boy had run from the park home to his stable.

Two hours later, Alexandra was staring at her husband, her cup of tea forgotten. She cleared her throat, adjusted her brain, set her cup carefully back into its saucer, and said, "I think it's an excellent plan, Douglas. We will leave very early, slip out through the back gate. James can arrange to have a hackney meet us over on Willowby Street."

"From there we will meet Captain Finch down at the docks. We'll be off to France with the morning tide."

"You've already arranged a packet?"

"Of course. One valise, Alex. Pack lightly."

She rose and shook out her skirts. She walked to her husband, wanting desperately to hold him close and protect him, but knew it wasn't possible. She smiled down at him, sitting there with his long legs stretched out, ankles crossed, a grin on his face. "You're enjoying this," she said slowly. "You wretch—you're enjoying this."

"It's been a long time, and no, I wouldn't really call it enjoyment. The danger does add some zest to the blood though, I'll admit. We'll have a time of it in France, Alex, and I won't have to worry about you so much as I do here. Let the villains scrabble about, wondering and looking for me, even believing I'm hiding here. Everything will be all right."

"Yes," she said, and sat on his lap. She buried her face against his neck. "Yes, everything will be all right."

"Remie will continue making his rounds. Also I've enlisted a good dozen of our friends to keep their eyes open and watch out for James and Jason. I want the boys kept safe."

"Yes," she said, and wanted to weep she was so frightened. "But you know they'll both be out leading the search."

"They won't get knives in their guts, Alex. They're smart and strong and fast. Ryder and I taught them to fight dirty. Don't worry."

She looked at him as if he were utterly mad.

THE FOLLOWING MORNING, three hours after their parents had left on a packet to Calais, James and Jason were in the breakfast room drinking tea. James said, "We're to go about our business, and if asked, simply say that Mother and Father are at home, resting."

Jason said, looking appalled, "Father would never admit that he needed rest. Can you imagine?"

"No, you're right." James frowned. "Actually, it was mother who said that."

"His friends won't believe that either. He didn't tell me if he took any of them into his confidence, but knowing our father, knowing he'll want us protected while he's not here, I wager he has. What then?"

"How about that he and Mother have traveled to the Cotswolds to visit Uncle Ryder and Aunt Sophie?"

"That could put them in danger, at least until the bastards realized they'd been duped and head back to London."

"All right. We could say they've gone to Scotland to see Aunt Sinjun and Uncle Colin."

The twins were still worrying over the problem when Willicombe shimmered into the breakfast room, making no more noise than a snake. There was tightness about his mouth, a bit of disapproval in his voice. "My lord, a young lady is here to see you. You were not included in her request, Master Jason. She is without an escort. Shall I send her on her way?"

"No, no, Willicombe, send her in. Jason, what will we say?"

"Let's say that Mother is feeling poorly and so Father took her to the seashore to rest. To Brighton. That'll keep the bastards busy trying to track them down there. Now, I'm off to see Miss Judith McCrae."

His brother gave him a thoughtful look, then said, "This evening, you and I are meeting with all our friends. We'll set the lazy sods to work, give them something better to do than roaming the brothels."

"I thought you had a meeting at the Royal Astronomical Society this evening?"

"The stars can wait," James said, then smacked his forehead with his palm. "Well, damn, I'm supposed to present a paper."

"The one on the silver cascade phenomenon you witnessed while you were studying one of Saturn's rings?"

James nodded, and began pacing the breakfast room. "Huygens was wrong about the rings being solid, Jason. They're not, which is why I saw that silver curtain pouring through—"

"James? Are you going to leave me in the hall all morning? You're worrying about Saturn?"

Both men turned to see Corrie standing in the doorway, Willicombe behind her, waving his hands, looking ready to call Remie. She'd rolled right over him. James could tell him that Hollis wouldn't consider trying to keep Corrie waiting, no man in his right mind would. "It's all right, Willicombe. This is Miss Corrie Tybourne-Barrett. She's a friend."

James took a step toward her, his hand outstretched. "Corrie, is everything all right? Where is your maid? Surely you didn't come here alone, did you? It's not done, you know, you shouldn't—"

"I must talk to you." She looked pointedly at Jason, who was staring at her, bemused.

"You make a mighty fine female." Jason gave her a blazing flash of white teeth that would fell any sentient female between the age of ten and eighty. "I'm off, James. I'll see you this evening." Jason flicked a finger over Corrie's chin as he went by. "Be careful, little one, big brother here is a bit on edge."

They stood there listening to Jason whistle, his boots sharp on the black and white Italian marble in the entrance hall.

"What's going on, Corrie? Oh, do sit down. Would you like tea?"

"No, no tea, thank you. I heard a very strange rumor, James."

James grew instantly still. Damn, she'd heard about the attempts on his father's life? "What rumor?" he asked very carefully.

"Juliette Lorimer."

"Juliette Lorimer? Who—oh yes, she's the girl who dances quite well and—What about her?"

"What do you mean she dances quite well? Is she so very special then? Don't I dance quite well?"

"Not yet, but you will. What's this rumor about Miss Lorimer?"

"I heard that she's decided she wants you, James. She intends to marry you. It's possible that she prefers Jason, but it has to be you because you're the heir."

James, fascinated, said, "Wherever did you hear that?"

Corrie stepped closer, went up on her tiptoes, and whispered, "Daisy Winbourne told me she'd heard more than a score of mothers and daughters alike wailing about it in the ladies' withdrawing room. Daisy's brother even mentioned there was going to be a bet soon at White's."

He paled. He shook his head, his eyes never leaving her face. "In White's Betting Book?"

"Evidently so. Soon now. Everyone wants to see you with her one more time before a wager is set. You know, see how besotted you look. Do you intend to marry her, James?"

"Damnation, of course not. I don't even know the damned girl."

Corrie smiled hugely.

"What is this? You don't like her?"

"Certainly not," Corrie said, and drew on her gloves. "Why ever would I like her?" She began whistling as she turned and walked out of the breakfast room.

He called out, the devil prodding and poking at him, "However, I will dance with her tomorrow evening at the Lanscombe ball. Then we'll see, won't we?"

She wasn't about to let him see the smile fall off her face.

That evening, James presented his paper on witnessing the silver cascade phenomena on Titan, Saturn's major ring, at the monthly Royal Astronomical Society meeting. There were thirty gentlemen present, star dabblers all, several of them who would believe to their dying breaths that the Earth was the center of the universe, that heretic Galileo be damned. There were two ladies present, both wives of men delivering papers, and both of them stared at James until all he wanted to do was finish his paper and make for the door. James's paper was well received, primarily because it was short, although he knew most members believed he was too young to understand what he was seeing. He was offered two invitations by the wives, ostensibly to dine with their husbands as well.

He was back at the Sherbrooke town house by ten o'clock to see his father's library filled with friends, all of them sober as prisoners in the dock, cursing the air blue with outrage, demanding to be the one to kill the bastard after the earl.

"We have to find out who they are first," Jason said. "As I said, the only man's name we have is Georges Cadoudal, but when he died a while ago, he supposedly wasn't my father's enemy. Father is in France trying to discover if Cadoudal had children. It could be revenge, but again, since my father and Cadoudal weren't enemies, it doesn't make much sense."

"Children, particularly male children, can get all sorts of notions, Jason. If the father is dead, then it has to be the children."

"We'll see. Now, we have no other leads. Just keep your ears open for that name and any others you might discover."

James smiled to see his brother writing in a small notebook, doubtless the assignments he'd passed out. Jason was logical and he was smart. James knew that he'd assigned the proper man to the proper task.

By midnight, every young man in the room had a sense of purpose. They were going to save the earl of Northcliffe, become heroes in the process, and earn his undying gratitude.

As the brothers walked upstairs to bed, James said, "However did you come up with so many different assignments?"

"Not all that many since I assigned them in pairs. Johnny Blair, for example, knows most of the French in London since he's engaged to a Frog's daughter. Johnny is discreet as long as he's not drinking, and Horace Mickelby will keep him sober and alert. Reddy Montblanc, who's nearly blind in one eye, is nevertheless one of the best trackers in England. He and Charles Cranmer will check the area where the assassin tried to shoot Father. And on it goes.

"As for us, two nights from now, that French captain should be here. We'll see him ourselves. How did your talk to the society go?"

"Short and to the point, and I could see that all the old graybeards in the group wanted to pat me on the head. I wonder if Father and Mother are in Paris yet."

"They should be soon, if they're not already. As Father said, he has many friends there. Someone must know something or have heard something. There must be people who knew Cadoudal, and they'll know about any family. I hope Mother isn't speaking French."

"She really tries," James said, and laughed.

"She's lucky we're not living in the last century, with the advent of the Hanoverian kings. Can you imagine her trying to learn German?"

CHAPTER FOURTEEN

❧

The cock may crow,
but it's the hen that lays the eggs.

MARGARET THATCHER

IT WAS A balmy night for the first of October, but since Remie Willicombe's mother had told him it would rain by midnight, James wore a heavier coat.

He didn't particularly wish to go to the Lanscombe ball on Putnam Square, but he'd promised Miss Lorimer that he would come by, though he had no intention of staying. He had no intention of ending up in White's Betting Book either. One dance with Miss Lorimer, no more.

Jason announced he was going with friends to one of his clubs, making James poke his brother and ask him why Miss McCrae hadn't requested his presence this evening.

Jason had looked at him, frowning, and said he understood that Lady Arbuckle wasn't feeling well and Judith had stayed home to attend her.

The twins were meeting at White's at midnight to go to the docks, to the *Crooked Cat Tavern*, where the French captain was said to frequent.

When James finally saw Miss Lorimer, he had to admit she looked amazingly lovely, all in lilac, her huge sleeves included, which stuck a good six inches out from her arms, the material stiffened by wooden rods, his mother had told him, and wasn't that ingenious?

The lilac silk skirts fanned out around her, at least six petticoats keeping them afloat. Her hair was in a knot on the back of her head with a score of little ringlets falling over her forehead and cascading over her ears, like the silver particles of Titan.

He saw Corrie then, standing with her aunt across the ballroom, her gown a luminous white, the style simple, his father's hand visible in every lovely fold and drape, and he was quite pleased until he reached her breasts, and frowned. Too prominently displayed, he thought, and surely her Aunt Maybella should say something to her. It wasn't appropriate for an eighteen-year-old young lady.

Perhaps he'd help her improve her dancing after he'd kept his promise to Miss Lorimer. Certainly that would dilute the gossip, unless everyone knew that Corrie was like a sister to him, then dancing a waltz with her wouldn't count.

So Miss Lorimer had decided to marry him, had she? More likely her mother's choice, James thought cynically, as he made his way slowly toward her.

He discovered quickly enough that everyone had heard about the attempts on his father's life.

All his father's friends stopped him, questioned him, and raised their brows when he repeated yet again that his mother and father had gone to Brighton because his mother wasn't well, which sounded more stupid each time he repeated it.

"Alexandra has never been sick a day in her life," said Lord Ponsonby, "except when she had to lie down a moment to birth you and your brother, and she wasn't really sick, now was she?"

He agreed that no, sir, she wasn't really sick then, and wanted desperately to flee.

"Humph," said Lord Ponsonby. "Did you say Brighton, James? Something's fishy here, my boy, the sort of fishy that makes me realize what a bad liar you are. Your father now—an excellent liar—would stare you right in the eye."

James cursed under his breath. He was going to throw his brother over the balcony when he got home.

Miss Lorimer, at last, was in his sights. She was looking at him over her mother's shoulder, eyes glittering. No, he thought, *more than that. Assessing.*

When he reached her, she said, "Why, it is a pleasure to see you, sir. You are James?"

"Yes, I am James," he said. "Would you like to dance, Miss Lorimer?" and looked toward her mother, who nodded placidly at him.

"Yes, if you will agree to call me Juliette."

"Very well, Juliette." He took her white hand, lightly placed it on his arm, and led her onto the dance floor.

So light and graceful she was, utter perfection, truth be told. But she couldn't tell him apart from his brother? That hurt. The moment the waltz was over, he led her back to her mother. He bowed, retreated. The air in the ballroom was heavy, the weight of all the ladies' perfumes filling his nostrils, making him want to sneeze. He saw Corrie wave at him. He wanted to leave since Lord Ponsonby had probably told all his cronies that James was a miserable liar and they should hold him down and beat the truth out of him, but there she was, looking quite acceptable except for those breasts of hers that would make a man swallow his tongue and want to dive his hands into her bodice.

He walked up to her, flicked his fingertip over her cheek, and said, "The cream has done wonders. I do believe this is soft skin I feel."

He smiled and turned to Lady Maybella, who was wearing a blue silk gown that James wanted to tell her needed to have at least three flounces sheared off.

"You're here to dance with Corrie? You're in luck. I've scarce had her to myself this evening, so many young gentlemen wanting to dance with her."

"Please don't exaggerate, Aunt Maybella. There's not been more than a dozen or so," Corrie said, making James grin.

Maybella said, tapping him on the arm with her fan, "Not more than two dances, James. We don't want people to get the wrong idea. Besides, look at that hoard of young men coming this way."

James didn't see a hoard, but there were two gentlemen, one of them old enough to be Corrie's father, on a march toward her.

James gave Maybella a charming smile and led Corrie to the dance floor, aware of her fingers tapping against his arm, and eased her into the throng of dancers. "You're going to wear a hole in my sleeve. Whatever is the matter with you?"

"I want to help you," she said.

An eyebrow arched up.

"Your father. I can't bear the thought of anyone hurting him, James. Whatever would I do without him to tell me what to wear? Come, don't get all stiff on me. I've known your father all my life. I want to help find out who's trying to kill him. I'm smart. I'm fast. Let me help."

James sighed. He didn't even wonder how she'd found

out. What with all their friends investigating, it was bound to be all over London in fifteen minutes. Fact was, he was willing to wager that everyone in the ballroom was speaking about it. And mayhap that was good. He wanted to tell her that there was absolutely no chance he was going to allow her to get within one hundred yards of any danger, and so he said, "You've always been able to tell me and Jason apart." That distracted her, but good. She scoffed. She sneered. "I've always told you that you are yourself, very different from your brother."

"Miss Lorimer can't tell us apart, evidently."

"There, you see, you can't marry her, James. She doesn't even know who you are."

She had a point there.

Then the devil stuck his elbow in James's ribs and said words right out of his mouth. "Speaking of the Angel, Miss Lorimer looks so heavenly this evening, don't you think? She's wearing lilac, not purple."

"Angel?"

James nodded. "That's the name selected for her."

"By whom?"

He shrugged. "By the gentlemen, I suppose."

"Maybe she started the name herself."

"Who cares if she did? Don't you think it's accurate?"

"If you like perfection, then yes, I suppose so. I wonder what name I should select for myself. I know, how about calling me Miss Cream?"

He threw back his head and laughed. "Miss Cream? That's rich, Corrie."

"And that was a bad pun."

"How about Devil?"

"No, I'm not wicked enough, at least not yet."

"You will never be wicked," he said, stiff now, looking down at her breasts. "Well, you won't be if you'd just hoist up your gown a good two inches."

"This is the style, James. If I can get used to heaving

myself out there, then so can you. Stop dwelling on it. Now, if I can't be wicked, then you can call me the Ice Princess. I heard that a Miss Franks was called that some five seasons ago. She married a duke who was eighty years old and almost dead. Isn't that interesting?"

"Heavenly Lord Jesus," James said, and whirled her about, making her laugh, distracting her yet again. "You're getting better at this. Forget this Ice Princess. That will make the gentlemen want to teach you all sorts of things you're not going to learn for a very long time. Now, you've obeyed me, haven't you?"

"Obeyed you? About what?"

"You haven't danced with Devlin Monroe, have you? You haven't offered him your neck at midnight, have you?"

She laughed, a lovely rich laugh that made him smile. "I gave him a little nibble, nothing more." She turned her head about. "Can you see the mark, there, right below my left ear?"

He wanted to kick himself when he actually looked. "Remind me to beat you again."

"Ha. That first time you caught me by surprise."

His eyebrow arched up a good inch. "You think so, do you? I don't think I've ever heard you whine so much as you did that day."

Before she could answer, he danced faster and faster, until she was panting and laughing, barely able to catch her breath, hating her damned corset. When he slowed, she gasped out, "Oh, James, that is so lovely. When I want to smack you in the head, you have only to dance me into the ground and I'm ready to forgive you anything at all."

"You're getting more competent moving your feet. Stay away from Devlin, I mean it, Corrie."

"He took me to the Pantheon Bazaar yesterday," she said. "He wanted to buy me a lovely ribbon to thread through my hair—he thinks my hair is lovely, by the way, all sorts of interesting autumn shades all mixed together—but I'm a proper girl, and thus I didn't let him do it. It seemed rather intimate, particularly since he wanted to do the threading. Do you know he got so close with that ribbon that I could feel his breath on my nose?" She gave a delicious little shudder that nearly had him ready to kill.

He saw the glint in her eye, and got control. "Your aunt should never have allowed you to go off with him. I will have to speak to her about that. He isn't good husband material, Corrie."

"Husband material? Do you want to know the truth, James? I've been thinking about it, and I truly cannot imagine attaching myself to a man and changing my name. Goodness, I would be Corrie Tybourne-Barrett Monroe. As for a husband, he would order me about and expect me to do whatever he wants whenever he wants it." She looked thoughtful for a moment, her eyes narrowed. "On the other hand, I must be honest about this. I have passed Aunt Maybella and Uncle Simon's bedchamber before, and do you know what?"

James was certain that his eyes were going to roll back in his head. He didn't want to hear this. He wanted to go to China before he heard this. He said, "What?"

She leaned close. "I heard them laughing. Yes, laughing, and then Uncle Simon said, quite clearly, 'I shall nibble on your lovely self for a while now, Bella.' What do you think of that, James?"

Well, he had asked. He wondered if Aunt Maybella wore a blue nightgown. No, he had to turn his mind away from that. He said, "Stay away from Devlin Monroe."

"We'll have to see, won't we?" She gave him a sunny smile, then looked like she'd burst into tears. "Oh drat, the waltz is ending. It was too short. Someone stopped it before its time. I'll bet that Juliette Lorimer bribed them to

stop. I think someone should go speak to them. Perhaps—"
She gave him a hopeful look, but he shook his head.

"No, I have to leave now, Corrie. I like your hair nice
and simple, all braided on the top. You wouldn't look good
with an army of ringlets marching over your head. Or any
ribbons. Forget ribbons, particularly those bought for you
by a man."

Corrie supposed it was a compliment. She wanted another waltz and so she said, "I believe Devlin is beyond
that very fat lady, speaking to another young man who
looks remarkably wicked himself. Hmmm. Let me see if I
can get his attention." She went up on her tiptoes and
whispered against his ear, "I think I shall tell him my
name is the Ice Princess. I wonder what he will have to say
about that?"

But her performance was wasted because James wasn't
listening. He'd turned at the tug at his sleeve. It was one of
the waiters hired for this evening, and he pressed a note
into James's hand. "A gentleman said you was to have this,
sir. Right away, he said."

His heart began to drum, deep and sharp. He left her
without a word, and looked neither right nor left at the
young ladies who were staring after him. He walked
through the long row of French doors that gave onto the
Lanscombe balcony.

He stepped out, saw a couple embracing at the far end,
and wanted to tell that old roué Basil Harms that he wasn't
far enough in the shadows. He wondered what man's wife
he was seducing.

He walked quietly down the steps on the far end of the
balcony and strode into the Lanscombe garden toward the
back gate. He didn't have a gun, curse it, and perhaps this
wasn't the smartest thing he'd ever done in his life, but on
the other hand, there was a chance this was news about the
man who wanted to kill his father. There was no choice re-

ally. Besides, who would want to hurt him? No, it was his father they were after. The lights from the ballroom dimmed until he was in blackness and saw only the outline of the narrow gate some fifteen feet in front of him. He wasn't stupid. He looked all around him for possible danger, listened, but it was quiet. The man he was supposed to meet was waiting for him by the back gate.

What sort of information did the man have? James hoped he had enough money on him to meet his price.

He heard the rustling of leaves just off to his right. He whirled around but saw nothing, no movement, no light, nothing at all. Surely there would be no lovers this far away from the mansion. He waited, listening. Nothing. He was alert; he was ready.

It was at least ten feet to that narrow gate with ivy climbing up it, cascading wildly over the top, rather like that silver cascade over Titan. The eight-foot-high stone walls of the Lanscombe garden were also covered with ivy, miles of the stuff, thick, impenetrable. His steps slowed. He scented danger; he actually smelled it.

Suddenly a man came out of the shadows to stand at the end of the path, right in front of the gate. In a deep rolling voice, the man said, "Lord Hammersmith?"

"Aye, I'm Hammersmith."

"I have information to sell ye, me lord, all about yer pa."

"What do you have?"

The man pulled a sheaf of papers from his old black jacket. "I want five pounds fer the lot of it."

He had five pounds, thank God.

"Before I give you anything, tell me what you have."

"It's names, me lord, names and places the gentleman what gave me the papers said yer pa would want to see. Some letters too."

Five pounds. Even if it was worthless, it was worth the five pounds, to be sure.

James was reaching into his pocket for money when the man dropped the papers, jerked up a gun, and said, "Ye don't move now, me fine lord. Ye just stand there nice and straight and don't ye even wink an eyelash."

CHAPTER FIFTEEN

❧

Life is simply one damned thing after another.

ASCRIBED TO ELBERT HUBBARD

JAMES WAS ALREADY in motion. His leg shot out, clipped the gun, and sent it flying into the ivy against the garden wall. The man yelped, grabbed his hand. James was nearly on him when a thick blanket came flying down over his head and he heard the voices of two men, one of them whispering, "No, don't yell, ye fool. We'll jest bundle him all up like this so's he can't kick out and break our necks."

"I want to kick 'is balls off, Augie, kickin' Billy like that, nearly broke 'is wrist the bastid did."

James was jerking at the blanket, trying to find a corner, when a gun barrel nicked him on the shoulder, then another one hit him hard on the head. He was cursing loud enough to bring the watch when the pain bowed him to his knees.

Another blow on the head. He fell, swaddled in the thick wool, and knew no more.

Corrie's scream never came out of her throat. There was nothing she could do except yell and jump on them and likely get herself banged on the head with a gun, and what good would that do James? She looked on, horrified and enraged, and stuffed her fist in her mouth.

She watched them gather him up, then one of the men, much larger than the others, heaved James, still wrapped in the blanket, over his shoulder.

"Not a feather, this one. Let's git our braw lad out o' this place, quick."

Her heart was pounding loud enough for the Lord to hear, but she followed, her slippers light on the cobblestones as she ran toward the back garden gate. She watched them push the gate open, saw a carriage in the alley, two bays harnessed to it, standing quietly, heads down, at rest. One of the men climbed onto the bench and picked up the reins. It was Billy. He leaned back. "Git moving, Ben, ye want to tie our gent up good. He's a strong 'un, kicked me wrist so sharp it sent pins through me fingers. I ain't niver seen a man move like that. We'll keep an eye on 'im."

She watched them toss James onto the carriage floor, then jump up after him.

A man leaned out the window, hissed, "Go, Billy, scrabble 'em, now! We've gots a ways to go."

Corrie watched Billy click to the horses and wave the reins. The carriage slowly moved toward the entrance of the alley, behind the mansion, onto Clappert Street.

She didn't think, didn't weigh consequences. She simply ran after the carriage and leapt lightly up onto the back runner, grabbed the straps and pulled herself close to the carriage. It was the tiger's perch, and she knew it well. When she'd been younger she'd loved to ride in the tiger's perch behind James or Jason, singing at the top of her lungs, feeling the wind tearing at her old leather hat and braid, tearing her eyes.

The only difference between now and then was that she was wearing a beautiful white silk ball gown, lovely white slippers on her feet, and no old leather hat. Nor did she have a wrap.

It didn't matter. Three bad men had kidnapped James. Where were they going to take him?

She had to keep down, keep quiet, not fall off, and not let the men see her. Well, she'd certainly hidden from James and Jason enough times, following them, even plastering mud on her face so they wouldn't see her in the bushes, and they'd never known she was there, watching them wrestle, throw knives at targets, practice cursing. But this was different, she'd agree with that. What would she do when they stopped, well, something would come to her, it had to.

Why had they taken James? To get to his father, of course. The note that waiter had pressed into James's hand, all a ruse. He shouldn't have come out into the Lanscombe garden alone, the idiot.

Thank God she'd seen everything. She drew in a deep breath as the horses lengthened into a trot. The streets were nearly empty. Thank God for the half moon. She would figure out something. She had to save James. It was that simple.

She had no idea which direction they were going because they'd gotten nowhere near the Thames. Suddenly she saw a sign to Chelmsford. Ah, they were going east. Wasn't Cambridge in this same direction?

Corrie didn't know how much time passed. Her arms ached, her fingers were numb.

Whining never helped unless you did it to another person, so she gave it up and hummed to herself. She held on to those straps, that was all she had to do.

She remembered when James had picked her up and

tossed her into a pond near the back of her uncle's property. Unfortunately, her breeches, stolen from the charity clothes in the sexton's closet at the vicarage, got snagged on a tangle of reeds underwater and she'd nearly drowned. She would remember until she croaked how white his face had been when he'd realized what had happened and pulled her out. He'd nearly crushed her ribs he'd pressed down so hard to get the water out of her lungs. And he'd held the eight-year-old Corrie, rocking her back and forth, begging her to forgive him, until she'd vomited up the nasty pond water all over him.

Corrie didn't remember if she'd forgiven him or not, the miserable sot. Of course, the next week, he'd tied her to a tree when he wanted to take Melissa Banbridge for a walk in the woods and he'd seen her following them.

She'd gotten the rope untied, but couldn't find them. She'd slipped a half dozen frogs into his boots standing downstairs to be cleaned by the boot boy. Unfortunately, she'd heard one of the footmen say that for some reason they'd found a wagon load of frogs flying around in the mudroom and how had that come about?

Hang on, hang on, don't think about anything but hanging on.

The temperature dropped as the night deepened. How late was it? She had no idea.

They skirted Chelmsford. She saw signs for Clacton-on-Sea, and the carriage turned sharply to the right. They were going toward the English Channel.

She heard occasional voices from inside the carriage, but she couldn't make out any words. Had they unwrapped James? What if they'd killed him with those blows on the head? No, that was crazy thinking.

Was he conscious? Was one of the voices she'd heard his? He was all right. He had to be all right. He was fine; he'd have a headache, but he'd be fine. She had no idea what she'd do if he weren't fine. She'd take care of him, that's what she'd do, and then she'd kill him herself for being such a fool to go out into that garden alone.

The carriage suddenly pulled off the gutted lane onto one even smaller, so narrow that a branch hit her arm, nearly jerking her to the ground.

She pressed herself closer and prayed. She heard a noise and nearly expired on the spot. It was her own teeth chattering. Good God, was she going to freeze to death before this bloody carriage got to where it was going?

Finally, the carriage slowed. She saw a small weathered cottage at the end of a lane. The horses were now walking, then Billy pulled up.

He shouted back down, "This is the place, gots to be. Not too bad atal, nice and comfy, all 'idden away. Get 'is bleedin' lordship all ready, don't want no trouble from the lad! Oh aye, an' watch 'is bloody feet!"

Augie stuck his head out the window. "We've got 'm all tied up, the boyo ain't going nowheres, Billy."

"Good. If we croaks our fancy cove, we don't get no groats."

They'd taken James so they could blackmail his father into an exchange. Augie and Ben were talking, grumbling, and she realized they would see her for her gown was stark white and would shine like a beacon beneath that half moon.

Thank God Billy climbed down and kept to the front of the carriage. When he opened the carriage door, she slipped around to the other side and tucked herself against the back wheel. Her legs nearly buckled, and she was clutching at the wheel to keep herself upright. She was numb, frozen, more frightened than she'd ever been in her life, and she was going to save James.

"The lad weighs as much as me mither, only she weren't tall like this fellow, jest a little fat pigeon wot liked to smack me noggin."

"Shut up, Billy. Okay, bring 'im into the cottage. Funny

thing how the lad jest fell unconscious again. Take care, this boy's a wily 'un. I wants to 'ave me a boy like this 'un some day."

"That'd mean gettin' yer pecker up an' stiff," Augie said. "When's the last time that 'appened?"

Ben said, "It 'appened when 'is landlady beat 'im with a shoe, made him all lusty."

The men laughed and grunted as they carried James, evidently still unconscious, into the cottage. Corrie remained hugging the wheel, watching. They would have to do something with the horses. She waited until they all went into the cottage, then stumbled on numb feet into the trees and began to work her way around to the side of the cottage. At least moving made her thaw a bit and got the feeling back into her feet.

She crouched down outside the filthy window and looked in. It was just one room, with a narrow cot along the back wall. There was a battered table and four chairs and a very dilapidated area where it appeared they cooked. The fireplace was off to her right.

She watched them dump James on the narrow cot, then pull the blanket away from him. She nearly fell over she was so angry. Blood had snaked down the side of his face.

Billy slapped his face a couple of times, then stood straight, looking down at him. "Still under the willow, our lad. Augie, ye said 'e came back to 'is wits in the carriage?"

"Aye," Augie said. "Then when I tapped 'im a couple of times, jest to get 'is attention, our lad 'as the nerve to collapse again. 'E'll come around in a bit. I'm ready to gnaw off me elbow, Ben. Ye fix us somethin'."

Settling in, she thought, *they were settling in. For how long?* Closer to the sea, it was colder, but at least she was out of the wind. Suddenly it was dark. She looked up to see black clouds covering the half moon.

It was Augie who came out in a couple of minutes and led the horses to a small shed on the other side of the cottage.

She watched James, then watched Billy carry logs to the fireplace.

What to do?

She continued to watch James, and finally, she saw his hand move. She felt such relief she nearly shouted. She had the feeling he was looking at the men, his eyes barely slit open. He was thinking, trying to figure out what to do.

It was so cold now she was ready to tear a strip off her gown and go into the warm cottage waving a white flag.

She gritted her teeth, waited. The three men were speaking low, of nothing at all, really. She saw Augie rise and go check on James. "Still out, our boy is. I don't like this. We're to give 'im off to the bloke wot's paying us our groats and give 'im off alive."

"Ye think this bloke'll slit 'is throat, or ransom 'im?"

Augie shrugged. "Don't know. Ain't none o' our business. Mighty 'andsome young man, 'e is though, 'tis a pity whatever 'appens to 'im."

She watched Augie check the ropes that bound James's wrists and ankles. At least they'd tied his hands in front of him. Augie walked back to the fireplace where the two men were stretching out on the floor. "Aye, I knows I gots the first watch. Billy, I'll roust ye in two 'ours."

And Augie sat in a chair, looking at the fireplace. He looked all toasty warm, the bastard.

It was time. She had to do something. She smiled. As she skirted the back of the cottage, she saw now that the cottage was only about thirty yards from a cliff that gave onto a narrow dark beach. She ran to the shed and crept in. It was small and ramshackle. There were some old blankets piled in one corner, some farm implements, and piles of moldy hay. One of the bays lifted his head, but he didn't whinny, just snorted, thank God. She patted his great head, and he blew into her hand. "You'll suit me, my beauty, and your brother there will do nicely for James," she said against his warm mane. She saw that Augie had given them each a bucket of oats and water. Good. Now, all she had to do was get James out of that miserable cabin. She sorted through the rusted tools, stopped, and smiled.

James watched Augie walk back to sit in his chair. Soon Billy and Ben would be asleep. But how to get to Augie without waking the others? Could he take all three men?

He wasn't sure. His head ached, but other than that he felt all right. He knew he had to get his feet free, then he'd have a chance. But Augie would notice if he sat up and began working the knot around his ankles. He settled for loosening the knots around his wrists. Thank God they believed he was still unconscious, otherwise they would have tied his hands behind him, likely tied him to the bed as well. It was then he caught a flash of movement. He looked at the dirty window behind Augie's back. He saw something white waving back and forth, like a truce flag.

He blinked and refocused. Yes, it was still there. Augie's head was slowly falling forward on his chest.

James saw a face.

Corrie.

He stared at her as he slowly raised his hand so she could see that he had his wits together. He wiggled his fingers.

He saw that grin of hers, white teeth shining through the dirty windowpane across the room.

Then she was gone. She was going to do something, and whatever she was planning, he had to be ready.

CHAPTER SIXTEEN

*One good head is better
than a hundred strong hands.*

THOMAS FULLER

HIS EARS WERE on alert. He heard something on the roof, a light scurrying sound, or perhaps it was a branch of a tree swishing against the wood.

No, that was no tree nor animal up there. It had to be Corrie, light on her feet, but what was she doing? His brain seized up at thoughts of how she'd gotten here.

His question was answered in the next instant as smoke started billowing out of the fireplace. She'd bought him time to get the ropes off his ankles. James immediately sat up and began working the ropes. It took a couple of minutes before Augie, Billy, and Ben began coughing, and by then, the room was filling up fast with smoke.

Augie jumped out of his chair, yelling, "Boys, it's fire! Tar and damnation, this jest ain't fair! Quick, quick, we gots to grab up our cove and git out o' this bloody 'ell 'ole!"

In that instant, the cottage door burst open and a furious, whinnying horse pounded into the room, rearing, snorting, Corrie on his back, aiming a pitchfork right at Ben, who was standing closest to her, struck dumb with shock and horror.

Then all three of the men were yelling, trying to get out of the room, trying to avoid the horse and the pitchfork, its long tongs rusted but still sharp. Ben wasn't fast enough. She got him through the arm. He yelled and pulled out his gun, but James was on him, his leg slicing through the air, his foot kicking that gun right out of Ben's hand. Then James was rolling to get the gun as Augie fired at him. Corrie and the horse turned and rode Augie down, sending his gun flying toward the door. Augie was crawling as close to the wall as he could get, toward the open doorway and into the night. At the last minute he managed to snag the gun and stuff it into his pants.

The horse was maddened by the smoke, and wanted out. "James, throw me one of the guns!"

He grabbed Billy's gun right out of his hand and threw it to her as she stuck the pitchfork into the wall and rode out of the cottage on the horse.

James had only Billy to tend to, and it was easily done despite the choking, blinding smoke.

He was leaping over Billy, stopping just a moment to lean down and smash his fist into his jaw.

Corrie was sitting bareback atop the horse, the other bay just behind, waiting for him. She was covered in soot, grinning like a fool. "Hurry, James, hurry!" Even as she spoke, Augie fired from the cottage door, and the bullet whizzed by the horse's ear. The horse jerked back and reared on his hind legs, hurling Corrie to the ground. Both horses reared and bucked, running madly back along the rutted road, away from the cottage, and away from them.

James cursed as he ran to Corrie. She was struggling to her knees. "We've got to hurry, Corrie. Sorry, but no horses. Can you walk? Are you badly hurt?"

"Oh dear, there's Ben, holding his arm. I got him with the pitchfork. Let's go, James. I'm all right."

Each of them held a gun in one hand, James nearly dragging her after him. They ran into the woods that bordered the narrow road. There was a gunshot, more yelling—this one out of Ben's mouth—if James wasn't mistaken, since he was screaming about how the bitch stuck his arm with that nasty pitchfork.

Well, the three bastards had only one gun and no horses. He and Corrie were better off. He wanted to go back and pound them, but he wouldn't be surprised if they had more guns. He didn't think they did, but who knew how Augie's brain worked?

They ran through the woods, tripping over roots, until he couldn't hear any of the men yelling anymore.

"Hold, Corrie. Let's wait a minute."

She was breathing hard, gulping in air, and nearly fell against a pine tree, her arms wrapped around her chest, the gun dangling from two fingers.

James stood there, staring at her. Her once white ball gown was black with smoke and soot, ripped and grimy, one sleeve hanging by a thread. Her hair was streaming in wild tangles down her back and onto her face. She was still grinning at him, all white teeth against the black face, still panting hard.

James laughed, he couldn't help himself. "Well done," he said and grabbed her hand. "They've got to come after us, although I can't imagine how they're going to do it. Ben's got your pitchfork tong through his arm and he won't be good for much. Damn, I wish I knew how many guns they have."

"If they catch those wretched horses, we might be in deep trouble again, James. I saw that lead horse run off the road and head toward the cliffs, out in the open, where we can't go."

James frowned thoughtfully down at his boots. "I don't think they saw the horses or where they went. But if they do manage to catch them, they could go back to the shed and get the carriage. That wouldn't be good."

Her eyes sparkled. "Then let's take care of that carriage, James."

James was weighing the risks. "It's a matter of how much they were paid to take me. If it's a lot, then they will try their best to get me again."

"I hope it was a carriage-full," Corrie said, eyes narrowing. "Failure must really taste bad if you lose a lot of money. Let's not take the chance. Let's get that carriage."

It took them only ten minutes to make their way back to the cottage. Augie and the boys had pulled the blanket off the chimney. James quickly saw that the cottage, with its door hanging on its rusted hinges, was quite empty, except for the pitchfork with a bit of blood on its tip. No Billy, Ben, or Augie.

When they got to the shed, James picked up an old, rotted axe, grinned like the Devil himself, and destroyed one wheel while Corrie took the pitchfork to the other. When the wheels were in shards on the ground, James dropped the axe, rubbed his hands together, and said, "That's slowed them down. Let's go."

They were off again. Not more than a minute after they'd stepped into the woods, they heard Augie yell, "Tar and damnation, curse the young 'un! The little bastid ruined the carriage. I'll have to kick 'im into the ground when I gits me fists on 'im."

"He gave me no credit at all," Corrie said.

"If they try for us again, you can shoot him."

"Yes, yes, I think that's a fine idea."

There was generalized cursing, nothing really original, Corrie thought, from all three of the men as James and Corrie stood quietly, listening and smiling.

James whispered near her ear, "Do you know where we are?"

"I know we took a turnoff to Clacton-on-Sea."

"That far east," he said. He looked down at her, saw that she was shivering like a loon, and quickly took off his coat. Corrie sighed and hugged it close. It felt as warm as bread just toasted in the oven. "Ah, that feels good, James. You know, the thing is that after all that running, after hammering that pitchfork down on the carriage wheel, I was getting warm again. I think I'm shivering now because I'm still so excited."

"Excited, are you?" As a matter of fact, he was as well, the blood pumping madly through his veins, his head pounding, so filled with energy that he knew he could swim to Calais. But that would fade quickly. And Corrie, she'd been hanging on to the back of that carriage for a good three hours before they'd stopped. She was going to crash like a felled tree. He prayed she wouldn't get ill.

"Not quite so excited as I was just a minute ago," she said. "It's odd, isn't it, how powerful you feel?"

"Yes, it is, but it won't last, Corrie. I don't want you to get sick. Keep bundled up. Now, there's nothing else to do, but walk."

He stuffed both guns in his belt, took her hand, and off they went. They stayed inside the woods that bordered the narrow road. "They're going to be looking for us, so that means we need to avoid the main road once we reach it. All we need is a town."

"They'll be expecting us to walk back toward London," she said, and frowned. "They kidnapped you because they wanted to trade you for your father, James."

"Yes, I imagine so. Unfortunately, they never spoke the name of the man who'd hired them. I'm sorry I didn't tell you about the attempt on my father's life. I should have before you heard it from others."

"Yes, you should have told me. It's not as if I'm some sort of stranger, James. Everyone was speaking of it."

He stopped, faced her, and cupped her dirty face between his dirty hands. "Thank you for saving my hide. How did you know?"

"I saw the waiter hand you that scrap of paper. I know you very well, James. I saw immediately that it worried you, and so I followed you. I knew I couldn't help you once they had thrown the blanket over you, so I waited until the carriage started up, then I jumped on the back."

"You've always been an excellent tiger."

"Yes." He watched her fiddling with her hair. He could only marvel at her bravery. But she wouldn't see it like that, not at all. She would simply say it was the only thing to be done and wouldn't he have done the same thing as well? No, he would have gone after their throats, immediately. And maybe gotten himself killed.

He squeezed her dirty hand. "I was trying to figure out how to get off the rope around my ankles without Augie seeing me, and then I thought I heard something on the roof. Augie was already half-asleep and didn't hear a thing. You gave me the time. That was clever of you. You've a good brain."

She beamed. "Truth is, I nearly broke my leg getting on the roof. And you know that some of the planks on the roof are quite rotted through? I thought for a while there that I would crash through and land right on Augie's lap."

He laughed, then sobered very quickly. "I have some money so we're not destitute. However, we both look like we've been in a fight. Try to think up a story to explain our condition."

She shook her head, said quite seriously, "No, when we reach a farm, all we'll have to do is make sure the wife gets a good look at you. Even with all that smoke and soot on

your face, she'll swoon and sigh and give you her husband's food, and bed. If she looked beyond your beautiful
face, she'll get to your evening clothes. That will surely do
the trick if your face hasn't."

"A bad jest, Corrie."

"It wasn't a jest, James. You just don't realize, do you
that—well, never mind. Now, a farmhouse, that's just what
we need. I don't know what would happen if we had to
walk into a village."

They walked. Exactly twenty minutes later, they heard
horses' hooves coming toward them. James pulled her up
and they stepped farther into the trees. They watched
Augie, riding the lead horse, bareback, with a makeshift
bridle, leading the second bay, carrying both Billy and
Ben, a dirty bandage tied around Billy's arm.

"Only one bridle," James whispered. "It looks quite
amusing, actually. None too steady, any of them. I'll wager
that our three villains are London born and bred, far more
comfortable slithering about in a back alley than trying to
ride down prey in the open."

If he'd been alone, he would have tried to take one of
the horses, but with Corrie present, he wasn't about to take
the chance of her getting hurt since she'd already taken too
many chances. What if the roof had collapsed? What if the
horse hadn't obligingly crashed through the cottage door?
What if— He was making himself quite mad. She'd survived and so had he. But no more, he didn't think his heart
could survive it.

She whispered against his cheek, "I think we can take
them, James. You get Augie, who seems the most competent, and I'll bring down Ben and Billy. Just look, they're
sliding all over that poor horse's back. Let's just scare them
off."

He could only stare at her. She was right. "No, it's too
dangerous."

"Climbing up on that damned roof was more dangerous than this would be, not to mention riding in like a knight with a lance into that cottage. Give over, James. Be sensible."

This from a girl who was wearing a ball gown in the middle of the night, on the side of a rutted road, with three bad men ready to slit her throat.

It was taken out of their hands. At that moment, a huge boom of thunder sounded. Lightning slashed down, once, twice. The horses reared, terrified, throwing all three men to the ground. Another boom of thunder, another streak of lightning and the horses were off, racing madly, right down the road, away from them.

Ben was moaning, holding his foot, weaving back and forth. "Damn ye, ye bloody bugger!"

"Well, me bloody 'orse threw me too," Augie said, walking gingerly toward Ben and Billy.

"No, not the 'orse," Ben yelled. "Billy's the bloody bugger wot landed on me foot! I'm goin' to carve yer gullet out fer ye, Billy!"

"Ye'll not be able to catch me fer a good month, so shut yer trap. Besides, we was already wounded by that little chit who shouldn't have been there, the good Lord knows. Maybe she were some sort of ghost come to torment us."

"Ye've got a right big 'ole in yer brain," said Augie in disgust. "The truth of it is that a little girl done brought us low. T'weren't no ghost even though she was wearing that white dress."

Billy said, "Don't she know 'ow she's supposed to garb 'erself? Coming after the three of us dressed like that, her shoulders white and bare as Ben's ass when 'e's in the bushes. Boggles the brain, it does."

"Now that's a thought," Corrie whispered.

James was trying very hard not to laugh. They watched the three of them arguing in the middle of the narrow road. They watched until the skies opened up and rain flooded down.

It needed only this. James said, "Willicombe's mother was a little late in her prediction. It was supposed to rain around midnight."

"I can't imagine Willicombe having a mother," Corrie said, then winced when Ben cursed the rain and his foot blue. Billy joined in, cursing Corrie for the pitchfork in his arm. Augie stood there, hands on hips, watching his two companions in obvious disgust.

Since the leaves protected them a bit from the deluge, both were loathe to get out into the open. They stood another five minutes until the three men managed to hobble down the road.

"We're all going in the same direction," Corrie said. "Well, drat."

"That settles that," James said. "We're going to angle back toward the coast. There's bound to be a fishing village of some sort not too far from here."

"All right. At least we won't have to worry that those three buffoons will creep up on us. You know, James, we could get them now. What do you think?"

He shook his head. "Too much risk." Then he stopped cold. "If we could get Augie, maybe we could make him tell us who paid him to kidnap me."

Her eyes shone even as she was blinking furiously to keep from being blinded by the rain. "They certainly won't be expecting us, now will they?"

Lightning struck again and they heard a man yell.

"Let's go, Corrie. We certainly can't get any wetter than we are now, well, not much more."

They ran out of the woods and down the road after their villains, rain lashing against their faces, no moon now, only bloated black clouds. They could barely see the road ten feet ahead of them.

They came upon them quickly since Billy's foot was evidently hurting him, and Augie and Ben had to support him, Ben with only one good arm.

They slowed, listening to the men cursing.

"I never heard that word, James. What does—"

"Be quiet. Don't you ever say that word, you understand me?"

Corrie wiped her hand over her eyes and shoved her hair back from her face. "But it sounded like tit—"

"Be quiet. Now, here's what we're going to do."

Three minutes later, James moved quite close to the three, raised his gun, and fired directly at Augie's arm. A shot and a yell and more cursing.

As James thought, Ben dropped Billy to the ground, and Augie didn't know whether to grab his arm or draw his gun, and so he did both. The shot brought down a tree branch. Billy, hobbling, and Ben holding his arm, went for the underbrush.

They'd disabled all three of them.

"Drop the gun, Augie," James called out, "or the next bullet will be through your head. I have two guns, you know, so don't doubt me."

"Young 'un! Is that really you?" Augie's hand was protecting his eyes, desperately trying to see James through the heavy rain. "Why would you want to shoot ole Augie now? I ain't done nothin' really bad to ye—not even wot I was paid to do—I jest worried ye a bit, gave ye jest a bit of a tap."

"Drop the gun, Augie, this is the last time I'll tell you."

Augie dropped the gun, although the chances were good that it had held only one bullet and was now quite empty. But better not to take any chances.

"Good. Now, Augie, I'll not put a bullet in your head if you tell me the man's name who hired the three of you to kidnap me."

Augie, despite the rain, tugged on his ear, sent curses toward his feet, then sighed. "A man's got to guard 'is reputation, lad. If I tells ye 'is name, me reputation will be in the dirt."

"At least you'll be alive."

James aimed the gun at Augie's head.

"No, ye can't do that, can ye?—jest shoot me in the noggin' like I was a bad man—well, niver ye mind about that. No, don't shoot me. Well, damnation. Aw right, the bloke wot gave us the blunt, 'e said 'is name was Douglas Sherbrooke. Niver 'eard that name afore, so's I can't tell ye who the cove is. Now ye won't shoot me, will ye, young 'un?"

Both James and Corrie gaped at him. Corrie said, "But that doesn't make sense, James."

"As a twisted jest, it makes perfect sense."

"How old was this man, Augie?"

"A young 'un, jest like ye are, me lord. Hey, I heard that little gal's voice. I wants to wallop that little gal's arse but good. Ruined it all fer us, she did. Nearly burned down that lovely cottage and stuck that bloody pitchfork into Ben's arm. Not a lady, she ain't, a real disgrace to her folks, I'd say, going out like that without no chaperone, wearing white to make us think she were a ghost. As fer the 'orses, wot she did ain't—"

"Stop whining, Augie. She got you fair and square. If you don't think she's a lady, you can call her my white knight," James said.

"It's a disgrace, it is, 'er doin that to three growed men. Maybe if she'd been me kid, I could o' taught her how to nobble ye fine lords, nip groats right out of yer pockets, ye niver the wiser. Ye got guts, little gal, not much brain since ye rode that nag right into the cottage, but ye got guts, lots o' guts."

"Okay, Augie, the truth is that Corrie would make a horrible pickpocket. It's her face, you see. You know exactly what she's thinking. She'd end up sitting beside you in gaol. Now, you can yell for Ben and Billy to come out of hiding and then the three of you can take yourselves off."

"Yer a good lad, that's wot I told me boys, now didn't I?"

"I don't know what you said, Augie, since one of your friends hit me over the head."

"Well now, these things 'appen, these little puddles o' mud in life."

"Leave, Augie. Go away. I don't ever want to see your face again."

Corrie called out, "How much did this Douglas Sherbrooke pay you, Augie?"

"Little gals shouldn't concern themselves about men's business, but it were a good ten pounds to take ye, and another thirty when I gives ye over to this Sherbrooke bloke."

"I hope you haven't spent the ten pounds," Corrie said. "I wonder what this fellow will do to you when he discovers you've failed to deliver the goods?"

Augie groaned at that thought, then whistled for Billy and Ben.

Corrie, a lovely sneer on her face, and James, close to laughter, eased back into the woods, and watched the three men stagger back down the road.

"Now what?" Corrie said.

Lightning struck a tree branch. It fell, smoking, not three feet in front of them.

"Oh dear, is that some sort of bad omen, do you think?"

"I think it means that it's best to get back toward London. Augie and his boys aren't completely down, and they will lose out on thirty pounds and their reputations if they don't deliver me. Let's not take chances. You keep as warm as you can, Corrie. I don't want you to get ill."

"This night is surely a misery," Corrie said, and pressed close to James as they began walking down the road in the opposite direction from the three villains.

She began whistling a ditty she'd learned from one of the Sherbrooke stable lads. James laughed, couldn't help himself. He prayed she didn't know the words. Oddly enough, he couldn't think of another time when he'd laughed quite so much as he had on a night he firmly believed was going to be his last.

They walked along the cliffs, the wind howling louder now, full of both rain and the smell of brine. They could hear the waves crashing against rocks below them.

James suddenly saw the flash of a lantern, then another. The rain was lessening, thank God, and a bit of moon was shining through the bloated black clouds. James saw two boats pulled up onto the beach and at least six men in a line from the boats to the cliff where they stood.

He cursed.

A deep voice came out of the darkness, "Now what have we here, I wonder?"

CHAPTER SEVENTEEN

❧

JAMES TOOK CORRIE'S hand and squeezed it as he pulled her tightly against his side.

"We are here by chance only," James said toward the dark voice. "We're merely trying to find a farmhouse or a fishing village to pass the rest of the night."

"Not much night left."

"I don't have a watch. I don't know." James had one bullet left, no more.

The rain stopped and more moon shone down.

A man stepped out of the shadows, a gun in his hand and a black mask over his face. He was wrapped in a many-capped greatcoat.

This wasn't good.

He looked them both up and down, and Corrie could imagine his eyebrow going up behind that mask. "What the devil happened to you, my dear? Did your handsome gallant here promise you marriage then ravish you?"

"Oh no," Corrie said. "He would never do that, I dare-

say he's never thought of ravishment. And why would he
have to? I've known him all my life, very nearly. I saved
him from three very bad men who'd kidnapped him. We're
trying to go home. We don't mean anyone any harm. If
you're smuggling in diamonds for the new king, why, we
could help you. We don't care, truly we don't."

"You saved him?" The man laughed, actually laughed,
which meant he surely wouldn't shoot them in that instant,
didn't it?

Corrie nodded vigorously. "Yes, sir. I jumped on the
tiger's perch on the back of the carriage and then I
climbed onto the cottage roof, covered the chimney with a
blanket, and rode a horse into the cottage armed with a
pitchfork."

The man was staring at her, and James knew even without seeing his face that his look was one of pure disbelief.
The man said slowly, "You are making that up." He
straightened. "I am no longer amused. No lady would dare
such things as you've described. Why are the two of you
here, in this exact spot? In the middle of the night? Looking like you've been rolling in a ditch?"

"She told you the truth. We're only trying to get back to
London," James said. "Nothing more. But you're right,
she's not a lady—she's my sister."

"Your sister, is she? Now that's a lie that won't hold
more than two drops of water. And since that's a bald-faced
lie, then the rest of it must be as well. Come along, now. I
must decide what to do with you."

"It was worth a try," she said against his neck as they
walked in front of the man. The path was treacherous,
steep and winding, a good thirty feet down to the beach. A
half dozen men were carrying crates from a cave to two big
longboats at the shore.

"Sit," the man said.

They sat. The man whistled and a young boy came running up. He handed him the gun. "Keep an eye on them,

Alf, especially the girl." He laughed. "You wouldn't believe how very dangerous she is."

He walked away.

"I am dangerous."

"Don't alarm Alf," James said.

"Oh, all right. At least we can rest for a while." She leaned against him, and to James's astonishment, she fell asleep.

"Lawks," the boy said. "That girl jest fell over, she did."

"She's had a hard night," James said, put his arm around her and pulled her close.

He didn't fall asleep. He hadn't known there was still smuggling into Britain. Why, for God's sake? He remembered his father saying that French brandy was much better when it was smuggled in. There was something about the danger of it, the risk involved, which wasn't all that great, he'd admitted, that gave it an extra dash of heat, right to the belly.

One thing he was sure of: These scoundrels weren't out to kill his father.

The man with his very smooth, very educated voice was suddenly standing over them. James realized that he must have nodded off after all.

"Tired, are you?"

"The nap helped," James said quietly, not wanting to awaken Corrie.

The man, still masked, came down on his haunches beside James. "This girl—she's wearing a ball gown and you're dressed in evening clothes as well. You're obviously a gentleman and she a lady. It's also obvious that you haven't been dancing all night given where you are and your appearance. I'm inclined to believe that you were kidnapped and that perhaps she played a part in the rescue. But here's the problem. If I leave the two of you here, you'll tell Bow Street, and I wouldn't like that at all."

James said, "I don't understand why you're smuggling.

The war with France has been over for years upon years. I didn't even know smuggling still went on."

The man looked amazed. He stood up quickly. "I'm going to take the two of you with me, no choice, so I don't want any arguments from either of you. I'll put you ashore near Plymouth. Would you like me to guess your names, or will you tell me who the devil you are?"

"I imagine you already know who we are, don't you? Now, there's no reason to take us to Plymouth. If I went to Bow Street, what would I tell them? I don't even know where we are, exactly. I don't even know how long it's going to take us to get back to London. I have no idea who you are, and I haven't a clue what you're smuggling."

The man cursed. He tapped his booted foot on the sand. He looked back toward the men who were nearly finished bringing the wooden crates out of the cave, making their way toward the two boats that were already loaded down. "No, there's no choice, I can't take the—"

James kicked the man hard in his belly, knocking him backward. James was on him in a flash, his fist slamming against his jaw, hard, and he fell back unconscious. James grabbed his gun and took two steps back and gave his hand to Corrie, whose mouth was suddenly so dry she couldn't have spit on the wretched man if she'd tried her best. They heard shouts, saw the men running toward them, guns drawn.

James shouted, "All of you, stop right there or I'll shoot your leader!"

The men stopped dead in their tracks, then began talking amongst themselves.

The man twitched, his arm snaked out to grab James's hand, but Corrie was faster. She kicked his arm, then fell on him and shoved her knee against his throat. He stared up at her, saying nothing because he couldn't breathe, and because he didn't know what to say. She drew back her knee just a bit. "Now you know how dangerous I am," Corrie said, leaning down close to his face. "You're not a very competent villain, sir. James and I bested you without much effort at all."

James yelled out, "All of you, throw your guns into the boats! I'm not going to leave you defenseless, but I don't want you shooting at us either."

James looked down at Corrie, her knee still pressed against the man's neck, he, no fool, still lying perfectly still, and said, "Well done, Corrie, now back away from him. That's it."

Once Corrie was clear, James said to the man he would very likely recognize, "Now, I'm not going to take off your mask which means if I went to Bow Street I couldn't give them a description of you. Truth is, I don't want to know who you are or what you're smuggling. I want you to get up and walk toward your men. When you reach them, I want you to get all of them in the boats. Go, now, or I'll have to shoot you and you won't have to worry about anything at all, ever again."

"The two of you," the man remarked as he rose slowly to his feet, gingerly feeling his throat that had so recently enjoyed Corrie's knee. "I hadn't appreciated how very good you are together. It is a pity that—well, never mind." He turned and trotted down the beach toward the boats and his men. The man was standing at the bow, looking back at them. He cupped his mouth in his hands and yelled, "I ask only that you keep out of the cave!"

Within minutes the men were shoving the boats out into the water, then jumping in.

The man raised his hand in a salute.

"There's a ship, James, I can see it now," Corrie said, pointing.

"Yes," he said. "I wonder what they were smuggling."

"Maybe they left something in that cave. Let's go look."

James thought about it as he kept his eyes on the retreating boats. The sea was choppy, the wind rising.

"You know what? I don't give a good damn what's in the cave, if anything. Let's get out of here instead."

She looked disappointed, but nodded, taking his hand, and together they walked back up the path to the top of the cliff.

As they stood on the edge of the cliff, looking out toward the two boats, far distant now, nearly to the ship, the sky began to lighten.

"It's nearly dawn," Corrie said, wonder in her voice. "It seems more like three weeks have passed."

"Amen to that," James said. "I would swear there was something familiar about that man."

"I think you're right. It's probable we do know him or at least know who he is."

"A gentleman smuggler."

"He moved well. Of course he wasn't good enough to take the both of us."

James grinned, shook his head at her. "At this point I don't care who or what he is. I saw you shiver. Don't do that again. You don't want to get ill from this, all right? Just keep thinking how excellent you feel, how warm you are in my coat. Let's go, Corrie." She stretched a moment, then shivered again, a good shiver. "Actually, I am feeling excellent since that short nap. I must say too that when I put my knee on his throat, I remembered that was what I did to Willie Marker, and it made me feel even better."

"Poor Willie, and all he wanted was a kiss."

She shuddered.

"Now, I want you to keep that coat real close. Just keep thinking how good you feel. No illness, Corrie. That's one thing we can't afford."

The coat was wet, but she pulled it close. It was better than nothing. She looked at James, his white shirt damp, the wind slicing through it, making the sleeves billow.

It started drizzling again.

They didn't see a single living creature until after the sun was up. They heard cows mooing.

"Glory be, I don't believe it," Corrie yelled. "Where there are cows there have to be people to milk them."

Hand in hand, they ran in the direction of the mooing. There was a farmhouse, the back of it facing the sea, the front bordering a narrow road, and on the other side was a good-sized pasture and beyond the pasture, a forest of elm and maple trees. The house was built of gray stone, a hulking ugly house with a barn attached. At the moment, it was the most glorious structure either of them had ever seen.

"Oh, there's smoke coming out of the chimney. That means it's got to be warm in there."

They ran to the front of the house, panting, and James called out, "Is there anyone here? We're in need of assistance!"

From behind the closed door, an old voice said, "I don't give no assistance to no one. Go away."

"Please," Corrie said, "we mean no harm. We've been walking all night and are very wet and cold. Won't you please help us?"

"Yer rich coves, from the sound of ye." The door opened a crack, and a very old face, seamed deep by years in the sun, and eyes a bright, intelligent blue, peered out at them.

"Wot's this? Oh my, ye're both a rare mess, ye are. Come in, come in now."

The door went wide, and James and Corrie walked into the house, James ducking before the lintel would have knocked the top of his head off.

It smelled like vanilla inside.

"Oh, how wonderful," Corrie said, sucking in that wonderful smell, turning to the wrinkled old woman, swathed in a huge apron that covered nearly all of her. "What a delightful house you have, madam. Thank you so much for letting us in. And it's so very warm."

"Please, ma'am," James said. "We've been in the rain all night and I'm very worried about Corrie."

"Aye, I can see that," the old woman said. "I'm Mrs. Osbourne, me man is out there wi' the cows. Our milk is the best in the district. I'll give ye a cup o' milk, all nice and warm, that'll make ye jig again. Now, ye're both wet, let me find ye something to wear."

Mrs. Osbourne disappeared into another room, and James realized that behind the door past the kitchen was indeed the barn.

"Corrie, I want you to hang my coat over that chair and get yourself close to the fireplace. We're nearly home."

When Mrs. Osbourne came back after only a few minutes carrying a pail of milk, she said to Corrie, "Aye, little dearie, let me pour ye some nice fresh milk, then we'll get ye into some nice dry clothes."

Corrie drank the warm milk gratefully then handed the mug to James, who finished it off.

She followed Mrs. Osbourne into an old-fashioned bedchamber with a lovely big bed and a huge trunk at its base. Mrs. Osbourne left Corrie there to change into a long shapeless gown of indeterminate gray with a high neck and not a single ruffle or flounce. Corrie thought it was a lovely dress. She was humming as she stripped off her wet clothes and laid them all spread out on the floor, careful not to let them touch Mrs. Osbourne's blue rag rug. She could hear Mrs. Osbourne speaking to James, but couldn't make out her words.

She toweled off her hair and untangled it as best she could with her fingers. She was warm, her belly filled with the lovely milk, and she was more than ready to take on more kidnappers. Or smugglers. What an amazing night it had been. And James was all right. She'd seen to it.

She walked back into the sitting room. "Your turn now, James."

When James took the men's clothes into the bedchamber, Corrie said, "I thank you, ma'am. Lord Hammersmith was kidnapped. We both escaped and have been walking in the rain nearly all night."

"A lordship is he? Well, I suppose he should have a title attached to that beautiful face of his. I don't think Mr. Osbourne's clothes will fit him well, but at least they're dry. Would ye like to buy some milk?"

Before Corrie could laugh or reply, James came out of the bedchamber dressed in Mr. Osbourne's clothes. Corrie knew that beauty would have to be in the eye of a very biased beholder. The breeches, old and baggy, came only to his ankles. The dark brown cotton shirt didn't quite meet over his chest, which made him look very manly indeed, what with chest hair poking out. She didn't think she'd seen James's chest since he was sixteen. Should she tell him that he would look magnificent indeed if he'd take off those ridiculous clothes?

Probably wise not to say that. She didn't want to hurt Mrs. Osbourne's feelings.

"You look very natty, James."

"I'm warm and dry, as you are, Corrie. Thank you, Mrs. Osbourne and Mr. Osbourne as well. Once Corrie and I are home again, I will have the clothes returned to you."

"So ye're Lord Hammersmith, the young lady tells me. Ye've the look of a ducky lad. I believe that Mr. Osbourne had the look of ye afore the years wore on him and knobbled his knees, and all those dratted cows kicked him in the head too many times." And Mrs. Osbourne curtseyed to him. "I'll feed ye. Mr. Osbourne can sell all the milk this morning. Goodness, I already hear the wagons coming down the road."

After the most delicious porridge and eggs and toast either Corrie or James had ever eaten in their short lives, they both felt too tired and stupid to do anything except sit at that table and try to stay upright.

"Tired, are ye? Well, that's no problem. How about a

short nap afore Mr. Osbourne sees that ye get at least to Malthorpe, our village five miles down the road."

James was so grateful that he nearly fell over his feet as he rose from his chair. He walked to Mrs. Osbourne, picked up her hoary hand, and kissed her knuckles. "We are very grateful for your kindness, ma'am. If you don't mind, I would very much like for Corrie to rest a while. So much has happened."

"I'll have her in my own bedchamber, my lord, tucked in right and tight."

"Thank you, ma'am. If I can perhaps assist Mr. Osbourne with the cows—" He stood there, the words barely out of his mouth, smiling his beautiful smile, when suddenly his eyes rolled back in his head and he collapsed, hitting the edge of the table on his way to the floor.

CHAPTER EIGHTEEN

CORRIE HAD NEVER been so frightened in her life. Riding on the back of a carriage for three hours on the tiger's perch, the wind whistling up her wide sleeves, was nothing; climbing up on a rickety roof with a blanket— well, the list was long. But this was James. And he was sick.

Mr. Osbourne left his milking to strip James of his own clothes and put him into bed. He was still unconscious, his breathing heavy, and he was so very pale. Corrie couldn't bear it. She'd taken his coat and left him in his shirtsleeves. She said to Mrs. Osbourne, "Is there a physician nearby? I must have a physician for him. Please, Mrs. Osbourne. I can't allow anything to happen to James. Please."

"Well now," Mrs. Osbourne said, lightly laying her gnarly old hand on James's forehead, "there is old Dr. Flimmy, over in Braxton. Don't know if he's still alive, but he birthed my three boys, and all of them survived, their mama included. Elden!"

Mr. Osbourne stuck his head in the bedchamber.

"Send little Freddie over Braxton way to fetch Dr. Flimmy. Our beautiful boy here is nearly pale as a corpse." She saw Corrie's face blanch. "Sorry."

"Fever," Mrs. Osbourne said, shaking her head. "I know fevers, I do. Little Lemon, that's what I always called him when he was a boy cause his skin was this pale yellow color; did that boy ever have the fevers, one right after the other."

"Did you say Little Lemon was alive, Mrs. Osbourne?"

"Oh aye, his name is Benjie and he's got three young-uns of his own now."

"Then tell me what to do."

"Funny this is, I always use lemons for fevers. It's a jest, you see? Little Lemon and lemons for fevers."

Corrie swallowed hard. "You will make a drink for him, ma'am? Made of lemons?"

"Aye, that's it. While I'm doing that, you keep an eye on him. If he starts burning up from the inside out, you wash him down with cold cloths."

"Yes, yes, I can do that."

Mrs. Osbourne stood there a moment, staring down at James's still face. "I've never seen a more beautiful face on any living soul. That face shouldn't go to God just yet."

Corrie could only nod.

The hours blurred, but they did march on, very slowly. James was still alive, so hot that soon both she and Mrs. Osbourne began wiping him down with wet cloths dipped in the coldest water Mr. Osbourne could find. Corrie's hands cramped, but she didn't slow. She saw that Mrs. Osbourne was slowing down, and no wonder. "I'll keep doing it, ma'am. Please, you must rest now."

But the old woman kept stroking down James's chest, then when they managed to turn him onto his stomach, she stroked those cloths down his back.

He was so still, so deathly still Corrie couldn't stand it.

Finally, when he was on his back again, he opened his eyes and looked directly into her face.

"Corrie? What's wrong? You're not sick, are you?"

"No," she said, her warm breath on his cheek. "I'm not, but you are."

"No, that can't be right—" And then he was gone, eyes closed, his head lolling to the side.

Corrie's world stopped. She put her face right into his. "James, come back to me, please, come back. I can't bear this."

He began twisting and throwing away the covers, then suddenly, he was shivering, his teeth chattering. They piled blankets on top of him, but still it wasn't enough. The three of them managed to carry him out into the sitting room, and lay him right in front of the fireplace. Within moments, the room was so hot sweat was beading on James's forehead. Time passed. He calmed. The fever was down, thank God.

Dr. Flimmy arrived with Freddie in the early afternoon. An old man, but if his brain was still working he must know how to save the life of a young man who'd spent the night walking in the cold rain.

She watched Dr. Flimmy ease down on his crickety knees beside James. He lifted his eyelids, peered into his ears. He pulled the blankets down and listened to his chest. He put his ear against James's throat. He pulled the blankets down to his ankles, unaware that Corrie, who'd never seen a naked man in her life, was standing there, gawking. He hummed while he looked over every inch of James.

"Lawks," Mrs. Osbourne said, blinking, staring down at James. "Mr. Osbourne never looked like that even when he was a young sprite. Maybe ye'd best not be staring at him, Miss Corrie. Unless you're his sister, and I know ye're not. And ye're not his wife neither, else ye'd have a big sparkler on yer finger, given that he's a lordship. Ye haven't told me what ye are and how the two of ye are together. No, I don't

want to know. Now, ye turn yer back and let Dr. Flimmy
look behind his knees. That's what he always did to Little
Lemon."

Corrie didn't want to turn around. She wanted to stand
there and look at James until it became so dark she
couldn't see him, not even his shadow. She supposed that
meant the fire would have to go out as well because she
knew she could see him if there were embers in the grate.
Mrs. Osbourne was frowning at her, hands on her hips.
Sighing, Corrie turned around.

"Is he going to be all right, Dr. Flimmy?" When the old
man didn't answer, she turned her head to look at him. He
was kneeling close to James, James's arm was raised, and
he was kneading his armpit. She watched him poke and
prod, then he leaned over James's chest and raised his
other arm, and the kneading continued. At least he'd pulled
the blankets back up to James's waist, and that was a pity.
Dr. Flimmy finally came up onto his knees, calling out,
"Mrs. Osbourne, fetch your lemonade. Make it nice and
hot. And add some barley water to it. That's what he needs
right now."

Dr. Flimmy managed to haul himself to his feet, waving
Corrie off when she moved to help him. When he was finally
standing again, breathing heavily with the effort, he said to
her, even though he was looking down at James, "His lordship is very ill. Luckily he's also young and strong. You and
Mrs. Osbourne keep him warm, and when the fever comes
again, continue washing him down with the coldest cloths
you can stand. Pour lemonade down his throat or he'll
wither up and die. Don't want that lad to die, I really don't."

"I don't want him to die either," Corrie said, swallowing
hard. "I must get him back to London. There's trouble, you
see, and he needs to be home."

Dr. Flimmy began rubbing his neck. "You move him
and he'll likely not make it. Keep him here and keep him
quiet and warm."

Corrie's brain simply seized up. "But Mrs. Osbourne—"

"Aye, Corrie, we'll see to him. Now, let's get some of my special lemonade down his throat."

Surprisingly, at least to Corrie, James drank when they put the cup to his mouth. It took a long time, but she managed to get most of it down him.

He slept, unmoving, the fever gone, until that evening. Corrie was reading a tract on animal husbandry by the light of a single candle. Mr. and Mrs. Osbourne were long in bed, but not Corrie. Sleep was far away for her. Every few minutes, she looked at James. He was still quiet. They'd gotten some chicken broth down his throat. The fire was going strong. He had four blankets tucked in around him.

Suddenly, he moaned, his eyes opened. He looked straight at her. "I was relieving myself and you were watching. I was never so mortified in my life."

The memory flashed in her mind and she smiled. "I was only eight years old, James, and I really didn't understand what I was seeing. You scared the devil out of me when you dashed away and got yourself thrown. I thought it was my fault. I felt guilty for years."

"How did you know about my accident?"

"Your father told me. He said he wasn't clear on exactly how all that had come about, so I told him everything that had happened."

James groaned. "What did he say?"

"He was quiet for a moment, then he patted me on the head, told me he'd said exactly the right thing to you. It had calmed you."

"Am I the only man you've seen relieving himself?"

"Yes. Forgive me, James, but I was so very young and I worshipped you to the point of idiocy. I thought the way you did it was quite remarkable and ever so much easier than it was for me."

He laughed. He actually laughed, low and scratchy that laugh, then his eyes closed and his head fell to the side.

"James!"

She was on her knees over him, her palm on his forehead. No fever, thank God. She sat back on her heels and stared down at him. When he began muttering, she nearly fell over.

It didn't make much sense, but she knew he was worried. He muttered about his father and the man who'd called himself Douglas Sherbrooke. Then he spoke of the Andromeda constellation in the northern sky, of the accident Jason had had when he was ten years old, falling from the hayloft. Then he mentioned her name, and how she wouldn't leave him alone, how she was always there underfoot, and it was true, she was cute as a button, like his father said. The only time he muttered about wanting her in another galaxy was when he turned twelve and wanted to kiss girls. Corrie remembered he'd became quite good at escaping her.

Corrie came down beside him, and pressed herself to his side. She stroked her hand over his chest, his throat, his face. "James, it's all right. I'm here. I won't leave you. Everything will be all right, I swear it to you."

He stopped muttering. She believed that he slept.

Corrie counted James's money. There was enough. She spoke to Mrs. Osbourne, then gave the money and directions to the Sherbrooke London town house to an excited Freddie. The earl and countess were in Paris, but Jason was there. He'd be here as soon as he could. There was nothing more she could do but wait.

The next days passed with terrifying slowness. James was delirious, then he was in a stupor, lying so still she thought several times that he'd died. Corrie prayed until she was out of words, and then she prayed feelings, swearing to God that she would become an excellent person if only He would spare James.

There was no sign of Freddie.

She and Mrs. Osbourne rubbed James down with cold

wet cloths until their hands cramped and turned blue and wrinkled. Dr. Flimmy came once again, examined James's armpits at greater length this time, and announced that his lordship was improving.

Corrie didn't understand this, but she'd grab at any straw. "Will he live, sir?"

"He's better, miss, but will he live?" He didn't answer his own question, accepted a pound note Corrie gave him from James's coat pocket, drank a cup of warm milk, and allowed Mr. Osbourne to take him back home, since there was still no sign of Freddie. Something must have happened to him, Corrie knew it. Mrs. Osbourne walked around, tight-lipped, shaking her head. It was interesting though how she smiled whenever she looked at James.

The next afternoon, Corrie fell asleep, her head on James's shoulder, when a loud moo woke her. She jerked up, so exhausted that it took her a moment to realize that there really was a cow standing in the open doorway. She heard men's voices from just outside.

Was it Dr. Flimmy? No, probably neighbors here to buy milk. She placed her palm on James's forehead. He was cool to the touch. She nearly wept with relief. The cow mooed again. She came up on her knees when Douglas Sherbrooke appeared in the doorway, right in front of the cow.

If it had been God standing there, his sight adjusting to the dim interior, she wouldn't have been more ecstatic.

"Sir!" She dashed to him, throwing herself in his arms. "You're here! I thought you were in Paris, but you're not. You're really here. Thank God, thank God. I thought Freddie had gotten himself lost. I thought maybe someone had killed him."

Douglas held her close, patted her back. "It's all right, Corrie. How is James?"

She heard the fear in his voice, and leaned back, smiling up at him. "The fever broke. He's going to be all right."

She stepped away and walked back to where James lay in front of the fireplace, his bed for the past three days.

Douglas dropped to his knees beside his boy. He studied the heavy beard on his face, the pallor of his skin, the hollowness of his cheeks.

He placed his palm on his son's forehead. Nice and cool. He sat back on his heels. "Thank God."

"James!"

Jason dashed through the front door, smacked his head on the lintel, and nearly knocked himself out.

"Dammit, Jason, don't make me worry about both of you."

Jason, rubbing his head, cursing, weaved slightly as he walked to where his brother slept. "It's very hot in here."

"Yes," Corrie said. "It's supposed to be. He's had the fever, been so cold—" She swallowed, stared at Douglas, then at Jason, and burst into tears.

It was Jason who drew her against him, stroking her back, patting her head. "That dress is a fright, Corrie," he said against her temple.

She sniffled, swallowed, and managed a small smile as she looked up at him. "It's been so long, and I knew he was going to die, and I didn't know what to do. And I sent Freddie off to London, to your house, but he never came back and—" She sniffled, then grinned up at Jason. "He's going to live. The fever's gone."

"Yes, thank God and your excellent nursing," Douglas said. "Freddie arrived this morning, not twelve hours after Alex and I did. He'd gotten himself lost and robbed. When he came to the front door, Willicombe nearly fainted at the sight of him. All Freddie could say before he collapsed was 'James'."

"Is Freddie all right now?"

Jason nodded. He looked toward his brother, nearly jumped out of his skin when Mrs. Osbourne shrieked, "Lawks and Lordie! There are two of ye. Mr. Osbourne, come and look at this. There are two beautiful lads, not just one." And she opened the door from the kitchen back to the barn and disappeared.

Corrie said, "Mrs. Osbourne has very much enjoyed taking care of James, particularly when it came to washing him down with wet cold cloths. It isn't just his face she admires." Then she giggled, actually giggled. She stared up at Jason.

He was grinning. "I'm sure James was delighted to please Mrs. Osbourne."

James moaned and opened his eyes to see his father looking down at him.

"Hello, sir. Why aren't you in Paris?"

CHAPTER NINETEEN

❦

DOUGLAS SHERBROOKE WAS so relieved, so very thankful, that he could only stare down at his son as he stroked his hand over the thick black stubble on his face, and finally accept in his gut that he was going to be all right. It did worry him that James's eyes were still a bit glazed, a bit unfocused, but he knew that would change, James just needed time and rest. He leaned down and said, "Your mother sends her love. I nearly had to tie her up to keep her from coming with us, but I knew, as did she, that you didn't need the both of us hovering around you.

"The fact is, we never got to Paris. Your mother claims the Virgin Bride came wafting into our bedchamber in Rouen, said you were in danger. We just arrived back in London last night."

"They kidnapped me to get to you, sir."

"Yes, I suppose that's true, but I know in my gut that

this is more complicated than we thought. There were three men who took you?"

"Yes. Augie is their leader, Ben and Billy the other two, who weren't really very smart. They were from London, which means that they've got to be known. Just maybe Remie will find out all about them. Willicombe can send him into the stews and down to the docks to hire more lads to find out what this is all about."

"I'll pass that along as soon as we get back to London. Actually, by now I think that all of London is looking for you and Corrie. Ah, James, I recognize that look—you're hungry, aren't you?"

James thought about it for a moment. "Yes, I could eat one of those damned mooing cows. They moo all the time, sir. I swear I could hear them mooing in the middle of the night." He saw Jason with his arm around Corrie. "Jase, I'm glad you came. But I don't understand how—"

Jason said, "We'll tell you all about it after you've had something to eat. Where is Mrs. Osbourne?"

To Corrie's surprise, Mrs. Osbourne was standing in the door of the sitting room, knotting her apron in her veiny old hands, looking—well, looking utterly intimidated. Corrie couldn't blame her. Douglas Sherbrooke standing in the small sitting room was surely akin to a cardinal standing in the village church. Douglas, not stupid, rose and smiled at Mrs. Osbourne. He walked to her, took one of her hands as gently as he would take a duchess's and raised it to his lips, just as James had done. "Mrs. Osbourne, my wife and I are very grateful for your kindness."

"Oh, sir. Oh, dear, oh dear, yer lordship, it wasn't much of anything, now was it, sir? Would ye look at me, all dressed in this old apron, with this even older gown beneath it, but I couldn't take my gown away from Corrie, now could I, because she was wearing a ball gown that was all ripped up, really quite a mess, it was. Why I—"

"You look charming, Mrs. Osbourne. I would like to thank you for taking care of my son and his friend."

Friend? James, who had just drawn a nice deep breath, choked. Well, he supposed Corrie was a friend, but still, to hear it said that way—he coughed again. Corrie went immediately and dropped to her knees beside him, raised his head, and gave him lemonade to drink.

Jason looked at the two of them. It was obvious that she'd done this many times since James had become ill, so many times that it looked utterly natural. As for Douglas, he became very still. Then, slowly, he nodded.

"Och, my little Corrie, what a sweetie she is. Just this morning Elden was showing her how to milk old Janie, who gives the sweetest milk within fifty miles."

James swallowed the lemonade, closed his eyes a moment, and said, "Did you really milk old Janie?"

"I tried. I haven't quite got the knack of it yet."

"Would yer lordship like a cup of tea? And yer other boy as well?" She stood there, looking from Jason to James, shaking her head. "Two such beautiful young men in my sitting room. No one will believe it. And now a lordship as well, not that yer not beautiful, my lord, it's just that these two young gentlemen would make the angels weep."

"Trust me, Mrs. Osbourne, they've made me weep as well upon occasion."

James said loudly, "Corrie is the daughter of a viscount."

"Och, so what does that make ye, Corrie?"

Corrie rolled her eyes. "It makes me the girl who tried to milk old Janie, nothing more, Mrs. Osbourne."

Mrs. Osbourne wheezed with laughter, caught herself, and choked out, "I have real proper tea, my lord. James here has drunk two bucketfuls of lemonade, Corrie pouring it down his lovely gullet."

"Tea would be very nice, thank you, Mrs. Osbourne." Douglas turned back to James, picked up his hand, to touch him, to feel the life in him. "We brought a carriage. It's a good two hours back to London. How do you feel about that, James?"

"This floor is very hard, sir. When I complained, Corrie tried to lift me up to put more blankets underneath me. When that didn't work, she wanted me to lift my rump so she could slide the blankets in, but I swear to you I couldn't get any part of me off the floor."

Corrie said, grinning down at him, "So I rolled him over, slid in half the blankets, then rolled him the other way. The squabs in your carriage are soft as a bed, sir. James will think he's floating on clouds."

"And you've been kept warm too and that's good." The earl looked over at Corrie, who looked quite lovely with her scrubbed face and shiny clean hair. If Mrs. Osbourne's gown hung off her, it simply didn't matter. She'd dropped flesh, he could see it in her face, just as James had.

Two hours later, the Sherbrooke carriage rolled away from the Osbourne farm, leaving the occupants fifty pounds richer and short one employee, a foundling Mrs. Osbourne said they'd taken in five years before. Aye, Freddie was a good lad, slept in the Osbourne barn, did his chores right and proper. But no longer. Now, Freddie rode tall and straight on the tiger's perch, dressed in Sherbrooke livery from Willicombe's store of uniforms. The uniform bagged on twelve-year-old Freddie, but Freddie had admired himself so much that Willicombe didn't have the heart to have him change back into his old clothes. Douglas had told Willicombe to have a half dozen suits made up for him.

Tied securely to the roof of the carriage was a keg of old Janie's sweet milk, a lovely gift from Mrs. Osbourne.

James slept most of the way, propped up between his father and Corrie, Jason on the seat opposite them, ready to catch James if he fell forward.

Douglas had wanted Corrie to tell them exactly what

had happened, but he'd no sooner told her he'd informed her aunt and uncle that she was safe, than she gave him a sleepy smile and her head fell against James's shoulder. He looked to see that Jason was staring fixedly at his brother and the young woman sleeping so naturally against him.

Douglas wondered if James had yet realized the consequences of this mad adventure.

AUNT MAYBELLA AND Uncle Simon were seated in the drawing room with the twins' mama, all three of them drinking tea and worrying endlessly until Douglas and Jason helped James into the drawing room.

There was a good deal of pandemonium until James, deposited on the long sofa by his father and brother, two blankets tucked lovingly around him, said to Maybella and Simon, "I was so careful to keep Corrie covered as best I could because I was terrified she would become ill—and look what happened. I was the one. As Augie would say— tar and damnation."

And Corrie, on her knees beside the sofa, said without hesitation, "I wish it had been me, James. I've never been more scared in my life than that second night." She said to the room at large, "He was burning with fever, thrashing about so I couldn't keep the blankets on him. Then he fell on his back so still I was certain he was dead."

"I'm too mean to die," he said.

"Yes, you are, and I'm very happy about that, although stubborn is more the truth of it." She looked up then and said, "But he drank down all the water and lemonade I put to his mouth. And then buckets of tea."

James took a sip of tea, laid his head back against the soft pillows his mother had placed beneath his head, and said, "You should have seen Corrie riding that horse through the cottage door, a pitchfork held like a lance un- der her arm. She was, naturally, wearing a white ball

gown." He began to laugh. "Good Lord, Corrie, it's something I'll never forget as long as I live."

"Whatever are you talking about?" Alexandra couldn't
help herself fluttering around her son, her relief was so great.

"Corrie sporting a lance?" Uncle Simon said, and
turned to his niece. "Dearest, I remember when you were a
little girl and going through your knight-in-Medieval-
England phase. James taught you how to hold a long pole
without impaling yourself. I remember he stood there
laughing when you held that pole and ran full tilt toward a
chicken. But you actually did it this time on horseback?"

"I'd forgotten that," James said. "You missed the
chicken, Corrie."

"She was fast," Corrie said, "really fast and then she had
the nerve to run behind a tree."

James said, "And you rammed the pole against the tree
and the impact sent you flying back on your bu—well, on,
you sat down, really hard."

He cleared his throat even as his mother said, "James
tries to be careful in his bodily descriptions. He knows it's
appreciated by his mother."

"Ha," Jason said.

James said, "Well, Corrie wasn't running with a pole
this time, sir, she was on horseback, a bridle, no saddle, a
pitchfork under her arm, and she did it wearing her evening
gown."

"She ran at a tree?" Aunt Maybella asked.

It took another hour before everyone had digested the
entire tale. Douglas saw that his son was exhausted. He
rose. "The man who paid the three villains said he was
Douglas Sherbrooke. This gives me great pause. I don't
suppose that this man, Augie, used my name to taunt you,
James?"

James shook his head, very nearly asleep. "He'd never
heard of you, sir. He wasn't making it up."

"You're ready to fall off the sofa, James," Alexandra

said, lightly stroking her fingertips over his face. "Ah, look. Your hair is all shiny and clean."

"Corrie washed me, hair included, this morning."

"Oh," said Aunt Maybella and shot a glance at Simon, who wasn't paying attention. He was staring at the oak trees, their leaves beginning to sport their fall plumage. She heard him say under his breath, "That gold is very nice indeed. I have browns and wheats, but no gold that specific shade. I must get it for my collection."

He was out of the drawing room before Corrie could blink. She smiled after him. She saw several governesses with their charges in the park, and knew that they would be admiring her uncle, never realizing that he had no interest in them at all, just in those gold oak leaves.

Maybella was tapping her toe and staring at the lovely ceiling molding. Douglas said, "Er, let me get Petrie, who's doubtless waiting in the entrance hall with Willicombe and all the rest of the staff in this house, ready to fight over who gets to carry you on his back to your bedchamber."

But it was Douglas and Jason who helped James up to his bedchamber, Petrie and Willicombe hovering three steps behind them, ready if needed, Freddie three steps behind them, arms out, ready. James smiled up at his father and brother. "Thank you for coming to fetch us."

He fell asleep, hearing Petrie bragging how he could shave his lordship and not wake him up in the process.

CHAPTER TWENTY

❧❀❧

WHEN JAMES AWOKE, it was nearly midnight, his bedchamber dark, embers burning low in the fireplace, and he was as warm as a lovely pudding just taken out of the oven. He realized he needed to relieve himself and managed to get himself out of bed and locate the chamber pot. He was damnably weak and it infuriated him. He'd no sooner gotten himself back into bed when he realized he was starving. He focused on the bellpull then drew back his hand. It was very late. He lay back, listening to his stomach growl, wondering if he could manage to walk to the kitchen. Forget the food, then. At least he was at home and in his own bed. He wasn't going to starve, and best of all, he was alive.

Not three minutes later, the door to his bedchamber quietly opened.

His mother came into the room, wearing a lovely moss green dressing gown, carrying a small tray in her arms.

James simply couldn't believe it. "Have I died and gone to heaven? How did you—"

Alexandra set the tray down on the bedside table and said as she helped him sit up, "Petrie was sleeping in the dressing room, the door open. I had told him he was to awaken me the moment he heard you stirring. He did. Now, I have some delicious chicken broth for you and some warm bread with butter and honey. What do you think about that?"

"I would marry you if you weren't my mother."

Alexandra laughed and lit a branch of candles.

James said as he watched her, "I remember when I was a little boy, sick from something, I don't remember what it was, but you were always there. I woke up in the middle of the night and there you were standing beside me, holding a candle, and your hair looked like spun flame in that light. I thought you were an angel."

"I am," Alexandra said, laughed, and kissed him. She studied him a moment. "You're looking brighter, your eyes more focused. Now, I'm going to stuff you."

She pulled up a chair and sat watching her son while he ate every scrap on the tray. When he was finished, he sighed and leaned his head back against the pillows. He said, his eyes still closed, "When I awoke, my first thought was, where is Corrie?"

Alexandra made a low humming noise.

"She saved my life, Mother. I honestly don't think my chances of escaping those three men were all that good."

"She's always been a resourceful girl," said Alexandra. "And always completely loyal to you."

"I never really appreciated that until this happened. Can you believe she saw me taken and jumped right up in the tiger's perch, with no hesitation at all? Can you believe that? Wearing her damned ball gown."

"Well, as a matter of fact," his mother said, "I can believe it."

He managed a grin. "Ah, you and Father, always there for each other. Yes, you would have leaped up in that tiger's perch, wouldn't you?"

"Mayhap I would have pulled out the derringer I wore strapped to my leg and shot the villains. I would have made the effort to save my ball gown."

"You think to make me laugh? No, I can see you doing that, Mother." James sighed and closed his eyes again. "I can also picture Corrie in my mind, all of three years old. It was the first time I ever saw her. You were holding her hand when you introduced her to us. I'll never forget how she looked from Jason to me, back to Jason, and then she said, those big eyes of hers on my face, 'James.' "

"I remember. Then she left me without a backward glance, walked up to you, her head back so she could see as high as your face, and she took your hand. You were ten years old, I believe."

"She didn't want to let my hand go. I remember how embarrassed I was. There was this little faerie, and she would sit at my feet and stroke my hand."

"Remember when Jason tried to fool her into thinking he was you?"

"She kicked him in the shin. He started chasing her, all in good fun, then she saw me and tried to climb up my leg."

Alex laughed. "Jason was so certain that he had all your mannerisms, but she wasn't fooled."

"Miss Juliette Lorimer can't tell us apart."

"Ah, yes, Juliette," Alexandra said, studying her well-worn green slippers. "A lovely girl, don't you think?"

James nodded. "She dances well, is light on her feet, and yes, really quite beautiful. But the thing is, I could be Jason and she wouldn't know the difference."

"She and her mother visited on three different occasions during the time you were missing. We weren't here, but Jason was. He said that Juliette was very distraught when she realized he wasn't you."

James thought about that, but not too much. Weariness
dragged at him. He managed a lopsided grin at his mother.
"Thank you for keeping me from starving." And he closed
his eyes.

Alexandra leaned down and kissed her son. She straightened, stood there looking down at him for a very long time,
thanking God and Corrie Tybourne-Barrett for her son's
life.

"WHO ARE YOU?"
          "I'm Freddie, my lord, the new Sherbrooke
tiger," the boy said, puffing out his chest, an amazing feat
since there wasn't much chest to puff out. "No wonder you
don't remember me, real down in the chops ye were."

What there was, however, was a good deal of pride
standing here in his bedchamber. James smiled at the boy
wearing the Sherbrooke livery who had traveled to London
to tell his parents where he and Corrie were.

"I remember you now, Freddie. Why are you here?"

"I 'ad this gnawin' in me brain, me lord. I jest wanted to
make sure ye were still above ground like everyone were
sayin' downstairs. Everyone is mighty pleased ye survived.
Best thing I ever did was to come to yer folks' big 'ouse,
tell 'em where ye was, even though I nearly got me liver
sliced.

"And would ye look at what did transpire? Jest look at
me, me lord. Ain't I somethin' to behold? 'Ere, me lord, ye
want to feel this wool? Soft as a baby's butt, it is."

"Yes, it looks quite soft and you do look quite splendid,
Freddie. Forgive me that I didn't remember you, but I do
know what you did for Corrie and me. Thank you."

"No matter, my lord, ye was so sick I believed I'd be
bringing yer folks back fer a burying, but no, ye managed
to pull yerself out o' the casket. It was Miss Corrie who

saved ye. She's a tough 'un, she is, and she didn't leave yer side, no she din't."

"What did I hear about you nearly getting yourself killed trying to get to London?"

"Set upon, I was, set upon by a gang o' young toughs what wanted to pound me, fer the fun o' it. Not much fun fer me, I'll tell ye. They took the groats Miss Corrie gave me, even though I'd poked 'em down under my foot, but they found 'em. But I gets away from them and got here, looking real bad, but Willicombe knew I 'ad somethin' important to tell 'is lordship, so's 'e brings me right in."

"I appreciate your bravery, Freddie, and your tenacity."

Freddie nodded, thinking of the five pounds he now carried in his pocket, not under his foot, given to him by the earl himself, and ah, didn't it feel good lying against that soft wool of his suit, what Mr. Willicombe called his livery. Fine word, *livery*. Sounded like a dressed-up body part. Freddie rubbed his clean palms over the wool breeches. "Yer pa told me Mr. Willicombe ordered six suits fer me. Six! Can ye imagine that?"

"No," James said slowly, "I can't." James thought about his Uncle Ryder who took in abused and mistreated children, raised them, educated them, and best of all, loved them. How would Freddie do with his Uncle Ryder?

When Jason came into his bedchamber not long after Freddie had slipped away, still stroking wool, James said, "What about sending Freddie to Uncle Ryder?"

"Our very pleased-with-himself new tiger with his six new suits of livery? I don't think he'd want to go, James. He's so excited about being in the big city, can't stop talking about seeing the Tower of Lunnon where all the heads were lopped off. Don't you see? He's now worth something. He's now important to himself. He doesn't need Uncle Ryder."

"We'll at least get him educated."

Jason smiled. "He'll probably squawk at that, but I'll see that Willicombe brings a tutor around and keeps our new tiger in the schoolroom for a good two hours a day. Now, I'm here to tell you that Miss Juliette Lorimer and her mother are here to see you."

James was shaking his head even before Jason had finished speaking. "I haven't even shaved yet this morning."

"At least Lady Juliette would be able to tell us apart."

"That's the truth. No, tell the lady I will be up for a visit say, tomorrow afternoon."

Jason turned to leave, when James said, "Where's Corrie? You know, when I woke up, her name was nearly out of my mouth, and I couldn't smell her—it's a light scent, maybe jasmine. It feels strange not having her right here with me."

"No wonder. I haven't heard a thing. She left right after we helped you out of the drawing room. You don't remember saying good-bye to her?"

James shook his head. "Jase, would you call on her, see how she's doing? Oh, and what about Miss Judith Mc-Crae? Have you seen her?"

Jason gave him a remarkably austere look, which made him look like a carved Greek statue. "There's been no time, really. I did inform her once we had you home. I dare-say I will see her again."

CHAPTER TWENTY-ONE

❧

JAMES WAS SITTING up in bed, bathed and shaved by Petrie, who clucked over him until he was ready to hurl a book at him, when Corrie was ushered in by Willicombe, who was beaming, so pleased to be the escort to the Heroine of the Hour.

And James, eyeing her, said, all stiff as a vicar, "You really shouldn't be coming to see me alone, Corrie. You're a young lady; there are rules about this."

She cocked her head to one side. "Now isn't that ridiculous? I've run tame in your home all my life. Now I'm supposed to have a chaperone when I come to see you? To make certain that you don't do something improper, like ravish me in your parents' home?"

"It's more the principle of the thing, not really what could actually occur."

"Looking at you now, I'd wager all my allowance that you couldn't do a single improper thing. I bet I could arm wrestle you right now, James, and you'd be whimpering within a minute."

"That's the truth," he said easily, feeling himself smile from the inside out. Everyone was being so very kind, so solicitous, so deferential, it set his teeth on edge. And now, finally, here was Corrie and within a minute she had her fist to his jaw. It felt good. He perked right up. "I'll bet even Freddie could take me out."

Corrie grinned, but said no more. She stood there at the bottom of his bed, just looking at him.

"I liked your whiskers," she said at last. "It added complexity to that face of yours."

He arched an eyebrow.

"Beauty all by itself can get boring, don't you think, James? You know, it just sits there being perfect and soon one wants to yawn."

He said, without missing a beat, "And I miss your white ball gown, all ripped and filthy. That added needed complexity to your presentation as well. Look at you now—a nice clean green gown, nothing more, nothing less. No, it's of very little interest at all." He yawned, patted his hand to his mouth, and yawned again.

She struck a pose, one designed specifically to get his goat, but one that didn't work since he'd seen her perfecting it in a mirror. She hadn't seen him, thank the good Lord for that small favor. He waited, smiling, wondering what was going to come out of her mouth. She said, all the while tapping her fingertips to her chin, "You know, now that I think of it, I have to admit that since you were naked most of the time you were ill, lying helpless—you know, all sprawled out on your back—I don't recall being bored for a moment looking at you. No, I didn't yawn a single time."

James fully recognized what a fine whap that was to the head. He flushed, color rising over his cheek to his hairline.

She was grinning at him, knowing she'd bested him, a grin so wicked she should go up in smoke.

It was hard, but he got hold of himself. "Corrie, why don't you come here and help me drink a bit of water?"

She kept that big wicked grin even as she shook her head at him. "So you can pour the water over my head? No thank you, James. Now, I see that you can do nothing but ignore my insults, a rather pathetic ploy, don't you think? You're waiting to dish an insult right back at me. You've just got to think of one, and that's a problem since your brain is still lying in your head, doing nothing helpful. So, admit that this time I've left you sprawled in the dirt. Hmm, *sprawled.* What a lovely word." Then she poured him a glass of water, sat on the bed beside him, automatically slid her arm beneath his neck, and raised his head to drink. His face was nearly touching her breasts.

He breathed in deeply. "Ah, enough. That's good. Thank you, Corrie."

She set down the glass and arched her own eyebrow at him. "What is this? You're still too weak to tend to your own thirst?"

"No, I like you doing it for me. I like to smell you when you're so close."

Without thinking, she caressed her hand down his face, cupping his chin for a moment. "Did I smell interesting enough? Enough complexity in my scent?"

"Yes, enough."

She snorted, and he said, "You know, that snort, as distinctive and expressive as it may be, simply doesn't go well with your gown that makes your waist look no larger than a doorknob. As for the top of you, your damned neckline is much too low. You're supposed to be a modest young lady in her first season, not a seasoned nearly on-the-shelf lady who needs blatant advertising to lure in the unwary male.

"Ah, now look at you, ready to hurl the water carafe at me. You're taking my well-meant words in the wrong spirit, Corrie. I mean it only as a very small observation on the goods you shouldn't be presenting to the world in such remarkable detail, at least yet."

That was quite fluent; both of them knew it. James waited, feeling his brain spark. She stared off into space as she said, "I remember how my hands nearly cramped I washed you so many times, to bring your fever down, you know. Each time my hands went lower and lower." She looked at him straight on now and grinned like a witch. "Ah, James, I can say without hesitation that your goods don't need any advertising at all. But look at me, I'm such a pedestrian peahen, I need all the advertising I can do."

He flushed. Damnation, he flushed again and she saw it, and so he said, "For God's sake, Corrie, have your gown hoisted up a good two inches."

She smiled at him. "All right."

He couldn't think of a thing to say.

"Close your mouth, James, you look too much like Willie Marker after I told him no girl would ever marry him because he was such a lamebrained bully."

"I doubt Willie Marker has ever thought of marriage," James said.

"That's what he yelled at me," she said, and sighed deeply. "And then he tried to kiss me again. Isn't that odd? After I'd insulted him but good?"

"I suppose some males are aroused when a girl beats them over the head, metaphorically speaking."

She looked down at him, her fingers itching to touch him again, but naturally she didn't. He was no longer helpless. And so she said, "Enough about my gown. Tell me, how do you feel this beautiful morning?"

"My pillows have slipped down. I need you to raise them back up. My head hurts."

She rose to lean over him and fluff up his pillows. She straightened and looked down at him. "Shall I also rub some rose water on your brow?"

"Yes, that would be good."

She began humming, one of his favorite ditties actually, as she dampened her handkerchief in the water carafe and leaned over to dab his forehead. She wasn't wearing a wicked grin now, rather a look of utter concentration. "I'm sorry that I don't have any rose water, James. Do you think the water from the carafe is helping?"

"Keep rubbing, ah, yes, that feels very good."

She did, a slow easy motion, one that his body recognized. "The oddest thing happened this morning, James. I was walking with my maid to visit you and I saw Mrs. Cutter and Lady Brisbett. I'd met them both last week at some sort of dance and they'd been quite charming to me. Both of them cut me, looked at me like I wasn't there, and walked by, noses in the air. Isn't that amazing?" She paused a moment. "Or perhaps they are both shortsighted, but I did smile and speak to them again. It was very odd, don't you think? Not as odd as a boy wanting to kiss a girl when she's blasted him, but still odd."

There was a gasp from the doorway. It wasn't Petrie nor was it his mother with more food. It was Miss Juliette Lorimer, her mother in her wake.

Juliette drew herself up, advertising her lovely goods even more prominently than Corrie did, and to, admittedly, better effect, and said in a voice cold enough to chill the lemonade, "May I inquire what is going on here?"

James said easily, "Hello, Juliette. Corrie is kindly dabbing my forehead with carafe water, since we have no rose water. My head aches."

"You need softer hands to attend you, my lord," said Mrs. Lorimer. "Juliette, here is my handkerchief. You caress his lordship's forehead. Miss Tybourne-Barrett should not even be in here. She is alone, unlike you, who is with your mother. It is not at all the done thing. I should probably give Maybella a hint."

Corrie said, an eyebrow hoisted up, "Why ever not, ma'am? I have been nearly one of the family all my life."

"That makes no difference at all, missy, and so you should know it. You need to go home now. That's right, it's time for you to leave."

"But what about James's headache?"

"Be quiet, Corrie," he said, and closed his eyes against the battlefield that was now gathering cannon in his bedchamber.

"James," said Juliette, her voice sweet and clear, all of her being focused on him, "you are looking splendid. I swear you look nearly ready to dance. I am so relieved. I was so dreadfully worried when you disappeared. No one could explain it. Then, of course someone remarked that Miss Tybourne-Barrett had also disappeared. It wasn't remarked upon nearly as much as your disappearance, needless to say, and what a strange thing it was to have the two of you return to London together."

A deep male throat cleared at the doorway. The earl of Northcliffe himself said, "Ladies, I am here to invite all of you down for tea and some of Cook's excellent lemon seed cakes. Corrie, you will join us after you've finished bathing James's forehead. Ladies?"

Saved by his father.

There was no choice. Juliette looked longingly back at James, whose eyes were closed at the moment, gave Corrie a stare to scorch her eyebrows, then turned to follow the earl from the bedchamber.

"She's right, Corrie," he said, eyes closed.

"That your disappearance was more remarked upon than mine? Well, that's surely a fact. Who would begin to care about me other than Aunt Maybella and Uncle Simon? It's quite likely that Uncle Simon wouldn't even notice unless he wanted me to hold down a leaf so he could glue it."

That was quite true, and it made James very angry, for some reason he didn't want to examine.

"He told me this morning that he'd found an unidentifiable leaf lying there unremarked by the side of one of the paths in Hyde Park. He was quite excited about it, determined to locate the plant from which it had detached itself, and he could enjoy his excitement without remark from Aunt Maybella since I was again home safe and sound.

"Naturally Jason missed me. And perhaps Willicombe. How I wish Buxted was here. You remember Buxted, our butler at Twyley Grange, don't you, James?"

"Naturally. I've known him since I was born."

"Buxted was always helping me slip in and out, never gave me a scolding. He did caution me about London, though to the best of my knowledge he's never been here."

"What did he tell you?"

"He said that wickedness was all fine and good within the confines of the country, but you stir wickedness in a pot the size of London, and the good Lord's eyes near cross, Buxted was right, wasn't he?"

"Yes."

"Oh, look at you. You're all upset. Now, don't move, James, keep yourself relaxed and your eyes closed. Is your headache better?"

He sighed deeply. "Did your aunt and uncle speak to you yesterday or this morning?"

"Certainly. Aunt Maybella wanted every detail and Uncle Simon appeared to be listening, at least most of the time. They were still thrashing it about this morning until I was ready to scream. That's when I told them I had to come to see you." She paused a moment, frowning over at the pillow next to James's head.

"What?"

"Well, Uncle Simon started shaking his head at me— just shake, shake, shake—but he didn't say anything until I was nearly ready to leave. Then he looked at me, shook his head again, and said, 'Hunted down like a rat. Ha!' And then he laughed a bit, and looked bemused, something he does quite well. He always looks so handsome when he does it that even if Aunt Maybella is eager to smack him, she immediately wants to stroke him. Isn't that odd? Do you wish more water? Tea? The chamber pot?"

"Corrie."

She paused, looked down into his eyes. "Yes?"

He simply looked at her for a long moment, then said, his voice slow and deep, "My father told me you were an heiress."

It flew right over her head. "Heiress? What does that mean, James? Oh, I understand. My parents left me a bit of money to ensure that I would make a respectable marriage. That was kind of them."

"It's far more than a bit. You're an heiress, Corrie, and maybe one of the richest young ladies in England. Your father was evidently astute with his finances, and you were his only child. Your Uncle Simon has guarded your fortune well."

"That would be because he simply forgot about it," she said, not really attending him now, just looking down at the lovely Turkish carpet on the floor beside his bed. James saw understanding hit her square between the eyes, saw the narrowed eyes, seamed lips, and then the explosion. She jumped off the bed, her hands on her hips, a nice touch. Her voice was all the more angry for its calmness, he'd always admired the way she could do that. "I would like to know, James Sherbrooke, how your father knew about this fortune of mine and yet I, the person to whom this supposed fortune belongs, didn't know a single blessed thing? And why the devil would he tell you of all people? You have nothing to do with anything!" Her voice rose a bit, for emphasis. "This is absurd, James, why I believe it makes me quite angry. If I'm a bloody heiress then why didn't Uncle Simon bother to inform me?" She stamped her foot. He'd never seen her do that before.

Now it was his turn to goad her. "Just look at you, stamping your foot like a child denied a treat. Grow up, Corrie. Young ladies don't need to know about finances. It is not a subject that conforms to their abilities."

She stamped her foot again. "That's ridiculous and you know it, James Sherbrooke! *Finances don't conform to my abilities?* I have worked for at least four years with Uncle Simon's man of business! I know all about his bloody finances! Why did no one bother to mention mine to me?"

James realized that stoking the blaze wouldn't get him what he had to have, and that was her agreement. It didn't matter that he didn't want it, he had to have it, no choice. A bit of conciliation, he thought. "Well, maybe. You could have a point, but that's neither here nor there. My father told me about it because he wanted me to keep my eyes open here in London, to get rid of the fortune hunters if I saw some sniffing around you. My father said that where money was involved, there were no secrets. He's right. It was a matter of time before rumors of your personal wealth got out, and believe me, Corrie, you'd be besieged."

Corrie, rarely angry because it upset her stomach, forced herself down to a simmer. "Well, those rumors can't be out yet since I didn't even know about it."

He smoothly delivered a discreet salvo. "And maybe the rumors won't come out now in any case." He looked at her beneath his lashes, but she was tapping her foot, unaware of what he'd said so very well. James sighed, looked down at his hands, clasped on top of the covers. He said without looking up, "There are many rapacious men on the hunt in London, never forget that, Corrie."

Corrie threw her handkerchief on his face and began to pace back and forth in front of his bed. "Even though I am no longer yelling, I am still very upset about this, James."

"I understand, but you have to admit that my father's reason for telling me is a sound one. My father also told me, laughing his head off, what your Uncle Simon had said before he brought up the subject of your inheritance."

"And just what was that, pray?"

"You heard it already this morning. 'She'll be hunted down like a rat.'"

That brought her to a halt. "Uncle Simon said that?"

"Yes. He was worried about your, er, lack of experience in the wicked ways of London, not for long, naturally, since he had a new scientific journal that had just arrived in the post."

"Hunted down like a rat. What an image that brings to mind." She started to laugh. *"Hunted down like a rat,"* she gasped, and held her stomach she laughed so hard.

"It has a certain effect," James said. "My father laughed his head off too."

She was still laughing as she walked to the door. She said over her shoulder, now hiccupping, "Tell me, James, if finances don't conform to my meager female abilities, then what does?"

He said, his voice deep and rich, "You would have been the *parfait gentil knight*."

That brought her up short. Her face flushed with lovely color. She opened her mouth, then closed it. She nearly ran to the door, threw a big grin at him, and waved her hand. "You should rest now, James. I will see you tomorrow, if, that is, you don't mind me coming to visit you without an escort of twenty brawny young men to protect me from you and all the gossips," and she laughed some more, the witch, and was gone.

He could hear her whistling. She'd left him before he'd said what he'd had to say.

He cursed to the empty room. But not for long because Corrie's departure meant Juliette's return. His father gave him a look, and left him to his fate, which included Juliette's mother. James wished Petrie would come in and shave him again.

CHAPTER TWENTY-TWO

❧❧❧

CORRIE ARRIVED AT the Sherbrooke town house the following morning to be told by Willicombe that the younger lordship was in the estate room, doing a bit of work to resharpen his brain.

"He doesn't need papers to sharpen his brain, he needs a good argument," Corrie said, and waved Willicombe away when he would have announced her.

She opened the door quietly to see James sitting at his father's desk, a piece of paper in his right hand, a pen in his left hand, his head resting on the desktop. He was sound asleep.

She started to back out of the room, when he jerked up, stared at her, and said, "It's about time you got here."

"Why aren't you in bed?"

He stretched, rose, and stretched again, then yawned.

"You've lost weight, James. I will speak to your mother about this."

His arms dropped to his sides. "Don't worry. My

mother is stuffing food down my gullet every hour on the hour. You lost weight as well. Where have you been?"

"I chanced to meet Judith McCrae, you know, she's the girl who's very interested in Jason, if I don't miss my guess. Of course, every girl in London is interested in both you and Jason, but she seems different, more suited to him, perhaps."

Whatever that meant. He said, "She's the niece of Lady Arbuckle. How did you meet her?"

"She was coming out of a milliner's shop with Lady Arbuckle. They were having a very intense discussion, but when Judith saw me, she was all smiles. I don't think that Lady Arbuckle was pleased to see me. I suppose Judith knows that I'm a childhood friend and thus someone to be cultivated."

"Jason hasn't spoken much about her lately."

"No wonder, since his brother disappeared and could very well have been killed."

"I think he quite likes her too. Now that he sees I'm well again, he'll resume his course with her."

"I wonder what course that will be. Was Juliette camping out in the drawing room when you woke up this morning?"

"Well, she and her mother did visit not long after breakfast. I was in bed." He struck only a very slight pose since he was still too weak to goad her to his normal standards. "Do you know, I believe she enjoyed my company, her mother sitting comfortably in the corner, benignly watching the tableau."

"And I don't suppose you enjoyed all that dripping attention? All the cooing? Did she smooth her palm over your poor brow?"

"I can't recall a single coo, except maybe from her mother."

"Well, yes, that makes sense. You're the heir, after all. You know, James, I really can't imagine that she would want to marry you."

"Why ever not?"

"Juliette is very rightly aware of her own beauty. The problem is that you're more beautiful than she is. Just imagine, both of you could be looking into a mirror and she would come in a very poor second. I can't see her tolerating that."

James streaked his fingers through his hair, standing it on end. "Bloody hell, I've already let you distract me. You open your mouth and I forget where I was going. Now, be quiet and sit down, Corrie. I have something to say to you." He started to walk to her, to tower over her, intimidate her a bit, when he felt a wave of dizziness and quickly sat back down in his father's chair. He cleared his throat, then plowed forward. "Jason told me he saw you riding in the park with Devlin Monroe."

She sat herself down, spreading the lovely pale green skirt of her gown over the cushions beside her. She crossed her legs and began to swing her foot. She eyed her lovely slippers. They made her feet look positively small; and no heels. She could run and leap in these lovely slippers. She examined her thumbnail, whistled a little tune, waiting for him to explode. She'd known the signs since he was fifteen years old and so furious with his brother he'd put his fist right through a stable wall. Now that she considered it, she realized that she hadn't seen him lose control in a very long time, in fact, not since he'd become a man. He was now more reasoned and—

"Corrie, would you please pay attention to me?"

She looked up and smiled at him. "I was praising my slippers. They could chase down Augie and his cohorts. Aren't they lovely?"

Actually, they were, but he said, "Pay attention. Why the hell were you with Devlin Monroe? I told you to stay away from him."

"This was what you wished to speak to me about?

Whatever is wrong with Devlin? Surely he isn't one of these fortune hunters who would hunt me down like a rat? Why, he's the heir to a dukedom."

"Well, yes, but it's Devlin himself that's the problem. He is not the sort of man you want all that close to you, Corrie."

"Well, he hasn't gotten all that close. Yet."

"Very well. You force me to be blunt here. He keeps mistresses—not one, but several, and he likes to compare them, and announce results in his club, which happens also to be my club."

"Goodness." She sat forward, eyes alight with curiosity. "That is quite the oddest thing I've ever heard. What do you mean by comparisons? Like this girl has blue eyes and this one has brown eyes?"

"Never you mind that."

"Perhaps this girl wears her gown cut too low and that one—"

"Be quiet."

"Do you know of any ladies who keep several misters?"

He gritted his teeth until his jaws ached. "There isn't a male version of mistress." He shook his head. "Damnation, ladies can have lovers, and yes, I understand that some ladies have a string of lovers. But lovers are a different matter from mistresses. Devlin has kept as many as three mistresses at a single time. Three!"

Corrie rose, pulled a rose out of a vase, sniffed it, and said, "It sounds to me like you're jealous."

"No, I'm appalled."

Her brow went up as she stared at him.

"Well, maybe a bit jealous, but that's neither here nor there. Three mistresses is more than a surfeit, Corrie, it's wasteful, and it would be immoral if he were married."

"Do you think he'll continue to keep mistresses when he's wed?"

"I don't know. It doesn't matter."

"Well, good for him, I say. The more mistresses the better. Next time I see him, I will inquire about this. There must be rules and—"

He spoke over her. "You've distracted me again. Dammit, forget his bloody mistresses. Why did you disobey me and see him?"

Another sunny smile from her, and a shrug that made him want to walk across the estate room and shake her but good, but all he wanted to do was sleep. She said as she gently slipped the rose back into its vase, "Well, he asked me to go riding in the park with him. No one else had, and I really wanted the exercise, you understand."

He looked to the heavens, only to have her bring him crashing back to earth when she said, "I can now swear that Devlin isn't a vampire. The sun was bright overhead and he didn't get burned up. I think rather than seduce me, Devlin wants me to amuse him. He certainly laughed a lot after he got all the details of your rescue out of me. He allowed that if he were felled he would like me to minister to him as well as I did to you, even though I was going to have to pay for it. He wouldn't tell me what he meant by that." Now Corrie struck a pose. "Ah, James, I was thinking a bit about taking care of Devlin and the thought intruded—do you think Devlin is as pale as a specter all over or just his face?"

"Yes, he is." That said, James leaned back against the desk, his arms crossed over his chest. He crossed his feet at the ankles and finally, he closed his eyes. It felt wonderful, but he knew he couldn't go to sleep yet. He had too much to do.

"I think I can imagine Devlin lying there naked, on his back, like you. He would be so pale that if the sheet was well washed, he might disappear into it. I think a darker complexion is more interesting, say a more golden skin color, like yours."

"Jason and I have our father's swarthy skin," he said, and wondered when his mouth had detached itself from his brain.

"Yes, that's it, you're swarthy, only that word doesn't sound as golden as you are, it sounds more like a sunburnt pirate. Now, to be honest here, James, I believe there is no more beautiful a man than you. On the other hand, to be objective about this, you are the only naked man I have ever seen."

How had she gotten off on this? He nearly moaned when he realized that he was hard as the leg on his father's desk. He had to get back on track here. He opened his mouth, but she was off again. "Naturally," Corrie said, "I didn't tell him I was an heiress."

"No, you told him everything else." He slammed his fist onto the desktop, making the inkwell jump. What came out of his mouth then was unplanned and unwise. "Are you a complete idiot, Corrie? Do you have any idea what you've done?"

"Of course. I thought about it carefully and then decided that if everyone in London knows exactly what happened to you, everyone will be looking out for not only your father, but for you and Jason as well. You know, Devlin leaves his hat on to keep the sun off his face. And he did today as well. There, I admitted it. Such a lovely pallor. At least his face." The witch shuddered.

There was no hope for it. He said, all indifferent, "I don't suppose Devlin told you that your adventure with me was the cause of some, er, consternation?"

"Consternation? Actually, when I mentioned to him that Mrs. Cutter and Lady Brisbett had cut me, he just laughed and patted my hand and told me that it didn't mean anything and not to concern myself about it. He said, if it was all right with me, he would like to visit with my Uncle Simon."

No, James thought, Devlin wasn't going to offer for her, his parents would disown him if he offered for a girl whose reputation was in shreds. Besides he'd only just met her. And he didn't know she was an heiress, she was right about that. She was just a girl who amused him. What was Devlin up to? Why had he told her she would have to pay?

Better to get things straight right this instant. "We had an adventure, Corrie, didn't we?"

"It was a splendid adventure if you hadn't gotten so ill that it fair to scared the spit out of me."

He grinned at her cant, recognized Lovejoy. "Yes, all of London—everyone, Corrie—now knows about our adventure. And those few who didn't know, Devlin has now doubtless informed." He stared down at his fingernails, examining the small tear on his thumbnail. When he looked up at her, he smiled. "It appears that I won't have to hunt you down like a rat."

"Whatever do you mean by that?"

The estate room door suddenly opened and the earl walked in, saying to James, "This smuggler who briefly captured you and Corrie, I've been wondering who he could be, wondering if I've played cards with him. I've a hankering to go look at that cave, see if there's any clue as to what he's smuggling. You said he sounded familiar?"

"Yes, sir, sort of."

"Whatever is the matt—?" Douglas turned slowly to see Corrie sitting there on the lovely brocade sofa that Alexandra had known he liked and given to him. "Corrie," he said. "You're looking quite lovely, my dear."

"Thank you, sir. James was telling me about Uncle Simon muttering about me being hunted down like a rat."

"It would be best if you simply forgot about that, Corrie. I must see to something now. You will both excuse me." He turned in the doorway. "James, ten more minutes, then I want you back in your bed."

After Douglas had left, closing the door quietly behind him, Corrie rose, smoothed down her skirts. "Well, James, I was thinking about our smuggler too. I agree with your father—when this is all over, let's go take a look at that cave. I think you should take a nice rest now. You're looking a bit on the vampire side. Not quite as pale as Devlin, but still too pale for your swarthy complexion to look anything but weedy."

He rose slowly, his palms on the desktop. "If you attempt to leave, I will put you over my lap and smack you good."

Her chin went up. "I don't think you're strong enough to hold me down, much less raise and lower your hand with any force at all. I think it likely that if you take one step toward me, you will fall on your face."

"I could beat you in my sleep."

"You're looking flushed, James. I don't like it. Please sit down and try to calm yourself."

He rolled his eyes, nothing else to do. He really couldn't beat her, not here in his father's estate room. It struck him rather forcibly that such an action would not gain him what he had to have, not that he wanted what he had to have. "Sit down, dammit."

Corrie sat down, clasped her hands in her lap, and looked up at him like an inquiring pupil.

He said, all slow as a snail, feeling each word being pulled out of his throat, "This adventure of ours—it will be a tale that will doubtless embroider itself into a heroic saga when we tell it to our children and grandchildren."

There, it was out of his mouth, and those clever words had made sense, indeed, had sounded fluent and sincere, and the words were eloquent, calling forth images to charm the mind. But James had signed his fate with those bloody elegant words, a fate he'd known had to be his when his brain had begun functioning again.

CHAPTER TWENTY-THREE

❦

H E WAITED. HE felt strangely detached, as if his brain was sitting over on that bookshelf across the room, watching him, watching and laughing.

Complete and utter silence filled the estate room.

Corrie raised an eyebrow. "I beg your pardon? Are you delirious again, James? Shall I fetch your father? A physician? You're obviously not well and that worries me."

"Corrie, don't be stupid."

"I will be as stupid as I wish." She fiddled a moment with her mittens, the same lovely green as her gown and slippers. What came out of her mouth next nearly sent him over the edge. "Do you think that Devlin is going to propose?"

"All right, be stupid for the moment, but I can't. I'm facing the situation head-on here. There's no choice in this, Corrie, no choice for either of us."

Corrie jumped up, backed away three steps to behind the sofa, and stood there, staring at him, her hands on her hips. "Now you listen to me, James Sherbrooke. There is no situation to face head-on. There is no situation at all. Do you know what your problem is? You think too much, you weigh everything, churn it all around in your head, and then you make a decision. Many times you're exactly right but sometimes—like right now, right this instant—you skip happily to a conclusion that makes my brain hurt, so stop it. Forget this. Do you hear me? Forget it!"

He said quietly, "Two ladies already cut you. Don't you realize what that means?"

"Devlin said to forget it. I plan to."

"You cannot marry Devlin Monroe, unless, of course, you've a hankering to be a duchess rather than just a countess."

"What a stupid thing to say. I'm leaving, James."

"Where are you going?"

"To get some brandy from your father's library."

"Don't you remember what happened to you the last time you drank brandy? You and Natty Pole stole a bottle of your Uncle Simon's best, and ended up puking your guts out in the yew behind the house."

"I was twelve years old, James." But that stopped her.

He said, "I remember you were so sick you were lying there panting, and in the most pitiful voice you said to me, 'There's nothing else in me, James, even my heart has been puked out of me. I'm going to die now. Please give my apologies to Uncle Simon for stealing his brandy.' And then you fell into a stupor. No brandy, Corrie. I don't think I'm well enough to hold your hair out of your face this time."

She paused, her hand on the doorknob. She gave him a look of acute dislike. "Sometimes you are right, I admit it. You do have a point here. Very well, I will get myself a big glass of water," and she ran out of the room, light on her slippers, and that was because there were no heels on them.

He sat there and brooded. For God's sake, he didn't want to marry. Not just Corrie—and that thought was enough to make his eyes cross—but anyone. His father hadn't married until he was twenty-eight, a nice ripe year, his father would say, a year when a man finally realizes that there just might be something to this business of sleeping with a woman every single night and it was legal.

But he was only twenty-five. Three years of freedom were wafting right out the window, all because Corrie had chased after him to save him.

He cursed. Petrie said from the doorway, "My lord, you are flushed. Miss Corrie shouldn't have disagreed with you, thus elevating your choler and perhaps bringing back the fever. I wanted to tell her to take herself off, but then she did it herself. Now, I have a bit of barley water that your dear mother left for me to give you."

"Petrie," James said, eyeing his valet of five years and that damned barley water, "there are some things a gentleman must face, even though it might bring back his fever. Give me that vile stuff then leave me be. I swear I will drink it down before I traipse upstairs and fall into my bed."

"Her ladyship told me to tell you that she'd added things to the drink and that you would like it. Here, my lord. Drink it now."

James sipped the barley water, ready to spit it out, but to his surprise, it wasn't bad at all. He downed the entire glass, sighed, trudged up the stairs, and walked slowly down the long corridor to his bedchamber. When he was leaning his head against the pillows, he saw that Petrie had followed him, probably because he feared James might keel over. He lay there, wishing there'd been a different road to walk. He heard Petrie clear his throat.

"You'll choke if you don't speak, Petrie, so go ahead."

"It is my experience, my lord, that young ladies must not be rushed into weighty decisions. They must be treated gently, without—"

"Petrie, I do wish you could have seen Corrie ride

through that cottage door with a pitchfork under her arm. She stabbed one of the men in the arm. She is not fragile, she is not weak."

"Perhaps you were delirious at the time, my lord, and only imagined what she did. Perhaps, and many of us agree that this must be the case, you yourself managed to escape the three men. You found Miss Corrie in the shed, huddled down and weeping, and you yourself carried her to that farmhouse where you finally collapsed because you'd carried her for ten miles and given her all your clothes to keep her warm. Surely this is what happened, since it makes far more sense."

James could but stare. "You're telling me that Willicombe subscribes to this, Petrie?"

"As to Mr. Willicombe's beliefs on the subject, my lord, I cannot say."

"Why the hell not? You have a say about everything else in this damned house. Listen to me. Not only did she save me, she also stuck her knee in the throat of a smuggler. What do you think about that?"

"You're fevered, my lord, it is obvious. I will fetch your father." And Petrie walked out of the room, shoulders straight, head up.

James lay there and continued to brood. Maybe he'd spoken too quickly, hadn't given her time to let everything soak in.

Married to the brat. Dear God, this was something he'd never imagined when he was sixteen years old and had walked out of the barn, brushing hay off his clothes, a silly smile on his face, and she'd been standing there, watching him.

At least she'd been far too young to have a clue what he'd been doing with Betsy Hooper in that cozy back corner of the barn. He looked up to see the bedchamber door open; he was more than relieved to see his brother.

Jason was shaking his head. "You wouldn't believe what Petrie is saying about all this, James."

"Oh yes I would. He just unburdened himself to me after eavesdropping on my conversation with Corrie. I had not realized that he was such a misogynist."

Jason sighed. "It could be worse."

"How?"

"Corrie could be like Melinda Bassett."

James moaned. That she-wolf had decided she'd wanted either him or Jason, it didn't matter, and when she'd not gained her wish, she claimed they'd both raped her. It had happened seven years ago, yet he could still remember the awful impotence he'd felt at her accusations.

"Corrie saved us," Jason said. "She told everyone the truth. You'll have to say one thing about her—no one would ever think she'd lie about anything."

"Yes, she saved us, saved me again, dammit."

"You see? There are many more worse things in the world than Corrie. In fact, she's a heroine, only no one will admit it as long as she's not married to you. At least you won't have to worry about unexpected bad habits in your wife."

"That's true. I already know all her habits, bad and worse. Damnation, Jason, how could this have happened? I've never been sick in my bloody life. Why did it have to happen at this particular time?"

"When I think of what led up to it, I thank God you're not dead. Corrie's a good sort, James. Beneath that disreputable old hat of hers, a lady was hidden. You must admit you've been surprised with her transformation."

James looked glum.

"He's right, James. More to the point, you've no choice in the matter, none at all."

Douglas Sherbrooke walked to his son's bedside, lightly touched his palm to his forehead, nodded, and sat down in the big chair beside the bed. "Corrie came flying into the library to ask me very nicely if I chanced to have some brandy that wouldn't make her sick."

"Did you give her any?"

"Yes. I gave her my special Florentine brandy guaranteed not to disrupt the innards."

"There is no such thing," Jason said.

"True."

"Where is she, sir? Did she leave? Is she hiding in your library? Did she tell you why she wanted the brandy?"

Douglas nodded slowly. "After a bit of prodding. Blackmail, actually. I wouldn't give her any of my special brandy unless she told me everything. She folded, said that you felt responsible for what had happened and told her that you two had to get married. She then tossed back the watered-down brandy, burped, if I'm not mistaken, and left without another word."

"I didn't do it well," James said. "I mean I started out well, with a lovely sort of future metaphor about our children and grandchildren."

"Now there's an image to give me pause," Douglas said.

James waved that away. "Sir, surely she must realize that there is no other course for us to follow. I don't want to marry, at least right now, but there is simply no choice."

Douglas was tapping his fingertips together, looking fixedly at the painting on the opposite wall that James had bought in Honfleur three years before. A young girl was sitting on a rock, her skirts spread around her, looking over a green valley stretching below her. Douglas found himself smiling. The girl looked remarkably like Corrie.

Jason said, "I'm having our friends over this evening to report on what they've discovered, though I doubt it's much, else wise they would have come raging over here immediately. Shall we meet here in your bedchamber?"

James nodded. He suddenly felt so weary his bones ached. He closed his eyes. His father's voice, warm and deep, said close to his ear, "You're safe and you will get well, James. As for all the rest of it, things will work out."

"I think Devlin Monroe is going to propose to her."

That announcement brought two pair of startled eyes to his face.

"Why would Devlin do that?" Douglas said. "It makes no sense."

Jason said, shrugging, "She is an original. Devlin likes originals."

"She can't marry him," James said, "even though she does amuse him. She would kill him when she discovered that he still had mistresses waiting in the wings. She would run a pitchfork through his belly, then she would hang for it. I don't want to marry her, but I also don't want her hung."

Jason said, "Maybe I should speak to Devlin. Tell him what's what here."

"Yes, do that, Jason. Cut him off at the knees. The last thing I want is for her to marry him to save me. That's what she's doing, of course. She thinks it isn't fair that I have to marry her because of what happened."

"I'm off, then," Jason said, and his eyes darkened to near purple. And he smiled.

James said, "You know, with Corrie as my wife, I'll never have to worry about boring her with talk of silver cascades through the ring of Titan. I remember when I told her about my discovery—her eyes sparkled. Yes, sparkled, that was exactly what her eyes did. She listened to me, you know how she is—sits there, her eyes glued to your face, like she wants to grab the words right out of your mouth. She then told me to tell her about it again so she would be certain she understood everything." And suddenly, James remembered her eyes sparkling like that when he'd given her a doll on her sixth birthday. He'd happened to be buying a gift for his mother when he saw the doll propped up against a bolt of material. Pale white face, big red lips, and eyes that reminded him of Corrie's. He'd been embarrassed to buy it, even more embarrassed to give it to her, but she'd pulled it out of the paper, pressed it to her skinny

little chest and looked up at him, eyes sparkling. With
more, of course. With love. With adoration. He'd wanted to
run then; he wanted to run now.

"As I recall," Jason said, "you and Corrie used to spend
a lot of time lying outside looking up at the stars, you
telling her everything you knew."

"That was a long time ago."

"It was two months ago. I remember because you were
excited about Mercury coming so close to the earth."

It was true, dammit. So many evenings she'd sneaked
out of her uncle's house and they'd lain on their backs,
looking up into the heavens.

"She always wanted to talk about the moon; she's always been fascinated with the moon. And you know, she
doesn't need to talk, like most girls do. She's perfectly fine
with blessed silence."

James wondered if Juliette Lorimer's eyes would
sparkle if she'd attended his talk at the Astrological Society meeting.

Marriage to the brat. Dear God, how could such a thing
be possible?

CHAPTER TWENTY-FOUR

❦

THE FOLLOWING MORNING, James had drunk some tea and eaten two slices of toast when Corrie suddenly appeared in the doorway of his bedchamber. She walked in, dressed quite nicely in a morning gown of pale golden brown, with a lovely matching wrap of darker brown that added a touch of gold to her eyes.

He raised a supercilious eyebrow at her. "Hello, Corrie. Did you ever leave?"

"Whatever do you mean? Of course I left."

"It seems that you're nearly living here now. In and out, in my bedchamber, in the estate room drinking my father's Florentine brandy, you're everywhere, including in the kitchen to steal biscuits, Willicombe told me. When we're married, there'll be little change."

Not a word came out of her mouth, not even a curse.

"Did my father select that gown for you?"

"What? My gown? Well, yes, he did." She fidgeted a moment. "Do you like it?"

"Yes, it's lovely."

She waved that away. "Listen, James, your mother paid my Aunt Maybella a visit. It was just the two of them, and they had their heads together for a full hour. Since you're still on the weedy side, I had to come here to see you. I want to know why your mother was with my aunt."

She'd begun pacing, and he liked the way she looked, thank God. Then she tossed her wrap to a chair along with her reticule, turned to say something else and he saw that that damned gown she was wearing was nearly falling off her shoulders.

"Put your damned wrap back on. Your gown is cut far too low. I cannot believe that my father ordered up a gown that leaves you nearly naked to the waist."

To his surprise, she grinned at him. She shrugged her shoulders, slipped her fingers beneath the gown and tugged it down a bit more. "Actually, your father didn't know that Madame Jourdan winked at me when he ordered her to cut the bodice nearly to my chin." She actually leaned toward him and poked out her breasts. "It looks perfect, so you will hold your tongue."

James, without thinking, with no consideration at all, bounded from the bed and stomped over to her, so angry he was panting.

He grabbed her bodice and jerked it up to her chin. And heard a rip. Corrie didn't say a word, just stood there, staring at him.

He was naked.

"James," she said, looked down his body, and gulped. "This is a lovely treat, but perhaps your mother might walk in and what would she think? I'm an innocent young girl, and here you are, stark naked, and so very lovely that I'm ready to burst into song. And that male part of yours that I shouldn't know anything about, is gaining in stature, James. It's getting rather alarming."

He cursed, she was right; it seemed when he was angry

with her he got harder than the bedpost. Or maybe it was whenever he remarked upon her breasts, he got harder than— He stomped back to his bed and grabbed his dressing gown. He shrugged it on, tied the belt at his waist, and walked back up to her. He took her shoulders in his large hands. "I ripped your gown. I'm sorry."

"No, you're not. You must be feeling much better. You roared out of that bed ready to hurl me out the window."

"No, I just wanted to cover you so I wouldn't have to lie there in my bed and slaver."

She blinked. "Looking at me would make you slaver, James? You're not lying to me, are you?"

"No, dammit, I'm not lying. Now look at you, your right sleeve is hanging off and your gown is still so low it makes me want to howl at the moon."

"Hmmm, I must ask Devlin if vampires can howl at the sun."

He gritted his teeth. "Do not speak of Devlin Monroe to me again. Do you understand me, Corrie? Now, I trust you burst in on me to inform me of your decision to marry me?"

"I came to tell you that my aunt and uncle are already planning our wedding, at least they were until I told them I was not going to allow you to sacrifice yourself. I told them I was going to marry someone else, someone who actually wanted me."

"Do not say his bloody name!"

"All right. He came to visit me this morning. It turns out that Jason tracked him down at his club last night and told him marriage to me would do him in. Can you believe Jason told him I would kill him if he kept his mistresses? Actually kill him, that's what Jason told him. He also said that since he'd known me from the age of three, he knew what I was capable of. He asked Devlin—oops, I didn't mean to mention his name—if he were willing to tread the path of faithfulness until he stuck his spoon in the wall. Devlin said he laughed when Jason asked him that. Then he asked me if I would really kill him if he were unfaithful."

"And what did you tell him?"

"I told him I'd kill him deader than the dinner trout."

"And what did he say to that?"

"He laughed some more, told me then that there was no gentleman of his acquaintance who could safely marry me, given my stand on fidelity, despite all my money, unless the gentleman was teetering on bankruptcy, and the good Lord knew that such a gentleman would promise anything at all to get what he wanted, including—horror of horrors—fidelity. He laughed again, told me that when it came down to it, even the promise of murder wouldn't deter a man from promising anything, and then doing what he wanted. That was the way of the world. It's not right, James, just not right."

"My father has never broken faith to my mother, nor she to him."

"I suppose the same is true for Aunt Maybella and Uncle Simon. I don't think it's particularly due to Uncle Simon's fortitude in matters of the flesh. I think it would take too much time away from his leaf studies. What do you think?"

"I can't believe you've gotten me off on this ridiculous tangent. Will you marry me, Corrie?"

"No."

"Why the hell not?"

"I will never marry a man who doesn't love me."

"Are you saying that you would marry Devlin if he swore to be faithful to you?"

She appeared thoughtful. He wanted to strangle her.

"You will say no, dammit!"

"All right, no."

"Well, I swear I won't be unfaithful."

She sighed. "I do think Dev—our vampire—was wrong when he said that every man would promise anything I wished in order to get what he wanted. You wouldn't do that. I know you down to your beautiful feet. You would never lie about something so very important."

"No, I wouldn't."

"James, listen. You're an honorable man, too honorable for your own good, as a matter of fact, at least most of the time. The fact is, I don't want to get married. I'm only in my first practice season. I've barely begun to sow my wild oats, barely begun to learn the ins and outs of flirting.

"I'm too young to get married, particularly for such an absurd reason. You're too young too. Admit it. Marriage is—or was—the last thing on your mind before all this happened."

"I won't admit to that."

"Then I'll have to reassess how truthful you are."

"All right, dammit. I had no thought of marriage. For God's sake, I'm only twenty-five years old. You speak of sowing wild oats. Well, I have bucketfuls left to sow. But I will forego them because honor is more important. Stop whining. Accept what must be."

"But neither of us did anything wrong!"

"I will waltz with you until there are holes in your slippers."

"I imagine Uncle Simon promised the same thing to my aunt. She didn't get holes in her slippers, James, she got leaves. Bloody leaves! She told me once that on their honeymoon, Uncle Simon allowed her to press three leaves in one of his many books. However, he didn't allow her to label it. That sounds perfectly dreadful, James."

"I will not have you pressing leaves on our honeymoon."

"Ah, and what would you do on our honeymoon?"

He was close to swallowing his tongue. "There are standard things that a man and a woman do after they're married. Surely you know all about sex, Corrie."

"Well, not all that much, really. You mean to say that's what you would do rather than pressing leaves? You wouldn't be reading me treatises on the orbital rotation of Saturn in a cosmic dust storm?"

"No. Saturn would cease to exist for me. Saturn wouldn't exist for most normal men on their honeymoon, unless they were looking up at the stars and Saturn just happened to be shining down in their eyes. You see, most men think about only one thing, and on their honeymoon, they can—well, never mind that." James dashed his fingers through his hair. "Dammit, you need a bit of promised wickedness, don't you? Very well, I am going to strip you naked and make love to you until you are snoring with exhaustion."

"James, you've said quite a lot there. But the end of it— me lying there snoring—that doesn't sound very romantic."

"All right, I happen to know that you don't snore. You make little mewling noises. Now, listen to me. I will let you flirt with me, endlessly."

"Men do not flirt with their wives."

"Now there's a wise oracle speaking."

"Don't be sarcastic with me, James Sherbrooke. I'm not stupid. I know that Aunt Maybella would many times rather kick Uncle Simon than kiss him."

"You should see my parents. Last week I came around a corner and saw my father pressing my mother against a wall, kissing her neck. They've been married forever."

"Pressing her against a wall? Really?"

"Really. And I would do no less. I will nibble on your neck in a dark section of a garden, the night jasmine scenting the air. We will get along famously, Corrie. Now, I'm nearly ready to collapse, so say yes and leave me in peace."

"You don't love me."

And he said, the words pouring out of his mouth, "I can't imagine that Devlin Monroe told you he loves you?"

"No, he didn't. He told me he finds me a delight, his word. Don't get me wrong. Being a delight sounds clever indeed, but it's not what's important in marriage, James."

"Did you tell him that?"

"Oh yes. He said it was a nice start, didn't I agree, and I said I did, but I said it was only a nice preamble to say a picnic or a ride in the park, not marriage."

She'd routed Devlin; she'd sent him about his business; she'd turned him down flat. James grinned. Relief poured through him.

"I told him to think about it with more depth, and perhaps I would entertain his request at a later date."

James cursed. He wished his brain was working a bit more competently, but he was tired, and he wanted nothing more than to collapse on his bed and sleep until supper. He said, "We know each other, Corrie. We like each other, at least we do most of the time."

"You didn't like me at all when Darlene nearly nudged you off the cliff."

"You want the truth, Corrie? What I remember about that day is the feel of your bottom against my palm when I spanked you."

Her agile tongue dried up. "M-my bottom? You felt m-my bottom?"

"Well, of course. You have a lovely bottom, Corrie, from the feel of it. If you marry me, why then I can take your clothes off, stretch you out on your back, and rub you down with a nice damp cloth. Again and again, perhaps humming whilst I stroke that nice cloth over you, every little part of you. Do you think your skin is as white as Devlin's?"

"You didn't want me to say his name."

He laughed. "Embarrassed, are you? Well, picture yourself naked, Corrie, and I'm the one stroking my hands all over you, particularly your breasts, and you're not sick at all. In fact, you're arching your back against my hands. What do you think?"

"Oh goodness," she said, and turned to walk away. "Oh goodness."

"No." He grabbed her arm. "No, you won't simply walk

out on me this time. We're getting this settled right now, Corriander Tybourne-Barrett. My God, what a ghastly name. Do you think we will have to sign that as your name in the marriage registry?"

She was standing perfectly still, aware that his hands were running up and down her arms, and one arm was bare where he'd ripped her sleeve.

"If you don't marry me, then I will have to do something drastic."

"Like what?"

"I'm not going to tell you. Listen to me, brat, there is simply no choice. If you don't marry me, then both of us are thoroughly ruined. Don't you understand? Haven't you got your brain around this?"

"You wouldn't be ruined, James, that's absurd. If I simply go back to the country, I won't be ruined either."

He shook her. "That is so stupid, I can't imagine how you could let it out of your mouth."

"You're right, I'm sorry. It was bad." She looked down at his hands still clutching her arms. She pulled free of him and took several steps away from him, shook her fist in his face, and wailed, "You don't love me!"

He yelled right back. "And I suppose you love me?"

She stared at him, mute as a post.

"Well? Answer me, damn you."

"No, I won't, and don't yell at me again."

"Why won't you answer me? All right, keep still, it's a blessed relief, your silence. I know you adored me when you were three years old. Has that changed?"

"Things are a bit more straightforward when you're three years old, much simpler, not a single shade between black and white. I'm no longer three years old, James."

"All I have to do is look at your breasts and I know that well enough. Is that a blush I see on that brazen face of yours? All right, so you wish to string me along, like a trout on your fishing line. That is very female of you, Corrie, and I don't appreciate it. You say I don't love you—all this has happened too quickly. How can something like that happen in the course of a week? I do like you all the way to the soles of my feet; I admire you. I think you're too brave for your brains. I think you've been a twit more times than not, but the fact is we'll do very well together. Now, listen. We've known each other forever. My parents are very fond of you, and you of them—forget my grandmother, she hates everyone—and your Uncle Simon knows that you won't have to be hunted down like a rat if you marry me, since our marriage would have nothing at all to do with your blasted money. Everyone would be relieved. The gossip would stop. We would be blessed and smiled upon. No one would cut you, ever again. I would no longer be considered a ravager of young maidens. We would get along fine, Corrie. Enough of this." He hauled her against him and kissed her.

Corrie, who'd only been kissed by Willie Marker, nearly blacked out. Delight, that's what it was, and it swept over her with the force of a wave at the beach. His tongue touched her lips, pressing lightly. Without any hesitation at all, Corrie opened her mouth and nearly fainted with the lust that poured through her when his tongue touched hers. She knew it was lust; it had to be lust because it felt so very good. She knew lust was wicked because Uncle Simon was wont to say that the reason wickedness was so rampant in the world was because it was so utterly delicious. Well, with James, it was beyond delicious. This was something she'd never even known could exist, it—

"Oh dear, excuse me."

Corrie would have crashed insensible to the floor if James weren't holding her up.

James's brain nearly melted at the sound of his mother's voice. His heart, nearly pounding out of his chest, thudded to his feet. His sex, thank the good Lord, became instantly dormant. He knew he couldn't let go of Corrie, she'd fall in a heap.

He managed to pull his tongue out of her mouth and slowly, very slowly, he turned to say, hoping he wouldn't pant out his words, "Hello, Mother. Since Corrie and I are engaged now, she wanted to know what it was like to kiss."

Alexandra stood in the doorway, amused, horrified, and terribly aware that her son had his tongue nearly down a girl's throat. Corrie looked like a half-wit, which was a very good thing, she thought, shuddering, because in that instant she remembered the first time she'd kissed Douglas, and lost her head. As for James, he looked flushed, embarrassed, and—no, better not think along those lines.

What if she'd walked through that door two minutes from now? Oh dear. What was a mother to do?

She cleared her throat. "Welcome to the family, Corrie."

CHAPTER TWENTY-FIVE

❧

J AMES WAS DRINKING tea the next morning, actually sitting in his chair in the breakfast room, not propped up in his bed. And, glory be, he didn't feel like he wanted to fall off his chair and curl up on the carpet.

Jason said, as he handed him a bowl of porridge, "This is from Mrs. Clemms. She said you were to eat all of it or I was to stuff it down your gullet. If I didn't succeed, why then, she would come out here to stand by your right hand and sing opera in your ear until you'd licked the bowl clean."

"I didn't know Mrs. Clemms could sing opera."

"She can't," Douglas said, and grinned over the top of his paper.

James spooned up a big bite, and sat there, chewing, savoring the sweet honey she'd mixed in with the porridge, when his mother walked into the room, allowed Willicombe to seat her, then announced, "I will meet with Corrie and Maybella this morning. Your father thinks the sooner your marriage takes place the better," and then she picked up a slice of toast, smeared gooseberry jam on it, and took a satisfying bite.

James swallowed too quickly and choked. His father was halfway out of his chair when James raised his hand and said, "No, sir, I'm all right. I was thinking, Mother, just perhaps it would be better if Corrie and I met first."

"What is this, James? You've still failed to convince her? She's still threatening to bolt?"

James turned to his father. "If I give her more than a minute alone, she will talk herself into a panic. Yes, probably she'll bolt. She told me that it isn't fair, said she'd just begun to sow her wild oats, you see, whereas I've had seven more years to be as debauched as I please."

"Hmmm," said Corrie's future mother-in-law. "She has a point, James. I hadn't thought of it in quite that way. You know, the same was true of your father and me, only he was ten years older than I, and he knew ever so much more than I did and—"

"I don't think you should revisit the past, Alex," Douglas said. "You might not remember things in the way they actually happened."

"Well, that's certainly something good about getting older." She smiled at her sons. "One does soften things a bit through the haze of years. James, if you like, I can fetch Corrie and bring her back here."

"No, thank you, Mother. Since I'm feeling more fit this morning, I think I'll take Corrie riding in the park. But first, I must write an announcement." James excused himself, and said over his shoulder as he left the dining room, "I shaved myself this morning. Petrie predicted I'd slice that lovely vein in my neck. I swear he was disappointed when I didn't."

"And," Jason said, rising, "I am off to meet with several of our friends. None of them had news the other night, as you well know, but I understand from Peter Marmot that we're going to meet a fellow down in Covent Gardens. Supposedly he spoke about this Cadoudal fellow. There's probably nothing to it, but you never know." Jason fiddled with his napkin a moment, then said, his voice lowered, "Actually it was James who was supposed to go with Peter, but I don't think he's completely well yet; at least I don't want him to risk himself again so soon."

"I'll come with you," Douglas said, and threw down his napkin.

"No, Father, we've discussed this. We all believe strongly that you need to stay close to home for the next couple of days. The man who had James kidnapped must know now that he failed. I know he'll be coming up with something else very soon. Please, sir, let us see what we can find out."

"If you get yourself injured, Jason," said his father, "I will be very upset."

"Just don't tell James about this. He's liable to try to throw me into a wall."

"If you get yourself hurt, I'll throw you into a wall," Douglas said.

Jason gave him a cocky smile, leaned down to kiss his mother's cheek, and walked out of the breakfast room, whistling.

"Young men believe they're immortal," Douglas said. "It scares the hell out of me."

Young men? Alexandra thought about how her husband had gone off late one night in Rouen, quite alone, whistling, in fact, to visit with some ruffians who operated within the shadows of the flying buttresses of the cathedral. However, having been married for twenty-seven years, she didn't say a word.

CORRIE WAS CHEWING on her thumbnail, looking out over the long, narrow park across the street from

Uncle Simon's town house on Great Little Street, wondering what she was to do. Climb aboard a ship bound for Boston—a strange-sounding name for a city—in the wilds of America? Or, and this was more likely, just fold her tent and walk down the aisle, James at her side. And, truth be told, what was so wrong with that? When he'd kissed her, she wanted to fling him to the floor and pin him down. She groaned aloud, echoes of those absolutely amazing feelings that had sunk into the deepest parts of her, those feelings that had made her soar into the heavens the instant his mouth had touched hers, still rumbling inside her. She shivered at the memory of those little sparkles of lust.

Corrie shook her head at herself, then saw a young lady walking across the park, coming this way. It was Miss Judith McCrae, and so very beautiful she was. Maybe even as beautiful as Miss Juliette Lorimer, who'd lost James, and wasn't that just too bad?

At least if Corrie married James, he wouldn't end up with an awful wife like Juliette, who wouldn't appreciate how smart he was, how very clever and witty he was, who would whine if she had to lie atop a small hill and look up at the stars whilst James was peering through his telescope at the Andromeda constellation in the northern sky. Juliette would probably think that Andromeda was a new perfume from France.

Corrie sighed. When he'd slid his tongue in her mouth, a million stars had exploded in her head, Andromeda probably among them, and she knew that stars were only the beginning. Had it been the same for James? Probably not. He was a man.

Judith McCrae was nearly at the front door. What did she want? She barely knew the girl, knew only that she'd been flirting with Jason. She rose, shook out her skirts, and waited for Tamerlane, Uncle Simon's London butler, to announce her, which he did, his bright red hair shining in the morning light.

He stood in the open drawing room doorway, cleared his throat, and trumpeted, "Miss Judith McCrae of the Irish McCraes in Waterford begs to be allowed to see Miss Corrie Tybourne-Barrett."

Corrie heard a female giggle, and was that a choked laugh from Tamerlane? Then here came Miss McCrae walking gracefully into the drawing room, a big smile on her face, knowing she'd charmed with that clever introduction. Corrie smiled back at her, charmed indeed.

"How very delightful to see you, Miss Tybourne-Barrett. I understand from my Aunt Arbuckle that you and James Sherbrooke are to be married."

Corrie grunted.

"Do you think we'll be related?"

This was frank speaking, indeed. And vastly clever, so clever that you didn't want to smack her, you wanted to laugh, so that meant Miss McCrae was a very smart girl. Corrie said, "No, Miss McCrae, James and I have not decided to get married, so I'd say it looks bleak, our being related. Would you like some tea?"

"Please, call me Judith. I'd taken your grunt for a yes. I think Lord Hammersmith is a very persistent man, possibly as persistent as his brother. Persistent is a very nice way of saying that they are both stubborn as goats. But who knows? I am very persistent as well. Jason needs me, you know, just as Lord Hammersmith needs you."

"Miss McCrae—"

"Call me Judith," this said with a sunny smile that brought out the deep dimples on either side of her quite lovely mouth. Corrie sighed. "Judith, James doesn't need anyone, particularly me. This marriage, if there must be one, is being foisted on the two of us. Oh dear, I don't really know you, and here I am bleating out everything to you."

"I know, I sometimes do the same thing, particularly when something very deep inside me recognizes that I can trust another person."

Corrie cast about for someone she'd known who was even a little bit like this young lady, but she couldn't. Judith appeared to be unique.

"I didn't realize you knew Jason so well."

"Not well at all yet, but I do know that I want him rather desperately. I have never seen a more lovely man in all my life, but you know—that's not all that important, now is it?"

Corrie saw James quite clearly in her mind, and slowly, she shook her head. "No, I suppose it isn't, except when one simply wants to look at him, and sigh with pleasure."

"Yes, indeed. It makes my toes tingle to think of it. Now, I must make Jason realize that he wants me as desperately. What with the threat on his father's life, however, it makes it difficult to snag his attention. He is distracted."

"I would be too if someone were trying to kill my father." The way Corrie had snagged James's attention was to save him, then nurse him, perhaps not a preferred method of attracting a gentleman.

Uncle Simon walked into the room, his beautiful eyes focused on something only he could see, probably some blasted leaf he was creating in his mind that hadn't yet been invented by Nature.

"Uncle Simon, this is Miss Judith McCrae."

"Huh? Oh, you're not alone, Corrie." He blinked his thick lashes over his lovely eyes and bowed. "Miss McCrae, how very charming you appear to be. Naturally, one never really knows another, particularly when one has just met, don't you agree?"

"Only a very stupid person would disagree, my lord."

"And this is my uncle, Lord Montague." Corrie tried not to giggle as she watched Uncle Simon take Miss McCrae's hand, and give her his full attention for perhaps three seconds, just long enough for Judith to fully realize that although he might be a bit on the older side, he was still a pleasurable eyeful for the ladies.

Judith appeared to have more abilities with regard to gentlemen than Corrie did. Her dimples deepened, she looked up at Uncle Simon through lashes that looked thicker than Juliette's, and said, "I understand that you are an expert in the identification and preservation of all sorts of leaves, my lord. I found one in the park last Tuesday morning that I was unable to identify. Perhaps—"

"A leaf? You found an unknown leaf, Miss McCrae? In the park? Why, so did I. What an amazing coincidence. Please bring it over and we will compare leaves." He beamed down at Miss McCrae, seated himself, and said to Corrie, "It appears I am in luck. Your aunt is out shopping and Cook has prepared"—his voice dropped dramatically—"Twyley Grange cinnamon bread." Uncle Simon dropped his voice even further to a near whisper. "I myself brought her the recipe. She's been all atwitter, pumping herself up to do it, and so she has, finally. She has prepared six slices, nice thick slices. Since Miss McCrae is here, that means we can't split them, Corrie. Now it means that we each will get to eat two, unless either of you is perhaps trying to lose flesh? No, Corrie, you're still too thin." There was a doleful sigh here. "You'll need to eat both of yours, I'm afraid." He cast a critical eye toward Judith, whose figure was well-nigh perfect, and said thoughtfully, "A young lady can never be too careful with her intake of bread, don't you agree, Miss McCrae?"

"I have always practiced eating only one slice, sir. Two would make my cheeks fat. It has always been so."

"Excellent." Simon rubbed his hands together and yelled, "Tamerlane! Bring in the cinnamon bread, and quickly, man. It's possible that Lady Montague might return sooner than any of us would wish."

Judith shot Corrie a look, demurely seated herself, and waited for the cinnamon bread to be delivered. The twinkle in her dark eyes was outrageous.

When Tamerlane, with great ceremony, whisked off the

silver dome from the small platter, the smell of cinnamon wafted into the room. There was utter silence, then Judith sucked in her breath. "Oh goodness, do they taste as good as they smell?"

Tamerlane announced, "This is the exact recipe from Cook at Twyley Grange. They are beyond compare."

"How the devil would you know that, Tamerlane? Cook said she made a loaf of only six slices. Was there another slice and you filched it? Stuffed it down your own gullet? Actually robbed me of a seventh?"

"No, my lord, it was a measly extra piece that didn't fit nicely into the glorious loaf that Cook fashioned. She allowed me to eat it, to ensure that it would be to your exacting standards." Tamerlane beamed and passed the platter first to Miss McCrae. Judith grabbed a slice and had it in her mouth so quickly it set her nose to quivering. She chewed, eyes closed in bliss, before Uncle Simon could grab his slice off the platter, which he did soon enough.

Corrie was laughing so hard she was having trouble breathing. It gave Judith time to snag a second slice right off the plate beneath Uncle Simon's nose, back quickly away from him since he looked ready to grab it out of her hand, and say, her mouth full, "I don't think you're too thin at all, Corrie. Indeed, I was thinking that perhaps your face was a little on the plump side and you could cut yourself down to one slice—oh goodness, this is the best cinnamon bread I've ever eaten in my life."

Simon said, "You've already eaten two slices, and to the best of my knowledge, you weren't even invited here this morning, you simply arrived. You probably smelled them cooking and hied yourself over, your mouth open. You've had quite enough." He was talking around his second slice, the platter balanced now on his knee, his other hand covering it.

James walked into the drawing room to see Corrie

nearly blue, she was trying so hard to stop laughing. Then he smelled the bread and heard his taste buds sing hallelujah. The famous Twyley Grange cinnamon bread, the recipe guarded closely for well nigh onto thirty years, and now they were here.

"Ah, James, is that you?" Simon asked, and quickly slid the platter, now holding only two slices, behind his back. "You're looking quite well again, my boy. Not at all thin."

"Yes, sir, I am nearly fit again, and quite on the plump side," but his watering mouth wanted one of those slices, desperately. He forced himself to turn to the young lady who was trying to see that platter. James knew this was Miss McCrae, the young lady who'd managed to snag Jason's attention a second time—which was amazing—and then even a third time, something no girl had managed before. She was licking her fingers now, humming with pleasure. James, who knew all about the immense power of the Twyley Grange cinnamon bread, said, "You're right, sir, I'm a positive stoat. I'm not here to gorge on bread, although I would probably wish to, if I weren't so fat. Actually, I'm here to take Corrie riding in the park."

Corrie jumped to her feet, one eye on her uncle and the other on Judith McCrae, who was rising slowly, staring at James.

Uncle Simon swallowed and—it seemed like magic—another slice of bread seemed to appear in his hand and was fast moving toward his open mouth. "Take her," Simon said, and bit down, nearly shuddering with delight. "Now. Before she tries to nab the last slice."

"This is quite remarkable," Judith said, her head cocked to one side, thick black curls nearly hitting her shoulder. "I've been told that you and Jason are quite identical, but here, up close, I don't think you look a thing like your brother."

"I myself have been told that," James said. He took her hand, looked into those dark eyes of hers, and said, "You are Miss Judith McCrae, and I am James Sherbrooke. It is a pleasure to finally meet you."

"Thank you," Judith said. "I am pleasured as well." She stared up into those incredible violet eyes. "Perhaps Jason is a bit taller than you are, my lord, and now that I am standing only three feet from you, I do believe Jason's eyes are more violet than yours."

"That is ridiculous, Judith," Corrie shouted. "James has the most beautiful violet eyes in all of England, everyone has remarked upon that, and since Jason is said to be his exact twin, then how could you possibly believe that his eyes were more violet?"

"I suppose," Judith said slowly, never looking away from James's face, "that I could be wrong about the eyes. But Jason is taller, no doubt about that at all. And perhaps he is also broader in the shoulders."

James burst into laughter. Corrie whirled around to frown at him. As for Miss McCrae, James knew that she was trying to keep a straight face.

But Corrie, still hooked on Miss McCrae's line, leapt at that. "Broader in the shoulders? That is absurd, ridiculous! Even though James has been quite ill—nearly dead he was so ill—even so, his shoulders remained exactly the same, and that means he's perfect. Look at him—I've never seen more perfect breadth in the shoulders in all my life! The idea that Jason's—"

"Corrie," James said, reaching out to touch her arm, "thank you for defending me, the obviously inferior twin. Now, Miss McCrae has nearly pulled your leg clean off. Let go of the bait now, Corrie."

"But, she—"

"Let go."

Corrie stared from Judith to James, reviewed Judith's outrageous comments, her own responses, and felt like the village idiot. She said, looking down at her slippers, her voice soft, a bit sad, "I fear you might be right, Judith. I have been thinking, actually for some time now, that perhaps it is Jason I prefer, not James here, with his meager shoulders."

"You may not have Jason! Do you hear me?"

Corrie looked up and grinned like Uncle Simon when he found a new leaf.

"Oh," Judith said, gasping a bit, "I know when a table's been turned on me, and this one just flattened me. That was excellent, Corrie. You got me right in the nose."

Corrie was preening, James laughing, when Judith turned to Lord Ambrose and said, "And now, my lord, perhaps you would like to see the leaf I was unable to identify? Or James, I understand that you have an inquiring mind. Perhaps you would like to see my unidentified leaf?"

Simon jumped out of his seat, outraged. "Excuse me? What is this, Miss McCrae?" He waved the platter, that now held one lone slice in its center, at her, "You told me about the leaf, not anyone else, particularly James, who knows nothing at all about leaves, only what's hanging about up in the heavens. Besides James is nearly out the door, to take Corrie riding. I wish to see that leaf, Miss McCrae."

Judith grinned, fluttered her lashes at Simon, and said, "Perhaps if I could have that very last slice, sir, the leaf could be guaranteed to be yours."

Simon looked at that slice, thought about the three he'd already consumed, thought about the unidentified leaf that might be the brother to the one he'd found in the park, looked back at the slice, and said, "Show James the leaf." He ate the last slice, dusted his hands on his trousers, nodded to the three young people, and took himself off, humming.

"You, Judith, are quite amazing," Corrie said. "Now we know what's more important to Uncle Simon. I will have to tell Aunt Maybella." She slanted a look at James. "Maybe on a honeymoon, eating cinnamon bread would be the activity of choice?"

He laughed. "Possibly. We'll see, won't we?"

They heard the front door open, heard Aunt Maybella's voice suddenly ring out in outrage. "I smell it! Simon, where are you? You've eaten the entire loaf, haven't you? I will hide that unidentified leaf of yours, you miserable loon, you'll see! I want some cinnamon bread!"

"Let's get out of here," James said, and offered an arm to each young lady.

CHAPTER TWENTY-SIX

❧❦❧

JAMES GAVE CORRIE a leg up. Once she'd settled herself on Darlene's back, he mounted Bad Boy. "Both of them look like they've been eating your uncle's cinnamon bread. They need more exercise, Corrie."

Corrie only nodded. She was looking at Judith McCrae, who'd insisted on walking back to Lady Arbuckle's house only two streets away. Since it was a sunny day for early October, James had agreed.

"May I perhaps meet you at the Mayfair for an ice, say tomorrow?" Judith had asked Corrie. The date made, Judith walked away, her step bouncy, infinitely graceful.

"She wants Jason," Corrie said.

"Well, it might be that he wants her as well, but the truth is, you never know with Jason."

"I think she's as beautiful as Juliette Lorimer."

"So you don't like her?"

Corrie said, "Yes, I'm afraid I do," and said nothing more until they'd guided their horses through a gate into

Hyde Park. It was too early for the fashionables to be out and seen, which was fine with her. She wanted to gallop. However, James lightly laid his gloved hand on the reins. "Not yet," he said.

"Oh, goodness, you're still not well enough, are you, James? I'm so sorry, thinking things were like they used to be before—well, of course we'll walk the horses."

He reached out his hand and laid it over hers. "Will you marry me, Corrie? No more excuses about me making this dreadful sacrifice, no more whining about missing out on sowed oats."

"You don't think I should do well as a barmaid in Boston? It's in America."

"No, you would be a miserable serving girl. You would clout any man who was stupid enough to pinch your bottom."

Her chin went up. "That's not true. I could do anything I had to do in order to survive. If you were ill and it were up to me, I could drive a dray. I could make meat pies and sell them. James, I would keep you safe and well. You could always count on me."

He cocked his head to one side, staring at her. He studied the face he'd known for more than half his life, first the child and now the young woman. "You know, Corrie, I believe you would," he said slowly, and then he reached out and clasped her hand. "We will do well together. Trust me."

She sighed, shook off his hand, and click-clicked Darlene into a canter along Rotten Row.

The fact of the matter was, he thought, watching her gracefully sway in the side saddle, firmly in control, *she would do anything she needed to do, anything she had to do.* To save him. She'd already proved that. He sent Bad Boy into a gallop and was riding beside her within a few moments.

"Say yes," he said, his eyes between Bad Boy's twitching ears. Then he gave her a sideways glance. "I could teach you things, Corrie, things that would make you feel quite good."

Oh dear, she quite liked the sound of this. "What sorts of things?"

"Perhaps it isn't proper of me to get all into details just this moment, but on our wedding night—ah, yes, I'll just spit it out—think of me kissing the backs of your knees."

The knees in question froze on her legs. "Oh goodness, my knees?"

"The backs of your knees. That could be one very small thing I will teach you about. No, no more. You must wait. Now, the truth is, I sent our marriage announcement to the *Gazette*. No one will cut you now, no one will look at me like I'm a debauched rake. It's done, Corrie. My mother is likely meeting with your Aunt Maybella even as we ride. The wedding must be soon."

"If I were to agree, I wouldn't want it soon. I would want the biggest wedding ever seen in London. I would want to be married at Saint Paul's."

He smiled. "All right. Let's go back and speak to our elders."

"I haven't said yes, James. This is all supposition."

He grinned at her. "You are tottering close to the edge."

"Why are you being so damned agreeable? Are you still too ill to argue with me? You must be, because you like to argue and yell and curse. You like to pretend you're going to clout me. This agreeable side of you isn't what I'm used to. Are you tired, is that the problem? Oh dear, let me see if your fever has come back." And she rode Darlene right into Bad Boy, her hand outstretched, but she didn't touch his face because Darlene, who'd just come into heat, decided she wanted Bad Boy and what followed was a fracas, a good word that meant everything and nothing, the word that Corrie later used to describe to her uncle and aunt what had happened. Actually, fracas didn't come close to the chaos of two rearing horses: Darlene shrieking, Bad Boy snorting, amenable to what she wanted to do and trying to bite her neck and mount her, and James, laughing so hard he was nearly falling off his horse's back.

And in the midst of it all, Corrie, barely managing to stay on Darlene's back, shouted through her laughter, "All right, James. I'll seriously consider marrying you! I suppose it could be more fun than being a barmaid in Boston."

"Is that a yes or another supposition?"

She whispered, looking down at her black boots with their lovely heels, "All right."

"Good. That's done."

James wasn't about to admit to relief. No, he was facing the raw fact that his doom was now formally sealed, his not inconsiderable wild oats now headed for a deep well.

He met for two hours with Lord Montague, managed to keep his attention focused long enough to get the marriage contract finalized, all the while thinking that at least there'd be laughter in his life. Corrie might drive him mad, make him want to hurl her through a window, but at the end of the day, she'd have him holding his belly with laughter. And kissing the backs of her knees. He grinned. Imagine, kissing the backs of the brat's knees. *Life,* he thought, *was amazing.*

J ASON AND PETER Marmot hadn't found the man in Covent Garden that morning. One old woman, who was selling very well-made brooms, had said through healthy gums, "Old 'orace was lying on his arse today, the lazy sod, likely he was drinkin' 'is guts out, and all because he'd heard that a man wanted to poke his sticker in 'orace's belly."

This didn't sound good. They made plans to return that night. As it happened, however, Peter hadn't appeared, and so Jason had gone alone to Covent Garden. He simply walked about, turning down a half dozen prostitutes, guarding his groats, looking at every shadow that crept out of the many alleyways, keeping his hand close to his stiletto and his derringer. It was raucous, as it always was this time of night, yells, laughter, curses. He tried to blend in, all the while looking everywhere for the man Peter had described to him.

He didn't know what made him turn at the last moment, but thank the good Lord that he did. A man, masked, wearing a black greatcoat, came at him, not with a knife in his hand, but a blanket, and right behind him were two other fellows, both of them with blankets at the ready. Good God, was it Augie and his cohorts again, believing they would succeed at trying the same thing again?

With no hesitation at all, Jason drew his derringer and shot the man in the arm. He yelled, fell back. "Ye foul young sot! Ye shot me! Why'd ye do that? I niver hurt ye, not really, even that first time."

Ah, so it was Augie and his crew, and he believed he was James. "Where is Georges Cadoudal?" Jason asked.

He kept his pistol pointed at the man in the greatcoat, who'd dropped the blanket to the ground and was holding his arm.

"I doesn't know no Cadoudal fellow."

"You're Augie, aren't you? And you two must be Billy and Ben. I trust you're all feeling better than the last time I saw you."

"No thanks to that little gal," said Augie.

"Not much of a repertoire you fellows have. All you know is blankets?"

"Ain't nothin' wrong with a blanket or two. We doesn't want to kill ye now, anymore than we did the first time. We jest wants to take ye fer a nice ride again, only ye goes and brings a gun wit' ye. That jest ain't fair."

"Just like you did to my brother."

"What brother? Ye is ye, ain't that obvious? What's this brother stuff?"

"You kidnapped my brother, Lord Hammersmith. I'm Jason Sherbrooke, we're identical twins, you fool. So the man who hired you didn't bother telling you that, did he? Not very competent of him. No, you two hold still." To make sure they believed he was serious, Jason drew the stiletto from its sheath along his forearm. "Nice and sharp, a birthday present from my father; he eased it out of a thief's sleeve in Spain. The first one of you who moves gets my stiletto right through the neck. Now, Augie, tell me. Did this so-called Douglas Sherbrooke hire you again?"

"I doesn't know what yer talking about, young 'un! Aw, ye hurt me bad, ye hurt me real bad. I jest think I'll send me two boys 'ere to pin back those ears of yers."

"If you do, I will shoot you again, this time, in what you call a brain. So send them over here, come on, you puking cowards."

But none of the three men moved an inch toward him. "Come on, Augie, tell me about Douglas Sherbrooke. He hired you again, didn't he? He had you set up the pie man, hired him to start talking about Georges Cadoudal. So we'd hear about it and come. This Douglas Sherbrooke—is he young? Old? What does he look like?"

"I ain't sayin' nothin', boyo."

"All right, then. Augie, let's see if you have any more to say when I take you to my brother and we both beat all the wages of sin out of that stupid head of yours. You will tell us what's going on here."

Suddenly, with a sharp whistle from Augie, the two men threw their blankets at him, then all of them simply faded back into that malodorous black alley.

Jason got the blankets sloughed off quickly, fired his second bullet, heard a yell. He listened, but couldn't hear anything more now. He trotted to the head of the alley and stopped. He wasn't about to go into that alley alone, he wasn't that big a fool.

Well, damn. He'd not done well.

Where was the man who sold kidney pies? Old 'orace? But Jason knew even before he found the man's body, one alley away, that they'd killed him before coming after him, cutting off a loose end. He turned to see Peter Marmot running up, late as usual, but with a smile so charming, you didn't long want to punch him in the nose.

Peter stared down at the dead man, stabbed cleanly through the heart, and cursed.

Jason told him about the three villains. "They're the same three men who kidnapped James. I'll wager that this so-called Douglas Sherbrooke sent them after me, only they believed I was James. I didn't manage to keep hold of them, damn me for an incompetent. This poor old fellow, they gave him a name to repeat until it came to our ears—Georges Cadoudal—then they killed him, because, I suppose, he could identify them."

Peter said, "Let's try to find some friends of the poor man, see if perhaps they know anything about Douglas Sherbrooke."

Jason said slowly, "The fact is, Peter, this Douglas Sherbrooke knows all about Georges Cadoudal, knows that my father is worried about him, and thus it's his name he uses to draw us out. He's got to be Cadoudal's son—but why is he after James in particular? Wouldn't I do as well if his motive was simply to draw out our father?"

But they didn't find anyone who would admit to knowing Horace until an urchin, with the help of a sovereign tossed to him from Jason, told them his name was Horace Blank, "'E made a fetching kidney pie, allus gave me one. I'll miss old 'orace. 'E lived ov'r in Bear Alley, up on the third floor, right under the eaves." And then he bit down on the sovereign, grinned as big as a full moon, and was gone.

They walked to Bear Alley, found Horace Blank's small lodgings beneath the eaves, and trudged up the narrow dark stairs and went into Horace's room. The small room was surprisingly clean, with a slatted bed, a small trunk at the bottom of it, and all along the far wall an oven, pans, and many ingredients he used to make his kidney pies. It smelled delicious.

"I never ate one of his pies," Peter said, and shook his head. "I really don't like this, Jason."

They parted company, Peter to gamble at a new gaming hall, owned by a friend of his, so Jason knew he wouldn't walk out of the place so poor he'd have to shoot himself, and Jason, to return home to change quickly into his evening garb, then off to Lady Radley's mansion, for a ball. To see Judith McCrae. James had told him about her visit to Corrie and the cinnamon bread farce. "Funnier than anything I've seen at Drury Lane," James said, and Jason wished he'd been there, to snag a slice for himself, maybe right out of Judith's mouth. Would she bite him? Now there was a lovely thought.

H E WAS GRINNING when he first saw her across the ballroom floor, dancing with young Tommy Barlett, so shy he was staring at Judith's neck. No, it wasn't Judith's neck that held Tommy's attention. Jason began making his way toward her, speaking to friends and enemies alike, politely nodding to his parents' friends as well, and smiling at the score of young ladies, and some not so young, who were giving him soulful looks that made him want to run in the opposite direction.

"Hello, Miss McCrae. Hello, Tommy. That is a lovely necklace, isn't it?"

Tommy Barlett, still breathing in Miss McCrae's lovely perfume, lust pounding through his young healthy veins, was slow to turn. "Is that you, James? No, it's you, Jason, isn't it?"

"Yes, I'm Jason."

"What necklace?"

"The one you've been staring at that Miss McCrae's wearing. Around her neck. Never once did you look away from that lovely necklace."

"Oh, I wasn't—that is, goodness, is that Mr. Taylor I see over there, beckoning to me? Thank you, Miss McCrae for the dance. Jason." And Tommy was off, nearly galloping across the ballroom.

"What was that all about?" Judith asked, as she stared after Tommy. "He acted like he was scared to death of you."

"He had good reason to be."

"Why? You didn't say anything to him. Come, Jason, what was that all about?"

Jason grinned down at her. "You smell good."

She came up on her tiptoes and sniffed his throat. "So do you."

He never knew what she would do next. It was sometimes unnerving, but more often, it was delightful, like now. She'd sniffed him. "Thank you. Tommy would probably have attacked you if I hadn't intervened."

"That shy young man? I doubt that very much. The dance was over. You didn't intervene in anything at all. What was that about my necklace? Did I tell you that it belonged to my mother?"

"No, you didn't. It's unique."

"So Tommy was admiring it. What, pray, is wrong with that?"

"Shy Tommy was staring at your breasts, not your necklace. He was sly, but I could tell."

"Oh," she said, blinking up at him. "I thought he was modest, dreadfully shy, not sly. Goodness, a budding young rake?"

"That's Tommy all right," Jason said. "I see people coming this way. Let's dance."

"The people you're referring to," Judith said as he

slipped his arm around her and danced her to the middle of the floor, "are all young ladies. After you. Unfortunately they're clutched together in a gaggle, not at all a good stratagem. Perhaps I could give them other approaches—to circle you, perhaps, or to form a wedge and force you into a corner where they would have their way with you. Lower that supercilious eyebrow. You know very well they're not coming to see if I know any new gossip or to compliment me on my necklace. Actually, I shouldn't want to be alone in a dark room with them."

"Nonsense," he said. He whirled her around and around until she was laughing, holding on for dear life, and her perfume smelled like—what? Not roses. He didn't know.

"Oh goodness, there's Juliette Lorimer frowning at me. She must think you're James. Can't she tell you apart?"

"Evidently not," Jason said, "even though my shoulders are so much broader than my brother's." He danced her through a throng of glittering gowns and jewels. *So much wealth,* she thought, *so many beautiful women.*

Jason slowed a moment and grinned down at her. "I have heard of your gluttony. I must say that initially I was appalled until James reminded me of the time he and I managed to steal an entire loaf of Twyley Grange cinnamon bread off a windowsill, reverently placed there to cool. James and I split the loaf, and wanted more."

"I could have eaten the entire loaf—unsliced—in under three minutes. I had a mere taste, only two slices. You should have seen Lord Montague—he actually hid the plate from me behind his back." And she started laughing. "What a wonderful gentleman he is. And so very handsome."

"He is going to be my brother's uncle-in-law. Amazing, that."

"So Corrie finally succumbed?"

Jason shrugged. "Evidently so. James is a good talker, he could convince a vicar to share the coins in his collection plate. Corrie wasn't a big challenge. She also says you're as pretty as Juliette Lorimer. I think you might be prettier. Thing is, unlike Juliette, you've got kindness in you, not to mention more wickedness than one would dream possible in a gently nurtured girl."

"Ah, and I have guile, Jason. Lots of guile."

"Not that I've ever seen. Indeed, sometimes I think you too candid, too open, what you feel is there for all to see on your face. Take care, Judith. The next time you accept a dance from a young gentleman who looks innocuous, look at his eyes. If they don't remain on your face, turn him down."

She laughed, actually laughed at what he'd said. She clutched her fingers into his coat, and laughed more.

He became alarmingly stiff. "I saw nothing funny in that advice."

"No, no, it's not that, Jason. While you said it, you were looking at my bosom."

"That's quite different," he said, and stopped because the music had ended, at least five seconds before. He lightly touched his fingertips to her cheek. "Lovely necklace," he said, and left her not two feet from her Aunt Arbuckle.

He heard her laughter float after him. He didn't dance with any other lady, merely thanked his hostess and took his leave. He wanted to tell James what had happened at Covent Garden.

They had to find Georges Cadoudal's son before he managed to get his hands on one of them.

CHAPTER TWENTY-SEVEN

"There is nothing more to be said, Northcliffe. I know nothing at all about any of this."

Douglas Sherbrooke nodded. "I know that, but the fact is, you knew Georges Cadoudal. You were in Paris when he died after Waterloo. Back in 1815?"

"Yes, of course. It isn't a secret."

Douglas looked down at the relic who was old enough to be his own father. A powerful man, was Lord Kennison, still, even though he was more fragile in his appearance than he'd been six months before. Because he loved his brandy too much, he had gout, and his right foot was resting, swathed in bandages, on a brocade hassock.

He had to make certain that Georges was dead, and Lord Kennison was his best bet. "How long had Georges been ill?"

Lord Kennison closed his eyes a moment. Even his eyes hurt. "Good God, Northcliffe, I thought you knew. Georges didn't die of an illness. Someone shot him down in the street. An assassination, no other word for it. He died perhaps two hours later, in his own bed. I arrived after he'd expired, his family around him. Of course, Georges was quite mad."

"Yes, I know." Mad and a genius, was Georges. "He had family, did he not, my lord?"

"Yes, certainly. A son and a daughter. The son is about the age of your boys. I understand you knew his wife, before they were married."

Janine, he thought, *who'd pretended I had impregnated her because she'd been too ashamed to admit to her lover, Georges, that many men had raped her.* He nodded. "Yes, I knew her. I never saw her again though, not after 1803. It was a very long time ago, my lord."

"Poor Janine, she died of the influenza before Georges was killed. Georges's sister-in-law came to live with them, kept the house. You ask me, Douglas, I'd say that she was a little bit more fond of Georges than a sister-in-law should be. But no matter. They were both past their first youth. And now Georges is long dead. You didn't shoot him, did you, Northcliffe?"

Douglas was staring thoughtfully into the fireplace, watching the flame lick around a new log, burrowing in to catch fire. He shook his head, still looking into the flames. "I quite liked Georges, but maybe he never believed that. I can imagine someone shooting him because, from everything I heard over the years before Waterloo, he never ceased in his attempts to assassinate Napoleon. So many men would have liked to cut his life short, and evidently someone did." He did look up now. "It wasn't me. I was at home, with my two ten-year-old sons and my wife. I had nothing more to do with politics by then."

"Ah, but a couple of years before, you were in France."

"Yes, but that was a rescue mission, nothing more than that. Nothing nefarious. I didn't see Georges."

"Whom did you rescue?"

Douglas shrugged. "The Conte de Lac. He died five years ago, at his home in Sussex."

"Could anyone have believed you were there to kill Georges?"

"No, that's quite impossible. It also makes no sense. If someone believed that I was responsible for Georges's death, why would they wait fifteen years for revenge?"

Lord Kennison shrugged. It even hurt to shrug, and wasn't that too much to kick a man while he was down? "I'm tired, Douglas. I can tell you nothing more than you already know. The children, as you've already decided, must be behind these attempts on your life. As for Georges, he never said anything about you, at least not in my hearing. I don't believe there was any enmity there. You remember Georges—if he hated someone, he hated all the way down to his soul. He wouldn't shut up about how he was going to pull out their tongues. So if it is a child's revenge, then where did they get this hatred for you?"

"I don't know. As you said, it makes no sense." Douglas rose. "Thank you for seeing me, sir. As you know, it was the duke of Wellington who sent me to you."

"Yes, he told me. Poor Arthur. So many problems clutching him around his throat. I told him to quit, to leave all the mess, and let others deal with it. He wouldn't ever do that, of course."

"No, he wouldn't," Douglas said, and took his leave. He rather liked Lord Kennison, who was probably a lot more honorable than his heir, who was so debauched he'd given his wife the pox.

When he walked out to his carriage, it was to see both Willicombe and his nephew Remie standing there, guns at the ready.

THREE DAYS LATER
SHERBROOKE TOWN HOUSE

James and Jason stepped into the drawing room to see Corrie and Judith seated close on the large sofa, their heads together.

"Good morning, ladies," James said as they walked into the room. "Willicombe said you were working on wedding plans." *Whose wedding plans?* he wondered, sneaking a look at his brother, who, in turn was staring at Judith Mc-Crae, a look on his face James had never seen before.

Corrie looked up at him, had decided during the long previous night to give it up, jumped to her feet, and flew to James, grabbed him to her, and hugged him tight. He grunted with the enthusiasm of her greeting. She looked up at him, lightly touched her fingertips to his chin. "No more whispering. I'll say it out loud for the world to hear. James, I've decided to marry you, decided that maybe it won't be so bad at all. I know most of your bad habits already. If you've more, you'd best not tell me because it might tip the scales the other way."

"I don't have any more," James said, and heard Jason snicker behind him.

"At least none that would make you break things off."

"I will speak to Jason about this later."

"Corrie, I do appreciate you coming right out with your consent, but the fact is I've already spoken to your uncle. Everything is in motion."

"Yes, I know, but I didn't want you to think I was a pathetic, gutless female who didn't know her own mind."

"I haven't ever thought you were gutless. Pathetic—not for at least a couple of months now." He saw she would question him and shook his head.

"All right, I'll wait. I just wish that Jason had managed to catch Augie, Ben, and Billy. Just imagine Augie thinking it was you again—and using the same blanket trick again. Did he think you stupid?"

"Probably so," Jason said, and found himself staring at his brother, and his soon-to-be sister-in-law. Imagine, Corrie Tybourne-Barrett, a sister-in-law.

James found that his arms went around his betrothed very naturally. Well, he'd hugged her since she was three years old, that wasn't so unusual. She felt good against him. He closed his eyes a moment and breathed her in. He was used to her scent, would have known it was her in a dark room, but now there was a light overlay of jasmine. "Your perfume?" he said against her hair. "I like it."

"Your mother gave it to me, said your Aunt Sophie swore by it, claimed it worked on your Uncle Ryder from fifty feet. She claimed he always came running, like a hound after the fox."

"Ah. I think I could chase you down. When I caught you, I wonder what I would do to you? Sniff you, I suppose, to make sure you're the right fox, but then? Hmmm. There's always the back of your knees.

"Now, you should probably release me, Corrie. There are two other people in the room and all this affection might give them a headache."

She leaned back in his arms to look up at him. "A headache? Why on earth would seeing me clutching you like the last slice of cinnamon bread give anyone a headache?"

"Jealousy," he said, and without thought, he kissed the tip of her nose. He set her away from him. "Willicombe," he said to the three occupants in the room, two of them paying not a whit of attention, "is bringing tea. Jason? Judith? Listen to me now. Tea is coming."

Corrie heard a giggle and peered around James to see Judith McCrae throwing pencils at Jason.

"Whatever did he say to invite the attack, Judith? Good shot, right in the chest. Pencils could be dangerous, I suppose, so you'd best be careful."

Judith, holding a final pencil between her fingers, ready

to dart it at Jason, turned, grinning. "This fellow, standing here all straight and tall, looking more dangerous than a kilted Highlander, tells me that it is hazardous for me not to wear a necklace. Without it, a man doesn't have any justification."

Corrie was on the point of asking what that meant when Willicombe entered, looking in each corner of the drawing room, as was his habit, before clearing his throat and saying, "Cook has prepared some nutty buns. She apologizes that they aren't the Twyley Grange cinnamon bread, but the men she hired to steal the recipe ended up being bribed and gorging themselves on the real item and falling into a swoon." He beamed at them. "A room of young people who are looking at each other with such affection. Such a tepid word, *affection*. Perhaps it is more along the line of fondness and warmth, at least I hope it is more, since two of you are now being fitted for leg irons," and Willicombe raised a questioning brow at Jason, who picked a pencil up off the floor and hurled it at him.

"Leg irons," James muttered. "I begin to believe Willicombe as much a misogynist as Petrie." Corrie poured tea and Judith passed out the nutty buns. James said, "Our grandmother adores these nutty buns. Oh dear, Corrie, you will have to gird your loins; she's nasty, she will malign you, given no encouragement at all, but you know that, she's gone at you often enough. But now that you'll be one of the family—it doesn't bear thinking about how she will treat you."

Judith stopped chewing her bun. "Your grandmother will be unkind to Corrie? How very odd. Why ever for?"

Jason laughed. "You don't know our grandmother, Judith. She dislikes every female who's ever had the misfortune to swim into her pond, including our mother, including her own daughter, including Corrie, who is, I understand, an abomination or something of the sort."

Corrie shuddered. James patted her hand, and said, his voice thoughtful and low, "I've been thinking that maybe we should live in a lovely house I own in Kent."

"Where did you get a house in Kent?"

"It's one of father's lesser houses, one built by the first Viscount Hammersmith."

She took a bite of her nutty bun and licked her lips. "Where is it?"

"Near the village of Lindley Dale, right on the Elsey River."

She finished off her bun, licked her lips again, this time James watching her tongue, wanting suddenly to lick her. Her throat, her left elbow, her belly—he had to get hold of himself.

She said, "Does it have a name?"

"Yes. Primrose House. It's not big and grand like Northcliffe Hall, but it would be ours, hopefully for a very long time since I don't wish to see either my father or my mother depart this earth until the next century."

Corrie simply couldn't imagine living with this man. Living with him at Primrose House. Just the two of them. Goodness, she was used to living with Aunt Maybella and Uncle Simon.

Living with James? She thought of her last kiss and his tongue in her mouth, licked her lips again, met his eyes, and flushed to her hairline.

"I believe," James said slowly, his eyes on her mouth, "that I want to know exactly what you're thinking."

At that moment, Willicombe ran into the room. "My lord, Master Jason, come quickly! Quickly!"

Corrie beat all of them out of the drawing room. She ran through the open front door, stopped short on the top step, and stared.

There was her soon-to-be father-in-law standing over an unconscious man wrapped in a huge black cloak, rubbing his fist, Remie standing near, his right foot planted on the back of another man, this one burly and unkempt, who was moaning and twitching.

Douglas looked up and grinned. He rubbed his fist again and said, "That was fun."

James and Jason ran to their father and Remie, and stared down at the two men. James said, "Who are these men, sir? Do you know them?"

"Oh no," Douglas said cheerfully. "Remie spotted them lurking across the square."

"Aye," said Remie. "His lordship decided we'd let them come to us, which they did, the bloody fools. Your father thinks we'll have a nice chat when the bastards get their brains working again." He kicked the man, who moaned again, shuddered, then didn't move.

Douglas leaned down and hauled the man he'd flattened to his feet. He slapped his face, once, twice, shook him. "Come on, open your eyes and look me in the face." He shook him again.

There was a sudden blur of movement. Without thought, Jason knocked Remie out of the way, kicked out with his foot and knocked the gun out of the man's hand who'd just come around a bush, that gun aimed at the earl. He grabbed the man's hair, lifted his head, and sent his fist into his jaw.

He looked up at his father. "He came very fast. That makes three of them now. James, are these three the same men who kidnapped you?"

James shook his head. "I've never seen these three before."

The man Douglas still had about the neck said in a whine that made Corrie want to kick him, "We ain't meant nothin', milord, jess wanted to snag a couple of groats."

Remie said as he dusted off his livery, "I think I would like to speak to these two, my lord, maybe open up their heads a little, see what falls out."

"We'll both do it, Remie."

A boy's voice said from behind Judith, "I seen 'em, milord, speaking to a cove, er, man, over on the other side of the square. A big man, wot was, er, were wearing a hat and a greatcoat."

James turned to Freddie, whose English had improved within the past week, although he'd heard the boy muttering that "wot were wrong wi' the way I speaks anyways," when he'd been informed that he was going to be educated. It was Willicombe who taught Freddie two hours a day.

"Well done, Freddie. Let's you and I go over to where you spotted this man and see if we can find any clues."

"Lawks," said Freddie, and patted his trousers, straightened his sleeve, presented James a proud pose in his beautiful new livery. "Let's be off then, my lord. We'll find somethin', er, something."

"Yes, hurry, both of you," the earl said. "Now, I think these two fine specimens should spend some time in our stable, if you don't think they'll upset the horses."

Remie and Jason bore the men off, and Douglas went in to write a note to Lord Gray, a gentleman he knew in Bow Street.

As for Corrie and Judith, they watched Jason and Remie haul the three men away. "This," Judith said quietly, "isn't what I planned to see when I came to visit."

"No," Corrie said. "Do you know, Judith, maybe you and I should spend some time with these fellows as well."

"You mean if the gentlemen don't glean any information from them?"

"Exactly." And Corrie cracked her knuckles, something she hadn't done since she was ten years old.

Judith laughed, shaded her eyes with her hand, and said, "I wonder if James and Freddie will find anything. Who is that boy, Corrie? Isn't he a bit young to be employed by the earl?"

"Freddie is very special," Corrie said. "Very special indeed. Did you hear how much better he speaks?"

"You're teaching him to speak proper English?"

"Actually, it's Willicombe," Corrie said. "I daresay that the earl would do about anything for Freddie." She smiled at Judith. "We can come back this afternoon, perhaps have our own little talk with those two villains." And that was what Corrie told the earl just ten minutes later. "My lord, I think you should reconsider calling in Bow Street. Let me go question these men. I know I can convince them to talk to me."

Judith nodded, eyes narrowed, nearly growling. "I should like to pry their mouths open as well, my lord."

Douglas looked at the two young ladies, whom, he suspected, had as much guts as his wife, and said slowly, "Perhaps this note to Lord Gray can wait for a while. Yes, let us try to break them first."

Willicombe, however, was dead set against this. Indeed, he stood in the entrance hall, six feet from the front door, so pale he looked dead.

He was breathing so fast, Corrie was afraid he would faint. She stepped up to him and slapped him hard.

"Ah, oh goodness, a hit in the chops by a young lady." Willicombe said on a moan. "But since the aforementioned young lady rescued one of our boys, I suppose that—" He stopped, drew a deep steadying breath, and said, "Thank you, Miss Corrie. I think I shall have a nutty bun if there is one left."

And he tottered off.

CHAPTER TWENTY-EIGHT

"HE RAN LIKE a young man," James said to his father, Freddie nodding vigorously at his right elbow.

"A young man," Douglas repeated. "Yet again he comes, this son of Georges Cadoudal." He looked at his son. "Why, James? Why?"

"When we get him, we will find out. Everyone is looking for him, Father. It won't be long now." James pointed across the park. "He hurled himself into a hackney and the driver whipped the horses up, fast. We had no chance to catch him."

"Well, we have three of his men. I've decided that we'll let Corrie and Judith speak to them tomorrow." He smiled at James's look of utter horror. "The young ladies claim they will make the villains tell us all. But now, let's try our hand at breaking them."

James rubbed his hands together. "Let's do it. Freddie, go fetch Master Jason, tell him we're going to have a chat with our villains."

Douglas said, "If none of us has any luck, I will send off my note to Lord Gray. He can send one of his men here to take them away. At least they won't be of any further use to Georges's son."

Two hours later, Douglas had to admit defeat. The men were being paid extremely well to keep their mouths seamed. *Indeed, it was more than money,* James thought, since he'd offered them five hundred pounds and been refused. There was real fear in their eyes. They simply said over and over that they didn't know nothin', that they'd just wanted to snag the rich bloke's purse, no, no, they didn't know any cove what called hisself Douglas Sherbrooke—a young man? No, they knew no young men. And on and on it went until Douglas called a halt. James and Jason wanted to bash their heads together, but Douglas allowed that he didn't want two dead men buried in his stables. He would turn them over to Bow Street, let Lord Gray's men bust heads and bury them in gaol.

All three men were depressed, but were forced to smile because Alexandra had invited Lady Arbuckle and Judith as well as Lord and Lady Montague and Corrie to dine with them that evening. Her reason, she admitted to her husband, after he'd nibbled on her neck, forgetting for a good long while that he was supposed to be fastening her ruby necklace, was to see the two young ladies with her sons.

"I want to observe how they treat each other, how they behave with their relatives, and with us."

"You've known Simon, Maybella, and Corrie forever. You know how they relate to us."

"Ah, but don't you see, Douglas? I don't know how they'll deal with Lady Arbuckle and Judith McCrae, and that's important. Also, I want to see if I like Judith. I've never before seen Jason so drawn to a young lady. Maybe she's rotten to the core, maybe she wants him for his looks, maybe she has a terrible sense of humor."

Douglas shook his head, patted her cheek, looked down at her breasts, swallowed a bit, and turned to straighten the cravat that his valet had pronounced perfect ten minutes before. He said over his shoulder, "Poor James. He had no chance to see if there was a young lady out there to win his heart. Now he'll never know."

Alexandra looked at her husband's broad back, watched his nimble fingers twitch his cravat this way and that. "You had to take me on, if you will remember, Douglas. You had no chance to find the love of your life either."

"Ah, there is that, isn't there?" He brought her against him, pressed up her chin with the lightest touch of his fingers. "We turned out all right, didn't we, Alex, what with you wanting to make love to me whenever you would pull me behind a door or clear off a table or—"

"How very odd, my lord," she said, her fingertips stroking his jaw, "I seem to remember that it was you who couldn't keep your hands off my fair person. Now, I must say that you didn't see James stick his tongue down Corrie's throat. He looked utterly absorbed, Douglas."

"Down her throat? Now, that's something that a gentleman much enjoys. Naturally he enjoyed it. What man wouldn't? But there's Juliette Lorimer and—"

"No," Alexandra said firmly. "Were James to prefer her, I would travel to Scotland and move into Vere Castle with Sinjun and Colin. I think Juliette might be tolerable until she realized that James got more admiring looks than she did. And her mother—oh dear—"

Douglas laughed, hugged her, careful not to disarrange her lovely hair, as he lightly bit her earlobe. "It was Juliette's mother who alarmed me as well, truth be told. All right, let's see how our respective young ladies behave toward their elders. Corrie and Judith, two lovely names.

"Ah, it was you, Alex, you, who were always after me, always lurking around corners, waiting to nab me and—"

She gave him a comfortable fist in the belly.

Truth be told, the young ladies behaved splendidly, but the fact was that all conversation was centered around the person out to kill Douglas.

"A madman," Simon said as soon as he'd swallowed the bite of vermicelli soup. "A very nervy madman. Did you say you think he's young? Well, young madmen are the nerviest, but that doesn't mean they're frothing at the mouth. You know that, Douglas."

Douglas, looking down at his own soup, said, "I know, Simon. Also, this young madman is very probably the son of Georges Cadoudal. For whatever reason—be it mad or not—he is committed to killing me. Is he truly mad? I wonder."

Maybella, who was eyeing Lady Arbuckle's emerald bracelet with a bit of envy in her heart, said, "Georges Cadoudal's son. His father died when he was only ten years old. That means he's festered with hate for fifteen years. How very odd it sounds, and frightening."

"I agree with you, Aunt," Corrie said and took a spoonful of *codfish au gratin* from the footman's proffered dish. "There was also a daughter. We haven't yet been able to find out about either son or daughter."

"It's evil, evil," said Maybella.

Neither twin spoke.

Lady Arbuckle finally cleared her throat, looked at Judith, and announced, "I believe it is all nonsense. There is no revenge at work here. I am convinced it is some foul Frenchman from a secret French society bent on destroying the very fabric of English society. Killing one of the premier noblemen of the realm, it is their opening salvo." That announcement made, Lady Arbuckle returned to her *fillet of whiting a la maitre d'hotel*. She drew a deep breath, and for an instant, she closed her eyes, her fingers clutched around her knife.

Corrie said, leaning toward her, "Are you all right, my lady?"

"What? Oh, yes, Miss Tybourne-Barrett. The whiting is perhaps a bit too rich for me, that's all."

Judith lightly patted Lady Arbuckle's hand. "I myself find it a little rich, Aunt. Why don't you try some fricasseed chicken? I have found it quite tasty."

Lady Arbuckle accepted the chicken and nodded as she chewed a small bite. "Yes," she said, "it's an excellent fricassee. Thank you, my dear."

James said, "It's a pity that Lord Arbuckle must remain in Cornwall, ma'am."

"Ah," said Judith, waving her fork, "my uncle adores being close to the Irish Sea. He is happiest when he is breathing in that salty air, feeling the sea winds ruffle his hair. Besides, the estate needs constant attention. He will not hear of another seeing to his responsibilities."

Douglas, who didn't know Lord Arbuckle well at all, was frankly tired of all the talk of his assassin, and was eager to learn more about this girl who might become part of his family. "I understand you come from Waterford."

She nodded, giving him a dimpled smile that Douglas found charming. "Yes, my family raises Arabians. It is a fine country for horses, you know, and Waterford is an excellent area."

"Who is there now?" James asked. "Jason told me that your father and mother were dead."

"My cousin Halsey manages things now. In any case, Halsey was next in line when my father died. The farm is called The Coombes and Halsey is Baron Coombes."

Jason picked up her fingers and squeezed them. "Judith has been alone too much of her short life, but Lord and Lady Arbuckle are seeing to her nicely."

"Yes, they are," Judith said, and leaned over to kiss Lady Arbuckle's powdered cheek. "My very first season. I never thought it could happen, but my dearest aunt—" She broke off, tears sheening her dark eyes.

Jason squeezed her hand again, then launched off on

one of his favorite topics—horses. He wanted to visit The Coombes, see the farm's operation, examine the stock.

The conversation continued to James and Corrie's wedding, which was to take place at St. Paul's in three weeks' time. Douglas shrugged. "I know the Bishop of London, Sir Norton Graves, a fine man who officiated at your christenings. He gave me a cocked eyebrow when I informed him that time wasn't in great abundance, and thus I had no choice but to tell him exactly why your marriage was on the prompt side. It turns out, naturally, that he'd heard most of what had happened already, albeit slanted in a far more scandalous direction. Sir Norton has many ears in society, and to his credit, he rarely believes what he hears. James asked that he officiate, and he agreed."

Corrie choked on an oyster patty. James immediately slapped her back.

"Are you all right?"

"Oh yes. It's just to have your father speak about our getting married in such a matter-of-fact way—sometimes I still can't believe it's going to happen. Good heavens, in only three weeks. It closed off my throat there for a moment."

James said, "It closes off my throat too. Don't dwell on it. We'll get through it. Now, I know you wanted a thousand people at least to overflow St. Paul's, all of them cheering and waving you on your way, but Corrie, it's not to be."

"Perhaps five hundred?"

James laughed, and his mother said, "Maybella and I believe that it is best if we have about thirty people to witness our drama."

James said, "I will ask several members of the Astrological Society to come. I wish you to meet them. Ah, perhaps you would care to come to a meeting with me, next Wednesday?"

"And I will show them you are getting the perfect wife. I will myself write and present a paper," Corrie said, and looked so wicked Jason nearly spewed a mouthful of wine on his mother's tablecloth.

"Yes," James said, his voice serious as his Uncle Tysen's when he was looking sin right in the face, "I think you should. I have already written about the cascade phenomenon. What should you like to present to the learned group?"

Corrie gave this some thought while she observed the roast goose on her plate. She picked up a roll, waved it at James, and said, "I want to speak about how vampires can come out only at night under bright moonlight, but not in the day when the sun beats down. That is, it beats down only occasionally here in England, which makes me wonder if English vampires have more freedom of movement than do, say, vampires from the Sahara Desert."

James rolled his eyes. "No more about Devlin Monroe. I saw him hanging about you yesterday. What did he want?"

"He tried to convince me that he would make a superior husband to you."

James, who took the bait swiftly, nearly leapt to his feet. "That damned bounder. That's more than enough, that's—"

"That was a jest," Corrie said and gave him one of her patented sneers that he hadn't seen since before she'd come to London.

Amidst the laughter, Alexandra led the ladies out of the dining room, leaving the gentlemen to their port.

"She got me," James said, red-faced, staring into his glass of port.

"Yes, she's quite good at it," his brother agreed, "has been for years." He sighed. "Unfortunately, I believe that Judith is as skilled as Corrie. She too could bait a dead man, make him leap up, curse, and rattle his bones."

"Yes, I've seen her do it," James said. "I do wonder what Devlin Monroe is up to, though."

"Nothing," said Simon. "Nothing at all. I myself spoke to him, told him Corrie had been in love with you, James, since she was three years old, to which Devlin replied that Corrie was too unripe in the ways of men and the world to know what was what, that she was too young to be forced into this marriage, that you were taking gross advantage of her, and that I should challenge you to a duel and shoot you. I thought for a moment that the poor boy would burst into tears. But then he got himself together and said it was a lovely overcast day, didn't I agree. Of course I agreed. Nearly every day is overcast. I didn't want anymore of his melodrama. I wanted him to leave. Is he really a vampire, do you think?"

Corrie had been in love with him since she was three? A child adoring an older brother, yes, he could see that, but was this how her uncle saw it? She loved him? As a man?

At that moment, the gentlemen looked up at the sound of running feet, raised voices.

Corrie threw open the dining room door and yelled, "Quickly! James, oh dear, come quickly!"

CHAPTER TWENTY-NINE

❧

WHEN THEY BURST into the stable it was to see that the three villains were gone, Remie was unconscious beside the door, and three stable lads were bound and gagged in the tack room.

The horses were distressed—neighing, tails swishing, shuffling about in their stalls.

James dropped to his knees to feel for Remie's pulse. It wasn't strong, but at least it was steady, and he was coming around.

Judith said, her voice high—too high—shaking a bit, "Corrie wanted to come out and question them the moment we left you. She knew you, my lord, would go all stiff and proper on us and deny us our chance. She didn't want to put it off until tomorrow, and so we told your mother that we needed to go to the ladies' withdrawing room, but instead we came out here and they're gone, escaped, and that means someone helped them."

Jason said, "Yes, that young man who was standing across

the square. He must have circled back, seen his men taken into the stables, observed the routine, then made his move."

"He succeeded," Douglas said, rising and dusting off his hands on his breeches. "Damn him. I will call for a doctor for Remie and send off a note to Lord Gray."

As it turned out, neither Remie nor the stable lads had seen who had assaulted them. Remie said he'd heard something, but then he'd been struck on his head and that left him on his nose in the straw.

Lord Gray, when he was drinking a brandy in the Sherbrooke drawing room late that evening, allowed he'd heard about the attempts on Douglas's life, told him he was now involved and would find the men responsible. "Since you have determined who the man is, why then, I will myself search him out," he said comfortably, tossed back his brandy, kissed Alexandra's lovely white hand, and took his leave.

No one believed him, even though they wanted to.

THREE WEEKS LATER

All seventy guests—forty more than originally intended—cheered wildly when James and Corrie, Viscount and Viscountess Hammersmith, came out of St. Paul's, and ran, hand in hand, toward the open landau, festooned with every white flower Alexandra Sherbrooke could locate in greater London. It was, to everyone's surprise, not a frigid, overcast day as all expected, but a cool, crisp, sunny day, unheard of for the end of October in England.

"It is because I am beloved in the celestial realms," Corrie had said.

James had laughed. "Ha, it's because those celestial realms are mightily relieved that I've saved you from being a fallen woman."

Corrie also confided in her new mother-in-law that she'd promised up good works for twelve months if God would send down sunshine on their heads.

"What good works will you do?" Alexandra asked.

Corrie looked perfectly blank. "Do you know, I didn't believe it would work at all, so I have no idea. I was expecting rain and thick fog up to my knees. This will require thought. I don't wish God to believe that I wasn't serious."

Jason was saying to Judith, "All is forgiven and soon to be forgotten. Corrie saves his life, and now they're married. Rules are sometimes the very devil."

"I think they're perfect for each other," Judith said. She moved a bit closer, came up on her tiptoes, and whispered in his ear, "Corrie told me that James gave her only one hint about what would happen on their wedding night."

Jason didn't so much as twitch. "And what would that be?"

"He was going to kiss the backs of her knees."

Jason laughed, couldn't help himself. And Judith, demure as a nun, looked up at him through her dark lashes and said, "You mean that he's lied to her? This isn't what he's planning?"

"Oh, I'm sure he'll tend to her knees," Jason said.

"And then I wonder what he plans."

"You are too young, my child, to even have a clue about what comes after knees." And he patted her cheek. "Or before knees, for that matter." As his fingers touched her face, Jason, in that moment, knew it was all over for him. The wickedness in those dark eyes, the softness of her skin, the way he felt punched in the belly whenever she was near, it fair to knotted his innards, knocked the breath out of his lungs. He realized his throat had closed, cleared it, and said, leaning close to her ear, "If he has any sense at all, he'll begin with her right knee. The right knee is more sensitive, you know."

"Oh goodness, I had no idea. Is that really true, Jason? On every female? The right knee?"

"I have proved it many times."

"Very well then. I will not forget that. Now, if James

were you and Corrie were me, I think I'd kiss each finger of his right hand and then lick each finger, very slowly."

Jason's breath caught in his throat. He was getting harder than the stone steps of St. Paul's. He pulled his eyes away from her, and shouted, "Don't let anyone kidnap him, Corrie, or you'll have to marry him again!"

She heard him above all the shouts and cheers and well wishes, turned, and waved, her laughter filling the air.

James pulled her against him and kissed her soundly, much to everyone's enjoyment. The landau rolled forward. As the afternoon progressed, all in society who hadn't been fortunate to receive a wedding invitation would hear about how the young couple were very pleased with each other, which was a good thing since they were tied together for life.

As for Jason, he patted Judith's cheek, and walked away, whistling. She stared after him. He baffled her.

Three hours later, after miles of observing countless farms, rolling hills, gentle stretches of forests, picturesque villages, and several great houses, they were at last nearing the village of Thirley sitting in the heart of Wessex. Not much longer now, and James planned to have her in bed not more than five minutes after that.

The day had grown colder, and there was wind now, making the carriage windows rattle, but James didn't care. And soon after they'd changed from the open landau to the carriage, it had become overcast, perhaps perfect for Devlin Monroe, curse him. James wanted to get Corrie up to a bedchamber, strip her to her skin, and begin an orgy of enjoyment.

By all that was holy, he was married. To the brat. It still boggled his brain when it hit him, made him blink to keep from crossing his eyes. The brat was his wife, and he could still see her—a three-year-old with sticky fingers, pulling on his pant leg to get his attention. Then she was a snaggletoothed six-year-old offering him a strawberry jam-covered muffin, a huge smile on that small mouth. And now she was sitting next to him, seemingly content to look at the passing landscape, her hands folded demurely in her lap. She was his bloody wife. A tress of hair had come loose and was hanging over her shoulder, escaped from her very pretty bonnet. Lovely hair, and that hank of hair was lazily pointing down to her breast. He wanted to touch that breast, wanted to caress her with his fingers, with his mouth. He began to ferment in lust.

The brat was his wife.

"Corrie."

She didn't turn. "Yes, James?"

"Not more than fifteen more minutes. I booked us the largest room in the *Gossamer Duck* in Thirley. My Aunt Mary Rose says it's fresh and clean, and the bed in the big corner room that overlooks the town square is so soft it makes you swoon."

"Oh dear."

"It's all right. We're married now. We can talk about soft beds and no one will be shocked."

"I know. All of this—it's rather alarming. I'm eighteen, supposed to be innocent for at least another year, but just look at what has befallen me. I'm riding next to a man who wants to rip my clothes off and do things to me about which I do have some ideas about since I was raised in the country and have eyes in my head."

"What has befallen you is going to be fun. Listen, I'm going to help you sow your wild oats. We're going to sow those oats together until you're exhausted and tell me you're glad we're together because no other man could sow nearly as well as I do, particularly Devlin Monroe."

She whirled around to face him. "That made not one whit of sense, James Sherbrooke. A girl sows wild oats with gentlemen precisely like Devlin Monroe, gentlemen she knows are wicked, not gentlemen who are honorable and too kind for their own good."

She saw him like that? He said slowly, "You think I'm honorable, Corrie?"

"Of course you are, you idiot. We're married, aren't we?"

"You don't think Devlin would have married you if you'd rescued him from kidnappers?"

That brought a thoughtful look. "Do you know I'm not really certain. I think Devlin finds me amusing, you're right about that. However, I don't think he would like to face me every morning across the breakfast table, even assuming that he's able to sit across from a breakfast table, even if curtains were drawn against the morning sun."

"You think I'm kind?"

"Of course you're bloody kind."

"I don't like the way that settles in my guts. It makes me sound like a perfect weak-kneed sot. Like Sir Galahad, who couldn't hold his sword properly and was always bungling about."

She laughed, the little witch actually laughed. "I've seen your knees, James. They're not weak, they're as nice as the rest of you. As for not holding your sword properly, I remember very clearly how you and Jason were fighting with swords in the forest so your father wouldn't catch you, and you forced him back into a bog. Sir Galahad was a wonderful knight, it's his name you don't like."

"Weak-kneed sod. On the other hand, Jason once knocked me off the cliff over Poe Valley."

"I'll wager you landed with your sword still in hand."

He laughed. "I did, as a matter of fact, nearly sliced myself in the belly."

"Well, I will say that a woman likes a man to hold his sword properly."

He stared at her. Surely she didn't know what she'd

said, even though she was raised in the country and had eyes in her head.

"Now, I am bidding a fond farewell to my wild oats. My heart isn't broken, not really, since I am determined to make do with you since there is no choice in the matter.

"I asked Aunt Maybella to tell me exactly what was going to happen other than having you kiss the backs of my knees. I wanted all the fine details. Do you know what she said?"

The coach hit a rut and he grabbed the strap to keep himself upright. "No, what did Aunt Maybella say?"

"She screeched, 'Knees? He wants to kiss your knees?' And she went on to tell me that this was something a gentleman told a girl so as not to send her running. I told her that was fine, I understood, but then exactly what were you going to do? After the knees? She said you'd begin shaking. I didn't believe her but I see I was wrong. You are shaking, James, I can see it. She said that means you're overwhelmed with lust, a good thing, she said it was, but she knew you were a gentleman, and even if you were too young to mind your manners, you were very fond of me and would, therefore, not attack me in the carriage. She smiled then and said hopefully she was wrong."

He was mesmerized. "Did she tell you what she smiled about?"

"She was smiling about lust, and she was thinking about lust with Uncle Simon. Can you imagine that? I cannot bear to think of Uncle Simon kissing Aunt Maybella's knees, James. Parents aren't supposed to do things like that."

"Maybe, maybe not. My own parents, well never mind that. Come, Corrie, what did she say then?"

"Nothing. Do you hear me, James? She wouldn't tell me anything. She rolled her eyes and told me to be agreeable to whatever you wanted—unless I found it so repellent that I feared for my modesty—and all would be well. I wanted to clout her, James, and then you know what she did? She started humming."

"She didn't mention that I was going to try to be agreeable to whatever you wanted as well, unless of course I found it repellent and feared for my own modesty?"

"You have no modesty."

"Anything else from Aunt Maybella?"

"Well, no. She did pat my hand before she left my bedchamber, and said that were she I, she would be content to look at you not wearing a stitch of clothes, and agree to whatever you wanted. Being a very observant girl, I'm inclined to agree with her."

James gulped. Aunt Maybella looking at him and he was naked? He didn't want to think about that. He said, "I had a chat with my father as well."

That floored her, as he'd hoped it would, and James tried not to laugh, when she said, "What? You mean you don't know what's going to happen either, James?"

"I have sort of an idea, Corrie. My father drew me some pictures, said to study them closely as he didn't want me to muck it up."

She ran her tongue over her lower lip, making it all damp and shiny, and he wanted to drag her down to the floor of the carriage, and he wanted his tongue on her bottom lip, making it shinier, wetter, and then—

"Er, do you happen to have the pictures with you?"

He stared at her, unable to believe what came out of her mouth, and then he threw back his head and laughed and laughed.

She was tapping her fingers, leaning toward him, all impatient. "Well, James, do you?"

He looked into her eyes, eyes lovelier than he'd believed them to be an hour before, and wasn't that odd? "No, I memorized them, then burned them, like my father told me to. He didn't want Jason to see them yet, you know, wanted to preserve his innocence until he was ready to get himself wedded."

"Hmmm." Tap, tap, tap, went her fingers. "Perhaps you could re-create them. Do you have any paper? A pencil?"

He slowly shook his head. "Corrie, why are you worrying about this? You already know what's going to happen and so do I. Now, kiss me, before I shake myself right out of the carriage."

And so she did, and it was close.

"Ah, thank God, we're coming into Thirley."

CHAPTER THIRTY

JAMES SAT BACK in his chair, his fingers against his chin, and tried not to laugh as he watched his wife of not many hours at all trying to play the courtesan. He didn't know who was having more fun, Corrie or him. He realized she'd been planning this, and he wondered how far she'd go. All the way to her white skin? He hoped so. He hoped so mightily.

He'd dreamed of having her naked within five minutes of arriving at the *Gossamer Duck*, but it wasn't to be. The innkeeper, Mr. Tuttle, was voluble in his greetings and insisted that his missus serve them some delightful tea and scones.

When at last he'd gotten her into the large, corner bed-chamber, the door locked, she'd told him to sit down and not move.

As he watched her twirl her pelisse around on her finger and send it sailing toward a far chair, he realized that even when she'd begun sneering at him some three years before, mocking him whenever he came close, he'd enjoyed himself. She'd never bored him. He remembered spanking her, feeling the softness, feeling a spurt of lust that had made him feel guilty, because, after all, she was Corrie, just Corrie, the brat.

She pulled off her gloves and tossed them after the pelisse.

James forced himself to sit back in his chair, his chin propped on his steepled fingers, legs stretched out, crossed at the ankles, and said, "Women wear too many clothes, Corrie. You should have begun your seduction when you were wearing only your chemise. What do you say I help you get to that stage?" He was praying that she'd say yes. He was in bad shape, didn't know, in fact, how much longer he could last. He was going to shake himself right out of his chair and wouldn't that be humiliating? He really didn't want to jump her, but it was going to be close. He had to hold himself steady.

He rose slowly, unable to sit there any longer, and stretched, and Corrie, all sense of wicked adventure whisked instantly out the shadowed window, stood there, her hands over her breasts, and looked horrified. What she saw on his face was something she'd never seen before. He looked close to violence; he looked determined; he looked to be in pain.

James wasn't a clod. He'd hoped she would leave her girl's modesty at the door, and he admitted that she'd tried, and thus her order to him to sit himself down and not move and she was going to entice him beyond endurance.

Well, he was beyond endurance right now and she'd only gotten rid of her pelisse and gloves.

He had to get a grip on himself. His father had told him that it was best to begin as you meant to go on, and that advice clearly translated to not mauling his wife on their wedding night. And then he'd frowned, shaken his head, and when James wanted to ask him what was wrong, he said only, "Life is a powerful and surprising thing. Unexpected things happen. Enjoy it, James."

"Why do you have your hands over your breasts and you've still got your clothes on?"

She licked her lower lip again and James stared at that lower lip. He was breathing hard, his sex harder than his breathing; he prayed she wouldn't see the wild urgency in him, he didn't want to scare her witless. Damn, that lower lip of hers . . .

"Stop looking at me like that, James."

Like what? Like he wanted to lick every inch of her? He hated being that obvious, but just couldn't help it. "All right."

"I'm covering myself because you're not lying on the floor, unconscious, moaning with fever, helpless. You're strong now, James, you're quite yourself again, and you want to do things to me that I've only seen animals do. It makes me feel quite strange."

"Strange how?"

"Well, perhaps I could walk the three steps to you and kiss you. What do you think?"

"Do it."

She hesitated only a moment, then walked the three steps, coming to within an inch of him, and raised her chin. She stood on her tiptoes, pursed her lips, and closed her eyes. She kissed his chin.

"Try again."

She opened her eyes, looking into his beloved face, a face so beautiful as to make a grown woman cry, and smiled. "Helen of Troy was nothing compared to you."

"Blessed hell, I hope not."

"You know what I mean." She kissed him on his mouth this time, but hers was seamed tight.

James raised his hand, only one hand, and lightly touched his fingertips to her mouth. "Open up, a little bit," and his breath feathered her skin. She opened her mouth without hesitation and felt his warm breath on her flesh, tasted him, and it was wonderful.

"Ah, that's good," he whispered into her mouth, and Corrie wondered how kissing the back of her right knee could be better than this. The feel of his mouth, his tongue, the heat of him, it made her want to fling herself against him and send them both to the floor.

Or to the bed. She walked into him, backing him up, until she shoved, and he went down on his back in the middle of that marvelous goose-down mattress.

She came down over him, laughing, wanting to sing and moan at the same time, so happy she was kissing him all over his face.

He kissed her back; his hand slid down her back over her bottom and stayed there. This was no spanking. This was something else entirely different. Corrie reared up and stared down at him. "Oh dear, James, your hand—"

"Clothes," he said, "too many clothes." He reared up, setting her on her feet in front of him. "I'm in a bad way here, Corrie. Now, I'm going to strip you down to your beautiful hide," and he wasn't civilized about it at all. He ripped and pulled and tore, and his breathing was harsh and fast.

Well, it wasn't the lovely lace wedding gown, she thought, and grinned. If he could do it, then so could she. She began ripping open his clothes, kissing his chest when she pulled off his shirt. Soon, both of them were naked, she, still standing in front of him, James, sitting on the bed, his hands about her waist, and her breasts weren't more than three measly inches from his mouth. He stared, swallowed, thought he'd burst. "Your breasts—I knew they would be nice, but I hadn't expected this." He sounded like he was choking. She didn't move, couldn't move. Corrie stood there, her hands on his shoulders as he raised his hands and cupped her breasts. He closed his eyes, breathed in very deeply, pulling her scent into the depths of him. Because his eyes were closed, she took the splendid opportunity to look down at him.

He wasn't at all like he'd been when he'd been ill. He was big and growing bigger. All because he was holding her breasts? She liked his hands on her, but staring down at him, watching him swell—"James, you're not the way you were."

He wanted to fling her on her back, this very instant. Her breasts—he wanted his mouth on her, he—"What? What way was I?"

"Oh goodness, not like this. This can't be right."

He realized through his cloud of lust that she was looking down. He in turn stared at himself. He was hard and big, ready to explode. What did she expect? Oh hell, she didn't expect anything. "You saw me naked, Corrie, when I was ill."

She swallowed. "Not like this, James. Never like this. This isn't like any of the animals I've seen."

"I'm not a horse, Corrie, I'm a man and you've got to know we'll fit together." Oh God, he wanted to weep, perhaps even howl, but most of all, he didn't want to have to say another word, he wanted to come inside her, deep, deeper still until he touched her womb. He groaned; she jumped.

"Oh dear, James, what's wrong with you?"

It was enough; it was too much.

"It's lust, isn't it?" she whispered, eyes alight with appalled excitement.

"Yes." He grabbed her around her waist, lifted her and tossed her onto her back. He came down over her, fitting himself between her legs. The touch of her, the scent of her flesh, the sound of her breathing, harsh and loud, it pushed him right to the edge and shoved him over.

He knew in some small corner of his brain that he was a clod; his father would disown him if he ever found out.

But it didn't matter, couldn't matter. There was only the here, the now, and the two of them, and he wanted her more than he'd ever wanted anything in his life. He raised her legs, looked at her soft flesh, lightly touched her, and that was all it took. He was shuddering so violently he knew he was going to spill his seed, right here, and he knew that couldn't happen, just couldn't, or he'd have to throw himself off the cliff into Poe Valley.

He parted her with his fingers, didn't think about any consequences at all, and came into her. Oh God, she was tight; nowhere near ready for him, but it didn't matter. He couldn't have stopped himself if someone had dumped buckets of cold water on him. He went into her, hard, felt her maidenhead. He closed his eyes at the knowledge that he was the first and that he would be the last. He looked down at her white face, her eyes filled with tears, and he said, "Corrie, you're mine. Never forget that, never—oh damn, forgive me—" and he pushed through her maidenhead, kept pushing until he touched her womb, and then it was all over for him. He reared back, yelled to the ceiling of the bedchamber, then stared, frozen, down at her, and collapsed heavily on top of her. He managed to kiss her ear.

He was dead, or very nearly, and who cared? He felt wonderful. He felt whole. He no longer felt the surge of lust that had driven him mad; he felt complete, his world was perfect, and he was very sleepy. Hit to his soul, he was. He kissed her cheek, tasted the salt of her tears, and he wondered only an instant about that, and fell asleep, his head beside hers, dead weight on top of her.

Corrie didn't move, wasn't about to move. He was still inside her, and she was content to lie there absorbing the feelings, letting the pain ease away from her, feeling his sweat drying on her body, feeling the smooth pumping of his heart against hers, feeling the hair on his chest against her breasts. He'd touched her breasts, touched between her legs—looked at her—and come into her like he was going to ram through a door.

He gave a light trilling snore. He was asleep? How

could he be asleep? She didn't want to sleep. She wanted to pace the bedchamber, perhaps stagger a bit because she hurt, deep inside, but it was fading quickly now. Her tears were drying and itching her flesh, and he was heavy on top of her, and he felt wonderful, big and solid, perfect, truth be told, and he was hers.

He was also still inside her, but not so much now. She was naked, James was naked, and he was snoring lightly in her left ear, and what was one to think about that?

The room was cooling down. She tried to move, but couldn't. Should she wake him up and ask him to pull himself out of her, perhaps cover himself before he went back to snoring?

No. She managed to pull the counterpane over both of them. That was better. It was nearly dark, the light dull and gray as it filtered through the window curtains.

She clasped her fingers together at the middle of his back, lightly squeezed. Her husband, this man who was once the boy who'd tossed her into the air when she was a little mite of a thing, and he'd tossed her one too many times and she'd vomited on him. She didn't remember doing that, but her Aunt Maybella would laugh even today when she remembered it. "James," Aunt Maybella said, "didn't pick you up again for at least a year."

And she remembered very clearly when he'd explained her woman's monthly flow to her when she was thirteen and he barely twenty, a young man, but he'd done it, and he'd done it well. She realized now that he'd been embarrassed, had probably wanted to run, but he hadn't. He'd taken her hand, and he'd been kind, matter-of-fact, then told her the cramping in her belly would go away soon. And it had. She'd trusted James more than anyone in her life. Of course, he and Jason were gone much of the time, to Oxford, then young men turned loose on London. He'd been so very grown-up when he'd been home, and that's when she'd learned how to sneer.

Corrie sighed deeply, tightened her hold around his back, realized that he wasn't inside her any longer, and fell asleep herself, his breath warm and sweet in her ear.

J AMES WANTED TO shoot himself. He couldn't believe what he'd done.

And now Corrie was gone. She'd left him, probably returned to London to tell his father and mother that their precious son had first ravished her and then fallen asleep on top of her, not a sweet or comforting word out of his mouth before his head had hit the pillow.

He rose, shivered because no one had come to light the fire in the grate, thank God, and saw that her valise was in the corner. He felt immense relief. She hadn't left him.

There was a knock on the door. "Milord?"

"Yes?" He looked around for his own valise.

"It's Elsie, milord, here with hot water for yer bath. Her ladyship said ye'd be wanting it."

Five minutes later, James sat in the large copper tub, hot water lapping at his chest, his eyes closed, wondering what the devil he was going to say to his wife of, what was it? Oh yes, his wife of approximately six hours. She'd sent up hot water for him. What did that mean?

At least she hadn't left him.

The hot water sank all the way through him, and he let himself sink deeper until he was nearly asleep again.

"I had no idea that this marriage business would require you to sleep for a week to recuperate. How do men accomplish anything at all, if—" She stalled.

He didn't open his eyes. "Thank you for sending up the water. It's nice and hot, as I like it."

"You're welcome. You're looking quite lovely in that tub, James, all sprawled out, just hints of what's under that water."

He cocked open an eye at that. Corrie was gowned in a

lovely green wool, her hair was up in a knot on her head, but her face was pale, too pale. "I'm sorry I hurt you, Corrie. I'm sorry that I rushed you. How do you feel?"

She flushed. She'd thought she was beyond that, believed nothing could make her tongue-tied or embarrassed, not after what he'd done to her, but here she was flushing like a—a what? She didn't know; she felt like a fool, and somehow a failure. "I'm quite all right, James."

"Would you wash my back, Corrie?"

Wash a man's back? "All right. Where's the sponge?"

"Here's a cloth." He brought it up from the depths of the water. Where had that cloth been? She swallowed, took the cloth, and was relieved to move behind him.

That long stretch of back, the muscles well-defined, smooth, and she wanted to throw that wretched cloth across the room and smooth soap over his back with her hands, feel him, let her fingers learn him.

She rubbed soap on the cloth and went at it.

He sighed, leaning more forward.

"Do you want me to wash your hair?"

"No, that's all right. I'll do it. Thank you. That was wonderful."

He held out his hand and she dropped the wet cloth into it. Then he started washing himself.

"Men have no modesty."

"Well, if you wish to watch, there's little I can do to stop you."

"You're right," she said, sighed, and went to sit in a chair across the room. She sighed again, stood up, and pushed the chair much closer, not more than three feet away from him in his tub. James grinned, went underwater, and then washed his hair.

He knew she was watching him and that felt good, actually. Surely she must like him, surely she'd forgive him if he asked her just right.

"It won't be like that again, Corrie."

"Rinse the soap out of your hair."

He went underwater again, then came up, and shook his head. Dear God, he was so unutterably beautiful, it hurt.

"I promise you it won't. I am very sorry about your first time. It was ill-done of me."

"It was rather fast, James, rather rough, truth be told. You didn't kiss my knees."

He gave her a lopsided grin. "I swear I'll take excellent care of your knees next time. Do you still hurt? Did you bleed?"

Frank speaking indeed, she thought, and shook her head, staring down at the toes of her slippers.

"I thought you'd left me."

That brought her head up. "Leave you? That never occurred to me. You and I have been through many adventures together, James. I consider this one more, not a pleasant one, but—"

James rose. What could he say to that? "Could you hand me that towel?"

She simply couldn't move, couldn't look away from him, standing there naked and wet, and she wanted to lick every drop of water off him. She gulped, tried to get hold of herself, and threw him the towel. Then she watched him dry himself. How could one gain such pleasure from so mundane a thing?

He knotted the towel at his waist. "When you take your bath later, do allow me to wash your back."

The thought of that nearly sent Corrie whimpering to the floor. "All right," she said, and then slapped her hand over her mouth.

James laughed. "Allow me to dress and we can eat our dinner."

It was over dinner that James, seeing that Corrie was staring into her soup, said, "Please don't fret, Corrie. We'll get everything right, trust me."

"Oh, no, it's not that, James. I was thinking about my new father-in-law. I can't help but be worried."

"I know," James said, and took a bite of cold mutton. "Jason is going to do everything but sleep in Father's bed to keep him safe. Also, there are more men than you can imagine trying to trace the Cadoudal children. All we know so far is that they're no longer in France, haven't been in quite some time."

"And there was their aunt, you know, their mother's sister. I wonder what happened to her." She was stirring her fork through the applesauce beside her pork kniver.

"I still have trouble believing it's Georges Cadoudal's son, since he and my father parted friends."

"You said that your father rescued Janine Cadoudal. Surely she couldn't have hated him, couldn't have taught her children to hate him. He saved her."

"Yes, and evidently she offered herself to him. But father was coming back to a new bride, namely my mother, and so he refused. When she discovered she was pregnant, she told Cadoudal that my father had forced her, and the child was his."

"Oh dear, I can see that such a story would make Cadoudal furious."

"Yes. Cadoudal kidnapped my mother, as revenge, took her to France, and when my father and Uncle Tony found her, she was miscarrying a babe. In any case, Janine confessed the truth to Georges, Father and Mother returned to England, and that was the last time he ever saw Cadoudal."

"So she had a child."

"My father said he heard something about the child dying, then there was nothing more."

"I've always loved mysteries," she said, her fork set on her plate now, as she leaned forward toward him, her chin resting on her clasped hands, "but I don't like one that could hurt my new family. We'll figure it out, James. We must find the son."

"Yes."

"James, you're looking at me again."

"Well, yes, you're my dinner companion."

"No, you're looking dangerous and determined. You were wearing the same look before you ripped my clothes off." She lowered her voice, leaned over the remains of her pork kniver. "It's lust, isn't it?"

Slowly, James rose, tossed his napkin on the table, and held out his hand. "How do you feel?"

"Full and—"

"Corrie, between your legs, are you still sore?"

She picked up an apple, polished it on her sleeve, took a tiny bite, then smiled at him. "I think," she said, "that I'm ready for my bath. You said you would wash my back for me."

He nearly shook and shuddered himself out of the small private parlor.

CHAPTER THIRTY-ONE

❧

JASON LOOKED INTO Judith McCrae's dark eyes, felt himself fill with an odd mix of contentment and an excitement so powerful he wondered how a man could bear it. "Your eyes are darker than mine, at least at this moment."

"Perhaps," she whispered.

"My brother was just wed."

"Yes."

"I remember looking up—was it the Ranleagh ball?— and there you were, staring at me all the while waving that fan, and my heart fell into my shoes."

She drew back, but her hands still clutched at his arms. "Really? Is your heart still there? In your shoes?"

He grinned down at her. "My heart even collapses into my boots when I wear them."

"I am nearly twenty. Did you know that, Jason?"

"You do not look your age."

A giggle escaped.

"Does this mean you're near to the back of the shelf?"

"Your wit—well, I never thought of it like that, you know, being unacceptable to a gentleman because I was no longer as young as say, Corrie. I never considered that I would move in London society. The thought of going to London with the express reason of finding a husband, it simply never occurred to me. But then Aunt Arbuckle swooped into my life, brought me here, and introduced me to everyone."

"Why didn't you assume your aunt would introduce you into society?"

"There were fallings out, I guess you could call them, amongst everyone in my family. But no longer, thank God. I will tell you something, Jason. I was rather bored, I admit it, until I saw you—yes, it was the Ranleagh ball. I'm not an heiress like Corrie."

"Why would that matter to me?"

"Well, you are a second son, Jason, no matter that you were born minutes after James."

"I'm rich," he said abruptly. "My legacy from my grandfather will keep me from penury. I can support a wife. I am thinking of breeding horses, Judith. It is something that suits me; unlike estate management, which suits James quite well. When the gods were casting the die, everything seems to have sorted out properly."

"You mean you don't mind being the second son? You don't mind not being the future earl of Northcliffe?"

"Blessed hell, of course not. You said you never considered coming to London to find a husband. Well, I never considered being the earl of Northcliffe. My brother will make a fine earl when his time comes. And I, well, I will be myself and surely that is not too bad. Had you expected some burning sort of resentment on my part?"

"Perhaps. It seems to me that it would be natural to resent not having what he will have."

He grinned down at her. "I would heartily detest dealing

with all the problems my brother will have to handle as a matter of course. We've some tenants who make the vicar curse. No, I'm free to be what I wish and free to do what I wish. I am a very lucky man."

He paused a moment, looked down at his boots, perhaps to see if his heart were there, and said, "I have been giving this a lot of thought, and I believe I should like to visit Ireland, go to The Coombes, to see your cousin's operation. Is he a welcoming fellow, your cousin?"

"Ah, I'm certain he would much enjoy having you."

"Good. Ah, there is also the Rothermere stud in Yorkshire. The Hawksburys live there. Their eldest son is my age. Perhaps you would like to see a stud?"

"Perhaps," she said, and her fingers tightened about his arms. "I might even prefer traveling to Rothermere above visiting my cousin. Rothermere is new to me, you see, and thus of more interest. You are very strong, Jason. I've observed that in you."

"My mother likes to tell James and me that the moment we could stand, we wanted to pick each other up. When I was three, I managed to hoist James over my head for perhaps one second. My mother, as I remember, applauded, which, naturally, didn't make James happy at all. I don't remember this, but my mother says that he stomped a toy wooden block on my foot he was so mad. I had a very fine childhood. Did you, Judith?"

Was there a flash of pain in her fine eyes? He couldn't be sure. He wanted to ask her, but he sensed, deep inside himself, that she would back away from him if he tried to probe. She was an exciting mixture of shy and wicked, reticent and confident, combinations that drove him mad even while his heart speeded up. He realized too that he wanted to hold her close, tell her that he would care for her until the day he died, but he said nothing. He wasn't yet certain what was in her mind. He wasn't a patient man, but he knew to his bones that with her, patience wasn't a lame virtue, it was a necessity. He wondered at it, but accepted it, just as he was prepared to accept her, her shyness and her wickedness, and anything else she could dish up.

"My childhood was fine indeed, Jason. There were some bad times, of course, as there must be in life. Happiness comes and then it goes, as does unhappiness."

He said, lightly touching his fingertip to her chin, "Are you happy now, Judith? Now that you've met me?" She shrugged, began to fiddle with his cravat, and fell silent. He felt pain, at a girl's seeming rejection? He'd simply never encountered such feelings before. Could he have been mistaken in her? No, that wasn't possible, surely. She seemed inordinately fascinated by his cravat. He said nothing, waited.

Finally, she raised her face to his. "Am I happier now that I've met you? It's odd, you know. When there is someone who is important, you forget that there was ever another life. You live from one burst of happiness to the next. Of course in between, there is uncertainty and plain misery, for you don't know what the other is thinking, feeling."

She'd spoken eloquently, he thought, and she was right. With her—and he admitted she was important to him—he'd felt more than his share of misery. And uncertainty, such uncertainty. "Perhaps in the future, bursts of happiness will overtake all other feelings. A not-too-distant future, if you please, since I am close to expiring with anxiety."

"Perhaps." And he saw the wickedness in her eyes, hot and wild, and he wished he had her naked beneath him right at that instant. "Do I make you happy, Jason?"

He said nothing at all, looked at her mouth, her small ears with the pearl drop earrings dangling. She punched him in the arm. He laughed. "So you are expiring with anxiety? I'm glad you see my point now. Yes, Judith, you have made me happy."

"Can you tell me what your parents think of me?"

She cared about him, there was absolutely no doubt at all in his mind. He wanted to ask her to marry him, right this second, but something held him back. She wasn't ready for that, he knew it to his boots. It had happened too quickly, he was reeling, his guts twisting and roiling about, so how must she be feeling? She was young and innocent, despite her nearly twenty years. Since he wasn't stupid, he said easily, "My parents are very fond of you, just as I am. Can you doubt it?"

"I haven't met many people who would be pleased to welcome a stranger."

"That is a pity. Perhaps you would like to spend more time with them before we continue on this path to more happiness for you?"

"I don't know," she said. "Perhaps."

"They know you well enough right now, Judith. They believe you quite clever; my father even said you were charming. I raised an eyebrow at that, but he said, yes, it was true. You'd charmed him, he said, and then he remarked that you were as bright as a new penny."

He saw clearly that she liked the sound of that, but she had to pick and prod and doubt herself. "But they don't really know me, not like they know Corrie. She's already like a daughter to them."

"That's true, naturally, since she's been in and out of Northcliffe Hall since she was three years old. She's been a sister to me for year upon year. I do hope, however, that James doesn't think of her as a sister; I can't imagine anything more hellish than that. Now, my parents are returning to Northcliffe Hall on Friday. My father is satisfied that all inquiries are moving ahead and he is no longer needed here. I am accompanying them, naturally, with Remie and three other runners Lord Gray recommended to guard my father. Perhaps you and Lady Arbuckle would like to come with us? For a nice long visit? Would your aunt like that, do you think?"

"I must speak to her." She looked up at him through her lashes and said, "I believe, though, that she wants me to marry an earl."

He laughed, couldn't help himself. "Like my father, you have charmed me as well. You're as wicked as any man could wish, Judith. Hmmm, wouldn't your aunt prefer the scion of a duke? Like Devlin Monroe, Corrie's vampire?"

"So now I am old and wicked, both at the same time."

"Yes, and I am immensely grateful for it."

"I wonder, should I like Devlin? Possibly, but he saw Corrie and it was all over for him."

"Even the mention of his name drives my brother wild with jealousy, though he doesn't realize yet that it's jealousy he's feeling and not repellent thoughts about fangs coming out of Devlin's gums beneath the light of the moon." Jason leaned down and kissed her, couldn't stop himself. She was a lady, dammit, but he didn't want to give her a peck on the cheek. No, he wanted a deep, wet kiss, his tongue in her mouth, and that is what he did. She was shy, her lips closed, and he felt her jerk in surprise when his mouth touched hers.

Was he the first man to kiss her? Obviously he was. She didn't know what to do. Dammit, no tongue in her mouth as yet. The thought that he would be the man to teach her everything made him want to sing to the dimpled plaster cherubs that adorned the corners of the ceiling in the Arbuckle drawing room. When he forced himself to step back, he said, "I will write to your cousin at The Coombes. Perhaps he would like to see me sooner rather than later, since it seems that you and I might be drawing closer."

"This drawing closer business—Jason, I am only recently arrived in town. What about that earl who surely must be waiting in the wings somewhere, just waiting to pop out onto my stage, doubtless reciting lovely verses to my eyebrows—"

He kissed her again, a light kiss on the tip of her nose,

and left her, whistling. She stood there in the middle of Lady Arbuckle's drawing room and listened to his boots striding solid across the marble entryway, heard murmured voices, then the opening and closing of the front door. Then there remained nothing but the soft silence of the early afternoon, soft drizzling rain pattering lightly against the windows. Did it always rain in England? Well, truth be told, it rained more in Ireland. She was alone. It seemed to her in that moment that she had been alone most of her life. She wondered what would happen. He had very nearly asked her to marry him, hadn't he? She hugged herself. She knew it, felt it deep within her, and wondered at it. He'd all but asked her.

J ASON ASKED HER for the exact direction of The Coombes that evening at a musicale at Lord Baldwin's spacious town house on Berkeley Square. Judith gave it to him, and said, voice as demure as a nun's, "I am considering visiting Italy whilst you arc in Ireland with my cousin, studying his breeding methods, eyeing his horses, and attending races."

Jason felt a sock of lust that nearly knocked him over; he knew he was getting hard, just standing there, for God's sake, just looking at her.

He said in that easy voice of his, "I understand that Venice is lovely in the fall. Not too cold as yet, the winds still calm over the canal. My brother and I visited Venice some three years ago. And yes, both of us got drunk enough one night to fall into the canal."

"I think perhaps I should prefer Florence. There are so many splendid artists working there. No drunken young gentlemen to disturb me."

"There are drunken young gentlemen everywhere in the world to disturb you, don't fool yourself."

She giggled, shaking her head at him. "When you visit

The Coombes, you will be attending the races with men who will surely try to fleece you."

Jason said, stroking his chin, "I might do some fleecing of my own. Now, I'm not at all certain about Florence. All those splendid artists died out centuries ago. Unfortunately, I fear their thousands of paintings, all of the Madonna and Child, will endure forever. We will never be free of them."

She was hiccupping she was trying so hard not to laugh. He patted her cheek, and left her, saying only over his shoulder in that offhand way of his that he was meeting with some friends.

She called out, serious now, "You mean there might be some information about your father?"

He only shrugged and left her again, this time without turning back.

Judith watched him until he was gone from the immense ballroom. She turned when Lady Arbuckle said, "He hasn't asked you to marry him, has he?"

Judith said slowly, "No, not yet. He is very beautiful, don't you think?"

Lady Arbuckle said matter-of-factly, "All consider the Sherbrooke twins to be the most handsome men in England. They will probably only grow more so as they get older, just as their Aunt Melissande has. She's at least forty-five now, surely past any excuse for beauty, but it just isn't so. Young men still swoon when she passes them on the street or see her across a room. The twins will be no different, for they are cast in her image, an odd thing, but there it is. Their parents have never been pleased about this miscarriage of heredity."

"And one of these perfect young gentlemen will propose to me. That is quite remarkable, isn't it?"

Lady Arbuckle started to turn away, then stopped, searched Judith's face, and said, "I have heard that the younger son, the one who you believe will propose to you, is not as constant as his brother, Lord Hammersmith. I have seen it myself. Jason Sherbrooke sees a young lady who pleases him—as you have pleased him, Judith—and he devotes himself to her entirely, for a short while—and then he is gone. Will he actually propose marriage? I don't know, but I must doubt it. I suggest you take great care, Judith. He is a wild young man, more honorable than most, perhaps, but I was told that he keeps a mistress on Mount Street."

"I did not know that," Judith said slowly. "I wonder what she looks like?"

"I daresay it isn't appropriate for you to know that. I daresay that you shouldn't even admit to knowing what a mistress is." Lady Arbuckle paused a moment, studied her face. "However, I doubt she has your looks or your charm."

"I hope that is true."

"I wonder," said Lady Arbuckle slowly. "I wonder what will happen. I wish to leave soon, Judith. That soprano from Rome made my eardrums ache. I wish to write my husband, to see if he is well."

"I am sure he is just fine. I'm ready, Aunt. Jason said that he was going to meet friends. I wonder if instead he was going to Mount Street to visit his mistress?"

"I would guess the mistress."

"Do you think he wanted me so much he had to go to her?"

Lady Arbuckle laughed. "I don't think a man ever needs stimulation in order to visit a mistress."

CHAPTER THIRTY-TWO

JAMES FELL ONTO his back, mouth open, trying to suck breath back into his body. Beside him lay his new wife, who, if he was not mistaken, was smiling like a fool even as she yawned.

When he could finally speak again, he said, catching up her hand in his, "The backs of your knees excited me infinitely."

"Ha!"

He grinned up at the ceiling. "Very well, you wish me to be truthful here." He turned on his side and looked down at her. Her hair was tangled and wild around her head, her face glowing, her body languid, so soft he wanted to begin kissing her ears and work his way down to her heels. "I'll skip the prelude. To kiss your belly, that was rather fine, Corrie."

She moistened her mouth with her tongue. She was embarrassed at his frank speaking, he saw it, and was charmed. "And kissing you and caressing you with my mouth, between those lovely long legs of yours—"

She came up against him and bit his shoulder. "You will not embarrass me, James Sherbrooke, do you hear me? You won't speak anymore of kissing my belly or touching me all over and kissing me all over until I nearly shook myself out of my skin."

He laughed, pulled her tight against him. "I pleased you."

She bit his shoulder again, then licked it. The taste of him excited her, made her feel soft and compliant, and perhaps that wasn't all that good a thing, but for the moment, pressed naked against him, she would accept it. She whispered against his warm flesh, "How do you know you pleased me, James? Perhaps I am still waiting to be pleased, still anxious and afraid that there is really nothing pleasant at all with this sex business."

He nibbled on her ear, got a mouthful of her hair, and, without saying a word, moved his hand down her back until he was spreading his fingers across her hips. She waited, wanting, wanting, but too embarrassed to ask him to—then those magic fingers of his curved inward, and when they touched her, eased inside her, she sucked in her breath, wrapped her arms around his neck, and kissed him.

"Damn," he said into her mouth, "it's a good thing I am a young man. You nearly killed me, and now you want me to pleasure you again, five minutes later."

"Five minutes? That long?" He looked into her eyes as his fingers found her. When her eyes went wild and his fingers sent her into her orgasm, he took those lovely cries into his mouth.

He came into her, hard and deep, his eyes nearly rolling back in his head. She was nearly squeezing the breath out of him she was clutching his back so tightly, and when she whispered against his neck, "James, I would kill for you," he was gone. He wondered in those incredible moments, if he would ever slow down with her. Or she with him.

He doubted it, he thought later, doubted the feelings he had for her that made him instantly hard, the feelings that were growing almost faster than he could accept, and wasn't that a fine thing? It was James who pulled the covers over them.

He fell asleep, her soft mouth whispering kisses all over his face. Had he known what she was thinking, sleep would have been the last thing on his mind.

NORTHCLIFFE HALL

Douglas Sherbrooke looked meditatively at the thin slices of ham on his luncheon plate, so thin he could see his fork through them. "I wonder what our eldest son is doing at this moment."

Alexandra pretended confusion, which made him laugh. "You mean right now? When he and Corrie should be consuming food in the inn parlor since it is time for luncheon? He is your son, Douglas; both of us know exactly what is going on at this exact moment."

"Perhaps he is sleeping. A man must restock himself."

She cleared her throat. "He is only twenty-five. I doubt much restocking is necessary. Whatever he is doing, there is no food involved." She rolled her eyes. "I'm his mother; it's difficult, but I suppose I must accept it."

Her husband grinned at her. "You believe our Jason is still a virgin?"

He felt peas hit his face. He began to pick them up and put them on his plate.

She said, resting her chin on her clasped hands, "I happened to catch Jason after his first encounter with a girl."

That caught her husband's attention. "How is that possible? I've always told them never to let their mother, well, as to that they were under strict orders—"

"I know what you told them. I know everything, Douglas, never forget that. Jason was unlucky. I happened to be walking out of the tack room in the stable when he nearly ran me down. He gave me this sloppy grin, realized who I was, and turned beet-red and started stuttering. And I said, 'Jason, what is wrong with you?' even though I well knew what had happened up in the hayloft. Our boy gulped once, twice, then said, 'It was the most wonderful thing in my life!' Then he looked perfectly horrified at what he'd blurted out to his mother, and ran away. Oh dear, Douglas, he was fourteen."

Douglas, wisely, didn't say a single thing.

Alexandra sighed, tucked down two more bites of ham, and said, "It's a blessing James doesn't consider Corrie a sister. That would be disastrous."

"My lord!"

Douglas was on his feet in an instant. "What is it, Ollie?"

Ollie Trunk, a grizzled veteran on the never-ending search for bad men, a successful Bow Street Runner for twenty-two years, stood in the doorway, ducked his head in deference to an earl, then said, "I jest got a message from Lord Gray, my lord. He says one of his boys caught up with this young man wot was trying to hire a couple of toughs to come after ye, my lord, no doubt about that."

"You caught the young man?"

"Well, as to that, he got away, fast and sly he was, but Lord Gray's boys managed to nab the two toughs and dragged them in to see Lord Gray so's he could rattle their brains, which he did, and they told him it was ye the young feller we were after, and he were offering buckets of groats to help him kill ye." Ollie paused, then frowned, a habit of such long-standing that his brow seemed furrowed through and through. "Lord Gray says he believes yer right. This is revenge, my lord. Revenge, through and through, and this young 'un ain't going to stop until we stops him. Lord Gray is sending two more lads from London to help us keep ye safe. Northcliffe is a mighty big place, even bigger than Ravensworth, so's we gots to find scores of hidey holes."

Alexandra said as she slowly rose, "Thank you, Ollie. Lord Gray wrote nothing else?"

Ollie Trunk blushed. "Actually, my lady, the note is fer his lordship here. I was jest so—"

"I appreciate your attention," Douglas said, and held out his hand. Ollie gave him a twisted-up piece of paper. "Do you wish two more men, Ollie?"

"Yes, my lord. We'll nab this man, this son of Georges Cadoudal. Aye, it's revenge. That can make a young man's blood hot." And with that, Ollie nodded, blushed again when he looked at Alexandra, and backed out of the dining room.

"But why," Douglas said slowly, "is the young man's blood hot?"

At that moment Hollis sailed through the door, cleared his throat, and said, "Some years ago, the earl of Ravensworth used Mr. Ollie Trunk's services. All worked out well."

"I wonder what trouble Burke had," Alex said. "So you approve of him, Hollis?"

"As to that, my lord, we will see. The proof of his abilities will be obvious to all, in due course."

That was for certain, Douglas thought, aware of the small derringer in his jacket pocket. Then he looked at his butler, really looked.

Hollis glowed, no other word for it. He was standing so straight, Douglas thought he must have gained at least three inches of his younger height back. "May I inquire as to your progress with your lady, Hollis?"

"She is very near to the sticking point, my lord. I dare say that another day or two in my company will have her yelling yes."

Alexandra said, "I can't imagine why she wouldn't be singing hallelujahs at the thought of being your wife, Hollis. You are magnificent, any woman would bless her stars to marry you."

"Just so, my lady, just so. As you may remember, Annabelle knew my precious Miss Plimpton. Her present hesitation is because she is concerned that my feelings for Miss Plimpton may still be too strong."

"Good God, Hollis," Douglas said. "Miss Plimpton has been dead these forty years!"

"Forty-two years and six and one months, my lord."

Alexandra said, "That is surely enough time to cleanse out all residual feelings you cherished for Miss Plimpton."

"That's as may be, my lady," Hollis said. "But Annabelle frets. She wants my heart whole."

"And will she have your heart whole, Hollis?" Alex asked.

"As you said, my lady, forty years have passed. I have told Annabelle that an old heart has more free space in it than a young heart, more room to take into itself the most profound of feelings and sentiments."

"When will we meet her, Hollis?"

"She, my lord, has consented to have tea with you and your ladyship this very afternoon. Actually, I am here to inform you of this felicitous news. Ollie's news was perhaps a bit more important, so I allowed him to precede me."

"Er, that is quite splendid, Hollis. Have Cook make her lemon seed cakes."

"It is done, my lord. Annabelle will be here at precisely four o'clock. I, myself, will fetch her from that lovely quaint village of Abington, where she has resided now for nearly four months."

"Abington is a charming village," Alex said. "Does Miss Trelawny have relatives there, Hollis?"

"It is Mrs. Trelawny, my lady. Annabelle has been widowed for many years now. She's all alone, but her husband left her a neat competence so she is quite comfortable. I, naturally, will make her more comfortable than she is now."

"Why did she select Abington to live?" Douglas asked. "It is lovely, to be sure, but not the center of anything I can think of."

"I much enjoy Abington myself, my lord, indeed I have spent a good deal of time there over the years, going through the church records. They extend well back into the thirteenth century, if you can believe that. It turns out, my lord, that Annabelle also admires the church, and indeed, that is how I met her, walking to the rectory."

Douglas nodded, thinking of the sheaf of ancient church records he'd bought from Noddington Abbey, and given to Hollis years before.

Douglas rose when the door closed on Hollis. "I must speak to Mother." He sighed. "I do not believe it would do Hollis's prospects any good if she is present to meet Mrs. Trelawny."

Alex said, "No, she would likely have Hollis's lady running from the Hall, shrieking or crying. She is so remarkably healthy. It quite makes one shudder."

He laughed, walked past her, only to turn and lift her up in his arms and swing her around. She was laughing down at him, his face nearly in her bosom, when the door opened and a familiar sour voice said, "Unseemly! Disgraceful! Why haven't you taught this girl how to behave, Douglas? You have been married to her more years than I can bear to count, and still she is poking herself out and encouraging you to wildness."

"Hello, Mother."

"Hello, Mother-in-law."

"I have decided to have my luncheon in here. You will both sit down since I have matters of grave concern to discuss with you."

Douglas said from his impressive height, still holding his wife in his arms, "Do forgive us, Mother, but Alex and I have very important matters to attend to. We will visit with you at dinner."

"No! Wait, it's my maid, the slovenly creature, she isn't—"

They missed the last, thank God. The two servants who saw the earl and countess dash from the dining room, laughing like children, cutting off the dowager's moldy voice, would have cheered, if Hollis wouldn't have berated them endlessly for such behavior.

"Miserable old besom," Tilda, the downstairs maid, whispered to Ellie behind her hand. "She'll live forever, my ma told me, said her meanness keeps her healthy. She said she wouldn't doubt if she kept a flask filled with rum in her bedchamber."

"I'll ask that poor maid of hers," said Ellie. "Rum? Hmmm." The two of them laughed.

Douglas and Alexandra ran, hand in hand, into the bright cold afternoon, to the gazebo that Douglas's grandfather had built on a small hill above an ornamental pond.

CHAPTER THIRTY-THREE

❧

"SIT DOWN, MY dear," Douglas said. "We've things to speak about."

Alexandra sat watching her husband pace up and down the length of the gazebo.

Douglas said, "Talking to you about this helps focus my brain. Georges's two children and his sister-in-law left Paris immediately after his death."

"Yes."

"I received a message that the children traveled to Spain, but soon thereafter they were gone again. I still don't know where they ended up. Nor have I been able to find out what sort of financial situation they were in at the time of their father's death."

Alexandra said matter-of-factly, "There must be sufficient money, for the son has funds to hire men to kill you."

He nodded. "The son is currently in London, but that could change in an instant."

"He will make a mistake, Douglas, you'll see, and we'll get him."

"I'll tell you, Alex, the thought of this young man hiding behind a tree, just waiting for me to come into his gun range, is beyond galling. I want him; I want him on my own terms."

"I've begun to wonder about the warnings that Lord Wellington received. Maybe the son arranged for you to learn that Georges Cadoudal was involved. Maybe, when he used your name, he wanted you to know exactly who he was. He wants drama, attention. He wants you to admire his prowess, his perseverance."

"He wanted me to know he was coming to kill me? Aye, I see. A warning then. That first time he shot at me was a warning. He wanted me to be afraid, he wanted to play with me before he killed me, but before he killed me, he wanted me to know who he was. I wish we knew why he's doing this."

It was time, Douglas thought, as they walked back to the Hall, time for him and his sons to bring their attention closer to home. When they stepped into the elegant entrance hall, still hand in hand, the three servants who observed them would swear that the earl and countess had enjoyed a splendid interlude in the gazebo. Douglas, realizing this quickly enough, kissed his wife thoroughly, and then he left her to work in the estate room. He sat at his desk for ten minutes longer, then walked quickly to his bedchamber, where he found his wife sitting on a chair facing the large windows, humming as she mended one of his shirts. She smiled up at him, a dimple deepening in her cheek, and slowly began to unfasten the long line of buttons on the front of her dress. He thought that being married a good long time wasn't a bad thing. The years tuned minds together, at least some of the time. The years added more space in the heart, just as Hollis had said.

He leaned down to kiss her, his hands already busy with hers on those buttons.

* * *

A T PRECISELY FOUR o'clock that afternoon, Hollis opened wide the double doors to the drawing room, stood there, tall, straight, thick white hair flowing beautifully, nearly to his shoulders, looking just like God. He waited until he had the full attention of the earl and countess, and said grandly, "May I introduce to you Mrs. Annabelle Trelawny, born in that lovely town of Chester."

"With such a splendid introduction," came a soft low voice, "I fear you will be vastly disappointed."

Annabelle Trelawny looked like a small, plump fairy, light on her feet, ever so graceful. She also looked at once embarrassed and so pleased she looked ready to burst her stays.

"Do allow me to seat you here, Annabelle," Hollis said, and led her tenderly to the very feminine chair opposite the earl and countess. "Are you comfortable, my dear?"

Annabelle straightened her skirts, smiled up at Hollis like he was indeed God, and said in a soft, well-bred voice, "Oh yes, I am perfectly fine, thank you, William."

William? Douglas supposed he knew that Hollis's first name was William, but it had been so very long, he doubted if he could have recalled it on his own. William Hollis, a good name.

Annabelle Trelawny didn't have the look of a rapacious grandmother; she had sweet, deep crinkles around her eyes and mouth, from laughter, Alex thought. And such a sweet face. Her hair was dark with silver threaded through, her eyes a rich dark brown, intelligent eyes that saw a lot. Her skin was soft, unblemished. When she spoke, her voice was as kind as her face. "My lord, my lady, it is gracious of you to invite me to tea. William, naturally, has told me so much about the both of you, and your sons, James and Jason."

Alex was trying to motion Hollis to sit down, but he

would have none of it. He remained standing behind his beloved's chair, looking both austere and infatuated, an unlikely combination, but it was true. "James isn't here at the moment. He and his new wife are on their honeymoon. Our son Jason will be here shortly. He is looking forward to meeting you, ma'am. May I pour you a cup of tea, Mrs. Trelawny?"

Annabelle smiled a smile so sweet that it was obvious why it had smitten Hollis, and nodded. "I prefer a bit of milk, my lady."

It was Hollis who delivered his beloved's tea and tenderly placed it in her white hands. "Allow me to bring you the tray of cakes that Cook prepared, Annabelle. I know you like the almond biscuits."

Annabelle proved her liking for almond biscuits, eating three of them, all the while nodding and smiling and listening, saying little until Jason came into the drawing room, windblown, dressed in buckskins and an open-necked white shirt, showing his tanned throat. He came to an abrupt halt, and said immediately, "Are you Mrs. Trelawny? It is a pleasure to meet you, ma'am," and he walked to where she sat, picked up her hand, and lightly kissed it.

"I am Jason, ma'am."

Annabelle gazed up at him, and said slowly, "You are quite a delight to behold," and gave him a smile less grandmotherly than the one she'd given his parents.

"Thank you, ma'am," Jason said, so used to looks like hers that it didn't faze him. "Hollis has told both my brother and me that we are only bearable. It is you, ma'am, who is Hollis's delight."

Now that was smoothly done, Douglas thought, eyeing his son with approval.

Hollis cleared his throat. "Master Jason, I fear that this display of polite affection is a bit on the overdone side."

"Hollis, are you jealous?"

Hollis puckered up, looked like God readying to blast

the stone tablets. Jason, surprised and dismayed, wished he could take himself back to the paddocks.

Annabelle said easily, wanting to pat that very lovely hand of his, "I don't blame William for being jealous, Jason. You are quite the most beautiful young man I have ever seen in my life. Goodness, you don't look a thing like your parents—oh dear, that wasn't at all what I should have said. I do apologize."

Douglas said, "My sons look exactly like their aunt, something that fries my innards everytime I am forced to face it. It fries my wife's innards as well."

Annabelle laughed at that. "I have always found it amazing how blood manifests itself in people, particularly in children. Is it true that your brother looks just like you, Jason?"

"It is true, ma'am." He turned to Hollis, who was still standing stiff as a poker. "May I bring you a cup of tea, Hollis? I know that you like a twist of lemon."

Hollis unbent to his beautiful young charge. "You may, Master Jason."

Douglas was relieved to see Hollis unpucker. He had never seen Hollis display such emotion, particularly an emotion so low as jealousy.

Alexandra said, "Tell us, Jason, what does Bad Boy think of the new mare you brought to him?"

"He's in love, Mother. I left him mooning, his head resting on the paddock fence, gazing upon his beloved with bloodshot eyes, since I doubt he slept much last night, thinking about her. The mare isn't in heat yet, so she just swishes her tail at Bad Boy. There might be a bit of a wait for him."

It occurred to Alexandra that such talk of mating horses wasn't all that appropriate in the drawing room. She smiled at Annabelle. "So you are from Chester, Mrs. Trelawny, so very close to the Welsh border. A beautiful city and countryside, both my husband and I enjoyed ourselves when we visited the area."

Hollis said, "After Annabelle's mother died when she was a child, her father took her to live in Oxford. It was there she met Miss Plimpton and enjoyed vast numbers of hours in her company. After Annabelle married, she left Oxford. I believe you told me that you and Bernard traveled extensively."

Annabelle nodded. "Oh yes, my husband wasn't happy breathing the same air for too many weeks in a row. He had to be off, and he took me with him."

Jason said, "Speaking of travels, Mother, did you and Father ever visit The Coombes in western Ireland? That's where Judith hails from."

"I don't believe I've heard of The Coombes," Douglas said.

"I'm going to write her cousin, see if I can't pay him a visit. Oh, Father, would you like to come riding with me later? I think exercise would calm Bad Boy down."

Alexandra said, "If you really wish to, Douglas, then I will get my gun and ride beside you."

Douglas patted his wife's hand and said to Annabelle, "We've had some problems here. My wife is concerned. She wants to protect me."

Hollis cleared his throat. "I have told Annabelle what has been happening, my lord. She has advised that we must remain calm, that we should observe every new face we see closely, for signs of evil, for this assault on your lordship is evil, she believes, and evil cannot be hidden if one is vigilant."

"Er, thank you, Mrs. Trelawny," Douglas said quickly, seeing that Jason was regarding the lady with something close to awe.

"Yes," Alexandra added, "we are grateful for your perceptions."

Ten minutes later, Alexandra was left alone with Annabelle Trelawny while Hollis saw to a problem in the kitchens. She said immediately, "You mustn't worry that

Hollis is still heartbroken over Miss Plimpton. Hollis always knows what he's about."

"Oh no, that doesn't really worry me," Annabelle said comfortably. "He's right. I did know Miss Plimpton." Annabella actually shuddered. "She was six years older than I and fancied that she knew everything. She was officious, my lady, but of course I would never tell my dear William that. I'll never forget one time when he visited Miss Plimpton. I hadn't yet left the house when I heard her tell him that her soul was fashioned in exactly the proper way to assist his soul to perfection. I would have thrown a vase at her, but dear William said something to the effect that his soul needed all the help it could get. Her death was really rather stupid, rather in keeping with her character. She was so busy telling one of her father's parishioners all the errors of his ways that she didn't see a step and fell off it, hit her head, and it was all over."

Alexandra said, "Blessed hell—er, excuse me—but how very amazing this all is."

"Well, perhaps I shouldn't be pouring out all this vinegar, but the fact is, if Miss Plimpton had lived, she would have made the poor man miserable."

When Hollis came back into the drawing room a few minutes later, the ladies merely exchanged a glance and that was that. A perfectly pleasant conversation followed among the three of them, about nothing and everything. Annabelle patted Hollis's hand several times, easily done since his right hand was sitting very close to her shoulder, and said, "I have imposed myself for an exceedingly long time on her ladyship, William."

Hollis hurried around the chair to assist her, although she didn't need any assistance at all. By visual reckoning, Alexandra thought she was at least fifteen years Hollis's junior. Was his name really *William*? But, the odd thing was, they looked very natural standing side by side, and when Hollis took her arm, he gave her such a sweet smile

that Alexandra thought it matched hers, and hers was po-
tent indeed.

When Hollis reappeared that evening at the dinner hour,
he gave everyone a placid smile and announced that he and
Annabelle were going to be married. Soon, he added, since
a man couldn't count on hanging about forever, and besides, a man wanted his wife with him at Christmas, when
he placed a present in her hands and earned her gratitude.

"What sort of gratitude could Mrs. Trelawny show Hollis?" Jason wanted to know as he watched Hollis glide in
his stately manner from the drawing room, but he knew.
The thought of Hollis and Mrs. Trelawny even kissing,
much less taking off their clothes, made his innards cramp
up. His father, knowing exactly what he was thinking,
threw his napkin at him, and said, "Gratitude is gratitude at
any age. Never forget, Jason, if a man has the will and the
parts, he'll do just fine until he's planted deep."

Jason was hard-pressed not to hoot with laughter, but
one look at his mother's face stilled him. He cleared his
throat. "Judith and Lady Arbuckle have finally agreed to
come for a visit. I believe they will arrive tomorrow."

"Excellent," Jason's mother said. "I have this feeling
that we should perhaps get to know Judith McCrae a bit
better. What do you think, Jason?"

"Oh yes," Jason said. "Oh yes," and he left the dining
room, whistling.

CHAPTER THIRTY-FOUR

❦

JASON LOOKED LIKE a proud parent as the girl he planned to marry said to his father, "I have heard that Jason can tame any wild animal he finds."

How did she know that?

"It's true," Douglas said slowly, his eyes on his son, who looked so besotted he was in danger of drooling. "He found an injured marten when he was five years old. The marten allowed Jason to wrap him in his coat and bring him home. He kept it in his bedchamber for two weeks. There have been a long line of creatures for him to tend since then."

Judith saw that Jason wanted to know how she knew this and said simply, "Lord Pomeroy told me. He said he should know, since you burped up milk on his shirt when you were eight months old.

"I also heard it said that you even train cats to run in the cat races."

"Who told you that?"

She lowered her eyes just a moment, a maneuver Douglas recognized and admired. "Why, I believe it was Corrie's vampire who told me that. Devlin said he'd always wanted a racing cat, but there was some sort of approval that had to be granted. Is this true?"

Her dark eyes twinkled outrageously as she added demurely, "Devlin also told me that the cat races were held during the day, so what was he to do?"

"He should sod off," Jason said under his breath.

Douglas said, holding his grin back, "The Harker brothers, old now, but still in charge of all racing rules, demand to know the bona fides of anyone who wishes to race cats. Jason here, even though cats don't treat him to infinite trust as do other animals, still race well for him." Douglas arched a black brow. "You spoke of Corrie's vampire. Did you know that Devlin's grandfather, the old duke, never left his house for the last five years of his life? Kept all the windows covered, not a hint of sun did he allow in. So Devlin is evidently following in his path, is he?"

"He does wear a hat when the sun is strong," Jason said. "I think James wants to drive a stake through his heart, a rather black heart, according to James. With his bare hands, I believe I heard him say."

"Oh dear," Alexandra said under her breath and stared helplessly at the open doorway where the dowager countess of Northcliffe stood, those bright old eyes of hers glued on Judith.

No hope for it, she thought, and rose, sorry that she hadn't had the time to warn Judith. "Mother-in-law, this is Miss Judith McCrae, here with Lady Francis Arbuckle, her aunt. Judith, this is Lady Lydia."

"Ma'am," Judith said, rising immediately and giving the dowager a graceful curtsy suited for a duchess. "It is a pleasure to finally meet you. Jason has told me about you."

"He has, has he?" The dowager humphed loudly and took herself to a large winged chair and sat herself down.

"I asked Hollis to fetch me some nutty buns. Where are they?"

"Why don't Judith and I find out?" Jason was on his feet, his hand reaching for Judith's when the dowager said, "Oh no. I want the girl to remain here. Jason, you go get my nutty buns for me. Now, girl, you have a cheap Irish name. Who are your parents? How is Lady Arbuckle related to you? Where *is* Lady Arbuckle?"

"She went to her room, a headache, I believe."

Douglas said, "Mother, Alex already told you about Judith. She isn't here for an inquisition. Let Alex pour you a cup of tea and give one of your lovely smiles to our young guest."

The dowager said, "Young lady, do you know that the Virgin Bride visits the ladies of the house?"

Judith, mouth ajar, said, "No, ma'am. I haven't yet met the Virgin Bride. Jason has mentioned her, as did Corrie, but I don't know anything about her."

"She is a ghost, you ninny, a real ghost that my dear son Douglas refuses to admit lives here. The poor thing was left widowed even before she was a wife, and thus her name. I don't believe it, of course, but my daughter-in-law here—who has more hair than she deserves and the color simply doesn't fade, which is a pity since it is such a vulgar shade—and wouldn't you think it would as she's gained years? She believes in the Virgin Bride, claims that she's visited her innumerable times, but will this famous ghost bother to tell her the name of the man trying to kill my son? No, she won't, and I am tired of it all! I don't think the Virgin Bride finds you worthy anymore, Alexandra. She finds you paltry and loose, always sticking our your bosom so that men will admire you, and wouldn't you think that such a bosom would disappear as she's gained years?"

"Er, I really couldn't say, ma'am," Judith said and shot the countess an agonized look. Alexandra merely rolled her eyes, poured the tea, added exactly one small teaspoon of milk, and carried the cup to her mother-in-law.

The dowager eyed the tea, handed the cup back to her and said, "There is too much milk in there. It looks soggy. I have told you countless times how to prepare my tea, yet you still can't manage something even that simple."

Alexandra smiled down at the old woman she'd known and suffered nearly thirty years of her life. Something unfamiliar washed through her, something hot and deliciously free, and it filled her brain to overflowing. She never stopped smiling. "If you don't like the tea, ma'am, I suggest that you pour it yourself." She set the teacup down on the small table beside the dowager and walked away.

The dowager was so shocked by this unexpected behavior that she was speechless, for perhaps nine seconds. "It is your responsibility as the countess of Northcliffe to pour the tea, young lady! I didn't want you to be responsible, but my poor Douglas had to marry you, so that was that. But look at you, speaking back to me, your words all sly and mean—"

Douglas rose, tall and straight. He looked at his mother dispassionately, wondering why he'd allowed her reign of terror to continue for so very long. *Respect,* he thought. Damnable respect drummed into his head from the cradle, even though it wasn't merited in his mother's case. He said easily, every inch the earl, "Alex is right, ma'am. If you don't like your tea, then pour it yourself. Now, I want you to try for a bit of charming conversation with our guest."

"Why is she even here? Our Jason is far too young to be wed. Poor James, nearly as young as Jason, having to shackle himself to that little baggage, Corrie Tybourne-Barrett and—"

Douglas walked to his mother's chair, leaned down, and lifted her out of the chair, his hands in her armpits. He straightened, and she dangled by a couple of inches off the beautiful Aubusson carpet upon which she'd dumped countless cups of tea because it was a rug that Alex had bought and placed in the room. She was very heavy, his mother, probably nearly as heavy as he was. He looked her straight in her eyes, even managed to smile. "You will not say another derogatory word about Corrie. You will not say another derogatory word to my wife. Indeed, you will not say another derogatory word about anyone. Do you understand me, Mother?"

The dowager shrieked, threw her head back and shrieked to the ceiling. Douglas, instead of letting her down, merely carried her to the drawing room door, kicked it open, and carried his mother away, still shrieking, but now she was adding some quite unrestrained curses. They heard him say calmly, "That is rather vulgar, Mother."

The dowager shrieked again, louder.

Alexandra stared after her husband, her look bemused. She said at last, "Well, it's about time, don't you think, Jason?"

"Yes, Mother, you did very well and so did Father. Judith, you don't realize it, but something very unexpected just happened. My grandmother isn't a very nice old lady—well, truth be told, she's a harridan. My mother has always let her walk on her back, always been kind even when that old witch tortures her mercilessly, but no longer. And Father actually carried her out of here. Oh, I can't wait for James to hear this. Well done, Mother, well done."

"I wonder if she will be kind to Corrie," Alexandra said. "I also wonder what threats your father is making at this moment."

"I can't imagine anyone not being kind to Corrie," Judith said, still staring at the open drawing room door, where muffled shrieks still sounded.

Jason laughed. "She even manages to insult Hollis. I do wonder how long it will take grandmother to realize she's no longer in charge here."

"I trust your father. Her reign is over." Alexandra stood,

her arms crossed over her chest, her chin up, her eyes hard. "It was over such a little thing," she said, shaking her head. "Never again will that old woman make my stomach ache." She turned to Judith. "Well, such a spectacle for a guest. I am so sorry, not about what I did, not about what my husband did, I'm sorry at the timing of it. Nearly thirty years— all this time I've swallowed my bile and tried to keep the peace." She began rubbing her hands together. "I cannot believe it took me so very long to put an end to it. Now, I need to speak to your father, Jason, if he is finished with the old bat. We can develop a strategy. What do you think?"

Alexandra didn't wait for any advice, just sailed out of the drawing room, head high and shoulders squared.

Jason said, "James told me that he and Corrie were going to live at Primrose Hall, a charming house that the first Lord Hammersmith built. He was probably thinking of the insults Corrie would have to endure were they to live here. Now? I wonder. Shall I show you some interesting statues in the east garden, Judith? They're rather unusual. I think you might like them."

CORRIE TURNED ON her side, kissed her husband's mouth, and said, "James, please wake up, please."

James was instantly awake. "What is this? You want me in the middle of the night? What's wrong, Corrie? You're shaking." He pulled her into his arms, holding her so tight she had trouble breathing. "Did you have a nightmare? It's over now, all over."

She pulled back from him. "No, it wasn't a nightmare, James. I was awake, she woke me up. It's you, James, not your father. Oh goodness, it's you. It was the Virgin Bride, I know it was. She visited me because I'm now a part of the family."

James stared down at her. He believed in the Virgin Bride, but he would never admit to his father that he did.

He didn't want to see his father's look of amused contempt directed at him. He'd heard stories about how she'd appeared to his father, but still, the earl wouldn't speak of the ghost without copious sneers and mockery.

He rubbed her back, ran his hands down her arms. "It's all right now. That's it. Now, tell me what the Virgin Bride told you."

"I woke up, felt you next to me, and I was smiling. I was thinking about kissing your belly." She reared back in his arms and made out his face in the moonlight. It seemed to her that suddenly James was too still, that he'd almost stopped breathing. "Are you all right, James?"

"No. Yes. Kissing my belly? No, no. I'll get over it. Tell me more."

"All right. After I kissed your belly then I thought about what else I could do to you—"

"Er, about the ghost, Corrie, start talking about her right now, or else I might be on my knees begging you to do what you were planning."

"Really? Oh goodness, James—oh yes, the Virgin Bride. Well, I was awake and then I sort of drifted off. But I wasn't asleep, I'm positive about that. Then she was there, beside the bed, and she was looking down at me. She looked all floaty, sort of wispy, but I could see that she was beautiful, with lots of long, pale hair. She didn't speak, at least I don't think she did, but it felt like she was speaking to me, in my mind. She said it was you, James, said you were in danger. She didn't say anything at all about your father, just you. What is going on? Oh God, what are we going to do? We're alone here. Do you have a gun?"

"Yes, I have a gun." He added with barely a pause, "I will buy one for you as well, all right?"

That calmed her as nothing else he could have said. He knew her that well.

"All right, that's good. What shall we do?"

"I think," James said slowly, kissing her forehead, "that it's time you and I went back home."

"I'm afraid, James."

"Yes, so am I. Now, can you put this out of your mind until morning?"

She was quiet for a good minute. Then she twisted in his arms and shoved him onto his back. She smiled down at him even as she began to push down the covers. "About your belly, James—"

CHAPTER THIRTY-FIVE

❧

IT WAS MIDNIGHT, a time when James, in decent weather, could be found lying on his back on some close-by hillock, gazing up at the stars. But for Jason, midnight was the time to sleep. He awoke with the sun on most mornings, his head clear, full of energy, and ready to take on the world. He many times passed yawning servants in the corridors of Northcliffe.

Moonlight spilled through the windows since Jason refused to have the heavy draperies drawn. If it weren't so very cold, near to freezing this night, the windows would have been open, cold air on his face, and a pile of blankets to his chin.

He was dreaming of his grandmother. In his dream, he saw her as a young girl. The thing was, though, she looked just like she did today, her face all mottled red with rage and disbelief because his mother had finally told the old woman her reign of terror was over. The only thing different was that his grandmother looked smaller, not different

or older. Suddenly, she was yelling at another girl he suddenly saw hiding behind a chair. She threw a doll at the
girl.

His dream suddenly changed. His grandmother became the marten he'd saved when he'd been a small boy,
and the marten's breath was warm on his face, its body
heavy on his chest, down the length of his body as well
and that was strange. He couldn't breathe, there was
something—

Jason woke up, no blurry mind, all of him there and
alert, to find Judith lying on top of him, kissing his face.

His heart jumped; the girl he loved was actually here, in
his bedchamber, sliding about on top of him, and it wasn't
a dream. He was able, barely, to keep his voice slow and
easy. "Judith, you've turned me into a bucket of sentiment
and lust, but when all is said and done, you shouldn't be
here in my bedchamber at midnight, doing what you're doing, which is a great pity."

She laughed, her warm breath fanning his mouth. Then
she kissed him again, just a light, tentative kiss, because he
knew she had no experience.

"Judith, why are you here?"

She didn't laugh. He heard nervousness in her voice.
"Jason, I came here because I want you. I want you more
than you can begin to imagine. I want you more than I did
just a minute ago. Don't send me away. Please."

Jason didn't know how it happened, but his arms were
around her back, tightening. She felt soft against him, and
he knew that within moments he would be hard against her
belly and surely that would scare her witless. He kissed her
then, keeping his tongue in his own mouth.

She liked that. When he managed to pull himself free,
he said with great urgency, "Judith, you shouldn't be here,
it isn't right. I love you, I've told you that—"

She reared up a bit. Her face was shadowed, but he
could see those dark eyes of hers clearly enough. "You've

never told me you loved me. You've always played around the point. And then you've gone off to your mistress."

"Very well, listen to me now. I love you. There, is that clear enough for you? Now, you must leave. I can't accompany you back to your bedchamber because there is no doubt at all in my mind that someone utterly unexpected would magically appear in the corridor and see us."

She laughed.

"No, listen to me. I'm perfectly serious. Something would wake them up, and they'd come out into the corridor to see us skulking back to your bedchamber. So go now, while I'm still able to let you leave me. You can count on the fact that I'm not off to see any mistress."

Her eyes were dark, even darker now at midnight. "I don't want to leave you, Jason. Don't you want me?"

"Even though you're a virgin, you can answer that question, Judith. Surely you can feel me against you."

She squirmed, and he thought he'd die. "Yes," she whispered against his mouth, "I feel you. I know that part of you somehow comes inside me, and that sounds very strange, but I've decided that I want to learn all about it tonight. I'm nearly twenty, after all. I want you to teach me."

"I can't do this, I just can't." It took all his will to flip her off him and over on her back. When he immediately turned to look down at her, he wondered if it had been such a fine idea. He was balanced on one elbow. His left hand was free to stroke her hair, to touch her cheek, her lips, her chin. She was wearing a virginal white nightgown, a soft white wrapper over it, tied at her waist. His hand hovered then touched her throat. He leaned down and kissed her.

The hand that was on her throat an instant before was suddenly touching her breast. He leaped away from her, rolled off the bed, and came up, breathing hard, to stare down at the girl he loved, lying on her back in the middle of his bed, every naked delightful inch of her only two very soft muslin layers away from him.

She ran her tongue over her bottom lip, an action that nearly made him howl. "You're incredible, Jason."

"What? Oh." He grabbed his dressing gown, but she came quickly up on her knees and pulled it from him. "I would like to stare at you for a while. I've never seen a naked man before and I've heard that every single inch of you is beautiful. I would like to see for myself that this is indeed a fact. Is that all right?"

"No, it isn't a good idea. If you look at me even another second, I will leap on you, and it will be all over for both of us."

"I think I'd like you to leap on me."

"No, there are consequences to leaping, consequences you wouldn't like."

"What does it matter?"

He could but stare at her.

"You love me."

"Yes, but—"

"Then why can't you be with me tonight? Why does it matter if we wait?"

He said, his voice austere, like his father's when he was set upon teaching one of his sons a lesson, "Because a girl is to be a virgin on her wedding night."

"Does that mean that you want a wedding night with me? Couldn't we just pretend that this is our wedding night?"

He was shaking, couldn't help it. He was so wild with lust he didn't know how he could put words together. He could actually feel his common sense being eaten away around the edges. He said, desperate now, "You want a wedding night now? But what if I get you pregnant? Such things happen, Judith, surely you know that. I can do things to lessen the risk, but—"

"What?"

He closed his eyes a moment. "I can withdraw from you before I spill my seed."

"Oh. Well, then." She gave him a siren's smile. He didn't see it clearly, but he saw enough of it to nearly stutter himself into the floor. He said slowly, "Th-that would mean marriage."

"Yes, I suppose it would."

Jason knew he was ready for marriage, knew he wanted to marry her, and here she was, wanting him, eager for him, and she didn't want to wait.

Who cared?

He was breathing hard when he pulled her up against him. She was soft and willing and her hair fell nearly to her waist, thick, wonderfully soft hair, hair as dark as her eyes, contrasting dramatically with her skin that was as white as a cloudless moon. And he said into her hair, "If I get you with child, then we will wed very soon, all right?"

"Yes," she said between kisses, "all right."

He was twenty-five, old enough not to be awkward or selfish or too fast, but it was difficult. When he had her naked, he wanted to take her in that instant, and he saw the invitation in her eyes, saw it clearly, knew that she wanted him, but he had to make this very nice for her. How could he do that when he was ready to explode? Her hands were all over him, and she was encouraging him, parting her legs to bring him closer against her. When he was trembling he was in such bad shape, she lifted her hips to bring him into her. Oh God, it was more than a man could take, but he sucked in a deep breath and told himself he had to hold back or he would be consigned to that group of pathetic dolts who lost their wits when a naked woman was lying beneath them, their legs spread. No, no, he had to stop thinking like that. He looked down at her, and knew this was her first time and he wasn't about to muck it up. When his mouth was on her, she began shaking. Then she was sobbing, deep in her throat, hitting her fists against his shoulders. When she reached her orgasm, Jason looked at her face as his fingers now caressed her. Astonishment, that was the first thing he saw in her wide dark eyes, then tearing pleasure, and her eyes went wild and blind. He eased the rhythm of his fingers slowly, very slowly; he came over her and came into her, slow and deep. To his surprise, she began to move against him, drawing him deeper, and he nearly fell off the cliff when she cried out in pain. "Hold on to me, Judith. Just hold on." He gritted his teeth, and went deep, deeper, and when he touched her womb, he couldn't hold back any longer. He didn't want to yell to the ceiling, someone would hear him. He managed to keep that in his brain, but it was difficult. He swallowed his cries, his body heaving over her, and then as suddenly, every thought in his head, every feeling that had raced through him—all of it was hovering around him, indistinct and blurred, like the softest of veils, and it was easy and fine, and he eased down on top of her.

"You didn't come out of me."

He froze. "No," he said slowly, "I forgot."

"It doesn't matter," she whispered against his ear, "it doesn't matter."

He managed to kiss her before he fell asleep beside her.

WHEN JASON AWOKE just after sunrise, he was grinning like a fool. Delicious memories raced through him in an instant. He turned, but she was gone.

Well, of course she was gone. He fell over onto his back, stretched, and wondered when she'd left him.

Marriage to Judith McCrae. It would be a very good thing. He imagined, a fatuous smile on his face, making love to her every night, or perhaps twice or even three times a night, then waking up with her every morning. The good Lord knew that he could pleasure a woman in the mornings as well. Himself too. That was a fine image, a fine future for the both of them. He wondered if she'd stop trying to twist him up, keep him guessing about her feelings, keep him off-balance, as if she didn't want him to know her all the way to her soul.

Jason whistled while he bathed, whistled while he strode down the wide corridor to the stairs, there to take them two at a time, going down.

At the bottom of the stairs stood James, Corrie just behind him.

James said without preamble, "Good. You're here. I told Corrie you were up with the servants. We're here because the Virgin Bride visited Corrie last night. We left to come home immediately."

Corrie stepped forward, stood there at the foot of the stairs, staring up at him, her head cocked to the side, quiet for the moment. Finally, she said, "There is something different about you, Jason. Are you all right? You look rather vacant, and somehow immensely pleased with yourself."

Jason said not a word to that, just came down and hugged her to him. "My new little sister. The only thing is you've been my sister for fifteen years already. Now, both of you, come into the dining room, and tell me what the Virgin Bride had to say." He held on to Corrie, even as he said to his brother, "I trust you have pleased my little sister."

James thought of her mouth on him, and coughed.

Corrie immediately said, "Why are you asking him since I'm the object of the pleasing? Can't I answer that?"

"No, you cannot. Be quiet. James?"

"I would say," James said slowly, looking from his brother to his wife, "that the two of you have the same look on your faces."

"Oh dear," Corrie said. "How is that possible? Jason, surely you haven't—"

James said, his voice so quiet not even the Virgin Bride could hear him, "Is Judith McCrae here?"

"Yes, she is. Now, as to this look on my face, I ask that you both forget it. She has agreed to be my wife. I will fetch some tea from the kitchen. James, take your bride into the dining room."

"HAS JASON SHOWN you the infamous gardens with all those lovely shocking statues?"

Judith's eyes sparkled at Corrie's question, but she looked around to make sure they were alone before she whispered, "You mean those lovely shocking statues that all appear to be having the time of their lives?"

Corrie laughed. "Yes." She drew a bit closer. "Which was your favorite?"

There wasn't a blush on either face. "The one where the man is kissing her in a way one would have to say is rather intimate."

Corrie gulped. "Ah, what a remarkable coincidence. There are at least fifteen statues and yet we both like the same one. Yes, that one is my favorite as well. It wasn't before I married James, but—oh goodness, this isn't at all proper, is it? Well, the fact is, I really didn't understand what the male statue was doing and what that meant, if you know what I mean."

"Now I know exactly what you mean," Judith said, then lowered her head. "Since Jason tells James everything you must know that I went to Jason's bedchamber last night and seduced him, but the fact of the matter is—"

"The fact is that if I'd only had the chance, I would have tried to lock myself in a small warm room with James as well. It doesn't matter. You and Jason will be married soon now." Corrie leaned closer. "The truth is that there was simply never the opportunity, blast it. Nor did James, curse him, give me the least little hint." She sat back, smiled, a soft smile that held memories for the rest of her days.

"Will you stand beside me, Corrie?"

"I should be delighted. Is this wedding to be soon or will your Aunt Arbuckle insist upon a long engagement and huge numbers of people spilling out of St. Paul's?"

"I want it to be very soon." Judith blushed, actually blushed. She pressed her palms against her cheeks. "Oh goodness, all I can think about is sitting on Jason's bed, staring at him, and he's standing there perfectly naked. Ah, he looks so very fine."

"Oh my," said Corrie.

"It was remarkable."

Corrie felt both embarrassed and wicked, a delightful combination, but she knew that anyone could walk in on them, and she didn't want to have to face Jason after hearing about his midnight encounter with Judith. She cleared her throat. "Tell me about how my mother-in-law finally buried the old bat."

When James walked in a few minutes later, it was to hear Corrie and Judith laughing. That pleased him, and he smiled even as he said from the open doorway, "I have come to fetch both of you. Father wants to tell you where all the guards are stationed here at Northcliffe. He doesn't want any of you getting accidentally shot." He paused a moment. "Ah, he also wants to hear if either of you have any more ideas, even though he swears that you're weakheaded, Corrie, what with your tale of the Virgin Bride visiting you. However, he is loathe to let me out of his sight, so what is one to believe?"

Corrie jumped to her feet. "Yes, I want to hear what your father has to say. How many more guards are there?"

"Two more."

"He hasn't told me to my face that I'm weak-headed. Do you think he will?"

"My father is an excellent diplomat. You are still too new to the family to be blasted. However, now that I think of it, your sneer and my father's aren't all that different." He gave each girl an arm.

Lady Arbuckle wasn't present, Judith telling them that her aunt was resting quite happily in her lovely bedchamber, drinking tea and eating toast.

Annabelle Trelawny was there, as she was nearly every day now. Today, though, her sweet smile was tinged with worry. She said, "I hope you are not displeased at my presence, my lord, but William believes that I have a fine brain. He wanted to see if I could be of any assistance at all. Now, this dream of Corrie's."

"It wasn't a dream," Alexandra said.

"Ha," Douglas said.

"The point of the whole thing," Corrie said, sitting forward, her hands clasped in her lap, "is that the Virgin Bride made it clear to me it is James who is in danger. Then she sort of faded away."

"Then why was I shot at?" Douglas said.

"I don't have an answer to that, sir."

"It's perfectly obvious that she would come to you since you're now James's wife," said Alexandra. "It doesn't mean she isn't worried about Douglas as well, but since you are now James's wife, he must be your first concern."

Corrie said, "I wonder why she didn't tell me who was behind this?"

No one had an answer for that. Alexandra said, "I have sometimes thought there are things she doesn't know. In other words, a ghost isn't omniscient."

"But she knew you were taken by Georges Cadoudal," Douglas said, then looked like he wanted to shoot himself. He closed down tighter than a clam, didn't say another word.

Annabelle's lovely white brow furrowed in concentration. "Why wouldn't any young man want to kill the people he believed responsible for his father's death?"

Douglas said, "That's a good point, Mrs. Trelawny, but Georges and I weren't enemies; I had nothing to do with his assassination. Surely his son must know that. But it hasn't seemed to matter."

"And now James has been added to the list. Why on earth would Georges's son want to kill James? They must be about the same age. They've never met."

The discussion continued until Hollis cleared his throat. "Cook wishes to feed all of you now. My lord, my lady, you will please rise and come into the dining room."

"Ah, William," Annabelle said as Hollis assisted her, "you are such a masterful speaker. Wellington should beg you to deal with those ridiculous French. Can you imagine, they're rebelling again?"

"Oh yes," said Hollis. "The French must needs fight against themselves; they must needs fight against others. Disagreement and perversity sing through their blood, poor blighters."

CHAPTER THIRTY-SIX

❧

The Devil gets up to the belfry by the vicar's skirts.

THOMAS FULLER

I T WAS THE end of November. In England, in Corrie's
experience, that meant unrelenting cold, so much wind
you couldn't keep a bonnet on your head, and endless in-
vading dampness that made your bones ache and your
teeth chatter.

But not today. Today in southern England, at least, the
sun was high overhead and clouds were fat and white
against a brilliant blue sky. There wasn't a hint of fog, not
a breath of wind, only abundant sweet fresh air that
wafted about your head, making you smile and breathe
deeply.

"Just incredible," Corrie said to one of the hunting dogs
that trotted at her side, his tail a waving flag, as she walked

toward the stable where James, Jason, and a half dozen stable lads were breeding the new mare to Bad Boy.

In her pocket she carried the small derringer James had bought her two days before. She'd practiced firing it, and James admitted yesterday afternoon, after watching her shoot for some ten minutes, that she was a natural. He sounded peeved about her skill, and that made her grin at him, wickedness overflowing in that grin, and he picked her up and whirled her around and around until she was dizzy and laughing so hard she could barely hang on. Then he'd carried her into a small maple copse and laid her down on his coat beneath a fir tree. Ah, so very nice that was. So it had been on the cold side. Who cared? It wasn't cold at all today. Hmmm.

Corrie was smiling even as she quickened her pace. She heard the mare whinny, heard Bad Boy stomping. She came to the paddock, leaned her arms against the wooden railing, and looked toward James.

No, she saw immediately, it wasn't James, it was Jason. How could she have been deceived even for an instant, no matter that he was standing some thirty feet away, examining Bad Boy's front hoof?

Where was James? He should be here. But then she knew, and her heart plummeted. He was in danger.

She shouted, "Jason! Where is James?"

Jason dropped Bad Boy's hoof and strode over to her. "Good morning, Corrie. I expected James to be here before now. He's probably in the estate room reviewing documents with Father. He'll be here sooner or later. Stay, Corrie, James would want you to."

She was torn. James was on his way here. Very well, she'd wait. She settled herself on the paddock railing. Two minutes passed. "I can't do this. Something's wrong." Jason, who'd been breathing a heartfelt sigh of relief, froze in his tracks. She said to the back of his head, "Forgive me, Jason, but I'm worried. I'll go look for him. I'm afraid. You must be careful too, Jason. This man who is after James, he might not know that you are not he."

Jason turned and walked to her, squeezed her arm. "Yes, I know, and yes, I understand you very well. I will be surrounded by people. But I wish you would stay here, where James knows you are. He's probably still in the house; when he comes, he'll bring Judith here with him." He grinned up at her there, still seated on the railing. "If she's going to be the wife of a horse breeder, she should understand what it's all about." Then he took her hands in his and separated them, held them tightly. "Don't, Corrie. Everything will be all right, I promise you."

"But you can't know, you—"

"Ah, Mrs. Trelawny is here in her very smart landau. Excellent. Stay still, Corrie, and stop worrying." He gave her another pat and shouted, "Lovejoy, let's see how the mare's doing. That's right, that's right, bring her out, slowly, SLOWLY! All right, that's fine. Hold her still now."

Bad Boy wanted the mare desperately. Jason had covered Bad Boy's front hooves with soft cotton stockings so he wouldn't hurt her. Corrie felt for the derringer in her pocket and was reassured. She watched, paying no attention to the trembling horses, her ears alert for James's voice. Where the devil was he? Was he with Judith? She looked up to see Jason pull his watch out of his pocket, say something to Lovejoy, then come striding toward her. She would have sworn there was worry on his face, but when he looked at her, it was gone.

"I have an appointment with one of the Bow Street Runners. Stay here, trust James to come for you, I mean it. It's important you remain here, Corrie."

She watched him nearly break into a run toward the hall. Something was wrong, very wrong indeed. She was to stay here? Why, in heaven's name?

* * *

DOUGLAS RAISED HIS head at the gentle tap on the estate room door. He paused only a moment before calling, "Come."

The door opened quietly to show Annabelle Trelawny's smiling face as she leaned into the room. "Oh, forgive me, my lord. I'm looking for my dear William." She stepped into the room now, looked around. "Oh dear, don't tell me that you're alone?"

"Do come in, Annabelle. Yes, I'm quite alone."

"I thought William might be with you. He is very fond of you, enjoys being in your company."

"And I enjoy his company as well. You did not receive my message, Annabelle? I had a lad take it to you several hours ago, telling you that Hollis left to execute an errand for me today. I didn't think you would wish to spend time here without his being present."

"What errand did you send him on, my lord?"

If he considered her question impertinent, Douglas gave no sign. He said easily, "There is information coming in at Eastbourne. I believe it will answer most of our questions. I am very sorry Hollis isn't here, Annabelle."

"As am I, to be sure. However, my lord, I would pray that you not underestimate your own charms."

"My charms, Annabelle?"

She pulled a long-barreled dueling pistol from her cloak pocket. "As a matter of fact, my lord, I am delighted Hollis isn't here. He would have been in the way, would have tried to save you, and who knows? I might have had to shoot him.

"That you sent him away, I thank you, my lord. I am relieved." She smiled at him. "Let me also thank you for sending the lad. I knew everything had to come to an end soon, but the right circumstances hadn't yet presented themselves. But now all is as I would wish it. William is gone, Lady Alexandra is off visiting Lady Maybella, and

Jason is at the paddocks. It is now just you and me. It will happen now." She looked quickly through the crack in the door, then turned back to him. "No, my lord, do not move. I am quite a good shot. I fancied you were getting close, perhaps you were even ready to set a trap for me, my lord, but here I am, springing it before you were ready."

Douglas sat back in his chair, his arms behind his head. "You duped us all, madam. You have a rare talent."

"You only say so because you were the one deceived, my lord."

"Tell me, Annabelle. Were the stories you told my wife about Miss Plimpton anywhere near the truth?"

She laughed. "Ah. William's precious Miss Plimpton. I never met her, of course, but I suspect you figured that out, didn't you?"

"Yes, a pity. I did not lie. I am glad that Hollis isn't here. You also deceived him."

Douglas looked at her with such contempt that she shouted, "I had to use the old man! There was no one else to give me entrée into this wretched house."

"You did it very well. Now, you are English. How could you be related to Georges Cadoudal?"

"His wife, Janine, was my sister, well, halfsister, really. My mother was English, and I was raised in Surrey. She named me Marie because she believed that useless Frenchman who was my father would be pleased, perhaps leave his wife for her. I did not go to France until months before Janine died. I took care of Georges and the children."

"What is your name?"

"Marie Flanders. My dear dolt of a mother dressed bonnets for all the wealthy ladies in Middle Clapton. A meager existence. She died far too soon, with nothing."

"Why do you wish to kill me, madam?"

"I am going to kill you because you betrayed my sister. You raped her, made her with child, and left her."

Douglas rose slowly as he spoke, splayed his palms on his desk, leaned toward her. "You know that is nonsense, Annabe—Marie. Why do you really want me dead? Come now, the truth. After all, you're going to kill me. What difference does it make?"

She gave him a wonderfully warm smile. She leaned toward him, whispering, "No difference at all, my lord. You want the truth? It's money, my lord, all your money, and your house, and your lovely title, once you are dead. Naturally one would wish to dress it up, claim a motive of pure vengeance, of righteous revenge, since it sounds so terribly tawdry and common to claim simple gain. Ah, I do believe she is here now. It is about time." Marie turned her head just slightly. "Come in, my dear."

Judith McCrae slipped in through the door, and softly closed it.

"I have checked, Aunt Marie. No one is in the house, other than some servants floating about. Everyone is out watching the horses mating. I should be there too, but now I won't have to endure that disgusting display." As she spoke, Douglas walked slowly around the side of his desk and stood against the bookshelves.

"Hello, my lord. From the look on your face, I have a feeling that you are not altogether surprised."

Douglas took small steps toward the sofa, as if he was going to sit down. "No, I'm not surprised. I hoped I was wrong, for my son's sake. No one had as yet brought in your name, but I knew I would have to. You wanted my son to give you entry to my house, just as your aunt did with Hollis, and you managed to snag him, something no young lady before has managed."

"It was not difficult. Jason is a man, my lord, just a man."

"And you sat in on all our meetings, learned of our thoughts and plans. My wife was ready to welcome you into the family. Do you know she told me she was blessed, to have two such fine daughters-in-law practically at the same time."

For the first time, Douglas saw the resemblance between daughter and father, or perhaps he simply wanted to see it. Those eyes of hers were cold and dark with rage and purpose. "I watched you slap Jason on the back, acknowledging that you knew he'd had his pleasure with me. I would have liked to stick a knife in your heart at that moment."

Marie Flanders said, her eyes on that closed door, "Damnation, I should have realized this sooner. His fine lordship here was baiting his trap last night. There is no more information that you're waiting for in Eastbourne, is there?"

Judith said, "It doesn't matter. He's a fool, as are his sons. There is no trap. You're wrong, Aunt Marie."

"No, I'm not. Why do you think he kept inquiring about Lady Arbuckle? He was pushing us to act. And that note he sent me, telling me Hollis wouldn't be here today. It was to lure me here, lure me into acting."

Judith shook her head. "You give him too much credit. Fact is, I didn't really pay attention to what he said. I had to give Jason my attention or he would have wondered what was going on. Do you know, my lord, I really preferred James. But Corrie already had him by the collar."

Douglas never took his eyes off the two women. "James didn't realize that until—well, that isn't any of your business is it?"

"No, and I don't care. Aunt Marie, I'm bored. I wish to get this over with. I don't wish to kill any of the servants. They've been quite kind to me, so we will do it here, now, and slip out through the gardens."

Douglas said slowly, "Both of you have much to answer for."

"If ever we answer, my lord, you will not be here to hear it."

Douglas called out, "James, Ollie, signal your men. Come in now."

But James didn't come from his post behind the glass doors. Neither did Ollie Trunk.

Jason walked slowly into the estate room, his arm at his side, a gun held loosely in his hand. "James is missing, Father."

Douglas looked at Judith. "Where is my son?"

"Why, my lord, he's with my dear brother."

JAMES FELT THE trickle of blood slide down his face. His head hurt from the blow, but his brain was clear. He could think, he could understand, and what he both saw and understood was a young man he'd never seen before, a young man who was tall and well-made, dark-haired and dark-eyed, and this young man wanted to kill him.

James shook his head, started to get to his feet.

The man said, "No, stay right where you are. Ah, I see you've got your wits together again." He stood, walked to James, and stood over him. "Hello, brother. It's such a pleasure to finally meet you face-to-face."

James looked up at him, saw the gun in his right hand leveled at his chest. "You've kept yourself hidden very well. You're Georges Cadoudal's son, aren't you? We were right about that."

"Yes, he was my father, at least in name."

James understood a great deal in that moment, but it still didn't make any sense. "You seem to believe that my father sired you. You weren't terribly subtle what with using Douglas Sherbrooke as your name. What is your real name?"

"Douglas Sherbrooke is quite real enough."

"How did you come to believe that you are my father's son? How did you come to take his name?"

"I assumed my rightful name when I came to England to kill you and that dishonorable bastard from whose seed I come. It seemed only just to take his name."

"What is your real name?"

The young man shrugged, but never did he look away from James's face and the gun aimed at James's chest. "My father and all my friends in France called me Louis. Louis Cadoudal. My father died insane, did you know that?"

James shook his head. "We knew he'd been assassinated."

"Yes, an assassin shot him, and all believed he died from that, but his brain had already rotted. There were only a few who knew it. He spoke of so many things in his mad deliriums, of how your father had raped my mother; but then he would frown, and say no, rape wasn't involved at all. Of course those were simply words spun from his madness. But I realized the truth of it the moment I saw your father. Our father.

"Don't you think I look like him, brother? You and your damned twin, neither of you look like him, but I do. I am his firstborn son, not you, and I look like his son."

"No, you don't," James said calmly. "You're lying to yourself. You are dark like him, and you are tall like him, nothing more." James knew he had to stay in control, knew he had to be ready. "Let us agree that my father sired you, Louis—"

"He did, damn you!"

"Very well, if he is indeed your father, it makes no difference to the succession. I am the firstborn legitimate son, so I ask why do you want to kill me? It gains you nothing but the hangman's noose."

"Ah, that a brother of mine could be so stupid. It will gain me everything. You see, my first goal was to kill your bastard of a father for what he did to my mother, but then I decided that if I killed him, it wasn't enough. He'd robbed me of my rightful life. My aunt arranged for a document that shows marriage lines between our father and my mother, dated before he married your mother. All of it legal. I will be the earl of Northcliffe, wealthy beyond my wildest dreams, and it will be justice."

"No, it will be murder. My father didn't rape your mother. He rescued her from a French general, a man who was giving her to his cronies. He brought her back to England for your father. It was a bargain he and Georges Cadoudal made. My father wasn't ever involved with your mother."

"A fine tale that. Make my mother out to be a whore, to sleep with dozens of men."

"She was raped. Listen to me."

"No. I'll wager both you and your brother lapped this up like cats, huh? But all of it is a lie. My father said—"

"You already said that your father was mad, that he would say one thing, then retract it. It is true that he first believed my father had raped your mother, but when it was all sorted out, he admitted he'd been wrong, particularly when your own mother finally told him she didn't know who had made her pregnant since so many men had raped her."

"You want me to believe that I am some unknown man's spawn? You puking liar! Goddamn you. No one raped my mother but your damned father. Before she died, my mother told my aunt—her own sister—that it was the truth, told her that no one had raped her except for the earl of Northcliffe and that I was his son. God, I'm going to love killing you."

"This aunt of yours—she lied. Ah, let me guess her name. Is it Annabelle Trelawny?"

Louis laughed. "Certainly she is my aunt, just as I am my father's son. I will become the next earl of Northcliffe. I deserve it. It is just." He raised the gun.

CHAPTER THIRTY-SEVEN

❧❧❧

*J*UDITH, *NOT JUDITH.* But he'd heard the damning words out of the women's mouths—out of Judith's mouth, all that exquisite detail, and he understood it, surely he did, but he couldn't seem to bring it into his brain and make it real to him, all the way to his soul. That cold recitation out of her mouth, the small derringer pointing at his father's chest, it brought him focus, it enraged him. They'd figured out that Annabelle Trelawny had been involved, but Judith? He looked at his father, realized in that moment that his father had come to suspect Judith as well, but he hadn't said anything, even when the three of them had met the night before.

She was standing no more than ten feet from his father. Why had his father come from behind his desk?

He knew the answer, of course. He expected James and Ollie to be hiding behind those draperies covering the glass doors onto the gardens, not him.

"Do come in, Jason," Marie said. "No, I can't tell you

and your brother apart, but since my nephew has James, then you must be Jason. Do drop your gun, my boy, else I'll put a bullet through your father's chest. My precious Louis managed to cosh James on the head and drag him behind the stables. He is very likely dead now."

"No," Jason said. "My brother isn't dead."

Judith looked at him, but didn't move the gun from his father's chest. "Is this some sort of twin communication?"

"I don't know, but he's alive."

"It won't be long. My brother is stronger than any man I've ever seen. He's been waiting for this day. He's ready," Judith said, then she smiled. "I wish to thank you for inviting me here to get to know your family, Jason. The truth is that I never wanted to come here; I only wanted to kill your father and be gone, but there were always people with him." She turned to Douglas. "Even here, in your own home, your wretched wife never left your side, until now. Oh, I see now. Your precious wife isn't part of your trap. Is Corrie part of it or just the three of you? Ah, yes, the men to do the bad business, leave the little females in a closet where they can have hysterics in private.

"Well, I'm not a weak, hysterical female, my lord. I demanded to be the one to remove you from this earth, even though my brother wanted the pleasure of it. Ah, Jason, do I see you considering perhaps throwing yourself at me? If you lift so much as a hand, I will shoot your father. Did I surprise you, Jason, when you awoke with me kissing you?"

"You know you did."

"I had thought you would come to me, but that old crone, Lady Arbuckle, told me that you would never sleep with a woman who wasn't your wife while under your father's roof. The witch told me that if I had an ounce of breeding, I would know that."

"No, I wouldn't have come to you."

"Do you want to know why I came to your bedchamber?"

"I was fool enough to believe that you cared for me."

"Poor boy, did you really believe that? It was originally James I wanted, but Corrie was already in the picture, and I didn't want to kill her. I believed I had you, but then Lady Arbuckle—that ridiculous vain old bat—told me that you were wild, not as honorable as your brother, and were known to keep a mistress. She told me you flirted with young ladies, made them fall in love with you, made them believe that it was marriage you had in mind, then walked away. It wasn't going to happen to me.

"And that's why I came to your bedchamber at midnight. I knew that if you took my virginity you would feel honor-bound to offer marriage, and so I would win. We were under your precious father's roof, now weren't we? A young gentleman, no matter his true nature, couldn't get away with seducing a virgin without marriage, now could he? And that would mean that I could stay here as long as I needed to with no one wondering about it."

Jason said to the girl whose lovely wicked eyes were now cold as the ice floes in the North Sea, "I loved you, Judith, and I was ready to ask you to marry me. What Lady Arbuckle told you wasn't the truth. Why do you think she said that about me?"

Judith laughed. "I have no doubt at all now that the old bitch told me that in an effort to protect you; she doubtless hoped that I would give up trying to attach you since you were such a flighty scoundrel, and that would mean that I couldn't use you. And so I did what I had to do. I will admit that it was no hardship. I believe I shall have to punish Lady Arbuckle for her pathetic attempt at betrayal. You're every bit as honorable as your brother, aren't you?"

"Judith, my love, let's end it."

Douglas said, drawing away her attention, "You want me to believe that your brother is planning to kill my son?"

"Oh yes," Marie said. "As Judith told you, he's ready. My dear, I told his lordship why I was doing this, that you and I have maintained the fiction for Louis, poor boy, such a romantic he's always been, wanting revenge and justice for his dead mother, believing implicitly that it was only right and for him to be the next earl of Northcliffe."

"Yes," Judith said. "I even told him it wouldn't be healthy for his soul if he killed his own father. He believed me."

Douglas had stepped a bit farther away from Jason. "Is Louis such a fool that he actually believes this lie you've told him?"

"He's not a fool, damn you! The truth is that *I* wanted to kill you. Now, I am really tired of all this. Jason, you weren't to be involved. I am sorry about that, but it will make things easier for Louis when he comes back to claim his title."

Jason said, his voice low and vicious, "You lie to yourselves, both of you. England will fall into the sea before Louis Cadoudal becomes the earl of Northcliffe."

"Oh, it will happen, Jason. It will happen." Marie was smiling as she raised the derringer.

Douglas said quickly, "Why did you foist this charade upon two innocent children, Marie? You wanted what wasn't yours, you were bitter because you were a bastard, your mother was poor. You saw your chance, and you took it."

"How very smart you think yourself, my lord. When I found out how Janine had been involved with you, when she finally told me how she'd lied to Georges, it was then that I started thinking what could come of it. Only a fool doesn't take a risk when there is such a huge gain."

Douglas looked again at Judith. "She has made you want to be a murderess. You can still stop this madness, Judith."

"I am sorry to say, my lord, that I agreed immediately when she presented her plans to me. Am I bad? Oh yes, I think so."

Her smile was so very lovely, her eyes filled with intelligence and beauty and cleverness. But there was so much more. Jason saw clearly now, saw the darkness in her, and beyond that, nothing more.

Judith smiled at him, a smile filled with such disregard he felt it to his soul. "I never could tell you apart, not like Corrie, who can tell which one you are from your shadow. Now don't move. I'm an excellent shot, as is my aunt. Your plan might have worked if James had been here, and that silly little Bow Street Runner."

Jason met his father's eyes, and nodded, nothing more.

Douglas said slowly, "So Lady Arbuckle is another victim?"

"Well, she certainly isn't my real aunt. Just look at that face of hers, the ugly old cow. To gain her cooperation, my brother and two of his friends took over their country home, Lindsay Hall, in St. Ives. She was to introduce me to London society, and I would meet you. In exchange, her husband would live. A fair trade, don't you think?"

"And is Lord Arbuckle alive?"

"I don't know," she said.

Douglas said to Judith even as he moved another couple of inches away from Jason, "You ordered Lady Arbuckle to keep away from the family, didn't you? And that's why she's kept to her bedchamber."

"Yes, my lord. I no longer needed her. I had my real aunt here, already completely accepted in your precious household. Annabelle Trelawny—what a stupid name, but one she believed Hollis would find romantic, and he did, that pathetic old man."

"He's not all that pathetic, Judith," Marie said. "He still has most of his teeth. Almost as many as I have."

Judith laughed, a contemptuous laugh that turned all of Jason's raw pain and soul-numbing fear to rage. He felt another bolt of anger for Hollis, a man so honorable and good, his soul shined through his eyes.

Jason wanted to leap on her, put his hands around her neck and squeeze the life out of her, but his father grabbed his arm and steadied him.

Marie said, "It was a treat to listen to you stumble around, to know that I could have poisoned all of you at any time, but Judith wanted to kill you, so what could I do? Don't move, my lord, because if she misses you, then it is I who will shoot you."

Douglas said, "You want to know what I see, madam? I see a young girl who wants what isn't hers and is prepared to kill to gain it, a young girl you've twisted into a monster. As are you, her aunt. Did Georges ever see through you, madam?"

"Yes, but it didn't matter. The madness had him, made him a pathetic creature. But he endured, remembering scraps here, telling Louis things he shouldn't have. It cost me very little to hire a man to kill him."

Judith didn't seem to care that her aunt had killed her father. She said, "Enough! I don't wish to kill everyone in this house. I must shoot you, my lord." She flicked a look at Jason. "And you too, I fear, Jason. A pity. You really are such a beautiful lad."

L OUIS CADOUDAL WAS nearly over the edge. James felt numbing fear, felt his heart pounding heavily against his chest; he didn't want to die; he didn't want to leave his family, leave Corrie. In that instant, James saw Corrie's face, saw her smiling up at him, touching him, kissing him. She loved him, had always loved him, but now she loved him as a woman loved a man. And he would give his life for her, he always would have. It had happened so suddenly, this knowledge that he wouldn't want to continue if she were no longer in his life. And he knew if something happened to him, it would destroy her.

James felt calm flow through him, and determination.

He wasn't going to leave Corrie, ever. He knew that he had to control this madman, and that meant keeping him talking. He said easily, "You know, Louis, your English is quite fluent. How did you manage that?" And as he spoke, his fingers were sifting through the ancient hay that covered the rotted floor, to find something, anything, to help him.

Thank God it did the trick. Louis Cadoudal took a long deep breath, the wild color in his face faded, and he even laughed. "After my father died, we went to Spain. And after that, Ireland. I even had an English tutor. Since I was young, I learned to speak your ridiculous language without an accent. If you are wondering, my father had rich Irish cousins, a very good thing. My poor father, how he wanted to go down in history as the man who'd dispatched Napoleon. But he didn't. He loved you English, wanted me to be an English gentleman, and it appears that is exactly what is to happen."

"I don't think so. Everyone knows about you, Louis. How can you imagine that you can simply kill me and my father, present forged marriage lines to the magistrates, and expect them to welcome you into the fold?"

"How arrogant you English noblemen are. You think me stupid? I will kill both you and your father, then I will simply leave. I won't return for several years, but when I do, I will have witnesses to say that I was in Italy, and that I only just discovered the marriage lines in my dead mother's trunks. There might be those to suspect me, but there will be no proof. Your brother, Jason, will be the earl. He will step down, naturally—if we and our aunt decide to let him live."

"Who is we?"

"My sister and I, of course. She is, at present, dispatching our father to hell, where he rightfully belongs. Judith told me she didn't want my father's blood on my soul, as if I would care. And you will shortly join our father in hell, brother."

James wanted to be surprised, but he wasn't. Somewhere, deep down, he'd wondered. "You're telling me that Judith McCrae is your sister?"

"Yes, of course. She will leave Lady Arbuckle in due course—another pawn who has performed her role sufficiently well—and come to Europe with me with our aunt, whom you know as Annabelle Trelawny. Both will return with me eventually and take their places at my side."

James couldn't help himself, the words flowed out of his mouth. "And what about Corrie? Is Judith going to kill her as well?"

"Ah, that little wife of yours. I must say that I was quite impressed with her ingenuity. Imagine a young lady in a ball gown jumping in the tiger's perch on the carriage back, then charging like a knight into the cottage to rescue you. A pity she got you away, I so wanted to kill you then, but it wasn't to be."

James had felt through nearly all the straw he could reach, and was losing hope. Then his fingers touched something cold and hard. It was an old bridle bit, still attached to one leather rein. It was solid and heavy. It took him precious moments to pull it close enough to tuck it into his right hand. He had it; now he had to ready himself. He'd have only one chance.

He saw that Louis was smiling, and that frightened him. He'd rather have a madman angry than amused.

Louis said, still smiling widely, "Yes, I find myself very impressed with your young wife. I have discovered recently that she is also an heiress, that she lined your pockets, stuffed them to overflowing actually. Perhaps she will be ready for a new husband in a couple of years. A young gentleman who is well-traveled, such as I, can certainly please her as well as you. What do you think, brother?"

James prayed harder than he ever had in his life when he lurched up to his knees and hurled the bridle bit at Louis's face. "I'm not your goddamned brother!"

* * *

"GO TO HELL, my lord," Judith said, and fired the derringer, the shot sounding loud and sharp in the drawing room.

Jason screamed "No!" and threw himself in front of his father at the moment she fired.

At the same time, another voice yelled, "No, Judith! No!" And there was another sharp report.

Corrie saw Jason leap in front of his father, saw Judith's bullet slam into him, then saw her own bullet hit Judith through the neck as she was turning toward Corrie's voice.

At the same time, Annabelle Trelawny, or whoever she was, whirled about, the dueling pistol aimed at Corrie. But Hollis, now coming up quickly behind her, shoved her to the floor. He stood there a moment, staring at the first woman he'd loved in more years than he could remember, and said, "It is enough, Annabelle. It's over. Give me the gun."

"I'm Marie, you ridiculous old man." She raised the gun to shoot him when another shot rang out. She grabbed her chest, stared for a moment at Corrie, who was now on her knees on the carpet, holding her derringer in both hands, the smell of gunpowder sharp and powerful in the still air. Slowly, Marie swayed where she stood. She looked over at Judith, who lay on the floor, blood gushing from her neck and out of her mouth. Then she fell, making little noise, her skirts cascading around her.

Corrie heard a noise, a keening sound, and realized it was coming from her own throat. Douglas held Jason in his arms, tearing open his shirt to bare the wound. He never looked up, but his voice was more urgent than she'd ever heard it. "Corrie, quickly, fetch Dr. Milton here right away. Hurry."

Douglas wasn't even aware Corrie had run out of the room. He was aware that Judith was probably dead, lying on her side not ten feet away, the derringer beside her, her aunt lying not far from her. He was looking down at Jason's still face. His son had saved his life, the last thing Douglas would have wanted. Then Jason's eyes slowly opened. "I brought her here, Father, I brought her here. I'm sorry."

"No, Jason, you didn't know. None of us realized. Be still now, don't move. I swear to you that everything will be all right. Corrie's going to get Dr. Milton. She shot Judith and her aunt. I think both of them are dead. Even though your brother hates it, I'm very pleased that Corrie is such an excellent shot."

A small smile touched Jason's mouth, then his head lolled to the side. At that moment Alexandra came running into the drawing room, saw her husband holding their son in his arms, rocking him back and forth, his face leached of color but the rage in his eyes still burning deep.

"Jason? Oh God, Douglas, oh God. Where is James? Oh God, where is James?"

CHAPTER THIRTY-EIGHT

❧

THE BRIDLE STRUCK Louis squarely in the nose, all of James's strength behind it. The force of the blow knocked him back, and he yelled with the shock of pain and furious surprise. Blood spewed from his nose. He howled as he jerked the gun up, but James was faster. Even as he fired, James was rolling toward him. The bullet struck the floor, sending rotted splinters flying upward.

James was on him in an instant. He was aware of a sharp stab of pain in his head where Louis had struck him down, and ignored it. He grabbed Louis' wrist and squeezed, feeling the bones crack. He wanted that gun. He wanted to shove it down Louis' throat and pull the trigger. Louis' nose was broken, blood still gushing out. But he was strong, and death was in his eyes and in his brain. He wanted James to die; he wanted to take his place, and he fully intended to.

They grappled, rolling across the hay-strewn floor, rot-ted through in many places since this old barn had been abandoned many years. They were of nearly equal strength, but it was James's soul-deep rage that gave him the edge. He knew it, nourished it, let it fill him. He heard the words come out of his mouth, so calm he sounded, the rage banked, "I'm going to kill you, Louis. I'm going to kill you right now." James jerked down Louis' arm until the gun was between them. James felt Louis' wrist break, heard him moan, but it didn't matter. Louis drove his knees into James's back. James nearly buckled with the pain, but he managed to hold on. He drew the gun lower, lower, until it was pointed at Louis' chest. He looked down into the young man's eyes, the young man who wanted to obliterate his family for no other reason than he believed he could do it. All the rest of it, a lie woven to justify his greed.

James squeezed the trigger.

The bullet slammed into Louis Cadoudal's chest. His body heaved, arched upward. Then he fell back. He looked up at James, opened his mouth, his blood bubbling out. "Brother," he said, then he said no more.

James threw himself to the side and jumped to his feet, breathing hard. He was alive. Alive. He didn't waste time on Louis. He grabbed up the gun and began running. He was a half mile from the Hall. And Judith was there. Had she and Annabelle Trelawny killed his father?

JAMES CAME RUNNING through the front doors of Northcliffe Hall at the same time Dr. Milton arrived. Neither man spoke to the other, James because he was breathing too hard. Hollis was there, tall and straight, but his face was pale. "In the drawing room," he said, then watched both men run into the room.

For the first time in his seventy-five years, Hollis didn't know what to do. His mind was a barren wasteland. He walked slowly after Master James and Dr. Milton into the drawing room, and stood there by the door, guarding all of them, he supposed, and then he simply prayed. He looked up to see Ollie Trunk, the Bow Street Runner, stagger through the front doors. Hollis said, "The doctor is here, thank God."

Ollie whispered, "The blighter got me, Hollis. He got me!" And he collapsed onto the front entrance hall.

It was in that moment that Hollis came back into himself. No matter what had happened, it was up to him to make things right. He knelt beside Ollie Trunk and said, "You'll be all right, Ollie, you'll be all right. I'm here now."

Douglas looked up at Dr. Milton, saw James, and thought he would yell with the relief of it. He slowly raised his palm that he'd been pressing hard against Jason's shoulder and saw that the wound was bleeding only sluggishly now. "The bullet struck him in his left shoulder, too close to his heart, dammit; it's still in him. It looks bad. Charles . . . please hurry." He recognized in that moment that he'd been scared when Freddie had come to them in London and told them that James was ill, but it was nothing compared to this. His boy had saved his life, damn him. Douglas was beyond fear now; he planned to kill Jason himself if only he would survive this.

James stood there, white-faced, watching his father move aside for Dr. Milton, looked at his father's hands, covered with Jason's blood. He watched his father take his mother into his arms, and they stood there together, holding each other, making no sound, their eyes on Jason. Then he heard someone whisper his name.

"Corrie, oh God, Corrie," and she was in his arms, pressed hard against him, and she was whispering about Judith and Annabelle Trelawny.

Judith, he thought. *Judith.* Then he saw the blanket covering a body some feet away from where Jason lay on the sofa.

"I killed her, James," Corrie said, but she didn't cry,

held on tight. "I shot her just as she fired at your father, only Jason ran in front of him, then I killed Annabelle Trelawny because she was going to kill Hollis. She's really Judith's aunt."

"Good for you," he said against her hair. "I'm very proud of you, Corrie, more proud than I can say. You belong to me. Don't you ever forget it."

She became perfectly still against him, then she sighed, a soft deep sigh and leaned into him, her head on his shoulder.

They stood silently until Dr. Milton looked up and said, "I will not lie to you, my lord, my lady. It will be a close thing. However, Jason is young, healthy, and very strong. If anyone can pull through this, he can. Now, we must get him upstairs in his bed, and I must get that bullet out of him."

TWO NIGHTS LATER

"I knew he was going to die," Douglas said, his face in his wife's hair. "At midnight, his breathing hitched and then it just stopped. I knew he was dead, Alex. I nearly died myself. I held him against me, then I shook him, I was so angry at him for throwing himself in front of me. Then, thank God, he started breathing again."

She held him even more tightly. "He's all right now, Douglas. He will survive this."

"Yes, I know that now."

They weren't alone in Jason's bedchamber. James and Corrie were sitting very close together on a sofa that had been moved in, both of them awake when Douglas had brought Dr. Milton from his bedchamber to see to Jason.

Douglas said, "Jason didn't say anything to me, but he opened his eyes, Alex. Opened his eyes and he smiled. Then he fell unconscious again."

Douglas looked over at Dr. Milton, who took Jason's pulse, then lifted his eyelids. He said quietly, "He isn't unconscious, my lord, he's asleep. For the first time. His breathing is deeper now. I think he's escaped the fever." Dr. Milton rose, lightly touched his hand to Jason's shoulder, and straightened. "I think he will pull through this. Now, all of you, go get some rest. I will remain by his side."

No one left Jason's room, of course.

Douglas didn't rest for a very long time. James and Corrie were leaning against each other, finally asleep. Alexandra's head was against his shoulder, and he heard her soft breathing. He thought of Lady Arbuckle's ordeal; Douglas had sent Ollic Trunk, recovered from the blow on his head, back with her to Cornwall this morning, Hollis still clucking over him. Lady Arbuckle was scared to death for her husband, and no wonder. So was Douglas. He doubted that Lord Arbuckle was still alive, but he wasn't about to say it out loud.

No one had said a word about Annabelle Trelawny. Hollis had come into Jason's bedchamber that first evening, stood by the door, straight and tall. "I am ready to retire, my lord."

Douglas had looked up, realized what Hollis had said, and frowned. "What is this nonsense? You will not retire, old man. A family member does not retire from the family."

Hollis stared over at Jason, unconscious, his breathing so shallow it didn't seem like he was breathing at all. He looked at his bare chest, covered with a large white bandage. His boy was unconscious, his face still, too pale. Hollis's breath hitched. "I must, my lord. I am responsible for all of this."

Douglas was scared to death for his son, and here was Hollis, wanting to shoulder all the blame. He wanted to tell Hollis to go to bed and sleep for all of them, but one look at the old man's face, and he stilled. "You are not responsible for any of it, Hollis." He didn't say Annabelle Trelawny's name. He never wanted to say that name again for as long as he lived.

Hollis drew himself up even straighter. "I brought that

woman here. I was so besotted, my brain ceased to function properly. She used me, my lord, to make all of you trust her.

"I must retire, my lord. I have hurt all of you. I must somehow make retribution."

Alexandra, red-eyed from lack of sleep, worry, and tears, said, "I will think about this, Hollis. There will be fitting retribution for your crimes. Now, we want you to go to your bed. Drink some of his lordship's brandy. Sleep, Hollis, else you won't be able to carry out your punishment. Believe me, retirement is far too easy."

Hollis bowed, said "Yes, my lady," and left Jason's bedchamber.

Douglas looked at his wife. "Well done," he said. "I believe his shoulders were even straighter when he left than when he came in."

DOUGLAS WAS FINALLY dozing, dreaming of a day long ago when he'd first taken his boys fishing, and Jason had caught a trout and gotten so excited that he'd lost his balance and fallen into the water, losing that fish. Douglas was grinning at the memory when he came awake suddenly. He looked over at the ormolu clock on the mantelpiece. It was nearly four o'clock in the morning. Three branches of candles kept the shadows away from the bed, but the rest of the chamber was in gloom. Dr. Milton was asleep on the truckle bed three feet away. Both Corrie and James were asleep, as was Alexandra. The bedchamber was dead silent. What had awakened him?

He rose immediately and walked to Jason's bedside. He sat beside him, picked up his hand, a well-shaped hand, tanned, strong.

Jason opened his eyes and said, his voice a rusty whisper, "I suppose I am alive?"

"Yes, and you will stay that way," Douglas said. He

wanted to hold his son against him and never let him go, but that would hurt him. He lifted his hand, stroked it, felt the warmth of his flesh, the blood that flowed through his son's body. Thank God he was alive. Then Douglas wanted to yell at him. But he didn't yell, not quite. "I love you, Jason. I also fully intend to beat you to within an inch of your life for throwing yourself in front of me to save my life."

Jason smiled, then a spasm of pain made his eyes pale. "Judith?"

It was Corrie, now awake, standing behind his father, who said, "I shot her, Jason, the very instant after she shot you. She's dead."

Jason said nothing for many moments. Then he sighed. "It appears I'm not a very good judge of character."

"It appears none of us are," his mother said. "All of us were fooled—all of us. We liked her and accepted her as we did Hollis's Annabelle Trelawny."

Jason felt his mother's hand lightly stroking his forearm, saw his twin smiling at him from the foot of the bed since he couldn't get any closer. James didn't look good, Jason thought, didn't look good at all. Then he wanted to laugh because of the way he himself must look right now. Then he thought of Judith, her wicked eyes, her wit, her charm. He thought of those wild, urgent feelings she'd brought him, feelings he'd never experienced before in his life. He thought of her gone, forever. He didn't understand all of it, but it didn't seem all that important right now. When his mother whispered next to his face, "We love you. Rest now, Jason. Everything will be all right," he did.

EPILOGUE

Life is the greatest bargain, we get it for nothing.

YIDDISH PROVERB

TWO AND A HALF MONTHS LATER
NORTHCLIFFE HALL

James and Jason stood side by side on the edge of the cliff overlooking the Poe Valley. It was early afternoon, a windless, bone-cold day in early February. A thick gray fog was creeping up from the valley floor.

They could see their breaths.

"Dr. Milton said you're fit again," James said.

Jason said as he put his hand on his brother's arm, "I'm leaving for Baltimore next week. James Wyndham has invited me to live with them and work on their horse farm. He will teach me." He smiled then, the first smile James could remember seeing for a very long time. "He wrote that his wife, Jessie, can outride just about any jockey in the races. I could see him grinning as he wrote about how he was simply too big to beat her, and I knew he was laughing at himself for making excuses."

"Do you really want to go, Jason?" James looked at his twin's profile. He didn't think anyone would confuse them now. Jason's face was thinner, austere as a hellfire preacher's, his brilliant eyes shadowed, all the joy sucked out of him. His body had healed, but his mind, his spirit, were distant, even from James, who was closer to him than any other human being.

Jason didn't reply for several minutes, then he drew in a deep breath as he turned to his brother. "I must go," he said simply. "There is nothing for me here. Nothing at all."

"You know that isn't true. Father and Mother are here. I'm here. You can remain in England, buy your own stud farm, do whatever you wish."

"I cannot, James. I cannot. It's—" His gloved hand raised a moment, then fell back to his side. "Everything is too close to me here, just too close. I must get away."

"You're running away."

Jason arched a dark brow, smiled. "Of course. Ah, look, I do belive the fog will clear soon."

James knew in that moment that his twin's mind was made up. He would leave. James prayed he would eventually come to grips with the horror of what had happened here, forgive himself for loving Judith McCrae, a monster. "Yes," he said. "The sun will come out soon."

"I must tell Mother and Father. This evening. Will you stand with me?"

"I have always stood with you, and I will again, even in this. I really don't want you to leave, Jason. Dear God, how I wish everything could be different."

"Nothing can change now, James. Let it go."

James knew when he was beaten. "Do you know that

since Father moved Grandmother to the dower house, Corrie and I have decided to remain here, at least for a while?" He paused a moment, flicked his riding crop against his thigh. He wanted to tell Jason that their mother and father were worried sick about him, about the profound depression that had changed him from a laughing, carefree man into this silent one none of them really knew or understood.

Jason laughed, not the sort of laugh that made you smile back. It was a strained sound that held a good deal of loathing. For himself? James didn't know.

"It wasn't your fault," James said, unable to keep himself quiet, though he knew well enough that it was something that Jason didn't want to hear, didn't want to talk about, probably didn't want to remember for the rest of his life. But it had changed him, and James was scared for his brother, scared to his very soul.

"Ah, and whose fault would it have been then, James?"

That mocking voice was mocking himself, of course, and James hated it. "It was Judith's fault. It was Louis' fault. It was that dreadful woman's fault who used poor Hollis." He wanted to say that at least Hollis was smiling a bit more now, unlike Jason. "They were bad, Jason, bad to their black souls. There was nothing but greed in them. None of it was your fault."

"At least Hollis didn't retire."

James grinned at that. "Mother's punishment—forcing him to spend a week with our grandmother while overseeing her move to the dower house. He told me it was surely more punishment than a man deserved, even the man who'd believed himself passionately in love with a younger woman who was still older than our mother. Here he was, a loyal family member whose first mistake had occurred in the twilight years of his career. Mother laughed and laughed."

But Jason didn't smile at that, just nodded. "Yes, she

handled him well, used exactly the right touch. She gave him his worth again.

"I will miss you, James. We haven't been separated before, not like this." He swallowed, shut up, and drew his brother into his arms, holding him tightly.

Jason said finally, pulling away, "I must go, James, surely you know me as well as I know myself and thus you understand why I must leave. There is nothing for me here. I will be back, you know. But I must—" He simply stopped, looked out over the fog-shrouded valley, then turned and left him. James knew he didn't want him coming after him.

James stood on the cliff edge, the fog swirling about his legs now, the sun still hidden, and watched his brother stride to Dodger, who would be traveling to Baltimore as well. James had always said that Dodger was born to race the wind.

He looked after his brother until he was lost from view. He stood there for a very long time.

He was surprised to see that the sun had burst out, now shining brilliantly from high in the sky, the fog burned off. He was thinking of his brother, wondering if there wasn't something he could have said to change his mind, some new argument he could use to make him slough off the terrible guilt, when he chanced to walk into the hidden Sherbrooke gardens and see his wife staring up at her favorite statue.

The sun seemed to shine even more brightly. He felt a leap in his heart. He came up behind her, kissed her neck, then kissed the squeak of surprise right out of her mouth. "Did I tell you this morning that I love you all the way to my boots?"

She pulled him close, then went up on her tiptoes to kiss him. "No, you didn't. I like to hear those words, especially from you. Ah, James, I do love you so."

He smiled, kissed the tip of her nose, felt her burrow in even closer. "I see where your thoughts are, Corrie. I believe I am ready. I don't need any lunch even though I have been working very hard all morning and my ribs are bumping against my chest. No, if you must have me right this minute, I will sacrifice myself. I am yours."

Corrie Sherbrooke grinned like that masked smuggler whose identity hadn't yet been discovered, and hooked a leg behind his knee, sending him to the ground.

"It's not at all too cold for this," she said once she was lying on top of him. "I would have thought it was, not above a minute ago, but not now, James."

"That's because you're on top. Come along, Corrie, I won't be able to do my very best with my back frozen to the ground."

Douglas and Alexandra Sherbrooke watched their son and his wife racing across the lawn toward the gazebo.

Douglas said, "It's too cold."

"They're young. The last thing they need is more heat," said his wife as she hugged him. "I'm very glad that your grandfather built that gazebo. I wonder, do you think he was young once?"

Join top authors for the ultimate cruise experience. Spend 7 days in the Western Caribbean aboard the luxurious Carnival Elation. Start in Galveston, TX and visit Progreso, Cozumel and Belize. Enjoy all this with a ship full of authors, entertainers and book lovers on the **"Get Caught Reading at Sea Cruise"** October 17 - 24, 2004.

PRICES STARTING AT $749 PER PERSON WITH COUPON!

Mail in this coupon with proof of purchase* to receive $250 per person off the regular **"Get Caught Reading at Sea Cruise"** price. One coupon per person required to receive $250 discount. For further details call **1-877-ADV-NTGE** or visit **www.GetCaughtReadingatSea.com**

*proof of purchase is original sales receipt with the book purchased circled.

Carnival
The Most Popular Cruise Line in the World!

- -

GET $250 OFF

Name   (Please Print)

Address   Apt. No.

City   State   Zip

E-Mail Address

See Following Page For Terms & Conditions.

**For booking form and complete information
go to www.getcaughtreadingatsea.com or call 1-877-ADV-NTGE**

Carnival Elation
7 Day Exotic Western Caribbean Itinerary

DAY	PORT	ARRIVE	DEPART
Sun	Galveston		4:00 P.M.
Mon	"Fun Day" at Sea		
Tue	Progreso/Merida	8:00 A.M.	4:00 P.M.
Wed	Cozumel	9:00 A.M.	5:00 P.M.
Thu	Belize	8:00 A.M.	6:00 P.M.
Fri	"Fun Day" at Sea		
Sat	"Fun Day" at Sea		
Sun	Galveston	8:00 A.M.	

TERMS AND CONDITIONS

PAYMENT SCHEDULE:
50% due upon booking
Full and final payment due by July 26, 2004

Acceptable forms of payment are Visa, MasterCard, American Express, Discover and checks. The card-holder must be one of the passengers traveling. A fee of $25 will apply for all returned checks. Check payments must be made payable to **Advantage International, LLC** and sent to: **Advantage International, LLC, 195 North Harbor Drive, Suite 4206, Chicago, IL 60601**

CHANGE/CANCELLATION:
Notice of change/cancellation must be made in writing to Advantage International, LLC.

Change:
Changes in cabin category may be requested and can result in increased rate and penalties. A name change is permitted 60 days or more prior to departure and will incur a penalty of $50 per name change. Deviation from the group schedule and package is a cancellation.

Cancellation:

181 days or more prior to departure	$250 per person
121 - 180 days or more prior to departure	50% of the package price
120 - 61 days prior to departure	75% of the package price
60 days or less prior to departure	100% of the package price (nonrefundable)

US and Canadian citizens are required to present a valid passport or the original birth certificate and state issued photo ID (drivers license). All other nationalities must contact the consulate of the various ports that are visited for verification of documentation.

<u>We strongly recommend trip cancellation insurance!</u>

For further details call 1-877-ADV-NTGE or visit www.GetCaughtReadingatSea.com

For booking form and complete information
go to **www.getcaughtreadingatsea.com** or call **1-877-ADV-NTGE**

Complete coupon and booking form and mail both to:
**Advantage International, LLC,
195 North Harbor Drive, Suite 4206, Chicago, IL 60601**